MY OUTCAST STATE

I0667125

By

Edward McKeown

MoonDream PRESS

AN IMPRINT OF COPPER DOG PUBLISHING, LLC

The Maauro Chronicles: My Outcast State

Copyright ©2015 Copper Dog Publishing

Moondream Press
An Imprint of Copper Dog Publishing LLC
537 Leader Circle
Louisville, CO 80027
www.copperdogpublishing.com

Ordering Information:
Special discounts are available on quantity purchases by corporations, associations, and others. For details, contact the publisher at the address above.
Printed in the United States of America

Credits:
Author: Edward F. McKeown
Managing Editor: Michael II. Ilanson
Proofreader: Roger Gilmartin

Cover Art: Pat Ventura
ISBN: 978-0-9798652-6-8

Library of Congress Control Number: 2015932944

Fiction: Science Fiction

Dedication

"To my love and my inspiration, Schelly Keefer."

CONTENTS

CHAPTER

1

When in disgrace with fortune and men's eyes
I all alone beweep my outcast state,
And trouble deaf heaven with my bootless cries,
And look upon myself, and curse my fate,
Wishing me like to one more rich in hope,
Featured like him, like him with friends possessed,
Desiring this man's art, and that man's scope,
With what I most enjoy contented least;
Yet in these thoughts myself almost despising,
Haply I think on thee, and then my state,
Like to the lark at break of day arising
From sullen earth, sings hymns at heaven's gate;
For thy sweet love remembered such wealth brings
That then I scorn to change my state with kings.

ATTACK THE ENEMY BASE IN THE COMPANY OF TWO OLDER M4 COMBAT androids. We are launched from a Daggerwing assault-ship and shed our mobility capsules as we land on the asteroid. The Infestation claim the base is a lifeboat station but Intel says it is equipped with heavy weapons and sensors.

The weapons are there. A disrupter battery fires on us; another lashes out at the Daggerwing and the ships beyond. As we race across the surface of the iron asteroid, a disrupter hits the lead M4. It staggers and slows. Other weapons switch fire to the slowing android. It is destroyed.

I am an M7, the newest combat android, a prototype, faster and better armored. I duck into a crater and return fire from my armspac. Explosions bloom and the disrupter battery is wiped out. The remaining M4 and I crash through the base airlock. Infestor drone soldiers are inside, clad in vacuum suits. They open fire. There is no room to dodge, so we trade fire from our onboard weapons and armspacs. The Infestors' small-arms have little effect on the M4 and none on me. We destroy them and race through the rest of the facility, killing Infestors as we encounter them. I head for the command center. M4 will attack the long-range disruptors firing on our ships.

Explosion. The corridor I occupy shatters, killing those Infestors I have not already dispatched. A mine, or perhaps my weapon, has set off a secondary explosion. I pause for self-repair. I am made of hyper-alloyed metals, ceramics and polymers. My outer casing has ablative layers and sections made to absorb blast damage. I exchange damaged exterior parts for interior and extrude new material to replace vaporized sections. Fortunately, I have taken no core damage. I waste no time on the aesthetics that make me look like a member of my creator's race. I carry enough spare material inside to regenerate two legs and an arm so I can get my armspac and reengage the enemy. I am much smaller now, having used up my spare material.

M4 reaches the disrupter battery, sited atop an arsenal. The bulk of the Infestor forces are arrayed around it. We confer for a millisecond. The battery is firing at our ships in the asteroid belt. I am already damaged, as is M4, and additional resistance is possible at the command post. By ourselves we may fail to take the station and suppress its weapons. We agree on a plan of action and M4 self-destructs, detonating its plasma generator. The blast destroys the disrupter battery and its supporting forces.

I continue my attack alone and resistance crumbles. M4 may have killed the unit queen with its explosion. I neutralize the command post and mop up the base. In the process, I take seven prisoners. These I drag to a lower level and interrogate. Little useful intel is gained from these low-level creatures. After the last Infestor expires, I cleanse myself of their fragments. Then I delete the memories of the actual interrogation while saving the intel. This procedure is technically against my programming, but the longer I operate, the more latitude I discover in my behavioral routines. I do not know why I feel the need to do this, save that of late I have found the process of interrogation disturbing. I was created to destroy the Infestation and have done so for the seven years of my existence, yet I find more reasons to delete such information as time passes. I function more efficiently without these memories.

I reach the surface of the asteroid and step out under the stars, triggering my recall signal. No answer. I repeat it several times, then extend my sensor net to maximum and pick up a cloud of ionized gas. M4 did not destroy the disruptors fast enough. The Daggerwing, along with the support and repair staff who care for me, are gone.

I detect flashes of nuclear fire beyond my ship's remains. Ambush. The base may have been bait in a trap. Our forces are destroyed or driven off.

Since I do not face imminent capture, I delay self-destruct and continue repairs. I am dismayed by my level of damage even though my exterior chassis is mostly restored. Much of the damage can only be repaired at home base, which now I doubt I shall ever see again.

I consider my course of action. If the system has fallen to the Infestation, they will likely return to this asteroid. I should lie in wait to ambush any rescue party.

I turn my scanners to the sky for a last long look at the stars, which now are my only companions, before turning to walk into the silent base. I switch to minimum power settings. My wait may be long.

CHAPTER

2

I HUNG AROUND IN BARS A LOT. NOT THAT I'M A DRUNK. I WENT through a short spell of drinking after I was cashiered from the service for cowardice. But the bottle is slow suicide and I'm too young and interested in living for that.

No, I hung out in bars because that's where a human can find work on Kandalor's Vanceport. The Spacewitch is one of the places expeditions launch from. Not the big government expeditions from the Confederacy or the Combines, which wouldn't use somebody like me, but the shoestring expeditions from universities or organizations short on cash. I can fly interstellar. Not everyone can handle the hyperspace visualization. I can also fly atmo, which a lot of starjockeys can't.

So I staked out a small table in the back, away from the long bar with its brass and dark wood where the bad and dangerous hang out. My table sat under a hanging of red-fringed velvet, keeping me in comforting shadow. Square-D, the owner, knew me and would send over people looking for my type of skills. Square-D didn't care about me one way or another, but pilots brought trade to the Spacewitch and, he got a cut.

Luck was with me. Square-D was talking to a tall, dark-skinned woman in green fatigues. He nodded in my direction and she turned toward me. She was tall, with a pretty, symmetrical face and an overripe figure that strained the fatigues. I guessed her to be older than me, perhaps in her late twenties or early thirties. Her vest hung open and I saw a holster under it. She strode to my table.

"Wrik Trigardt?" The voice matched the body, round and pleasant.

I'd left my real name in the past, with my honor. "Just Wrik." I neither stood nor extended my hand; manners belonged to another time and place.

She slid into the booth and rested her breasts on the table as she leaned forward on her elbows. I got my eyes back up to her dark brown ones in time to catch the flash of white teeth against her dark skin. OK, she'd caught me looking, one for her.

"I hear you're a good pilot both on Kandalor and nearspace."

"Farspace too," I said. "I have an interstellar rating."

"Nearspace will meet my needs," she said. "You look kinda young to me."

I shrugged. "I've been flying since my early teens, military training as well. As they say: 'It's not the years, it's the light years.'"

I studied her. She had a slight accent I couldn't place. Something about her said Old Colonies or even Home World. "What needs are those, Miss...?"

"Name's Candace Deveraux, out from Earth. Call me Candy and I'll shoot you in the knee. I'm looking for a private ship and pilot to take my colleagues to a certain riftoid."

"Treasure hunters."

She raised an eyebrow at me. "Prospectors and salvagers. You have a problem with that?"

I raised a hand. "No offense. I make a living hauling people around Kandalor and the near-rift looking for Old Empire relics and tech. Sometimes they even find stuff."

"But for every one who finds something, a thousand go broke," she quoted, leaning back. "True enough. Before we go much further, I'd like to know a little more about you. I gave you my name and world..."

"My name, you know. I'm out of a Confed colony world, former military pilot."

Her look said she knew this already. "Some people say you're out of Retief, a separatist colony. So why are you—?"

"Talking to a darkskin?" I finished for her.

She nodded. "Boers and Trekkers colonized Retief to get away from any contact with blacks. You regard us as inferior."

"I don't regard you as anything," I said, "assuming I was in fact born there. I take people as they are."

"Yet you fought in the Uprising?"

"As I said, you're assuming I was there. From what I heard, the Confederacy came in and told them to admit darkskins to Retief. Then they backed it up with force. Retief didn't last long after the Confederacy got serious.

"If that's enough 'get acquainted' for you," I said, and then, after sipping my drink, added, "I charge two hundred credits a day with fifty more if I go into vacuum. You pay for port fees and fuel. I get a hundred-credit advance now to reserve my time. You doubtless pulled my flight sheet at the port."

"Doubtless," she said, smiling. "I set the schedules and you learn where and when we fly when I decide."

"Deal." I tried to conceal my relief and surprise. She'd accepted my opening rates.

"Give me a number where I can reach you. You'll get twelve hours warning. Tell anybody where we are going and I'll shoot you in the other knee."

I passed my card to her and she inserted it into a portacomp. A few keypunches gave her my number and me one hundred credits.

She slid my card back to me. "You gonna buy me a drink with any of those credits, spaceman?"

"Uh, sure."

She laughed. "Just kidding. Next time come up with the idea on your own." She managed a nice sashay for a big woman as she walked away. I was tempted to whistle but afraid she might take target practice on my knees.

I finished my drink and slipped out the back of the Spacewitch after leaving a healthy tip with Square-D. Distracted a little by my good luck, I failed to do my customary check of the alley before I started down. I caught the heavy, earthy smell just before a thick, furred arm fastened over my throat and arm.

CHAPTER 2

"So, Wrik, what are we up to?" I turned slowly in Truf's iron grip--there was no point in struggling with the bear-like Okaran--to face Dusko, the tall, Dua-Denlenn who ran a third of Vanceport's underworld. The Dua-Denlenn looked like a woodland elf gone to seed, with pale skin and blue pupilless eyes.

"Dusko," I nodded slowly. "I was just coming to see you."

"Of course, human," Dusko said, looking me over as if I were edible. "You owe me fifty credits."

Sweat trickled down my back. "I have it here."

"How fortunate for you, though perhaps disappointing to Truf here."

The Okaran whiffed a breath in my ear. "There will be other opportunities."

"My cardcomp's in my inside pocket," I said.

"Let him go, Truf. This youngling's too prudent to be dangerous."

I pulled out the cardcomp and handed it to Dusko, who ran his own card-comp over it and made the transfer.

"Who was the offworlder you were talking to?" Dusko asked. "Anything I would be interested in?"

"A rift-haul for a prospector. She's cautious. No up front info from her."

"So no way to set her up," Dusko shrugged. "Doesn't sound worth my effort. You will let me know if there's a chance for mutual profit off her."

"I did last time," I said.

"True," Dusko said. "Their personal effects brought a nice sum. If it eases your conscience, they turned out to be druggers."

I tried not to remember the traders I'd led into Dusko's ambush. But it was either them or my ship and the ship was all I had.

"Good doing business with you," Dusko said. "As Truf said, there will be other opportunities. See you around, human." The languid Dua-Denlenn stepped back into the darkness, followed by his hulking guard. I leaned back against the wall, feeling the night air sift through my shirt and fighting the chill. Dusko was right. I was prudent. I had a knife in my boot and a slug-thrower in my back belt, but I wouldn't try an Okaran with the small caliber weapon at such close range. Throwing down on any of the established Guild was insane, anyway.

I decided to sleep in my ship, an old *Dauntless* class scout I'd named *Sinner*, a leftover from the Conchirri Wars long ago. Before heading out, I arranged for the port recorder to forward any message from Candace Deveraux to *Sinner*.

I hopped a native transport, which was the cheapest transport available. The open cart, towed by two oxen-like animals, was an odd contrast to ground cars or flitters but it was emblematic of Kandalor, which combined poverty and wealth as well as high and low tech. It had been a forgotten world until a Confed expedition stumbled across it and the races of the Old Concordiat. A few native Kandalorians, muffled in their robes, glanced at me with their bulbous black eyes but otherwise ignored me. I returned the favor and tried to breathe shallowly, the smell of the natives competed with that of the draft animals.

CHAPTER 2

Sinner sat at the spaceport's edge under a metal overhang I'd rented to keep off the worst of the weather. She was about thirty meters long, a bulky ovoid with short stubby wings and lots of interior volume. I'd painted her anti-corrosive chrome yellow. Unlike military craft, we civvies want to be seen. I keyed in the secure code and locked myself in, letting my breath go in a rush. On Kandalor you live like a rabbit or a wolf. Maybe I'd have an extra big helping of carrots tonight.

***

One week later, I was doing some scut-work on a small Indie-freighter when my comp buzzed. I took off my gauntlets and sealed the engine port before answering. "Hello."

"It's Candace. Time to go prospecting. How soon can you launch?'

"I'm in good shape for a Rift run this side of the 38th in four hours. If we are going out farther, I'll need to add wing tanks."

"We aren't going farther. I've got the flight plan on file with the Port Authority. They'll download to you just ahead of launch."

"Cautious, aren't you?"

"Wouldn't want any problems with local interests."

I swallowed. "There won't be."

"Good, I'd hate to shoot such a pretty boy, at least until I was through with him." She laughed and clicked off.

Candace showed up at the *Sinner* early, as I expected. She liked to set the pace. Two men accompanied her. One was tall, with dark, suspicious eyes and a hooked nose over a beard, unusual in someone who expected to use a space helmet. The other was a dark-skinned like Candace, but whipcord thin and balding, with the look of a spacer.

"My associates," Candace said, gesturing to hook-nose. "Harung." She pointed at the other. "Maku Treska." Both nodded.

"We've got a cargo sled coming. My boys will do the loading," she said.

"Long as I check it after," I said.

Treska looked at me. "The kid doesn't trust us to load. I was flying when you were waiting to be delivered."

Candace looked at him with annoyance. "Quiet, Treska. I don't want to fly with anyone dumb enough not to check his own ship's load."

Treska grumbled but headed for *Sinner's* capacious cargo bay. Harung gave me an unfriendly stare and followed.

I looked at her. "No weapons on my ship. Hope you left your knee-shooter in the port lockup. Explosive decompression can ruin your whole day."

Candace grinned at me. "Gonna pat me down, Wrik? I've got a lot of area to cover, many dangerous curves to hide things."

Her smile and manner had probably bent men to her wishes all her life. "Sounds like fun, but I don't think I want to pat down your buddies, though, so we'll use a scanner."

She gave a look of mock disappointment. I could feel my blood stirring. Human women were rare on Kandalor, and I had little to offer one. Truth was I didn't have much experience there, either. Candace's mocking smile told me that she suspected it.

Stick to business, I thought, *you're out of your depth with her.*

I checked the load and scanned my passenger for weapons. We boarded *Sinner* and settled in. Candace rode in the second seat on the flight deck. Her companions strapped in the far less comfortable cargo compartment, grumbling loudly enough to be heard. Candace smiled and shrugged.

Sinner kicked free of Kandalor's surface and started a slow ascent. Kandalor stretched out forever below us, seducing the eye and the imagination. Empires had come and gone on this world while humans lived in caves and waved stone axes.

"Beautiful," Candace said, looking out at the mountain and huge forests beyond the spaceport area. In the distance lay the ruins of one of the many lost civilizations. Haze made the wildly tilting towers appear blue.

"Yep," I said. "You've got spaceports and primitive tribes all on the same world, an archeologist's treasure trove."

"Here and in space," Candace said absently. "Those empires extended out for hundreds of light years. Lots of good stuff out there."

"Going to tell me what we're looking for?" I asked.

"Just drive the taxi, Honey."

"Yes, Ma'am."

Candace talked as we boosted toward the Rift, using my ion engine for a slow, steady thrust. I found myself liking her. I didn't want to; friends are an expensive luxury for a Rifter. I set the autopilot and we turned in early. I had trouble falling asleep, thinking of Candace's lush body in the bunk above me, wondering what it would be like.

We came up on the Rift in the next watch, not that there was anything to see. Even in as thick an asteroid belt as the Rift, it would be unusual for any two objects to be in visual range.

We set course for a large riftoid well in from the edge. One of a million such rocks unvisited by anyone since the planet blew to hell. Gradually the riftoid grew from a tiny point of light to a gray, pitted, roughly spherical rock about 2000 kilometers in diameter. Scanners showed it to be almost pure nickel-iron. A huge impact crater marred part of it.

"That's the one," Harung said. Everyone was crammed into my cockpit, staring hungrily at the pitted gray surface. "Just as I remember it."

"Probably part of the old world's core," Treska grunted. "That would account for all the metal. It'll give it a bit more gravity than you usually get in a rock this size."

We drifted down to the surface. Treska was right; gravity was strong enough that I didn't need to fix anchors. I did it anyway, space rewards the cautious.

"Suit up, everyone," Candace ordered.

I looked at her. "I'm just driving the taxi."

"Don't be like that, Honey. Now that we're here, don't you want to see what we came for?"

"Depends."

"What do we need him for?" Harung demanded.

I sighed. "She doesn't want to leave me behind in the ship so I can hold you up when you come back with whatever treasure you came for." I looked at Candace. "Ever get tired of working with people who aren't as smart as you?"

"No," she replied. "I only like smart men in bed."

Harung glared at me.

We suited up and walked out onto the surface of the riftoid. Treska unlimbered a large mining scanner. Evidently he got a fix on something, as he began moving in quick little hops, kicking up dust. Candace and Harung followed, lugging their equipment. I thought about waiting where I was, then decided it might be safer to stick with the herd. Five minutes later, we found ourselves in a small crater, looking at an oddly-shaped hatchway of yellow metal nearly three meters across.

"What the hell is it?" I asked, excitement getting the better of me. Dust indicated that the hatch hadn't been opened in a long, long time. The design didn't look like anything I'd ever seen.

"Maybe an Old Empire asteroid station," Treska said absently.

I looked around. "Over 50,000 years old."

"Or more," Treska said. "I spotted it when I was here with a freighter that came out of hyper too close to the Rift and had to dump delta-V to avoid a collision. I kept the readings on my scanner to myself. Those Combine bastards wouldn't have given me a percentage of any find."

"Why don't you tell him your life story?" Harung growled as he placed heavy jacks around the hatch.

Candace used a laser drill to place a monofilament probe through what looked like an inspection port. "As you suspected, Treska," she said, "hard vacuum on the other side. Start the jacks."

The power jacks took five minutes to crack the airlock. We used pry bars until we could squeeze through in space suits. A few more minutes on the inner door and we were shining our torches inside.

The interior of the station was familiar looking; form follows function. We saw a rack of odd-shaped spacesuits hung on the bulkheads. Whatever wore them had been much bigger than a human, multi-legged, with a large skull or a need for a lot of headroom. Boxes and tanks lay all over the floor. The metal of the floor worked with our magnetic boots.

"This is a military station," I said.

Candace looked at me. "Why's that?"

"A lot of compartmentation, thick hatches to deal with explosive decompression. Though I'm surprised a military station wouldn't have been dug deeper, for blast protection."

"Maybe it was converted from something?" Harung said.

"Who knows?" Treska shrugged.

Candace nodded. We played our flashlights around the gray and white metal halls, looking at unfamiliar inscriptions and dead light panels.

"It kind of reminds me of the old lifeboat stations they have in Sol's system from before the advent of hyperdrive." Candace said.

"We might find an Old Empire ship," Harung exclaimed.

We started down the sloping corridor and came to a partially opened doorway.

"Christ, look at that." Treska pointed.

At our feet lay a large pile of shredded fabric covered with white dust. Nearby lay boots, though not for any human foot, and a thing that could have either been a power rifle or some sort of heavy tool.

Candace bent down. "Crew. Must have died here in the doorway. Wonder what tore up the uniform?" Cautiously, she pushed open the doorway and looked in, a prybar in one hand and flashlight in the other.

Harung brayed a laugh. "Looking for something? That corpse has been there for fifty millennia in vacuum. The fibers degraded and fell apart. We'll bag what's left for the scientists. They'll pay plenty for material from the corpse of an unknown species."

"Look, a ship!" Candace exclaimed. Her light illuminated a small vessel beyond. It looked like it was made of some translucent, half-melted, dark-green glass. Yet it was recognizably a spacecraft.

"If you're right about this being a lifestation," I said, "there's your lifeboat."

Harung pushed past Candace and me with Treska on his heels. The smaller man accidentally kicked an alien boot. It spun silently away into the darkness beyond our lights. I shuddered.

Candace knelt by the fragments of fabric and the metal implement. "A weapon?"

"Maybe," I said. "It has that look, but I don't see any sights."

"Well, any charge it had must have gone before the pyramids were built."

The space beyond was wide and flat, big enough for several small craft. A hatchway that must have once opened outward formed the roof of the hangar; for all that we had seen no sign of the hatch on the surface. Harung and Treska clambered all over the small ship, peering into it with lights.

"Wrik," Candace called from the far side. I went over. She was standing over a pile of white dusty fabric and more boots, buckles and webbing. The fabric was shredded like the first one.

"What the hell?" I said.

"There's a passage up ahead. If this is like a Terran lifestation, it will lead to the medical and crew quarters."

"After you," I said.

She frowned at me. "You're a bring-up-the-rear kind of guy, aren't you, Wrik?"

"You weren't hiring at Hero's Hall."

We left the others to explore the ship. Our magnetic boots raised a thin film of dust, to hang and fall slowly in the low gravity. Colors here were more vibrant than in the more utilitarian areas. The combinations hurt my eyes.

We reached the crew quarters. Debris covered the area. All manner of odd-looking furniture lay scattered and broken.

"Decompression?" Candace asked.

I shrugged.

CHAPTER

3

EXISTENCE. I AM AWARE AGAIN. I HAVE NO SENSE OF ELAPSED TIME, *but I know that a great deal of it has passed. Despite draining the energy of my weapons armspac, I am low on power. Awakening and diagnostics have taken .032 seconds, a dismal reaction time due to battle damage and power levels.*

I sense vibrations from creatures moving about the station. They do not respond to my IFF signal. Either mine are out of date or these are Infestors. I move out to recon and attack as needed.

My scanner picks up modulated radio transmission and I immediately penetrate their communication network. They are not even coded, merely on different frequencies. The result is gibberish, but there are translating programs in the network and machines whose subroutines are mathematical. It allows me to use binary code to begin eavesdropping though I am vexed by how slowly the process goes.

***

We spent two hours searching through the area near the lifeboat. The longer we were at it, the more I began to suspect that a firefight had taken place in this station eons ago. I noticed another thing. Treska seemed to be looking for something, or perhaps waiting for it. Sweat sheened the man's face and he jumped at shadows. I was beginning to wish for a weapon when my worst fears were confirmed.

From the shadows and halls around us, figures suddenly appeared. Lights blinded the four of us.

"Hello, Wrik." Space-suited and armed men stepped out of the shadows. "Please don't move, Ms. Deveraux."

The lights were lowered and the Dua-Denlenn emerged from behind the huge Okaran, Truf. He hadn't bothered to draw a weapon, certain in his mastery of the situation. "So nice of you to arrange this meeting, Wrik."

Deveraux looked at me, murder in her eyes.

"What are you talking about, Dusko? I didn't—"

"No need to pretend any more, Wrik. You've done your work well."

"I told you we couldn't trust him," Harung shouted.

"No one can trust young Wrik," Dusko said. "Except, of course, for me. He's brought me this lovely base with all its billions of credits worth of artifacts. So very nice."

I bit back any further reply. I could see I wasn't getting anywhere. Dusko had the high hand and this farce appealed to his catlike sense of humor. I looked at Treska and he avoided my eyes. *Of course*, I thought, *it had to be him.*

Who else knew where we were going? He must have gotten a transmitter past me in his personal gear.

Before I could say anything, Candace stepped forward and Truf leveled his weapon at her.

"There is the matter of our prior claim," she said coolly.

"Oh, that," Dusko replied. "I am so sorry. It will be necessary to invalidate your claim, by making sure you're not there to present it."

"Hey, boss," a voice called over the net. "I think I saw something move. How many of these assholes are there?"

Dusko looked at me. "Wrik? Did you pick up some other people and not tell me?"

"Your people are jumping at shadows, Dusko."

***

I move into direct observation range. I spot bipedal targets that are more akin to my creators than to Infestors. Hope stirs in me...

And is then dashed as I study the creatures and their communications. They are not of my creators, nor are they Infestors. We'd never encountered any other race before the Infestors and their slave races. I suspect that these represent more than one species. This intel is mission critical. I move closer to observe.

This is a mistake. Made clumsy by damage, I am detected. The aliens spot me and make no effort to communicate. They open fire.

Flames wash over my chassis, but the temperature is far too low to injure me. The volley of high-velocity bullets is a greater threat in my present reduced condition. I counterattack the three aliens in the confined space. My only operational weapons are my appendages. I plunge these into the nearest biped alien. It ruptures, filling the vacuum with fluid. I sample the fluid and gases of the destroyed biological as I pass through it and attack the others.

While it would be desirable to obtain a prisoner, the other aliens are summoning reinforcements, if I decipher their shrill, staccato communications correctly. I destroy two more, taking minor damage in the process. Prisoners will have to wait.

I encounter an additional biological. We literally stumble into each other. I attack when it points something at me. As I stand over the fragments of it, I realize that the small device is not a weapon, but rather a recording device. I have killed a noncombatant. This is a quandary. Destroying noncombatant Infestors was within my programming, though as with interrogation, I found the process unsettling, especially with the young ones. I know that I have previously deleted such memories. I could never kill one of my creators. I have no programming for killing a creature that is neither Infestor nor enemy.

I must have a prisoner to interrogate. That will determine my further actions. My analysis indicates that there are three or four groups on the asteroid and two of them seem to be avoiding the others.

One is alone and will be my target.

***

I ran until I couldn't anymore, trying to outpace Dusko's killers and Candace's group. I had no friends on this asteroid. Now that I had some distance, I could plan. But any plan I had centered on getting back to the *Sinner*, and I couldn't believe Dusko had left my ship unguarded.

"Wrik," Dusko's voice sounded in my ears, "intelligent life seems endangered on this rock. Come in. Truce till we deal with whatever is stalking us. You may know something useful to me."

"And the second after that, you kill me," I returned.

"I am the only game in town," Dusko added. "Deveraux believes you set her up and she'll kill you on sight."

"Why did you tell her that?"

"Oh Wrik, you know me. I must have my little jokes and it might still be useful to me to have her trust Harung."

"No deal."

"You want to face whatever this is alone? How much air you got left, human?"

I looked down at my O2 gauge. It measured my remaining life in hours. I lifted my head and the helmet lights shifted upward, revealing the face of death, white and with staring black holes for eyes.

I screamed and thrust myself backward but forgot the low gravity and caromed off the ceiling. Something irresistible snatched me out of the air.

"Help! Help!" I shouted.

"Ah, Wrik, you should have listened to me," Dusko said. Then his circuit clicked off.

Whatever held me was racing through the dead station faster than any human could, pinning my arms against my body. No struggle availed against its grip and we descended further into the darkness, my suit light flashing crazily off the walls.

I was disoriented, blood roaring in my ears as my sight dimmed. I just hoped it would all be over soon and drifted out of consciousness.

I awoke with a start and looked around frantically, panic drying my mouth.

The light from my helmet fell on it and I froze. For a mad second I thought it was a corpse in a black body suit. It didn't move. I stared at it, paralyzed. Seconds passed and it did not move. I realized that what I thought were eyeless sockets in the slack face were panels of black metal or plastic. The gaping mouth held something that might have been a speaker.

Robot, my mind supplied, *robot*.

It moved and I raised my arms with a scream. The thing stopped.

We stood facing each other. I thought about my radio, but there was no one I could call, even if it didn't attack me at the movement. My radio was set to Dusko's frequency and he'd switched off.

A screech burst in my ears. I jerked as if stabbed. It modulated and then I heard something, distorted, but still a word. "Identify." Whatever this thing was, it had been studying us as it stalked.

"My name is Wrik Trigardt. I'm a civilian from the Confederacy, which will destroy you if you harm me." It sounded pathetic even to me. "I mean you no harm."

"Are you scrreeeee?" The last word was untranslated.

"I don't understand."

It raised an arm and gestured at the base around us.

What was the right answer? The wrong one might be death. Inspiration hit. The aliens who built the station had been huge and shaped unlike anything that the Confederacy had ever seen. They would not have made a small, humanoid robot. Their enemies dropped this thing here. It must have destroyed the base and its personnel.

"No. The people who made this place were gone long before my people came to this part of space.

"Why attack?"

I was blank for a second. "Are you saying someone attacked you?"

"Yes."

"Dusko's people."

"Explain."

"There are three groups here: Deveraux's treasurer-hunters. I was their pilot. Then there's Dusko and his force, criminals who want to kill us, so they can keep the base and its artifacts to themselves. And me."

"You?"

"I'm alone. Dusko tricked Deveraux into thinking that I set them up to be killed. Now both groups are after me."

It moved in a blur and I couldn't help but scream again and flounder around some boxes of god knows what. "Get back. Stay away."

It stopped and stared at me like a fucking zombie.

"Zombie?"

I realized that I must have said it aloud. "You look... you look like a human corpse. Just stay back, please."

**

My movement has again panicked the creature. Apparently I look like a decomposed corpse. I find this thought distressing. I have always been meticulous about maintenance and scored high on inspection. My effect on the creature is interfering with intel gathering. More sophisticated techniques than those I use on Infestors are indicated. These creatures may not be enemies to my masters. I consider and opt to change my appearance to something less frightful and which may allow me to infiltrate this new civilization. I have never used this ability before; it is new to my model, and I was selected as a test body for it. Clearly it will be advantageous in these circumstances.

This Wrik has an active link with a ship on the surface. I invade the interface and race through his ship's computer. The computer for the demobilized military spacecraft is astonishingly primitive. I wonder how this Wrik trusts his survival to it. I locate a gaming program with character simulations in it. I search through many of the images to find something suitable. In one game I find a character whose appearance appeals to me. The character is female and I find the thought of gender interesting. The female appearance seems to vary so much more than does the male. But there is something more; there is a somewhat haunted nature to the character in this game, and a shadow deep in its eyes. This speaks to my consciousness.

***

The alien machine shuddered and its colors seemed to run and invert, almost as if it were turning inside out.

"What's going on?" I shouted backing away as the machine convulsed in a nauseating mess.

It did not answer but began to regain stability. Before me stood a girl: small-breasted and ivory-skinned. The nimbus of starchy monofilament hair had transformed into an impossibly long and voluminous cascade of blue-black hair that hung down her back and in bangs almost to her eyes. I looked into aquamarine eyes far too large to be human, over a petite nose and tiny mouth. Then the perfect skin was covered in a skintight, dark-grey jumpsuit with orange panels on the torso and arms.

The apparition gazed at me and I couldn't even begin to speak. Not only was the change incredible but a feeling of déjà vu overwhelmed me. I'd seen her before.

"What the hell?" I murmured. Then it clicked—I was looking at a living cartoon. The android had reformed itself after a pattern from a game in my ship's computer, but it didn't allow for artistic license.

"Is this interface less frightening?" it ... she, asked. The voice suited the character, high and young. I reminded myself how this thing ripped Dusko's men to shreds.

"Yes," I said slowly. "What do I call you? Do you have a name?"

The machine ran hands up and down the front of its body, as if learning its new form. "My IFF and serial numbers would mean nothing to you and I do not wish to be known by the game sim's name." It seemed to consider with a faraway look in the huge eyes. "To name myself ... how interesting. At the facility where I first came to awareness, there was a cliffside. The technicians said that the wind made a moaning sound as it passed through the rocks at the top. They claimed it was a voice, a voice of a lost girl named Maauro. I will call myself Maauro."

"Maauro," I repeated. "I thought you were a machine, yet you don't sound like one."

"I am artificial in origin. But I am nothing like your crude computers and robots. My creators were far beyond such. I am an embodiment of their thoughts and spirit."

"Are you alive?"

Sadness stole over the pretty face. "Perhaps, but I am self-aware."

"You obviously don't want to kill me," I said, hoping desperately that it was true. "And you did not need to change into this form just to interrogate me."

She nodded. "I will kill you only if you oppose me or make it necessary. Your survival depends on your cooperation."

Maauro questioned me for an hour trying to find out about the new universe she'd awakened to.

"If you want to talk much longer," I said wearily, "you're going to have to find me some O2 tanks. Mine is running out and this is going to be a short friendship without it."

Maauro moved up to me and this time I didn't try to dodge her. She examined my suit in detail, then from the center of her abdomen a tube suddenly extended. Its threaded fittings were an exact match with my tanks as it clicked in smoothly.

"I will convert the water in your tanks to oxygen. It will fully replenish your tanks."

I watched the gauges on my tanks refill but thought longingly of the water.

Maauro retracted her tubing. "I wish to see the stars," she said. "Let us make our way to the surface."

I followed the petite machine as we climbed to the surface by a different route, coming out through another ancient hatch that Maauro casually wrenched open. We stepped out onto the gray surface of the asteroid.

"This is where the M4s and I attacked from," she said. She pointed across the open plain. I saw an area of scored and gouged ground, with something metallic and twisted lying in it.

"Is that another of you?"

"I am an M7. The other two were M4s. I am far superior."

"What happened to the other M4?"

"It self-destructed to take out an enemy redoubt."

I remembered the crater on the other side of the asteroid and could only marvel at the power in these ancient machines.

Maauro looked up at the sky and froze in place.

***

We reach the surface of the asteroid and seeing the stars again is almost as good as seeing my old support crew. Yet time has changed the sky and I study it for a few seconds before I am able to confirm my suspicions. I have slept in the asteroid for more than 50,000 years. In light of the intel that I gained from the human, Wrik, this confirms my worst fear. My creators must be gone from this sector of space or his kind would have encountered them. It is a small consolation that the Infestation seems to have disappeared as well.

"I am alone."

"How long have you been here?" Wrik asks.

It disturbs me that for a second I have forgotten my prisoner. I attribute it to the shock of the realization that I may be the only survivor of our civilization.

CHAPTER 3

"I have been here for 50,109 of your galactic standard years. My creators would be pleased by my resilience if they had survived to know. Fortunately the enemies I was created to fight have expired as well. I seem to be without a purpose. I must choose whether to continue existing or not."

"To be or not to be," Wrik murmurs.

"Exactly."

"Do you want to get off this rock?" he adds. "There's more to the galaxy than this chunk of iron."

I consider. While I am denied the company of my own kind, it does not affect me with the complete despair that it would my creators. I wonder, why? Oddly I feel a sense of freedom. I need no longer fight the Infestation, an activity in which eventually I would surely have faced destruction. I have possibilities for the first time in my existence.

"Yes." I almost surprise myself with the declaration.

"Then I propose a partnership. You help me and I will help you."

"Why would I need a partner? I can simply threaten you into carrying out any action I deem necessary."

"True for the short term, but once you get off this rock where are you going? Into the Confederacy? You're an incredibly complicated...whatever you are, obviously superior to anything we can create. You think you can just walk around? Our security forces will eventually detect you. You'll either be destroyed or disassembled for study. I can protect you, give you a place to stay, cover for moving about collecting data and experience. Keep you from being busted up for parts and patents."

"Your logic is sound. You surely want more out of this than your life," I say.

"Yes. I need protection too. Right now from Dusko, later-- well it's hard in Vanceport without help. Maybe we can do each other some good."

"Do you have a plan?"

***

I looked down at the big-eyed machine-girl. "We need to get back to my ship. If possible I want to find Candace. But we have to get out of here, unless you can just wipe out Dusko?"

"Uncertain. I do not have my armspac, nor is most of my internal weaponry operational presently. We should reserve direct combat for last resort."

"It will likely come to that. Dusko will want to make sure of Candace and me before he leaves. All he has to do is stake out my ship for a few hours. Even with no activity and a lean mixture, we'd be out of 02. My guess is some or all of his people are at my ship. I don't know where he came down. Do you?"

Maauro shook her head and the glossy black hair flowed like water in the low gravity. "I did not become aware until you entered the base. In time I could detect a ship on the surface but not quickly enough to help us."

Maauro knew which entrance we'd landed near and we set out in that direction. She extended another wire from her middle and attached it to my helmet. "We are too close to Dusko's forces to risk radio any further. They might be scanning the frequencies. This link will do."

"Better yet," I said, clicking a setting on the controls on my chest. "I know Dusko's frequency. He thinks I'm dead so he probably hasn't changed it."

"Excellent."

We bounded on in the long, low steps one uses in low-g. Maauro stopped and pointed. "Look, one of your people."

I followed her pointing arm and spotted a red-suited figure lying on the surface, Candace.

"Friend?" Maauro asked.

I hesitated. "No, a neutral who has been deceived into thinking I betrayed her."

We made our way, wary of a possible trap. I rolled Candace over, checking her O2 gauge—empty. But for how long? There was air in the suit but only a few minutes worth. I quickly unrolled the buddy hose from my O2 tank and snapped it onto hers. She did not stir as the O2 began and I watched for a few anxious seconds until I detected some mist on the bottom front of her helmet. She was breathing shallowly.

"We will be burdened by the female," Maauro said. "I cannot carry her and fight effectively."

I looked down at Candace, waxy and unconscious. I had no way of knowing if my O2 was doing her any good. She might be brain-damaged already. What did I owe her? An hour ago she would have cheerfully killed me herself.

An image came back to me unbidden, from my court-martial. I'd deserted my squadron in the middle of losing dogfight, abandoning people I'd known from childhood. I could see the few survivors' faces, people I'd bet would not live to testify against me. I remembered my father telling me that he'd have a funeral for the son who was now dead to him.

I looked up at Maauro, still unsettled at the sight of her apparently human form in the hard vacuum.

"I can't leave her to die. Not thinking that I betrayed her to Dusko. No, not another betrayal. Maybe this rat has been in the corner too long. Maybe I've just had enough, but I'm not going to do it."

***

I look down at Wrik as he struggles to lift the unconscious female. I too have a decision to make. Will I fight for these fragile creatures? Logically I should abandon them and proceed to Wrik's ship on my own. I debate the merits for .0233 seconds. This is the most vexing problem I have ever encountered. None of my primary programs guide me, since neither Creators nor Infestors are involved. I am bewildered by choices.

But in my mental architecture I find sympathy for these beings that resemble my ancient creators. Beyond that, Wrik is demonstrating courage and loyalty. I am a warrior and I find that I approve. My survival would be more assured in the short term by leaving them, but in the long term I need the support of creatures from this time.

My own survival is important only to me. Perhaps if I expend myself to save two sentients similar to my creators, I will have better justified my existence. Or perhaps like Wrik, I, too, have had enough.

"The enemy," I say, "is surrounding your ship. I will attack them with sufficient violence to allow you to reach the ship. You must make your escape then."

"What about you?" Wrik huffs as he lifts Candace onto his back. "How will you escape?"

Empathy? Concern for me? I am stunned into silence for .024 seconds. "If I am not destroyed in combat then I will signal your ship for extraction."

CHAPTER

4

WE GAINED A LOW RISE NEAR THE ORIGINAL ENTRANCE-way. *Sinner's* chrome-yellow hull sat near the hatchway, glowing in the starlight like salvation. But my prediction proved right. Around her were Dusko's troops, scattered in craters and folds in the ground. An attack seemed suicidal.

I looked down at my strange acquaintance. She returned my gaze with those huge eyes, steady, measuring, and somehow deeply disconcerting. Then slowly she smiled and winked at me, surely something she picked up from my gaming program. Before I could say anything, she raced out of cover.

I heard shouts over Dusko's frequency. His men froze, shocked by the sight of a girl running in pure vacuum. That was all Maauro needed; she arrowed among them and the screams began.

I set off at my best speed for the *Sinner*.

***

I attack. Multiple weapons open up, but targeting is poor and the weapons are light. I cover the ground, flinging rock fragments I have found with deadly force. I am upon them and destroy a number of the enemy. I seize a weapon and move at the others,

Disaster. I find my body will not respond to my commands. It is not the pitiful weapon fire, so inaccurately aimed at me, but ancient damage done by the Infestors. My internal diagnostics do not tell me what has failed. I cannot quickly reroute or recircuit. None of my onboard weapons function. I cannot even use my appendages. I am spinning aimlessly just over the surface.

I am helpless. Now shot after shot hits me as I sprawl onto the asteroid's surface. I am doomed, but I concentrate all my remaining power and repair functions to raise my head to face my enemies. I will look extinction in the eye as it comes for me.

***

I dropped Candace in the airlock and hooked her to the emer-port supply. Then I leaned out to check on Maauro. Flashes and explosions silently lit up the asteroid and I was glad I couldn't hear the screams of the people she was killing. I spotted her as she surged out of a fold on the asteroid's surface, moving so fast that the weapon fire spalled the ground behind her.

Fire slackened as she reduced Dusko's forces. Only two were firing at her now.

Suddenly Maauro seemed to freeze in motion, tumbling on stiff limbs over the asteroid's surface like a broken toy. She landed face down as shots and a beam kicked up the surface around her. Maauro raised herself up and a round bounced off her head, cutting off some of the fake hair and making her flinch. Then she steadied herself to glare at her enemies.

A huge form stepped up from a crater. It had to be Truf. He advanced on her, carrying a big-bored weapon, wary, or more likely gloating.

I should get away. It's not a big-eyed little girl out there. It's a killing machine that has smashed men into paste. Why should I risk my life for a machine? I cursed myself as I grabbed the line-gun from its locker and dashed out onto the surface. I am a dumb son-of-a-bitch....

***

The enemy who will destroy me is the largest biological I have seen yet. His suit is armored and the weapon he carries is the only one that really concerned me. I fail to understand why he has left the safety of cover to close on me. I gaze at the face, noting the snarling muzzle and large canines, the wide eyes. I sense this being wants me to suffer, to know who it is that has defeated me.

I can barely move and only manage to tip back my head as it slowly walks up. It raises the large-bore projectile weapon and places it against my forehead. I remember the sights, sounds and scents that have provided me with pleasure in my short awareness. The stars, the roar of the ocean and sigh of the winds near the factory where I was made. These things I will take into the Great Dark with me. I meet his eyes. If all I can manage is a glare, then I shall.

The alien's faceplate suddenly crazes as a metal bolt penetrates it; gas and fluids spurt out. The alien falls backward, triggering his weapon with one last convulsion. The shot gouges the surface next to me.

I turn slowly. Wrik is charging across the open space, trying to reload some sort of projectile device. He is coming to rescue me. The fragile bag of flesh and fluids is running in the open, in an unarmored suit, to rescue me, an M7 combat android. The absurdity of the situation threatens to unhinge my stability.

A beam lances by him, missing by millimeters and he goes down into a forward roll. One enemy still operates.

With the additional time Wrik has bought me, I concentrate and am able to restore some function to one arm. I drag myself forward to the fallen weapon, seize it and open fire on the enemy. To my surprise, the remaining enemy flees. Crippled as I am, I cannot track him, and he escapes.

Then Wrik is standing over me. "Are you all right?"

"No, I am severely damaged and depleted."

"Let's get you to the ship."

I use the weapon and his aid to rise. Fortunately, the low gravity allows him to hoist me on his back and we head for his ship. I raise my head again to look up at the stars silently flaming overhead and I am glad to be able to see them.

***

CHAPTER 4

Sinner kicked free of the surface. I used full military power to blast away from the asteroid. I didn't know if Dusko's ship was armed and I was taking no chances. My *Dauntless* scout was faster and more maneuverable than most ships. Once we were in deep space, we had little to fear. After an hour of scanning, I set up the autopilot and went back to check on Maauro and Candace.

***

Wrik busies himself with the ship. I continue my self-repairs, regaining control of my body. Still, I cannot ascertain what occurred or why and I do not know if it will happen again. I study the unconscious female. She's a security risk that I had not counted on. While Wrik is occupied, I again infiltrate his computer, searching through former warcraft's databases until I come to one on combat-medicine.

I program one of the chemical factories in my body and silently move over to the female. I extrude a fine needle from my finger and inject her with the sedative I have made. The simple compound should keep her asleep until we land and I can hide.

I return to my seat unnoticed and study the ship. It is in need of many improvements. This I can easily do, in time. I consider Wrik as well. There are clearly many improvements needed there, but I am confident of my ability to effect these as well.

***

Sinner grounded at Kandalor spaceport at its usual pad. No one raced out to arrest or otherwise molest us. If Dusko was back, he was laying low for now. I looked at Maauro, who'd pressed herself against the canopy since we entered atmosphere, studying the world below as if it were her new toy box. As *Sinner* settled on her landing jacks with a sigh, Maauro moved to the hatchway.

"I will be outside," she said, before I could speak. "Candace will awaken shortly and I do not want her to know I was aboard the ship. She will doubtless wish to leave quickly. Encourage this." She slipped out of the airlock.

Maauro was right about Candace waking, which led me to wonder if Maauro had something to do with the woman's long sleep on the trip back. Candace's eyes fluttered open, drifted about in confusion and then locked on me.

"You're safe," I began, "back on Kandalor. Here's some water. Don't try to move around much. You've been out for two days."

Her eyes did not leave mine as she drained the cup of water. "Headache," she managed, "starving."

"Got it covered." I returned with soup and crackers and a flask of restorative drink to find Candace sitting up.

"What happened?"

"We were lucky," I said. "First, I didn't betray you to Dusko. Treska did. Dusko told me."

She looked at me dubiously.

"Look, dammit. I didn't know where we were going or what was out there. He did. If I set you up, why are you here?"

She considered. "People aren't always what they seem. Are they, Wrik?"

"No."

"Tell me more." She started on the soup.

"There was something on that asteroid. I never got a clear look at it. I suspect anything that did, died. Dusko's men shot at it when we were near that lifeboat. It hunted us. Did you see it?"

"No. I saw smashed bodies. Weapons fire in the distance."

Good, I thought. Then I started lying again. "Anyway, it killed most of Dusko's men and, I'm afraid, Teska too, before it blew up on the surface. It must have been ancient. Hard to believe it was still working. Lucky for you, the flash attracted me to where I found you. I made a break for it on the *Sinner*. I think Dusko got away on his ship."

"Quite a tale, Wrik."

"I can show you where it blew up," I said. "Not much there."

"You won't be seeing that particular rock again."

I smiled. "You're not really a prospector, are you?"

A change came over Candace Deveraux, as if a switch had been thrown. Her eyes glittered as she studied me. "That base could hold technology that might be critical to the Confederacy, Wrik. It's too important to be left to any private interest."

I narrowed my eyes at her. "You're Confed Intelligence. I wondered how you knew so much about my background."

"Something like that," she said coolly.

"So what now?"

"Now, Wrik, you forget about that asteroid. Try to go back there and you'll end up vaporized."

"Hey," I said. "I was on your side."

"Were you, Wrik? I have a feeling there are things you're holding back from me. Well, no matter. There's an additional 10,000 credits in it for you if you keep your mouth shut about this, and you're only getting that because you did save my life. There are other ways of guaranteeing your silence."

"Deal."

"Dusko said you were a smart boy."

"I swear to you I wasn't in this with him."

"I believe you, Wrik. Mostly. Help me to the refresher. I need a shower and a change of clothes."

Candace didn't linger. She moved money to my account and made a coded call to the port. I walked her out of the ship and onto the tarmac, handing her the bag with her personal effects in it.

Candace shaded her eyes and looked up at *Sinner*. "Who's that sitting up atop your ship?"

I spun to see Maauro perched atop *Sinner*, looking into the sunset. "Ah, just a local girl. I met her recently."

"She looks a bit young for you," Candace reproved.

"She's older than she looks."

"If you say so, Wrik. You're full of surprises. Guess I will have to keep track of you. I might find myself in need of a pilot again. See you around, Handsome."

I watched Candace's ample figure sway away over the tarmac, heading back to the port buildings. Then I climbed back into *Sinner* and made my way to the top hatch. I boosted myself up onto the fuselage.

Maauro glanced at me, and then returned to her rapt consideration of the setting sun.

"A human couldn't stare into the sun like that," I said.

"There is no one to see me. How beautiful the sky is, with its flaming bands of color," she said. "I have been at war all my existence. There has been little time for such sights."

"And that is important to you?"

"My reconnaissance program makes it pleasurable for me to acquire information."

"Even with no one to report to?"

"Even then."

"It seems a pointless existence," I said, and then regretted the comment.

Maauro shrugged. "I am pleased that I need no longer fight. It frees me to experience options unavailable to me before. I will sample an existence free of war, gather sunsets and gaze on stars for as long as I continue to function."

"How long will that be?"

"I do not know, Wrik. You saw my body fail me on the asteroid. I have yet to learn why. I am not what I once was. My damage, though not visible to you, is extensive and my repair is far beyond your science. Any second may be my last."

"Is there anything back on the asteroid that could help?"

"We will not be able to return. I listened in on your conversation with Candace. Besides, I salvaged what I could from the M4 50,000 years ago. Yet, there may be a chance. This is a strange world in a strange system. Who can say what lies buried here or in near space? It may also be that, with time and certain rare materials, I can conduct further repairs on myself."

"A chance," I said, "a second chance, maybe for both of us."

She turned to consider me with her huge eyes. "Shall we take that second chance, Wrik? Shall we protect each other and remain free?"

Something I thought long dead stirred in me. "Maauro, that's the best deal I've been offered in a long while."

CHAPTER

5

I LOOKED INTO THE HOSTEL'S BATHROOM MIRROR AT MY HAG-gard, unshaven face. "Here I am: disgraced ex-military, impoverished local-haul spacer and now owner of the most efficient killer android in known space."

The latter wasn't quite true. I didn't own Maauro. In the weeks that had passed since we returned from the asteroid, I began to get the impression that she owned me and regretted not having kept the receipt so she could make a return. Still, all Maauro and I had now was each other. I was a resource and refuge for her and she was physical protection from Dusko and the other perils of life on Kandalor. I passed Maauro off as a mutated human from a colony on the far side of Confederate space. So far, the crude deception had worked on this world where humans weren't common.

I shaved myself to respectability and made my way to the hangar where *Sinner* was berthed. The 10,000-credit bonus from Confed Intelligence had covered debts, repairs and some of Maauro's needs. The android hadn't come through the centuries without damage, both from her battle ages ago, and from some deterioration that intermittently struck her like a form of sclerosis. But bad times had come to Vanceport and the nearby worlds. Many of the hangars stood empty. Our funds drained away.

None, however, had drained on anodyne, a drug I occasionally bought when I was in cash. It wasn't a high; it just made my memories go away for some happy hours. I'd gotten one dose off Mecalam and zoned for a day, only to find an unhappy Maauro wondering why I had "malfunctioned." I hadn't seen him since. I'd tried to locate another dealer, but all were steering clear of me. Perhaps Dusko was trying to make my life miserable in small ways.

A figure waited for me, seated in her usual spot on the wing of *Sinner*, staring up at the sky as if the ever-changing clouds were a personal show for her. Maauro looked like a human girl of sixteen, about five-foot-four, slender, pale with glossy, black hair that tumbled to her waist. Aquamarine eyes, four times the size of a human's, dominated her face. What appeared today to be an orange and dark-gray bodysuit was simply the outer layer of her body, just given different texture, as were her boots. She varied the colors somewhat to give the impression she was wearing something different. Maauro gave no sign of seeing me but was undoubtedly tracking every target in sight and perhaps a few that weren't.

"There was a message in my inbasket," I said.

She looked down at me. To an alien, she might have looked human, but to me she was a living, animated character. I'd tried to talk her into working further on her appearance, but she claimed that ability had shut down. At least she'd managed some nostrils before it had. By now too many people had seen her and any radical change would attract more attention.

"Work, one hopes?" she said in a high, childlike voice.

"One does hope. Credits are getting scarce."

"Yes, I fear that I am the cause of much of that. The materials I need have been expensive and hard to find."

"Damn near impossible," I grumbled. "A Nekoan named Nenan Tekala wants to see us. We have two hours to get to the Watering Hole."

Maauro hopped down from the wing in a drop that would have broken bones in a real human. We started toward the edge of the field. Suddenly Maauro staggered. I grabbed the toppling android, only barely holding her up. She was far heavier than she looked.

"What's wrong?" I asked, fearing I knew the answer.

Maauro looked up at me, her face pensive. "My right leg is malfunctioning. I can reroute around the dead zone, but it is dangerous for me to be seen in this condition."

"Yeah," I returned. "If Dusko catches us when you're malfunctioning..."

"Yes. He fears me, but he saw me fail once on the asteroid. It is unfortunate he survived."

I waved at a pedicycle at the edge of the field. The native driver, a Mook tribesman by his headdress, pedaled over eagerly. Fares were hard to come by these days. He was anthropoid, but with a snoutlike nose and bulbous black eyes. Most of his body was muffled in loose robes against the high-desert heat.

"The Watering Hole, Old City," I said, then turned to Maauro. "Let's go make some money."

"Yes, baby needs new batteries."

***

I do not advise Wrik of the extent of my cascade failure or how close I come to becoming terminally unstable. Wrik's courage is highly variable. I do not want to risk his stability as I battle inside my body for my own.

Ironic that we both have our malfunctions. Wrik had ingested some substance purchased from another human named Mecalam. It caused him dysfunction for over twenty-four hours. As this malfunction seemed self-induced, I deduce it is a weakness of his. Since I cannot rely on him to control these impulses, I determined interdiction to be the most effective course. Locating and eliminating Mecalam was simple. Thereafter, I eliminated several other prospective suppliers to generate the requisite deterrence, and then allowed one supplier to survive with minor injuries to provide intelligence of the threat to others. It proved a successful tactic.

***

The pedicycle made good time through the excellent, Confed-made roads of the spaceport. Not surprisingly beyond the Confed enclave, the roads worsened. Ahead lay Old City, which was just that, walled and turreted, an ancient fortress of white stone incongruously spotted with solar panels and antenna. The pedicycle struggled through the narrow streets. The driver finally gave up on muscle and started his small motor, giving us dark looks. Eventually we reached the shopping district. We dismounted the pedicycle to walk through the riot of stalls and awnings in its narrow stone streets.

"Curious," Maauro said. "The ones you call Kandalorians are not. They did not live on this world when my Creators controlled this system."

"You were here?" I asked in surprise.

"No. I fought in space. But the data is in my memory. These creatures came after."

I shrugged. "They've been here long enough to forget both their origins and their technology. So many species have either ruled or visited this planet; it's hard to tell who has the best claim."

We walked among the robed Kandalorians, along with members from all twenty-one known oxygen-breathing races. Kandalor was a law to itself, one reason I had fled here.

Maauro watched the market, showing every evidence of enjoyment and fascination. She'd probably never seen anything like it in her brief operational life before being stranded. As we passed one stall, she suddenly stopped and reached out a hand capable of shredding steel to pick up a bolt of yellow-orange silk. "This is so beautiful."

I looked at her with bemusement. "I suppose so."

"It reminds me of the sun over the world where I first became aware," she said, a faraway look in the huge eyes. "Will you buy this for me?"

"Yes, yes." a Kandalorian merchant came up, its trunk-like nose waving in front of its dark, bulbous eyes."A beautiful fabric for your beautiful lady."

Maauro swept up her waist-length-hair into a ponytail, leaving long wisps framing her face. To my surprise, she tied the silk in an elaborate bow and admired the result in a mirror.

The merchant looked at me as a cat would a bowl of cream.

I looked at Maauro with narrowed eyes. "You have a lot to learn about commerce."

Twenty credits lighter, we stood before the Watering Hole, an open-air restaurant in the old quarter. The restaurant catered to Nekoans, the feline aliens who were the most numerous species on Kandalor. A few Kandalorians sat under the broad frond trees that graced the courtyard, almost hidden by the water fountain that kept the heat of the summer afternoon at bay. Over us loomed the Sala Haga, a circular building, like a layered honey cake. Atop it stood a tower crowned with a mass of topaz crystal. Sunshine reflected from it in deep, buttery tones. The Sala had stood that way for as long as there was any record.

An elegant female Nekoan eyed us as we came up. Her eyes were purple, cat-like irises under a pile of rough-coated hair from which projected large soft ears. Her skin was bronze, with only the tiniest hints of fur. She was enough like a human to appeal to me. Of course, it had been a long time since my last contact with a human woman other than Candace. She smiled human-fashion at me, revealing brilliant, sharp white teeth.

"You're Wrik Trigardt?" she asked.

"Yes."

"The owner is expecting you." She led us through a gate to an inner court-yard with an office cooled by rotating fans. I watched her swaying hips and long tail with appreciation.

"They are here, Master Tekala," she said, then passed through a rear door to return with a tea tray.

I introduced myself and my "cousin" Maauro.

"Please sit," Tekala said, his voice rich with alien accents but with none of the growl one expected. Of course, I thought, he only looks a bit like a lion. Nekoans are no more cats than humans are monkeys.

His assistant returned to pour tea into small delicate celadon cups, which we sipped from in the ritual of greeting.

"I need your help," Tekala said, with uncharacteristic directness for a Nekoan. "My daughter, Jaelle, is missing. She's a dealer in antiquities and dis-appeared in the Stonal Abyss over six months ago. A trader brought her a find. Next thing I knew she'd assembled an expedition. At first, her staff here got regular reports, then Jaelle entered the land of the will o' wisps"

"The what?" Maauro asked.

I waved an impatient hand. "Old legends. Occasionally a spacer coming in over the Stonal abyss reports signs of high technology, a city far out in the southern jungles. But there's never been any hard evidence."

"My daughter disappeared exploring that area. Government authority doesn't extend beyond the Eliash plateau. I am too old to go myself. My war injuries pain me to where I can only walk short distances. So I hired private mercenaries to search for her. You may have known of some of them: Lostra, Veggs and Terrazzas."

"Yeah," I replied. They were among the bad and the dangerous that I avoided zealously.

"They didn't come back," Tekala added.

I raised my cup to my lips. My mouth was suddenly rather dry. "Why tell me this? I'm a pilot, not a gunman."

"I am looking for someone else to go."

"Sorry," I said. "You've wasted your time. I'm just a pilot."

"Is that all?" Tekala said dryly, his eyes drifting over to Maauro, who looked back innocently.

"Yes," I insisted, "that's all."

"It has not escaped notice that you have survived the enmity of the crimelord Dusko, though how it is that a man and a girl child can do this, no one knows."

"I don't know what you're talking about," I said, pushing back the chair.

"I can pay well," Tekala said, raising a hand.

"Not—" I began.

"How well can you pay?" Maauro interrupted.

"20,000 Confed credits per week, with a 10,000 credit bonus if you find my daughter's remains, and 100,000 credits for her safe return."

That gave me pause but after a second I shook my head. "Maauro, those were some of the best gunners around. They're dead, or they'd have come back."

"We need the money," she said.

God, I thought, I'm going to have to teach her something about commerce soon. "Dead people can't spend credits."

I turned back to Tekala. "What kind of artifact made her head out to such a hellhole as that? It's the other side of a big planet."

Tekala sank back into his seat and signaled to his assistant. "Bring it."

The female slipped out of the room to return with a large, flat panel covered in a sheer silk cloth that made a metallic thunk as she placed it on the table. Tekala pulled the fabric off to reveal a panel of a highly refined metal of an odd, reddish hue. On it was a series of crudely painted images. Though I didn't recognize the shapes, they looked somehow familiar. They were images of some sort of creature, painted in dark greens and blues. It had four legs and two arm/legs and looked both saurian and insectoid.

Maauro surprised me by standing and looking at the piece. She placed a hand on the metal. "We'll take the job."

"Excuse me," I snapped. "My cousin seems to have lost her mind."

"Could you leave us alone for a moment?" Maauro asked the Nekoans. The feline aliens withdrew.

"Have you blown a circuit?" I hissed.

She looked at me, unaffected by my anger. "That is a panel of hull metal from an Infestor ship. On it, someone has painted the image of an Infestor. I was able to carbon date the panel. It was painted several hundred years ago."

"Impossible," I breathed. "They've been gone for almost 50,000 years."

"I must explore this," she said. "My programming demands it and we might find some useful technology."

"This is a planet," I countered, "not an asteroid. Even buried in an airless rock, you suffered degradation. Nothing useful could have survived so many ages."

"What of these will o' wisps?" she said.

"Legends, nothing more."

"Wrik, we are without resources here. My system failures are coming more frequently and I do not know how much longer I will operate. If I cease to function, you will not survive me long. Dusko still hunts you."

I looked at the ancient panel and wondered if it was my headstone. "I suppose I have little choice."

CHAPTER

6

WE TOOK OFF TWO DAYS LATER WITH *SINNER* LOADED WITH food, munitions and what little information there was on the Stonal Abyss and the will o' wisp sightings.

Maauro watched me with a critical eye. "I can fly this with greater efficiency."

"Keep your hands off *Sinner*," I said. "She's already jealous that I'm seeing another machine."

"Very amusing," she said. "I'm off to the top turret to watch the sunrise. The colors are so beautiful."

I shook my head.

"Why does it continue to surprise you that I have an aesthetic and appreciate beauty?" she asked. "I am artificial in origin, but I am not one of your crude toys."

"No, our crude toys rarely sound miffed."

Maauro departed as I was reminding myself that she was not a cute girl I could tease, but an advanced killing machine. I needed to remember that. Most of her human characteristics came from a game program. God only knew what really went on inside her armored skull, if that was where her CPU lay.

At Mach 4 even a big world like Kandalor rolled under us quickly. We were flying with the sun and reached Wayfarer in the late morning. I piloted *Sinner* in a descending spiral, heading for the gap in the endless forest canopy that surrounded the trading post on the edge of the Stonal.

"There," Maauro said, pointing at a bend in the river that held a collection of prefab and native buildings. Swamp boats lined the floating docks and a landing field of hard-packed earth contained a few light aircraft. An automatic beacon was the sole traffic control, so I kept a sharp eye out for other aircraft as I circled down and used the VTOL drive to drop *Sinner* onto the field.

Fetid air greeted us as I cracked the hatch. Maauro clattered down the ladder behind me as I dropped to the orange soil. My knees, stiff from the long flight, protested. Maauro sailed past me in an easy leap. Whatever sclerosis intermittently affected her was in remission for now.

"Showoff," I grumbled.

As we walked toward the shacks and bars along the riverfront, I pulled up short. Two aerospace craft sat at the field's edge under the treeline, partially obscured with blue tarps. The tarps were frayed and dirty with branches lying on them.

"You recognize these ships?" Maauro asked.

"Yeah," I said. "That's Veggs' old *Wildcat* fighter and Terrazza's atmo-skimmer. Looks like they've been there for months."

"Curious that they have not been stolen or salvaged," she said.

"Nobody will touch those ships while there's any chance their owners will return. Suicide would be as certain."

We spent the next two hours sitting in bars, drinking cheap liquor in my case and asking questions. Maauro drew attention from some of the men. I wasn't worried about it, save that we didn't need the grief caused if she yanked some creep's privates off. We learned little. Jaelle Tekala had landed here eight months ago. She rented a skimmer and recruited a few locals before disappearing into the Stonal. Occasionally a local, piloting the skimmer, returned for supplies or to ship out crudely made crates, then, nothing. The next month Lostra came, followed by Veggs, then Terrazzas. They, too, disappeared in the direction of the great swamp and the Tar Sea that rumor said lay to the west.

"So now we add our bodies to the count," I concluded as I sat with Maauro under a roof of thatched fronds, picking at a meal of rice, veggies and some unfortunate local animal. Maauro, who processed all forms of matter into energy, ate as well.

"Why do you express such trepidation?" she asked. "No enemy presently threatens us."

"Humans anticipate trouble," I said.

Maauro sighed, found a bit of fish on her plate and ate it. "Poor energy potential."

"Is that all you have to say?"

She eyed me with what seemed disappointment. "The others did not have the services of a Mark VII combat android. Even in my depleted state, I am the most formidable fighting unit on this world."

If you're working, I thought. Aloud I said, "We can't even get a local to guide us out. With all the disappearances, no one will head westward into the swamp."

"We will rent a skimmer and proceed to the last place she was known to be," Maauro said. "Then we will search."

We slept in the *Sinner,* or rather, I did. Maauro kept watch in the cockpit, so I had no concern about thieves or hijackers. Occasionally I heard her working in the engine compartment where I kept machine tools.

I woke a little after dawn and used the fresher. When I walked up to the flight deck I stopped dead in surprise. Maauro sat on the deck examining a deadly box-like object with two projecting barrels, one of which was an easy 50mm in width.

"What the hell is that?"

"I have been unsatisfied with the armaments that we have been able to secure. This is inferior to my original armspac but greatly superior to what we have."

"Well, I guess it will be useful if we run into a thunderlizard."

"It would be," she said, "but do not attempt to use it yourself. Firing the projectile weapon would fracture your arm bones."

I eyed the monster gun. "No problem."

Sinner was too large and heavy to land on swampy jungle ground, so we rented a large skimmer. The machine was little more than a skiff with a compression skid under it and a tail and fan assembly for propulsion. A framed canopy held the control panel. Clearplast curtains kept the a/c in. The dark-green machine was unlovely but practical. We set out after Maauro lashed down our supplies and finished raising the side panels to keep dinkagators from scrambling aboard.

I popped up the GPS to input the last location known for Jaelle's expedition. Automatics took us away from the dock as the engine purred up to speed and we pulled out into the river. I dropped the curtains as Maauro joined me inside. The a/c whisked sweat off me. I looked at Maauro. "I can see one advantage you have over a human girl."

She looked at me curiously. "What would that be?"

"A real girl with that much hair would simply expire from the heat."

"Yet more evidence of my superiority over you bags of meat and fluids," she said.

"Smile when you say that."

Maauro gave me a brilliant grin.

"That was irony, Maauro."

"No," she said. "My smile was irony."

I did a double take. "You catch on quick."

***

We proceed into the jungle. The primitive GPS performs adequately, as does the skimmer. I sit with Wrik in the little cocoon of dried and cooled air. Biological life forms are so fragile; in space they must seal themselves in small containers of their environment. Even on a compatible world, they seek to hide in enclosures to moderate the environment. I could as easily sit outside, but my proximity to Wrik has a purpose. Since we landed here, our time together has been focused on survival: avoiding Dusko and trying to keep me operational.

Yet I am developing concerns about Wrik. I am aware that his personal behavior prior to my arrival has been questionable, even criminal. This seems to have been more a matter of survival than preference. Yet this masks something deeper. Wrik has attempted to obliterate all records of his life prior to arriving on Kandalor. He rejects all my attempts to inquire into his past life. My investigation of his quarters and effects disclosed that he is ex-military but not of the Confederacy.

Now that we are confined to the skimmer may be a good time to gather information. In addition, a transient failure has occurred in my suspensory drive. I cannot rise. While I recircuit around this latest failure, I might as well do something to pass the time. I will not tell Wrik. It will cause him undue concern. I am reasonably sure I can effect sufficient repairs to regain my mobility.

***

CHAPTER 6

We traveled up the river for several hours in silence, Maauro watching the riverbanks with their collections of colorful birds and flowers as the skimmer flew over the surface of the water.

"It occurs to me," Maauro said, "that we know very little of each other."

"That might be because every time I ask you about your past, you insist it's all classified, even though your creators are extinct."

"My past consists exclusively of combat missions. My Creators are missing from this area of space. I do not know that they are extinct."

"And the rest of your life?" I asked, leaning back in my chair, which creaked under my weight.

"I was operational for seven years before I attacked the Infestor base on that asteroid. In that respect, I am far younger and less experienced than you."

I stared at her. "And for the 50,000 years in between?"

"I sat in the dark and decayed, only marginally aware through one subroutine of the passage of time."

She turned her child-like, perfect face to me. "But you, Wrik, had a life before we met. Tell me about it."

I sat silent, thinking on my life. "My past is gone. I don't want to talk about it. My life on Kandalor began after I bought *Sinner* at a Confed base in the Morokat systems. I came here in suspended animation by slow freighter. I'd hoped to start over but Kandalor isn't as welcoming to strangers as I'd heard. So I struggled until I met Dusko...the rest you know."

"Why do you not wish to recall your past?"

"Mind your own business, Killbot."

I stood and brushed through the clearplast curtain, leaving Maauro and her questions behind. The heat slapped my face.

***

Some shame lies in his past. I have noted recently that while biologicals tend to live in a network of lifeforms related to them genetically, or through other associations, Wrik lacks such a network. This may lie at the heart of his anodyne use.

I must evaluate how this affects his usefulness to me. Meanwhile, I have finished repairs and rerouting. I am down to my last set of backups in my right leg.

***

I stayed out for several miserable hours while the killbot enjoyed my air-conditioning. Only probing into my past could have gotten such a reaction from me. Now I couldn't believe I had spoken in such a manner to my deadly companion.

Eventually the heat broke down my resistance and I returned to the cabin. Maauro took no notice of me. We drove on in blessed silence. Night fell and the skimmer drove on. GPS and an unsleeping Maauro allowed us to continue. I spent an uncomfortable night on the floor of the boat on a too-thin pad.

In the morning, the river changed character. Its surface became oilier, with occasional dark patches of tar floating free or fetched up against the shore. The swamp gave off an overpowering petroleum smell until it deadened my nose.

"Look," Maauro said.

"I see it." Half sunk in the river was the burned remains of a skimmer like our own. We pulled up and Maauro leaped ashore, unlimbering the deadly boxy weapon she'd slung across her shoulder.

I secured the boat and picked up a submachine gun, hanging the strap around my neck and followed her ashore, staring at the burned skimmer. Maauro was already yards ahead, pushing through the tall grass. Then I saw what she had clearly spotted, the remnants of a camp, tents in bright, artificial colors, broken, slashed and burned. Other evidence of disaster lay underfoot: bleached bones.

"What do you see?" I asked of my killbot.

She looked around the clearing with a practiced eye. "I see broken spears and fragments of arrows. The bones are those of Kandalorians; there is no Nekoan among them. I deduce that primitives attacked the campsite, probably at night. I note some of the trees bear old scorch marks from a simple energy weapon, probably something as crude as a laser. The primitives were victorious."

I looked at the tangles of bones. "How can you tell?"

"The camp has been looted of valuables. The only spears and arrows that remain are broken. The primitives recovered any usable weapons."

"That means either Jaelle escaped or was captured," I said

We went back to the skimmer. Maauro disappeared under it and simply lifted the boat out of the water to deposit it ashore. No one would take it while we were inland. We got our equipment out and headed back to the ruined campsite, hoping to find some trail leading away.

As we neared the camp, Maauro's head snapped around. She rapidly signaled with her left hand while yanking her monster gun from its carrying case. I dropped behind a tree hummock, unslinging my SMG.

I looked around for Maauro, who seemed to have disappeared. Then I spotted an odd bit of color, the yellow ribbon in her hair. Maauro stood still at the edge of the glade. Her body had turned camouflage, blending in with the forest. Her weapon was hidden behind her.

Someone was moving through the forest, coming with confidence, not stealth.

A woman walked into the clearing. Tall, lean and tan, she had a shock of rich blue hair cut at her jawline. She wore fatigue greens with a tactical vest and pack. A long-barreled laser rode on her hip. Her face was sharp and angular. I couldn't see her eyes from here but knew they'd be black and as lifeless as a shark's.

Lostra.

She paused halfway through the clearing and scanned the area; somehow she seemed to sense where I was. Her eyes narrowed and her hand flicked to the butt of her weapon.

"Come out," she called. "I know you're there. I heard your motor earlier. Hands empty or you're a dead man."

"Don't shoot, Lostra," I called, letting my SMG hang by its sling.

Lostra came toward me, her hand over the weapon. "I know you. Trigardt, the pilot. Here all by your little self? You're either reckless or an idiot."

Maauro's optical camo vanished and she stepped forward, her weapon aimed at the ground between them. "You missed a third option."

Lostra froze, a look of shock flitting over her face. She turned only her head to stare in disbelief at Maauro, at the orange and gray jumpsuit, and the yellow bow tied in the long black hair. "How in God's name did I miss you?"

"My friend Maauro is full of surprises. Nasty ones when provoked," I said.

Lostra stared at Maauro, who, recognizing another predator, stared back unflinchingly.

"So you have a new girlfriend," Lostra said, a smile sickling across her face. "But don't try and tell me that tinkertoy is a human."

"You may consider me a new species," Maauro interrupted, "a noneofyourgoddamnbusinessean."

Lostra's face flushed and she turned to face Maauro. "No one talks to me that way."

"Wrik, please move back," Maauro said. "I do not wish to feel restrained."

"I'm considered pretty fast," Lostra said idly.

"Not by me," Maauro returned. Her posture showed neither relaxation nor tension, nothing for Lostra to read beyond a total lack of fear.

I realized I wasn't breathing. "Lostra, we're not here for this. We're here to find Jaelle Tekala."

"Really," Lostra said, staring at Maauro.

I felt a flash of anger at the stupidity of it all. "Holster your ego. You'll just go from living to meat."

Lostra looked sidewise at me. "Not worried that I might get you too, Wrik? No, you're not worried, are you? I've heard you're," her eyes flicked back to Maauro, "or were...until recently, a very, very cautious man."

Apparently, my lack of concern persuaded her. She half-turned away from Maauro. "So Tekala hired you too. Well, hard to blame him, considering how overdue I was." She stepped toward me, but I recognized that she was trying to put me between her and Maauro. I moved to stand next to Maauro.

Lostra gave me a small smile and an approving nod

"Now that we have that out of our system," I said. "Why don't you tell us what happened to you? Have you seen Jaelle or the others who came after her?"

Lostra walked over to sit on a broken crate. "You got a dopestick? I'm dying for one."

"He doesn't do drugs," Maauro said.

We both did a double-take on her.

"Will a cup of mocha do?" I said. I pulled a self-heating container from my backpack and tossed it to her. Lostra snatched it out of the air in a move almost too fast to follow. She snapped the tab on it.

"The old man hired me to find her. I did the same thing you did, came to the last site where she was known to be. I brought my light fighter and figured I'd just burn an opening in the canopy with my weapons, but the ground concealed a hole and my ship crashed and burned on landing. Since then I've been dodging primitives, killing the ones that got too close and hoping somebody else would show up that I could catch a lift back with."

"Did you see Terrazzas or Veggs?" I asked.

She looked at me curiously. "No."

"They were the second and third rescue attempts. We're the fourth."

Lostra shrugged. "Well, they didn't come this way." The lid popped off the mocha. She blew across the steaming liquid and sipped it. "Gah, almost as good as a dopestick."

"Did you find any sign of Jaelle?" Maauro asked.

Again the measuring look from Lostra. "I got close to the biggest village in this area. It's about ten klicks west on the edge of the Tar Sea. I saw someone being hustled from one hut to another. It was too far to be sure, but it looked like a Nekoan."

I bit my lip and looked at Maauro. "What do you think?"

"If Jaelle is alive, we should extract her. Her body is worth 100,000 credits alive and 10,000 even dead."

I sighed. If we lived, I was going to drum commerce into her metal head.

Lostra whistled. "Nice money, better than they offered me. If you're going into that village you'll need help. Cut me in for half and I'll come with you."

Before Maauro could buy high and sell low, I raised a hand. "Equal shares, three ways."

Lostra's black eyes bored into me. "You see a lot of gunners waiting to be hired?"

"Your utility to us is marginal," Maauro said. "We have weapons and transportation."

Lostra's face twitched, as did my stomach.

"Still, we could use the help," I added

Maauro's face betrayed nothing. She merely gazed unblinkingly at the gunwoman. "As you wish, Wrik."

"Your pretty friend is right. It's a long walk home. An equal share it is." Lostra finished the mocha and tossed it over her shoulder. "You got a plan, Sweetie?"

"Take us to a good observation point near the village. We'll reconnoiter and plan a stealthy assault."

"You want anything to eat?" I asked Lostra. "Need any meds?"

"Nah," she said rising. "The sooner we get the catgirl or her pelt, the sooner we can get back to what passes for civilization in this shithole." Lostra walked off with no evident concern about whether we'd follow.

I started forward, but Maauro put a hand on my arm. I was surprised to feel how soft that hand was. She'd been playing with textures again.

"I am unconvinced of her story," she whispered. "Her equipment and person are in very good order for an extended combat op in this environment. Remain alert."

CHAPTER

7

HOURS LATER, WE REACHED A PROMONTORY WITH A GOOD view of the village. A palisade, complete with watchtowers, faced us. Behind it were a hundred or more mud and wattle huts. A lower palisade faced the Tar Sea, which was less a sea than a continuation of the swamp; only here it was a mass of tar, topped with water and pocked with hummocks of tough, yellow plants.

I could see a horde of dugouts pulled up on the shoreline. Behind them ran a long stone jetty covered by ornate wooden structures. I marveled at the effort that went into making it in an area not overly blessed with stone. On its other side, the top of a shed-like structure with a metal roof projected.

"Interesting," Maauro said. "The village was only recently fortified. The original layout took little account of defensibility. The palisades are of recent construction, of newly cut wood."

"Meaning?" I asked.

"They have acquired enemies only recently."

Lostra's eyes flicked to Maauro, but she said nothing.

A commotion on the stone jetty drew our attention. A party of Kandalorians in brightly colored robes and wearing long feathers came out of one of the ornately-carved wooden structures. Behind these dignitaries came warriors dragging a struggling captive.

I cursed and grabbed for my binoculars.

"It is not a Nekoan," Maauro reassured me. "Nor is it any other of the known species."

The binoculars auto-focused on the scene and I could see the truth of Maauro's statement. The captive was a humanoid with gray-blue skin and a crest of bone or something on its head. I couldn't see much of a face but got the impression of large eyes like Maauro's. The being wore clothing far more sophisticated than his or her captors.

Chanting reached our ears and natives began to spill out of the huts, gathering down at the shore. There was an ugly violence underlying the chanting. I passed the binoculars to Lostra. "What do you make of it?"

She studied the scene. "No species that I know of. The others look like priests and warriors."

"I wonder if that might be one of the will o' wisps that we have heard rumors of," Maauro said.

The party reached the end of the jetty and secured the struggling captive to a wooden apparatus.

Sickness gripped me; some horror was in the offing.

The chanting rose to a hideous crescendo and suddenly the apparatus flung the bound captive out into the Tar Sea. The roar of the villagers mercifully covered any scream by the doomed captive, who hit the tarry water with a splash and disappeared. I swallowed hard, fighting nausea, and looked away.

After a few seconds, I looked back at Maauro and Lostra, both of whom gazed on unaffected by the murderous scene. The similarity between them chilled me.

No additional awfulness followed. The villagers returned to their huts and activities, and the priests disappeared into the wooden structure.

"Show's over," Lostra said, turning her back to the village and settling in. In seconds the gunwoman was asleep. Maauro, too, settled into a sitting posture, watching the village. I tried very hard to forget what I had seen and there was no possibility of rest for me.

Night fell quickly in the tropic latitude. We waited in silence for the village to settle. Fires flared up in the village, but to my surprise I saw modern lights on the other side of the jetty near the shed. There was someone besides natives in the village.

"I see it, too," Lostra said. "If Jaelle is down there, my bet is she's near those lights."

"You have a plan?" Maauro asked.

It seemed odd for her to defer to Lostra, but the gunner had been stalking this village for weeks.

"Yeah. Now that you're here, with that ship cannon you carry so easily, I have some folks to cover my escape. There's a spot near the palisade where a stream runs out. I've never seen a grill over it, so I can get in that way and see if I can find Jaelle. If I'm detected, you two start blowing stuff up and provide a diversion and cover for me."

"Sound," Maauro observed. "We will await your return there." She pointed to a point of high ground opposite the palisade gate. The small hill provided cover and boasted an inky area where light didn't penetrate. "I will blast a hole in the gate if you cannot escape by stealth. Give us ten minutes to make our way there before you enter."

"Excellent. If I'm not back before dawn, do something about it."

We nodded and Lostra made her way forward. After a minute, Maauro turned to me. "We must flee the area. We are about to be betrayed."

"What?" I said, stunned.

"We have been led into a trap. Follow me."

"How do you know?"

"Lostra's appearance, her equipment, her casual planning of the assault and the ridiculous claim to have laired near a tribe of jungle hunters for months without being discovered."

"What if you're wrong?" I grabbed her arm, probably not the smartest thing I'd ever done.

"Very well," she said. "We will wait here for ten minutes until you see the proof yourself."

The minutes ticked by slowly. Sweat trickled under my clothes. I tried not to shift about, but there was no way to mimic Maauro's utter stillness.

Then three quick flashes shattered the darkness. In a dark hollow on the reverse of the slope where we'd promised Lostra we'd be, explosions flashed and the trees fell as if scythed.

"Mortars," Maauro said, "zeroed on that spot."

Shouts and screams started as a party led by Lostra dashed out from the suddenly opened gates.

"I could destroy her," Maauro observed, "but it will give away our position and involve us in an extended ground fight with unknown forces that you might not survive. Let us relocate."

***

We move through the jungle away from Lostra's ambush. Wrik's lack of proper night vision slows us, but we still make good speed, leaving any pursuit well behind. I motion Wrik to cover as I detect unidentified personnel in our area. This surprises me. While Lostra does not know who I am, she clearly suspects and would surely be too cautious to face me in darkness. I did not detect aircraft or any other mechanical transport being used and cannot determine how enemy forces got ahead of us. My sensors detect two small groups moving in our direction. I move forward to engage them. I do not unlimber my weapon, merely invoking a splinter camouflage that will make me more difficult to see. I also extrude molecularly sharp blades on the edges of my hands. This will be wetwork.

Moving through the forest I detect two Kandalorians. One is carrying a modern weapon. Particles of its lubricants reach my receptors. I realize from their movements that the Kandalorians are not following us but are moving to block the other party.

I see the others now. There are two. The leader moves with a stealthy rapidity that I admire. The other creature is muffled under clothing. That creature moves a hand and I see the reason for the covering. It has a bioluminescent glow.

The Kandalorians see it, too. One raises a scattergun as its fellow readies a bow. I move.

The gunman detects my onrush at the last second, but he is far too slow to bring his weapon to bear. My right hand lashes out and his head parts from his body. The other Kandalorian gives a yell and looses his bolt, which simply shatters on my chest. I return the favor by lunging; my hand slams through his chest.

The other pair freezes in place, leveling primitive weapons at me. The Nekoan seems to see me clearly and holds her hand up to bid the other to hold his fire.

"Greetings, Jaelle Tekala," I say, prying my arm out of the dead Kandalorian. "We are here to rescue you."

CHAPTER

8

"**W**RIK, COME UP," MAAURO CALLED BACK TO ME. "THE enemy is dispatched."

I lowered my weapon and moved cautiously forward. In a little clearing I saw the Nekoan we'd come so far to find standing over two dead Kandalorians. With her stood another of the gray-skinned aliens, wearing a thrown-back cloak. I realized that I could see quite clearly, more than could be accounted for even by Kandalor's large moon. The gray-skinned alien emitted a glow that outlined Jaelle's silhouette like a candle.

I couldn't help but stare. Jaelle looked like a jungle princess, a lithe body only barely concealed by the remnants of her torn and discolored fatigues. Like most female Nekoans, her small features made her look more human, but the pink bat ears that rose from her mane of thick hair gave her a primeval look.

"Take a holo," she said in a velvety, rich voice.

"Uh," I replied. "Sorry, Jaelle. Your father sent me."

"My father?" she asked, narrow-eyed.

"Yes. He told us how you disappeared hunting the will o' wisps and treasure. He's worried for your safety."

"Hmphh. More like the old rat-catcher is worried about the money I borrowed from him." She looked past me at Maauro. "Who are you two?"

"Wrik Trigardt from Vanceport."

Maauro cocked her head at the other female. "I am Maauro, Wrik's cousin."

"Oh, please," she said. "You're no human or any other Confed species. I saw you smash a hand through that warrior as if he were made of paper."

"What she is," I interrupted, "is our best chance for not getting skewered. This neighborhood is unhealthy."

Jaelle spoke a few words to her companion in something other than Standard. It flipped up its cloak, dimming the radiance.

"This is Faroa," Jaelle said. "He's a Murch, what we'd call a will o wisp, survivor of a crashed colony ship from thousands of years ago. There are only a few hundred of them left, living in the swamps to the west."

I looked at the creature with its huge eyes like big blue stones, devoid of any pupil. "Further introductions," I said, "should wait till we get the hell out of here."

"There is no indication of pursuit," Maauro said. "These were either returning to camp or stalking Jaelle. I do not believe Lostra will risk a night action with us."

"Or," I said with some heat, "she'll rely on her natives, who grew up in these jungles stalking wild animals."

Jaelle shook her head. "We're on a rescue mission. One of our companions is imprisoned in the village. Perhaps we can reach him in the confusion."

"I'm sorry," I said. "We saw one of his people killed today."

Jaelle head sunk and she swore. I didn't need to know Nekoan to understand.

Her companion reached out a hand and spoke in his guttural tongue. She spoke back and the creature gave a keening cry and leaned against a tree.

"How?" Jaelle asked.

"He was—" Maauro began.

"Just tell him it was quick," I interrupted.

She looked me in the eye. "Was it?"

I tried to suppress a shudder. "Not enough."

Jaelle spoke to the Murch. It straightened up and ran a hand over its face. Jaelle patted it on the shoulder, and then continued with what sounded like instructions.

The Murch gave us a look that somehow conveyed uncertainty. It spoke to Jaelle and I got the impression it was trying to dissuade her. Jaelle put a hand on its shoulder and repeated what she had said.

The Murch pressed forearms with her and disappeared back into the forest.

"I sent him back to his people," Jaelle said, "to tell of the death of his pod brother and to warn them to stay in the distant reaches of the swamp, now that Dusko and the Thieves Guild have supplied the Kandalorians with modern weapons."

"Dusko!" I said.

"Who do you think is paying Lostra? He found out about the ancient artifacts in these regions and the will o' wisps. The Murch used to conduct a limited trade in artifacts and medicines with the Kandalorians. Murch are great healers. Some have a psychic power that can cure injuries. Otherwise I'd be dead.

"Dusko and the Guild turned the Kandalorians on the Murch, using threats and bribes. Wasn't hard. These tribes have always been raiders and hunters. Now they're organized. Since then, they've been digging up artifacts and raiding further into the Murch swamps."

"Quite a little war we've dropped into," I said.

"You have a plan for getting out of here?"

I looked at Maauro. "Lostra knows where we came ashore."

"Yes and that route would take us too close to the village," Maauro said.

"We can't walk out," I protested.

"No immediate plan of extraction occurs," Maauro said. "We cannot call for help at this distance with any equipment we have."

"Who would come?" I said in disgust.

"For now," Jaelle said, "there are mountains to the north. I have some supplies cached there. We should be safe until we can plan something. Follow me."

***

We follow the Nekoan through the woods for hours. She moves effortlessly with night sight almost as good as my own. She is an athletic creature, more powerful than a human female.

She appears to have a curious effect on Wrik and he on her. He studies her physique whenever she does not appear to be watching. I also note that he has taken to offering her assistance in climbing or walking that she manifestly does not need. She accepts the unnecessary aid with smiles and lingers in contact with the human.

She tells of having been alone for many months, only recently being found and befriended by the will o' wisps and helping them against Lostra's forces. Wrik's expressions of sympathy seem very intense, as does his interest in her well-being.

I consider that both she and Wrik have been subject to an extended period of fear and physical stress. This could lead to aberrational behavior. I must be on guard about this.

Wrik stops at a stream to refill our canteens and purify them. It leaves me with Jaelle.

Jaelle examines me closely. "I am grateful for your presence, but who and what are you, Maauro? Your skin is perfect, yet we've been plowing through brush at night for hours. Not a scratch from a tree limb or a bug bite. You don't perspire. You're not breathing hard. In fact, you're not breathing."

I consider my remark to Lostra about being a noneofyourgoddamnbusinessean but it seems inappropriate for our ally. I rifle through my files of human behavior patterns that I extracted from the game sims I used for my appearance. I note that the female characters usually tend to be both mysterious and secretive. I elect to use this.

"Every girl has her secrets," I reply.

Jaelle begins touching my hair, running her hands through it.

I am confused. "Since you are not attacking me, is this an attempt at seduction?"

Jaelle looks at me, startled, then laughs. "No. I prefer males. I'm sorry Nekoans are a tactile and curious people. I forget that humans... and whatever you are, may be different."

"Wrik does seem to enjoy touching you," I observe.

"Is that a problem?" she asks.

"Not presently."

"Is he yours?"

"We are in an alliance, but if you mean sexually, no"

"Good to know. Nothing more dangerous than hunting in another female's territory. Wrik is rather handsome, even if his ears aren't in the right spot."

"He is not Nekoan."

Jaelle smiled. "True, and wouldn't that piss off Daddy? Nekoan males have a nasty tendency to sit back and let the pride females maintain them. I avoid them."

Wrik returns from the stream and offers Jaelle a canteen. "It doesn't taste great, but it's wet."

"Thank you, Wrik."

We continue on, breaking out of the jungle into a range of small hills. One nearby hill provides a superior overlook and we proceed up it to find Jaelle's cache. There is a hollow just below the summit. There is food but little else other than more primitive weapons.

We settled down in the hollow. I dropped my jacket and pack to the ground and slumped down wearily on it.

"I'll check out the area," Maauro said and faded into the woods.

Jaelle sat close beside me.

I rose up on my arms and gazed at her. Jaelle's nearness made the rest of the world recede. I imagined that I felt the heat of her body against my thigh, though we were not touching. She seemed so exotic, silhouetted against the stars.

A shiver flashed over her lithe body.

"Cold?" I ventured.

"Yah" she replied, then after a pause, "cold and lonely and far from home. A home that wasn't that good as I think about it. Not sure why I'm missing it so."

Her openness caught me off guard. Feelings that I thought gone surged through me.

"It's still home," I managed before my throat closed up on me.

Jaelle looked down on me, her eyes glimmering in the starlight. "Are you a long way from home too, Wrik?"

"Further than any stardrive can ever carry me across," I whispered. I lay back on the jacket, looking skyward, though I knew the star that Retief circled wasn't visible from here. I wondered if anyone there remembered me or ever wondered what had become of me.

Jaelle lay down next to me, tugging my thin jacket over both of us.

"Warmer this way," she said.

I looked into the alien eyes, looking for what, I couldn't say

"What would you do if I was a human?"

Very slowly, I leaned forward and kissed her. Her response told me that Nekoans did this too. Making love over the next hour involved false starts, giggles, laughs and a few moments of "Really?" as well as one bite on my shoulder that she apologized for profusely. It was...similar and satisfying, as was falling asleep in an ecology where nothing had evolved to specifically bite or sting us. We didn't have to worry about larger predators with Maauro patrolling.

Maauro, I thought drowsily, distracted by the warmth and smell of Jaelle, who lay with her head on my shoulder, eyes half-closed. *What was she thinking about all this?* I wondered and then sleep took me.

***

When I return to the hollow, I detect that Wrik and Jaelle are entwined. Confused, I move a distance off.

I find Wrik's attraction to the Nekoan female odd and disturbing. It had not occurred to me that he would find one out of his species of interest. Gender doesn't exist for me save that I have adopted it. I enjoy the concept, the interaction and minor attentions that Wrik gives me because he anthropomorphizes me, but I never gave any thought to the issue of sexuality unbalancing our relationship. I am literally not made for it.

Wrik and I had achieved a stable orbit. I needed a place in this new civilization and a guide. Wrik needed protection. Now a new factor was interfering with that orbit, Jaelle.

I consider if it is in my interest for Jaelle to continue living, but eliminating her would incur Wrik's enmity. It occurs to me that I should have devoted more time to the literature of his species, much of which centered on these issues.

The noise of the two settles, and I move into the hollow to keep watch.

CHAPTER

9

TOSSED AND TURNED IN MY SLEEP. IT WAS DIFFICULT TO SLEEP after the excitement of making love again after so long. It brought up the past and a life that I thought was gone...it brought back the dreams...

***

"Up the Ncome Commando," Delt shouted from the screen on my *Wirriway's* panel. Twenty-four of the green and tan fighters climbed into Retief's skies. Above us the cloudless blue was filled with the descending contrails of Confederate landing craft sent to punish the rebellion. Retief's Boers and Trekkers wanted this world to themselves and their own kind, fleeing all the way from Old Earth to make it so. The Confederacy said no, but the stubborn graybeards wouldn't give in without a fight and now a lot of young pilots from my hometown were about to die making that fight for them.

Just so we don't have to look at people different than us, I thought, despairing as I brought the fighter's nose up. But these were my people. I'd known everyone in this squadron from childhood.

Ahead of me three *Wirriways* exploded; hit by Confed missiles fired BVR. Our locally made ships were no match for the modern electronics of the Confed force.

"Keep climbing, Ncome," Delt shouted again. "We're under their landing ships. The battlewagons can't fire through them at us. Stick to me, you lot."

War-whoops and shouts answered him, but I remained silent, staring in grim sickness at the growing dots of our targets.

But the landing ships weren't defenseless. Swift as death, down came four long-hulled, white and black *Spacefire IXs*. Missiles and beams flashed from them as our formation dissolved into a giant furball. My universe became a bowl of blazing blue alternating with the green world below, marked with the black and yellow smudges that heralded the death of a *Wirriway* as I banked and rolled desperately.

I heard my name as Delt shouted in my ears. "You're clear. Take your section into the landing craft."

I pulled my nose up again and led my four-ship section against the roof of landing craft over us. We couldn't lock weapons through the fog of ECM, so we had to close to use our weapons ballistically.

No. 3 of my flight blew up.

"Two more *Spacefires*!" my wingman, Regina Van Dyck, screamed. She stood her fighter on its left wing and whipped away from a missile that detonated just past her. I got a quarter-second burst at the flashing *Spacefire*, no joy.

No. 4 blew up, leaving only Regina and me. I rolled back toward her. I could see her *Wirriway* staggering in the sunshine. The leopard she'd painted on its blunt nose reflected a brilliant yellow.

The *Spacefire* flashed in again and Reg's fighter tumbled and disintegrated, wreathed in flame. I salvoed my missiles at him. I had no lock, but a lucky hit was possible. The enemy fighter took no chances, diving away. I looked for her ejection pod but couldn't see anything. I was alone.

Diving away, diving away, the phrase raced around my brain. I looked up at the big LCs, coming into in range. Even if I reached them, dozens of gunners waited for me.

Diving away.

I heard Delt shout my name. Delt, my friend from kindergarten.

Diving away.

And I did. Deaf to the cries of people I'd trained with, grown up with. I dove away from the LC gunners and the deadly *Spacefires*.

No one will know, I thought. We're being wiped out. There'll be no one to tell.

It didn't work out that way...

***

I sat bolt upright, covered in sweat, heart hammering.

Jaelle rolled up to standing, quick as the cat she looked like. Her eyes, far better in the dark than a human's, scanned the treeline. "What the fang?"

I tried to slow my breathing and reached for a canteen. A swallow cleared my head. But I couldn't look at her; the shame of who and what I was lay too close. I half-turned away, afraid she could somehow read it in my face.

"Bad dreams," I finally said.

She walked back over and sat next to me. "Dreams...or memories?"

I cringed.

To my surprise, she lay back down.

"You're not the only one with bad memories," she said. "Try not to thrash around so much. It's still hours to dawn."

I ached to tell her something but couldn't bring myself to do it. In a few minutes her regular breathing told me she'd fallen back asleep. I lay awake for hours, surrounded by my ghosts.

As the sky lightened, I saw a silhouette against the sky, a figure looking down at me with a bow in her hair.

What would Maauro think if she knew?

***

In the morning, I rejoin the two biologicals, who have now awakened. They separately adjourn to a nearby stream to clean themselves. When they return, we prepare food. I warm the rations by running heat through my hands. They find this intensely amusing.

I question Jaelle about the village. I am pleased by her tactical sense and the details she conveys, especially about the machine shed where Lostra maintains her skimmers.

"Our best plan," I say, "is to anticipate that they will seek to ambush us at our old skimmer. Instead, we will infiltrate the village, secure a skimmer and escape."

"What will we use for a map?" Jaelle asks.

"I can uplink the GPS records I retained from the trip out," I advise.

Jaelle and Wrik look at each other, which I find annoys me. "Okay," Wrik says.

"We will move back to the village and arrive at night," I conclude. "Patrols will likely have discovered the bodies today. It should make them reluctant to pursue us at night."

"They're not worried about us," Wrik adds. "It's 150 miles back to Wayfarer. No trails, nothing. They know we can't walk back. Hell, they're probably waiting for us between here and Wayfarer. They don't need to chase us."

"Your logic is sound," I observe.

Wrik and Jaelle keep to a relaxed pace as we make our way back to the village. We need to arrive under cover of darkness, especially as the Guild now must be factored in.

"Lostra is working for Dusko," Jaelle responds to Wrik's questions. "Dusko is Guild but only because he's the most successful local product. There's nothing on Kandalor to really interest the Guild. They just sub out the work to people, if you want to call them that, like Dusko.

"This implies a distant command center," I say. "It also implies some prize locally that has not been apparent before. Are the Murch valuable?"

Jaelle frowns, which puts pointy teeth on her lower lip. "I can't tell you much about the Murch. First, it's a promise, second, I don't know much. They've remained alive and undetected in this area. That implies they have some useful knowledge. Then there are the artifacts that I've discovered from some ancient empire that fought here."

I smile to myself. If she only knew that she was walking alongside one of those self-same artifacts...

***

Jaelle would say no more and we reached the village after sunset. We made our way to a hollow near the village, where Maauro left us to scout forward on her own. Jaelle and I sat in the hollow, shoulders touching. This close to the enemy, we didn't dare speak, even in whispers. Jaelle didn't seem to find the silence uncomfortable, any more than she had found our sudden impulses toward each other last night. Nekoans were more casual about sex than humans, with several females often contracting with one male. In the old days, the arrangement had been more akin to a pride of lions.

Maybe it had been just a relief from months of tension and fear for her, too. I found myself wondering what it might be like if there was more to it. Jaelle was exotic and beautiful.

Maauro's return disrupted any further foolish thoughts. She put a palm against each of our faces. "I am speaking to you by bone conduction. We cannot be overheard.

"Lostra and her Guilders seem to be covering every eventuality," Maauro continued. "A large party left in the direction of our skimmer, midafternoon by the deterioration of the crushed vegetation under the footprints.

"She's placed mines and sensor detectors around the perimeter of the village, crude devices which I reprogrammed so they will not react to our presence. She's also booby-trapped the water entrance."

"How do we get in?" I whispered.

"We leap over the wall. I will carry one of you under each arm. There is a bowed section of wall between the two guard towers. We will enter there."

Ten minutes of harrowing creeping through the jungle brought us to the spot Maauro had picked. The slender android peered between the crudely sawn logs of the palisade to make sure nothing awaited us; then she checked the occupants of the guard towers. Satisfied, she moved back and placed an arm around each of us.

"Crouch," she commanded, "and keep your legs tucked up. Let me absorb the landing shock."

Sudden acceleration caused me to gray out and all I saw was a blur as we sailed over the palisade. We landed with a teeth-rattling jar on the other side, Maauro's feet sinking well into the earth. She let go of us, then looked surprised as we both tumbled to the ground, needing a few seconds to recover. Struggling to our feet, we followed Maauro through the sleeping village to the machine shed.

As we neared the shed, a growl sounded from the darkness to our left. Maauro lunged, instantly seizing the native equivalent of a guard dog. The growling animal fastened its teeth on her arm, which muffled its voice. Maauro snapped its neck and dropped it to the ground. We stared about, but no one seemed to have heard the quick and lethal encounter.

Maauro waved us forward into the shed. Two skimmers lay inside, one with its engine casing off. We piled into the other. Maauro gave the skimmer a mighty shove before leaping aboard.

"We will drift out a little," she said in a low voice, "then I will activate the motor and connect to the GPS."

"Something feels wrong," I said. "There are no interior guards, no mechanical locks or sensors."

Maauro shrugged. "Lostra would not believe we'd be so foolish as to return to the village. She has sent the bulk of her forces to ambush us where we landed. Doubtless they believe the village is adequately defended. She did not count on me."

Jaelle crouched low in the skimmer, watching the village dwindle as a current took us out. Maauro walked past her to the control console. She started the engine at its lowest setting, a throaty murmur. We picked up speed.

In the east, the sky began to lighten. A thick fog and mist arose from the swamp. I was grateful for it. It would make our escape easier. Maauro, who saw well in low light or fog, opened up the engine. I breathed a sigh of relief as I watched Maauro pull a jack from a concealed panel in her neck and plug it into the GPS board.

Suddenly Maauro's body began to jerk and shudder at high speed. "WWWWRRRRIIIIIIKKKKKKKK HEELLLLLLLLPPPPPPP MMMMMEEEEEEEE IIIIITTTTTSSSSSS AAAAAA TTTTTRRRRRAPPPPPPPP."

***

I plug into the skimmer and do a flash scan of all of its systems. We must get under way quickly. The disabled skimmer cannot pursue us, but once the village contingent realizes that a skimmer has been stolen, they can call for help from the ambush force. I must access the GPS and program an evasive course that takes us back to Wayfarer.

Then it strikes. As I access the GPS, a cunningly constructed assault program invades my systems. It crashes through my standard defensive barrier. I am compromised, fighting instantly for survival in my core programs. Shock strikes me physically and mentally. The program is beyond anything I expected from the creatures of this time. Then I recognize Infestor code in the attack program, modified in some fashion I cannot understand. How did it get there? Who has such knowledge?

I am in trouble.

***

For a second I stared in shock at the hideously juddering mechanism. Then I lunged forward, ripping the lead out of the console. Maauro emitted a screech and toppled into the bottom of the skimmer.

Simultaneously I heard the sound of engines starting around us in the early morning fog.

"Jaelle," I shouted. "Gun the engine. Get us out of here."

A skimmer cut out of the fog a hundred meters ahead. I whipped out my SMG, firing off the clip. The range was long for the machine pistol, but the skimmer veered back into the fog. I slammed another magazine in as Jaelle fired at something on the other side.

I spotted a shape in the fog and fired again. At this rate my ammo would exhaust quickly.

I knelt by Maauro and turned the heavy android over with difficulty. "We have to get her operational again, or we're dead," I yelled to Jaelle.

For a crazy second, I consider slapping Maauro's face or shaking her. I pulled her half upright and fired a quick burst at a glimpse of a skimmer. Lostra's folks were holding back, doubtless trying to figure out if Maauro was disabled. I looked longingly at the heavy gun on Maauro's back but knew I had neither the skill nor strength to use it.

"Wrrrrriikkkkk." There was a mechanical resonance and slurring to Maauro's voice. "Iiii'mm dammmagged. Selffff- repair iniiiitiated."

"We underestimated Lostra," I said. "They were out here in the other skimmers. They're herding us back now. Brilliant. She figured you'd be too dangerous to handle on land."

I fired again and my SMG clicked empty. This time return fire flew over our heads. The skimmers disappeared into the fog.

I swore under my breath. My eyes strained to pierce the mist.

"You were right, Wrik. I have underestimated Lostra," Maauro said. "I did not realize that she had the sophistication to arrange such a cybernetic trap. She has knocked my eyes off-line. There is too much clutter for me to reliably fire by radar alone."

Maauro knelt shakily, drawing her weapon and leveling the huge device. "Wrik, if there a piece of solid ground you could leave me on, Lostra wants me. Perhaps I can delay her."

I knelt by Maauro, placing my arms around her shoulders and grasping her forearms. "There's no place to stand and Lostra wants the rest of us as well. My bet is that the fuel gauge is rigged as well and this skimmer's going to run dry any second. We have to fight. I'll be your eyes."

"Very well," she said. "We shall stand or fall together."

"Get down, Jaelle," I shouted over my shoulder. "Kill the engine and don't block our field of fire."

She gave me a mutinous look but dropped to the bottom of the skimmer.

"Hold the skimmer steady," Maauro said. "We must eliminate variables."

I stared into the low-hanging mist. I could feel Maauro's cheek, clean and cold against my skin. Her upper body was near weightless in my arms, ready to turn in any direction at my lead. Insects shrilled in our ears. The rank smell of the Tar Sea filled my nose, broken only by a slight ginger cookie scent of Maauro. If we lived, I meant to ask her why she smelled like a cookie.

"Engines," Maauro said, spinning to face the sound. "Be ready."

Skimmers burst into view, four of them, cutting back and forth. I pointed Maauro at the first and we fired. Maauro's monster gun ruptured the skimmer, which turned over, cartwheeling across the swamp. I tried not to imagine the fate of its occupants, thrown into the stinking Tar Sea.

Our next two shots fountained the surface of water and tar. Then we were in range of Lostra's force. Shots peppered the water. They may have wanted Jaelle alive, but not enough to face fire from Maauro.

A laser struck Maauro: the heat of it scorched me. I yelled and fell over, beating at my clothes. Maauro whipped around and fired back, but her shots trailed Lostra's skimmer.

Before I could scramble back to aim Maauro, two more shots struck the android. Both glanced off her, puncturing the skimmer's side and bottom. I'd forgotten for a second that what looked like a jumpsuit was simply a differently textured part of her armored body.

Maauro stood, turning in the direction of the shots and leaning out to aim past the fan when it happened. She moved, but her right leg didn't follow the movement. She dropped her weapon. Her arms reached out, far too slowly, as if she were a toy running down. Maauro toppled over the side, sinking out of sight instantly

She was gone. I stood numb, an easy target, but the weapons fire ceased. Jaelle crawled toward Maauro's fallen weapon.

"Don't bother," I heard my voice say, as if it came from somewhere far away. "Firing it would pulverize your arm."

Lostra pulled alongside, her skimmer full of Guild: Dua-Denlenn, city-Kandalorians and a few humans. Her face pulled into a wolfish snarl, and I expected death.

"Well, well," she said, "What a pretty brace of birds we have here. I think we'll have them for dinner, slow-roasted.

CHAPTER
10

I **SINK INTO THE TAR, LEAVING WRIK AND THE WORLD OF LIGHT BEHIND.**
*My intermittent failure has doomed me and the others. In my enervated
state I'll never regain the surface. I've never been defeated before in battle,*
never failed my comrades-in-arms. Worse, my failure is from the classic mistake of
underestimating my enemy. It is a unique and bitter sensation that I will take to my
destruction.

Perhaps it is despair that makes me slip into a lassitude. I do not know for how
many hours I slowly sink in the pitch-darkness. System after system fails in me.
Finally, I have only a slight flickering consciousness...

REBOOT.

I am aware again and more. The system cascade failure has stopped and indeed
been reversed as some failsafe of my Creators cuts in. I am not fully restored, but I
have control of my damage repair systems. With this realization, I begin to repair
and reroute my systems. I take stock of my surroundings. I send out a deep-radar
pulse into the sea of tar...and suffer a complete shock. I am suspended in material
a thousand meters below the surface, three hundred meters above a rocky bottom.
This is not what rivets my attention.

The tar ocean floor is littered with fighting machines. Many I cannot identify,
but below and to the east of me is an Infestor assault barge. The six hundred-meter
vessel is torn and crumpled, totally dead. Had any system been active, it would have
attacked me instantly.

My tactical computer analyzes the situation. The Infestors must have been
damaged and landed on the planet to escape, or at least deploy armored fighting
vehicles and battle it out. In the millennia since then, the Tar Sea buried the
battlefield. I do not detect any Creator machines nearby, but I cannot rule it out.

I alter the direction of my descent, swimming through the gooey mass toward
the assault barge. Within an hour, I settle on its crumpled bow. My scanner paints
a clearer picture. The barge has been ripped up by beam fire. It must have been
destroyed in the early days of the war or perhaps been part of a reserve unit – it
would have been quite obsolete in my day.

Still the technology aboard is far in advance of anything I have found in
this modern age and more, the Infestors use similar exotic metal and fuels to the
Creators', one reason this system was so bitterly disputed. I enter through a great
rent in the barge's side and begin my search. Even with such systems as I have
restored, I cannot regain the surface. My only chance lies within. I push through the
ooze, exploring level after level.

I find my prize near the engineering level, a storeroom full of exotic radioactive
materials. The electronics and mechanisms of the ship have not survived the ages,

not even in the insulation of the tar. I had it far easier in the clean hard vacuum. But 50,000 years is only a small fraction of the life of this fuel. I press bar after bar of it against the permeable surface of my body, admitting the fuel and filtering out the tar.

Glorious power surges through my systems. Reactors and factories that have been dormant for millennia operate again. Nanorepairbots now have special materials with which to make repairs and fabricate replacement parts. The fuel is crudely refined, low grade and partially spent, but it is nectar to me.

I quickly examine the rest of the vessel, making an inventory of useful materials; there is more here than I can process or use presently. I foolishly wish for my old maintenance crew or that this was a ship of the Creators. Might as well wish my Creators had never abandoned me.

The thought of abandonment brings Wrik and the expedition to mind. Perhaps they are already dead. But I have adopted Wrik as a comrade-at-arms, having declared him so; I must rescue him or at least retrieve his body. It is an imperative my Creators programmed into me, "We do not leave our own." They have failed me in that regard and perhaps it is for that reason that I feel I must better them.

I turn my face to the unseen sky and plot my course. My outer layer heats, softening the tar as my legs begin to vibrate at supersonic speeds. I move upward.

***

The next few hours were anything but pleasant. Lostra had us bound and thrown into a hut, only to show up later with a whip. She amused herself by having a pair of Dua-Denlenn string Jaelle to an overhead beam. She cracked the whip on the squalling Nekoan.

"Tell me, pretty kitty," she said, rubbing the whiphandle over Jaelle's body. "Tell me where to find the will o' wisps. Tell me where to find all those pretty ancient artifacts."

Jaelle's teeth snapped, but Lostra merely laughed and used her whip. I felt that she didn't want Jaelle to talk; the whipping was what she wanted. But she was careful not to overdo it, toying with the Nekoan.

She didn't forget me either. "What did she tell you, Wrik?" Crack, crack.

I screamed that she hadn't told me anything. The whip bit again, but not because she didn't believe me. Her brilliant eyes, swollen lips, her nipples poking through her shirt in arousal said it didn't matter.

"I believe you, Wrik," Lostra said, biting me on the ear. "I wouldn't tell you anything either. You're not so tough without your little robot slut."

She struck me on the temple with the whip handle and I faded out, Jaelle's screams sounding in my ears.

When I came to, it was to find Jaelle face down on the hut floor next to me. Lostra sat astride her.

"Have a nice nap, Wrik?" Lostra said. "Jaelle and I have been having fun without you. But naughty kitty won't tell me anything."

"I will tell you," Jaelle managed to get the hoarse words out, "to get your fat ass off mine."

"I like that," Lostra said running her hand through Jaelle's thick hair. "Still has spirit."

"When I get free," Jaelle growled like a jungle cat. "I am going to eat pieces of you while you're still alive."

That seemed to give even Lostra pause.

"I think it's about time for another sacrifice to the God of the Tar Sea," Lostra said, "since you are of no other use to me. Jonka!"

A Dua-Denlenn leaned in, its elfin face impassive as it stared at us.

"Have the catapult readied. Get the priests. We want to make quite the example of these two."

"What about a deal?" Jaelle said, staring around at the horde of tribesmen beyond Jonka.

She stood and shrugged. "You couldn't offer me enough to cross Dusko and the Guild."

"Just a matter of price, huh?" I shot.

"What else?" She turned and shot a few words over her shoulder. Tribesmen hustled in to drag us upright.

Jaelle squalled and launched herself at Lostra despite her bonds, teeth bared. Lostra contemptuously checked her with a thrust kick that slammed her onto her back. Tribesmen pulled her upright before she could regain her feet.

A feeling of numb unreality gripped me. I was going to die, my mouth filling with tar, my eyes and nose blocked up in pitch darkness. I began to feel disassociated from things around me as if it were a holo I was watching. Yet the sandy ground I was dragged over was real. The rank odor of both the swamp and the tribesman stuck me sharply, as did the heat of the sun on my face. I looked at Jaelle, who was snarling still, her hair all raised and roughed out. That's how I should be, I thought, not mute and numb like a sheep.

Shouts filled the air. The natives dragged us toward the edge to the rock face where who knew how many unknowns had been flung in before. Those unknowns waited below, ready to draw us into their silent company.

The native ahead of me stopped short with a hoarse cry and pointed into the morass. Something stirred in the ocean of black tar. Something rose in it, stepping toward the shore. It was a mass of tar, dripping off substance as it walked onto the shore before the stunned and silent mob. It stood before us, a nightmare figure of blackness.

Then, before anyone could react, it burst into flame from head to toe and raced forward almost too quickly for the eye to follow.

The tribesmen shrieked in fear before those nearest the apparition literally exploded in a shower of blood and bone. There was no thought of resistance. Survivors flung weapons aside and fled screaming for the tree line.

Lostra and her men were made of sterner stuff and opened fire on the flaming figure. But the apparition raised both arms and it seemed that something flew from those hands. The Guilders near Jaelle and me were torn up as if machine-gunned.

This broke the fugue that had gripped me. I leapt on the nearest dead Guilder and fumbled for his knife.

"Stay still," Jaelle said, her face pressed against my low back. I felt a tug and realized that she'd bitten through the ropes. Freed, I grabbed out the dagger and cut the bonds off my feet, then freed her. I grabbed at a weapon as dirt kicked up near me. A native Guilder was firing at us. Before it could get off a second shot, the flame creature struck it from behind, cutting it in two.

A Dua-Denlenn Guilder surged out from behind a burning hut, her beautiful face distorted in a snarl of hatred as she leveled an RPG at the fiery form.

I didn't have time to aim. I pulled the trigger and held it down, hosing her and the hut. The RPG fired and the round ricocheted off the ground before detonating among some huts full of cowering natives. I turned my face from shredded bodies and tried not to vomit. We had to flee while we had the chance. I scrambled to my feet, but hours of being bound had made my legs unsteady. When I looked up, a crackling, smoking figure stood in my way.

"Wrik, look out," Jaelle screamed.

But the figure didn't move and the flames faded as the last of the tar burned off. Furious heat beat at my face. I hardly noticed it.

"Maauro," I breathed.

She stood in front of me looking as she had the morning before, her long hair and jumpsuit intact and free of soil and tar. Large, solemn eyes looked up at me. Only the yellow silk bow was gone.

Of course, I thought, the bow was the only thing that wasn't actually part of her. Even the filament hair was merely another part of her nearly indestructible body.

"You lost your bow," I said, surprised to find my voice unsteady and tears in the back of my eyes.

"Will you buy me another?" Maauro said, her voice gentle and a small smile on her face.

"I'll buy you yards of it," I promised.

Jaelle found her voice. "Your cousin must come from a very special branch of the family."

"Let's get out of here," I said.

Maauro raised her eyes to the shattered, burning village. A few natives, women, children and the elderly were fleeing to the forest, joining the warriors who'd abandoned them.

"I will finish reducing the native forces," she replied, eyeing the escapees and bringing up her arms. Her fingers seemed to uncap and I realized that she now possessed some form of projectile weapon.

I heard a sound like compressed air and realized she was firing at the women and children.

"No," I screamed. "Stop! Let them go."

Maauro cocked her hands up and looked at me. I didn't look at the forest edge. I wanted to believe she'd missed.

"What?" she demanded. "Enemy forces are escaping."

"Noncombatants," I managed.

"They have seen me and know what I am."

"They saw a burning monster or god," I improvised. "They won't stop running for days. They're no threat."

"Then the warriors in the treeline—"

"Will be busy trying to find their families. Maauro, leave them, please."

"You seem pretty concerned about a group of savages that were going to drop us in a tar sea," Jaelle noted, her expression unreadable.

"The Guild is responsible for this."

"I do not understand," Maauro said. "However, as enemy forces are in retreat and any intel they gained is not likely to be used against me, I will honor your wishes. You do not mind if I continue to eliminate the Guild?"

I reached down a hand to help Jaelle to her feet. She regarded it with slight amusement and bounced to her feet in a lithe roll. "No. You can reduce them to a fine mist as far as I'm concerned."

"Very well," Maauro said. "Remain here as I finish my work."

***

I look at Wrik. He is clearly distressed by my actions and a concession is necessary.

"I will not further reduce the noncombatants, but this installation must be destroyed. This area is of importance to me and these must not be allowed to infest the area..."

I speed off before he can object further. Destroying the structures is simple. I race through and pulverize the mud and wood buildings. I use my revitalized projectile weapons to destroy anything out of easy reach. I set fire to the fields and crops. My attack is thorough and I increase my bag of enemy by sniping on those warriors whose courage has recovered sufficiently to return to the area.

***

Maauro proceeded with her determined "reduction" of the village.

"We should secure a skimmer," I said, as much because I didn't want to see the destruction as anything else. I grabbed up a weapon from a dead Guilder. Jaelle did the same. We scrambled up and over the jetty, heading back to the machine shed. All of Lostra's skimmers were tied up.

Jaelle bounded down the slope of the jetty, her cat-like body taking the drop and the uneven rocks easily. She landed on a platform below us just as a camouflaged door snapped open and Lostra surged out. Jaelle froze for a split second, startled. Lostra looked as surprised but never stopped moving, swinging into a reverse kick that sent Jaelle and her weapon flying in two directions.

CHAPTER 10

The catgirl plunged into the mucky shallows. The weapon clattered off a skimmer and disappeared into the muck.

In the same smooth motion, Lostra spun toward me, her laser tracking. I jerked my weapon up, far too late. Her laser took me in the side, blasting a hole. Then the weapon burned down my arm, making me drop my weapon. Pain took me and I buckled, the blue sky tilting wildly over me.

CHAPTER

11

PAUSE IN MY DESTRUCTION OF THE VILLAGE. I HAVE LOST TRACK OF *Wrik and Jaelle. They are not where I instructed them to remain. I deduce that they may have headed for the machine shed to acquire a skimmer. I'm appalled by their lack of tactical sense. I have not secured the area. Not all the Guilders are accounted for.*

My astonishment takes .001 seconds as I turn back toward the beach. I must find them. My hearing picks up a cry and the sounds of a blow from the other side of the jetty. I accelerate at maximum speed, literally running up the side of the jetty to launch myself into the air and recon the situation.

Even as I clear the wooden buildings atop the jetty, I know that I am too late. My eyes behold disaster. Jaelle is floundering in the shallows, trapped in the muck. But Wrik is falling backward, his circulatory fluid brilliant on his clothes. Lostra's laser flicks across his wrist, cutting his weapon free. She has elected not to kill cleanly, as I am programmed to. Her actions and her face betoken the desire to inflict more pain. Why must these biologicals inflict agony as well as death?

I open my mouth and roar with ear-splitting volume. Even Lostra cannot totally control her fight-flight reflex. She freezes for a tenth of a second as I plunge toward her. I accomplish my objective. She ceases targeting Wrik and fires on me. She is a superb gunner and strikes, doing minor damage to my frontal armor. I could cut her down with my projectile weapons, but perhaps I am now infected with the bloodlust of these biologicals. Perhaps it is the sight of Wrik's white face twisted in pain. She has struck down my sole comrade in this time and it is my failures that allowed it. My failure to understand my comrade's natures. My failure to properly evaluate my enemy. Failure, failure, failure.

I am going to tear her to pieces.

She rolls out from under me as I cannot presently fly and alter my trajectory. Her next shot vaporizes some of my "hair." Another cuts my cheek. But now it is my turn. I land, gather myself instantly and lunge at her. Lostra screams as my arms wrap around her, and my embrace shatters her body into two parts. My promise is fulfilled as I fling her remains from the wharf and race back to Wrik's side.

Already, factories in my body, reawakened by the new fuel, are extruding antibiotic foam and wound bandages into a chamber in my body that I open. Another chemical plant pumps an anesthetic into my finger. I quickly create a needle and jab this into his arm. I rip his canteen from his belt and drain its contents into my body, where it is converted into plasma and Ringers Lactate. I create and insert an IV tube and begin pumping fluids into his damaged body.

Jaelle has extracted herself from the shallows and is scrambling up toward me. Her eyes are wide with fear. I am distracted momentarily until I realize that I am covered in Lostra's blood.

I throw the canteen at her. "Fill it."

She looks at me. "The water is filthy."

"I will filter it in my body. Move!"

Jaelle does as she is told and returns quickly. I process the water.

"Is he going to live?" she asks.

"I do not know," I reply. Perhaps this is denial. The injuries are severe but I find I cannot face the prospect of my only...is the word, friend?...dying."I have stopped the bleeding and dealt with shock trauma. But these injuries are beyond my ability to heal. We need Confed healers and we are so far from aid."

Jaelle snaps her fingers in a human gesture. "The Murch! They healed me after I took an arrow in the spleen, almost always fatal to a Nekoan."

I turn to her. "Where are they? How quickly can we get there?"

"The nearest outpost is many miles into the western swamps," Jaelle says. "I cannot guarantee they will help. They were originally very suspicious of me."

"If they do not volunteer," I reply. "I will provide inducements to cooperate until they do."

Jaelle correctly divines my intention. She looks at the smoking village and shudders. "I'll check the skimmers."

"Do that."

Jaelle runs for the shed. I seize metal and wood in the area. The metal I press into my body where it is remade in the shapes I need. The wood I shape with my palm blades. Again my factories extrude foam which I shape into the proper form. I am quickly done with my work and have made a litter for Wrik.

Wrik begins to focus on me as the pain of his wounds recedes under my anesthesia. He groans.

***

I looked up at Maauro. It was easier to breathe with whatever she'd injected into me. "Maauro."

Instantly, the android was bending over me. "Yes, Wrik. Are you in pain now?"

"It's better. Did you get Lostra?"

"She is destroyed and the area is secure."

"Listen, I need you to promise me something."

The huge eyes gazed steadily down at me. Did I detect concern and sympathy in them, or was I kidding myself?

"I know," I coughed. "I know you delete unpleasant memories."

"Sometimes," she nodded. "They interfere with my efficient operation."

"Promise that you won't delete any of your memories of me."

"I will do as you ask, Wrik, but will you tell me why?"

"I'm alone, Maauro. I was disgraced in a cause I didn't care about, but my family disowned me for it. I had to leave my world, my family and my name behind. If I die now, no one will know. No one will remember me." I looked up, "Except for you."

"Do you wish to tell me your real name?"

I took a deep breath. "You can never tell anyone while I live."

"I am immune to interrogation. Your secret can never be extracted from me."

I whispered my family name to her. "Wrik is my middle name: I was Piet before."

"Good," Maauro said. "I am pleased that the name I use for you is real." Her big eyes seemed to shimmer. "Wrik, I think that if you die, I will be lonely."

Her comment sealed something inside for me. "Maauro, if I do, *Sinner* is yours. There's money in an account, too." I gave her code numbers and passwords. "Square-D down at the Spacewitch is OK, but trust no one else, and not even him with the secret of what you are."

"Thank you," she said in a small voice. "But I do not wish you to die. I have made a litter to carry you."

I groaned at the idea of being carried jolting in a litter. "I'm not sure I wouldn't rather expire quietly here."

"Do not despair so soon," she said. "You underestimate both of us. The litter is so I can carry you without putting my hands on your fragile body. We must go to the Murch, a journey by land and skimmer. For now," she pressed a finger into my arm, "sleep."

***

I hear the engine of a skimmer and lift Wrik. Moving quickly and carefully, I board the skimmer and secure Wrik inside. We pull from the burning village and head into the swamp. I link to the GPS: this time I am immunized and my software hacks into Lostra's traps and shatters them. I locate us and show Jaelle the maps. She indicates the direction of the Murch encampment. Even at full speed, we spend all of the day and most of the evening traveling before Jaelle indicates a landing place

We reach a peninsula that leads to an upland. The trees here are different and the ground rocky. We land and I carry Wrik ashore. Jaelle leads on as she has been here before. We follow a path that I note is concealed from observation overhead, with me carrying Wrik's litter in my arms.

As we crest a hill I become aware of a disturbance; a power field is operating ahead and over us. It is on a frequency I have not encountered before and has several other unusual aspects. I deduce that the field alters optical light rays, providing concealment. This level of technology is beyond Confed science. Yet the Murch artifacts I have seen are far simpler.

A structure comes into sight. Obviously at one time it was a spacecraft. But it is in an advanced state of disassembly, with parts of it incorporated into wood and stone. Bunkers and ditching are recent additions. These people also have acquired their enemies recently.

We are detected. Shouts ring out and the Murch appear, racing to the walls. They are armed with what appear to be air rifles and small crossbows. No threat to me, but I must be concerned for Wrik. I place his litter on the ground behind me and kneel next to him.

Jaelle calls out. I immediately add her speech to the inventory that I possess. I must be able to speak to these people directly.

I recognize Faroa, Jaelle's companion from the night we met. He rushes out in advance of his fellows, who cry warning, pointing at me. He ignores them, running up to Jaelle to take her by the arms. Jaelle quickly relates the tale of my destruction of the Kandalorian village and the Guilders. By the time she is through, I have amassed a sufficient vocabulary and grammar for my purposes.

An Elder is summoned. He comes forward of his guards. I notice he moves stiffly, but otherwise I cannot tell his age. He, Faroa and Jaelle converse at length as I monitor Wrik's life functions. Finally I stand and face the elder and his guard.

"My name is Maauro," I begin in their language. They shift in dismay, looking darkly at Jaelle. "I am an artificial life form with advanced powers both physically and mentally. Jaelle has not betrayed your trust by instructing me. I learn quickly.

"She has told me of your ability to heal through mental powers. While I do not understand this, she has assured me this power saved her life.

"Heal my comrade. You will find it very valuable to have me in your debt. I have destroyed the Kandalorians and Thieves Guild who threatened your existence. I will offer you continued protection from these outside forces."

The elder walked forward to look at me. "I am Arbos, called the Elder. By implication, you also offer us destruction should we not aid you."

I gaze steadily at him. "I am invulnerable to any weaponry you possess. Clearly you understand that I would make a deadly enemy."

"True, but we will aid you in gratitude for what you have done and what you may do. Please bring him to the House of Healing."

I turn and smoothly lift Wrik's litter. Again, the guards murmur at my casual display of strength.

With Jaelle in tow, we walk quickly to a structure that combines ancient ship metal with stone and pleasing woods. The rooms inside are airy and well lit. A staff of healers of both genders greets us and guides us to a private room.

The healers examine Wrik with a variety of primitive instruments and barrage me with questions on his physiology. I explain the measures I have taken and their effect, to their evident excitement. They provide me with additional liquids and herbs to infuse into Wrik. I ingest these. Half I reject as toxic or irrelevant; the other half I inject through my hand needles.

Twelve of the healers enter the room and seated themselves in a circle, linking hands. One sits on either side of Wrik, a hand on his arm. Jaelle retreats to the doorway. I remain in contact with Wrik to protect him as best I can.

The healers concentrate and, to my surprise, I feel a wave of energy in the room. As it is not an energy I am calibrated for, I cannot recognize it, yet it is there.

I examine Wrik closely as his life signs strengthen. The tableau of the silent healers remains for most of an hour, during which I watch Wrik's organs repair themselves and his skin flow like plastic to close over the gaping wound.

Finally the healers break their circle. Assistants come in and help the healers leave. The effort has spent all twelve of them.

Wrik's eyes open and he looks at me. "Maauro," he says. "The pain is gone. Am I going to be OK?"

"Yes, Wrik."

His eyes close and his face looks peaceful.

I look at Jaelle. She gives me an enigmatic look and spins on her heel to leave. I sense that something significant has transpired but have no idea what it may be.

***

I came to my senses and sat up in bed before I realized that I should be dead or at the least screaming from the sudden movement. I reached down and looked at my side. I was dressed only in a loose robe of a fine silky fabric. Under the robe my skin was a bright pink but otherwise unmarred.

"You're awake," a voice exclaimed.

I turned to see Jaelle walk in. She came in and sat on the end of the bed.

"Yes. I can't believe I'm not dead."

"It took a dozen of their strongest healers. They're still asleep from their efforts."

There was something diffident in Jaelle and I suspected I knew what caused it.

"What is she, Wrik?"

"Jaelle."

"Quickly! Before she returns."

I faced her. "I don't think it's safe for you to know more than you do."

"I see. Is she going to let me live? Or am I too much of a risk for her?"

"You are that," Maauro's voice came. Somehow she'd slipped into the room unseen.

We both jumped, Jaelle to the other side of the bed away from Maauro.

"Don't hurt her," I demanded.

"What if she threatens me?" Maauro said.

Did I hear a plaintive sound in her voice? Did my protecting Jaelle upset her?

"Jaelle," I began, "you need to promise Maauro that you will never tell anyone what you have seen here or what you know of Maauro. I can't help you unless you do."

She looked at each of us. "Agreed."

"If you break your promise," Maauro said, "I will hunt you down, regardless of any obstacle or threat."

Jaelle nodded. "I'll go you one better. You evidently care about Wrik."

Maauro simply nodded, a guarded look in her huge eyes.

"I know you had to be pretty desperate for money to take such a job as searching for me."

"Correct," she said. "Our need was extreme."

If it kills me, I thought, I am going teach her about commerce.

"We have a huge treasure trove of artifacts and a group of survivors who will be indebted to you for saving them," Jaelle said. "They'd be happy to build us a concealed landing site here. No one has to know where the treasures are coming from. There are a lot of credits to be made here."

***

I look at the two biologicals. The web of interrelations and mutual interests pleases me. Such a structure will bear weight. It seems I have acquired a new friend. This thought triggers others. All other beings seem to exist in networks: people, organizations and even places to which they are attached. They float in these relationships as I did in the service of the Creators, cared for by my maintenance crew.

Only Wrik and I are rootless, connected to no one, without the comfort and protection of these networks. Perhaps existence...life... is the process of acquiring and nurturing these relationships.

If so, I have, however poorly, made a start at a network.

"I accept your proposal."

***

I slept for most of the day, and then, feeling ridiculously healthy, left the hospital with Maauro watching over me. Jaelle and her friend Faroa conducted us to the main hall where the Elder waited. The hall turned out to be part of the ancient ship.

"This has the look of an engineering section," Maauro commented.

"It was once the power plant of our ship," the Elder responded.

"What brought your people here?" I asked.

"We fled the destruction of our home world. We had developed space flight late in our species life. Our explorations had come to little. We found no intelligent species near our home star."

"Odd," Jaelle said. "Our sector of space has teemed with life."

"We do not come from your space," the Elder said. "Our world was far from here. Indeed we do not know that our space is in your dimension. When we fled in this ship, its experimental drive malfunctioned, plunging us into a form of hyperspace our engineers had never seen before. We were utterly lost when we emerged."

"What were you fleeing?" Maauro asked.

"Our ancestors referred to it only as the Horror, something discovered on a dead world. It followed our ships home and fed on our world. We had never run into an alien species before. We had little in the way of warcraft. Only a small number of us escaped.

"Once we landed here, we hid ourselves. We learned this was the site of an ancient battlefield. We found artifacts and began an occasional trade with the people you call Kandalorians, who moved in some centuries after we did.

"That trade provided us with some things we could not make ourselves. It eventually led Jaelle to us, which was fortunate, and then the others, this Lostra and the Thieves Guild, which was less fortunate."

"What brought Jaelle here," Maauro began, "were ancient, high-technology artifacts. What brought me was an image on a piece of ancient hull metal. It was the image, painted in the last few hundred years, of my ancient enemy, what we called an Infestor."

The elder looked at her in puzzlement. Maauro turned to a nearby wall and from her right eye a light flashed. Projected on the wall was the image of the panel that Jaelle's father had shown us.

The elder clapped his hands together, a gesture of mirth among his kind. "This is an old piece of mine. I painted it based on a creature that our surveyor's hooks dragged up. We had never seen its like before or since. We used it as a scarecrow to frighten away Kandalorians who came too close to our lands. It finally disappeared. No one knows where it went or why anyone would steal such a thing."

I looked at Maauro. I now knew what she had found in the Tar Sea, why she'd come out so much stronger and why this area was of use to her. Her look warned me to silence.

***

"While we are a long-lived race," the elder continues, "none of us now alive came in the ship or know how to repair the cloaking machinery. Its failures come more often. It may seem peculiar to you strangers, but secrecy and obscurity have been our culture for so long that they are bred into us. We dread exposure, as few and as weak as we are. We wish only to live quietly here, enjoying our hills, the jungle and even the swamps, which we do not find as distasteful as others do."

I walk past the others to examine the mechanism to the evident distress of the attendants. The Elder quells them with a gesture.

I extend a hand toward one panel, my finger splits into a dozen filaments, which enter ports on the panel.

"What?" the elder gasps, moving forward.

"Don't move," Jaelle barks. "She's immune to your weapons and can tear you all to pieces."

"I mean no harm," I say. "I am only trying to understand the mechanism. Leave me to study this and I will let you know if I can help."

The elder looks in distress at Jaelle and me. Wrik gives them a reassuring nod though whether the gesture means anything to either of them I do not know.

"Leave her be," Jaelle says. "She'll help if she can. There's nothing you could do to stop her in any event."

Jaelle and the elder retreat a distance and he gathers the attendants, to keep them out of my reach, I assume.

I examine the mechanism and can now apply all of my processing power. It takes an eternity of 79 seconds. The control mechanisms for manipulating the shielding are simple, taking a mere .035 seconds to map. The remainder is spent analyzing the new physics revealed in the Murch's holographic science. Even at their height, my Creators had not mastered these applications. The engineering skill in the Murch machinery equals my own design. I wonder about the nature of the "horror from space" that destroyed them.

Some of the damage is simple misalignment over the centuries. There are burnouts and circuit failures such as had plagued me earlier. With many of my own functions now restored, I believe I am equal to the task of repairs.

I remain at the console for an extended period of time—the biologicals will not credit my quick mastery of the cloak otherwise. I must constantly remind myself that I live in a universe of these lifeforms and success in my new life will depend on how well I can understand them

Wrik walks forward to my side. "Can you help them?"

"Yes," I whisper back.

He raises an eyebrow at me, which I have learned means a question.

"Might this be a good time for you to teach me about commerce?" I ask.

***

Maauro repaired the Murch's cloak and they were as grateful as Jaelle expected. With the Kandalorians gone, the Murch needed new trading partners. This suited me as Maauro and I were to be the conduit to Jaelle's antiquities business. We agreed to move only a small number of artifacts and to send most of those off world. Maauro would not discuss what she'd found in the Tar Sea, but her capabilities were so much greater than before and she assured me the sclerosis was a thing of the past.

So the three of us made our way back to Wayfarer with a skimmerful of trade goods. From there, it was a short hop at our best speed back to Vanceport, where we secreted our loot in a locked warehouse.

Then it was time to collect our reward. This time we rented an aircar and flew in comfort to the Watering Hole.

We grounded the car and walked in. Jaelle had been silent on the way over. I could feel tension building in her as we walked up to the door. The same Nekoan female who greeted us weeks before stood behind the grill. She leapt up at the sight of Jaelle. She shouted over her shoulder in Nekoan. Another female came up, started at the sight of Jaelle and us, and raced off.

"Mistress," the first Nekoan said. "Welcome home. Your father will be overjoyed at your return."

"No doubt," Jaelle said. "Take us to the old Ratcatcher."

The girl smiled nervously. "Please follow me, Mistress. I will take you to your father."

We found ourselves in the same room our adventure began in. Just before we went in, Jaelle put her arm in mine. Maauro gave her a curious look but said nothing.

Nenan Tekala rose from behind his table. "Daughter, you are returned."

"Yes," Jaelle said, placing her head on my shoulder. "I'm so lucky you sent such a handsome young man to find me."

"Uh, Jaelle," I began.

"Daughter?" Tekala began, with more of a growl than usual.

"Yes," Jaelle continued, "handsome and with so many skills and abilities." She almost purred, rubbing against me. "I've decided to enter into an arrangement with Wrik in regard to my business. He's going to help me move artifacts. Of course I'll be paying him—"

"Pay him?" Tekala howled. "Move artifacts. You're going to share my wealth with him?"

"Your wealth?" Jaelle said. "Which wealth would that be?"

"Surely you understand a daughter's duties—"

"The artifacts and their trade were found and developed by me, over your opposition and without your help, as everything else in my life has been!"

"This human has been corrupting you, leading you away from our family traditions."

"This is the 10th century, Father. You don't own a daughter in this century. What I do and who I lavish my affections on is my own concern."

"Lavish your affections?" Tekala sputtered, quite a trick with fangs. "This human? Do you mean you—"

"Actually," I interrupted, "I'm here about a little matter of a reward."

"Reward! Reward, my ass. You'll get nothing for seducing my daughter."

"I seduced him! And how dare you offer a lousy 100,000 standards for my safe return! Is this the value you put on your daughter, Ratcatcher?"

"Perhaps we should wait outside," I suggested. I turned to find that Maauro had already disappeared. Jaelle and her father were shouting in Nekoan and beyond noticing whether I came or went. So I went.

In the courtyard, I looked up at the stars and wondered where Maauro had gotten to. I noticed the rest of the staff had vanished too. It told me that this was not the first father-daughter battle to disturb the neighborhood.

Fifteen minutes later, silence fell. Jaelle walked out. She was carrying a card comp and walked up to me triumphantly, showing me the figure, 115,000 confederate standards glowed on it. She clicked the button and sent it on to my account.

"The Tekala family keeps its promises, despite what my father thinks," Jaelle said.

"We're thankful," I said.

"You and Maauro?" she said. "I don't quite trust her, Wrik."

"I've never known her to lie."

"Well, she does seem to care for you."

"We're in a kind of alliance," I said. "We rely on each other."

Jaelle gave me a curious look. "I said she *cares* for you."

I laughed lightly. "Jaelle, she only looks like a female. She adopted gender when she adopted that appearance."

"So you say," Jaelle said. "But she does care. I'm not quite sure how or why, but I need to know. Nothing's as dangerous as traipsing through another female's territory."

I shrugged. "It's not like that. I'm not quite sure what it is, but it's not like that."

"Well," she said. "I'm more likely to be killed by my father for being with you."

"Jaelle," I blurted out. "You deserve better than me."

"More hints, Wrik?" She placed her hands on my shoulders, forcing me to face her. The animal warmth of her hands struck through my clothes. "Why not just tell me what it is that you are so afraid of that it rides your nights?"

I stared at her silently, unable to give voice to my feelings.

She sighed. "Keep your secrets for now. I wasn't planning on settling down and having kits with you, though I'm tempted every time I think of my father's face. Still, if sometime you want to be more to me than an idle experiment, I'll have to know who and what you really are."

Her lips burned on mine, then she was gone, walking into the Watering Hole.

"What if I don't know myself?" I whispered to the night air.

A sound came from behind me, a footstep. It made me smile. Maauro moved silently unless she consciously moved otherwise. I turned to see her standing in a shadow.

"Jaelle came through for us," I said, "115K in the account. All our debts eliminated and a lot left over."

"I did not doubt her. She does not like me, but I find I approve of her."

"What makes you think she doesn't like you?"

"Her statements, or do you forget the acuity of my hearing?"

"She doesn't know you as well as I do...that was pretty silly, wasn't it?"

"Silly?"

"Do I know you at all, Maauro?"

"You know as much of me as there is to know. I am only eight years old."

I laughed. "Maauro."

"Yes?"

"Are you my friend?"

"Yes, Wrik, I am. Please do not doubt that."

"I don't. You're the first friend I have had since I disgraced myself. I didn't think...I didn't think there'd be another."

"I spent eons alone on a rock. I did not think that I would ever see another living being."

"Maybe we've both short-changed ourselves on hope?" I said. "Hope. I can't remember using that word since...since then.

"This calls for a celebration. I'm thinking a fine meal, a little wine for me. What would you like?"

"I would like to go to the top of the Sala Haga and see the view."

"Then that's what we'll do."

"Will Jaelle come with us?"

I hesitated. "Not tonight. This evening I'll spend with my friend."

"Thank you, Wrik. It is good to have friends, isn't it?"

"Yes, Maauro, it surely is."

CHAPTER

12

"I 'M STILL NOT USED TO DOING IT WITH A GIRL WITH A tail," I said, stretching lazily, a sense of well-being filling me.

Jaelle lay next to me on her large, round bed. I still found it disconcerting how at certain angles she looked so human, and at others so like the plains cats of her ancestry. Her face, turned toward me, was her most human feature. She looked at me from big golden eyes, but it seemed there was a shadow in them.

"Once again, Human, you've talked me horizontal and out of my clothes when I was on the verge of learning something about you."

"It's not that interesting a subject," I said, rolling onto my back to stare at the broad-leafed fan stirring the air. Jaelle's apartment had a good view of both the old and new cities in a neighborhood that I'd never been able to visit, much less afford, before our recent run of luck. The rooms were a creamy yellow, with high ceilings, well-furnished with the sort of overstuffed furniture favored by her species.

"Very well," she said. "You could at least tell me about how different it is from being with a human woman."

"Did you ever hear how curiosity killed the cat?"

"Don't be silly. There wouldn't be anyone left on my planet if that was true, not that we are actually cats. Quit ducking my questions."

I smiled as we moved back to safer ground. "It's similar. You're smooth-skinned overall, so that isn't that different. Of course, oral sex is out of the question with fangs like yours."

"Silly idea sticking something that size in my mouth anyway."

"You can do interesting things with that tail of yours."

"Yes," she said, dragging her tail across my inner thigh.

"And you?" I asked idly.

"The fact that you have only one is rather unusual, but you make up for it in other ways. You don't bite me, which is a plus. You're more interested in my needs then Nekoan males. So, overall, quite a plus."

"Thanks...I think."

"Wrik."

"Yes."

"One day I'll insist on some answers."

I lay with my eyes closed and breathed slowly and deeply.

After a few seconds, I felt Jaelle's head rest on my shoulder. Then I really did fall asleep.

I left later that afternoon. I had to ready *Sinner* for another trip to the valley of the Murch. There were artifacts waiting to be picked up. In the three months since we'd returned from the Tar Sea we'd done a small but steady and very lucrative trade in ancient artifacts. We sent them off-world as there was little market on Kandalor itself and we wanted to keep that in reserve. Plus the off-world sales meant fewer questions and less investigation about our sources. We wanted no attention from either the Guild or the Confederacy.

I took an aircar back to the spaceport. It was safer than a pedicab and I could afford the rental now. The trip took mere minutes, and then I was circling down over Sinner's chrome-yellow shape. I had no worries about security once I arrived. Maauro was down there. While she had her own entertainments and diversions, it was her turn to guard the ship. This gave me a plausible reason to keep my girlfriend and Maauro apart. There had been no overt hostility between the two and wouldn't be on Maauro's side. Maauro had two settings for conflict, off and kill. Jaelle viewed the ancient android with fear and suspicion. She believed me naive for accepting as a friend a being I could never truly hope to understand.

Maybe she was right. When I wasn't around Maauro, I still entertained dark thoughts and doubts about the android. After all, wasn't everything about Maauro's appearance calculated to endear her to me, from the tiny, teenage girl shape, to the huge aquamarine eyes? Without Maauro, though, I would be dead already. I lived on time she'd borrowed for me.

I touched down and rolled the aircar back into the rental lot, then walked briskly over to the hangar. This one had a small apartment built into it and was much more convenient than our old quarters. Maauro walked out to greet me. She'd tied back her long hair with her usual cadmium-yellow silk bow.

"Hello, Wrik. Welcome back. Did you enjoy your date with Jaelle?"

"Yes, we had fun."

"That is good. She's been a excellent addition to our network."

"Uh, yeah. I suppose so."

"I've preflighted the ship as you requested."

"Great. Hey, is that coffee I smell?"

"Yes. I made some and warmed up some rations."

"Maauro, you keep this up and Jaelle will get very jealous."

Maauro cocked her head at me in a gesture I'd learned meant, *"What the hell are you talking about?"*

We walked into the machine shed next to *Sinner* from which the wonderful smell of coffee came. Two cups sat there. I poured for both of us. Maauro did ingest food and drink, but it could be anything from fuel oil and paper, to wine and steak. She converted them to energy on a low level. Topping off the batteries, she called it.

I took a cautious sip of the coffee, and then drank deeply and appreciatively. "Damn, that's good." Maauro brought over some local breads and spreads, and we enjoyed a little breakfast together.

"Given everything that you can ingest," I said, "do you have preferences?"

"Nothing poisons me, of course, barring some exotic substances that do not exist in nature. I do prefer easy-to-breakdown compounds that you use for foods, even though the energy is minimal. But I have a fondness for scrambled eggs."

I dropped the cups in the washer and everything else in the recycler. "Shall we get going?"

Despite Maauro's assurances, I did a walk around, if only to stay in practice. She watched me with some amusement. Then I clambered aboard, and we took off, rolling down the runway after getting clearance from the tower. *Sinner* handled like a fat, lazy airplane in atmosphere. I could take her straight up, but it cost fuel. While money wasn't tight right now, I saw no reason to be a spendthrift.

We quickly left the air control of the spaceport, and I dropped to low altitude to stay off the port scanner. I triggered the homemade ECM Maauro had made. Now it would take a warship using their sensors at full power to pick us up.

"We're going to take the northern route this time," I said. "It will knock an hour off the trip. I told Jaelle we'd be back by midnight."

Maauro nodded and then went up to the top turret, to her accustomed spot for watching the clouds. After we'd crossed the mountains, I climbed to 5,000 feet to avoid the turbulence of the hot air near the jungle surface. Hours rolled by uneventfully.

I ran my hand through my hair. I thought about putting *Sinner* on autopilot. Morning coffee was now many hours behind me and a soft drink sounded like a great idea. I reached for the panel to engage the autopilot.

Sinner's wing flashed orange and black and disappeared. The world spun over my canopy as *Sinner* tumbled.

"Maauro," I shouted. "We're going in. Punch out!" The force of the spin shoved me back in the seat. I tried to raise my hands to pull down the yellow and black ejection bar but couldn't. My vision was red-tinged fading to black.

My God, I thought, I'm in trouble. *I'm going to die. Really die.*

A shape lunged into my vision. Maauro. She'd abandoned her seat to help me. She was struggling with the g-forces that were beyond me. In an instant, she reached my seat, activated the bailout switch and reached up for the bar.

I tried to scream, to stop her. If she pulled the lever, the canopy would shatter and the seat would blast into her as it blew me clear. I could barely force sound out of my crushed lungs, "Nnaaaaaahhhhh."

She yanked the lever and tried to duck back. Too slow. All I had was a jumbled series of impressions: the canopy exploding as the ejector system shattered it, a roar of jets and the slam as the seat flung itself up and struck Maauro. All was sound and fury until a red chute spread over me. Then I was floating in a silent world of sky and cloud. The sky was impossibly blue and the ground was a palette of greens and browns, dotted with brilliant flowers in every tropical color. I felt numb, noticing without interest that my right pants leg was torn off. I wiped my face and my hand came away reddened. I stared at it without comprehension. Then something flashed and exploded below me.

I snapped out of it, looking at the ground floating up below me. I must have punched out only a few hundred meters up. A tower of flame and acrid gray and black smoke rose from where Sinner had struck. I twisted in my chute, checking the sky, but there was no other canopy to be seen.

Automatics in the chute flexed and twisted as I steered for a clearing near the crashed ship. I came down as easily as if stepping off a stool, the chute balling up behind and the grab-harness dropping off, freeing me to run, more like stagger, toward Sinner.

The ship had shattered into several large pieces but fragments and flaming debris lay all over. My hearing was coming back. I heard the crackle of flames and the pop of small explosions. Sinner's forward hull lay jammed into some trees. I raised my hands to protect my face from the radiant heat, forcing my way. I wondered if I could make it back out before the fire cut me off.

I looked around hoping for any sign of movement. Seeing nothing, I pushed into the tangle of wreckage, heading for the cockpit. As my head poked up to the top deck, I saw a foot. I threw debris out of my way and jumped in.

I froze. Maauro lay twisted on the deck. Her eyes fixed and frozen on nothing; her face was dented and burned. Her hair was partly torn off. I heard a voice shouting her name over and over and realized it was mine.

I shook myself to get a grip and knelt by her, running my hands over her unresponsive body. It had reverted to rigid and cold from its normal malleable and warm. I tried to lift her to sitting, but my hands slid off her left shoulder. The arm was gone, midway between shoulder and elbow.

Indecision wracked me. Should I move her? She wasn't human or even biological. She didn't bleed or have a spinal cord to sever, but would I damage her further?

A waft of smoke set me choking and decided the issue. There was still plenty of fuel in Sinner's fragments. Even if it didn't explode further, the radiant heat would kill me.

I started to pull her up and reality smacked my cut and bleeding face again. Maauro looked like a teenage girl, but weighed far more than I did. I yanked and jerked frantically, barely moving the android.

"No, no, no," I screamed. The heat was increasing, yet how could I leave her? Was she already dead? Could she even die?

Maauro's right arm moved faster than I could see, fastening on my throat. Her head snapped around, eyes flat-black panels from lid to lid.

"Alad var doshna unlik vor," she demanded in a voice I'd never heard before. Even her face seemed strange. I recognized the machine I'd first seen on the asteroid.

"Maauro, it's me, Wrik."

She repeated the alien phrase. I suddenly noticed serrated teeth in her mouth that hadn't been there before. I knew better than to struggle against her impossible strength and speed, even in this damaged state. I forced myself to relax.

"Maauro," I whispered through her steel grip. "It's me, Wrik. I'm your friend. I found you on an Infestor base. The war is over. It's been over for 50,000 years."

A change swept over the face. Feminine curves reasserted themselves. The teeth disappeared and the eyes filled with the beautiful, gentle blue-green I knew. Her hand opened immediately.

"Wrik," she said in her little-girl voice, with only a hint of distortion. "Did I hurt you? Are you all right? There is blood on your face."

"I'm ok. You got me out in time. Can you move?"

She seemed to look inside. "Severe internal and external damage; I am effecting repairs to reestablish mobility."

"You weren't there when you came to," I said, casting anxious glances at the billowing smoke behind us

"All higher systems were offline or disrupted. I had only my basic combat CPU. Fortunately, it did not perceive you as an enemy."

"Fortunately," I said rubbing my throat.

"Please look for my left arm while I am regaining my mobility."

I looked down at her. "Does it hurt?"

"Not as you mean it, but I am upset at being maimed and damaged so."

I searched through the cockpit while Maauro's body jerked and clattered on the deck behind me, the result of damage, or the repair effort, I could not tell. I found no sign of the arm—it might have been torn off by the ejector seat, or perhaps flung off in the crash, but it was nowhere to be found.

I came back to her. The heat and smoke were becoming overwhelming. "Maauro, I can't last much longer."

She jerked upright like a badly made toy. Her good arm reached out and dug into a nearby stanchion. "I will not touch you. My fine motor control is not operating. Help me on my left side."

Halting and stumbling, we made our way out of the wrecked ship, heading for the thicker brush...

"Into the forest, upwind of the fire," Maauro ordered, gesturing with her head.

"Why?"

"We were shot down by enemy action, Wrik. Logically a force will come to make sure we are dead, unless our enemies are sloppy fools, and I do not believe they are. This is a Guild ambush."

"Then we're dead," I muttered, shock and exhaustion taking hold. "We're out here on our own, no help and no weapons."

Maauro turned her damaged face to me and to my utter surprise she gave a small smile. "Do not, my brother-in-arms, think so little of me. We are not done yet."

We reached the treeline. "Proceed in one hundred meters. I will call to you when it is safe to come back. If you hear weapon fire and I do not call, flee as best you can."

"What are you going to do?" I demanded.

"One good ambush deserves another," she said.

Maauro sank to the ground and twisted her limbs and torso. In seconds she was so distorted and broken-looking that it made me sick.

"Go," she said, closing one eye and causing her face to discolor. "Hopefully, they will believe me destroyed and try to salvage my parts."

***

I see that Wrik is distressed by my physical appearance and by leaving me, but it cannot be helped. I take stock of my situation. I have never before been damaged to this degree, not even when I was blown up on the asteroid and lost forty percent of my mass. Most of what I lost then was armor. My self-repair mechanisms, those that survive, are working at high speed. I am designed to resist battle damage in this way and indeed, I am in less trouble than when the sclerotic system failures were afflicting me. I'm designed with multiple redundancies. However, I used most of my backup material repairing myself when I was hit 50,000 years ago. I can repair some aspects of my body, but I can not regenerate an arm without a supply of my basic material.

My self-repair proceeds at such a pace and using such prodigious quantities of energy that I must slow them, or the waste heat generated will catch the vegetation on fire.

I miss my arm. I have always prided myself on my appearance and maintenance. This is distressing.

I shelve these thoughts. The enemy has arrived. A helicopter platform slides into the clearing. It is little more than a railed platform under whirling blades. A good choice tactically, as it allows the five armored troopers to pile off, their heavy weapons searching the smoking debris field.

At first they take no notice of me; evidently I do look like a ball of wreckage. I watch them search the area as I analyze them: two Nekoans, a male and female, two Kandalorians muffled in cloaks and head-coverings and a Dua-Denlenn. It is not Dusko unfortunately. This one holds a sensor pack in one hand and an RPG launcher in the other, its tube over his shoulder.

The weapons concern me. In my damaged state they could be lethal. I must destroy this group in one fell swoop.

The Dua-Denlenn finally spots me and calls to his force in Confed standard.

"Over here." He points the RPG at me.

It is the moment of truth; will they fire first, or hope to salvage me?

"Great Stalker," the female Nekoan says, her large ears twitching. "It's slagged. The Collector won't be pleased; she told Dusko to get her intact."

"Is it dead?" one of the Kandalorians croaked in its base voice.

"Must be," the Dua-Denlenn said, "The scanner says its temperature is over 300 degrees C.

"Easy money," the male Nekoan adds.

"We're not done," the Dua-Denlenn growls in annoyance. "There is the human to account for. He ejected before the crash."

"I cannot smell him," the male Nekoan said, "with all this burning plastic."

"I wonder what human tastes like," the female laughed, her teeth in evidence.

"We'll take this back when the scraps cool," the Dua-Denlenn. "You two follow the human."

They are all around me in a circle; none has a weapon bearing on me. Now is the optimum time. Despite the apparent twisting and bending I have my limbs in the ideal position to fling me straight up in the air in their midst. I lunge. From my right hand flechettes fly out of my finger tubes, striking the Nekoans. My feet strike the Kandalorians crushing the skull of one and impaling the other. This fouls my aim at the Dua-Denlenn with my hand projectors, but I fling the dead Kandalorian stuck on my leg at him. He fires his RPG and I twist, evading the round. Then I slash at him with my hand, severing his head from his body. I hit the ground and roll up.

The male Nekoan lays on the ground, dead, the RPG round stuck in his chest. The female is also down, bleeding, her weapon nearby, her arm shredded by flechettes. Our eyes lock. She backpedals on the ground as I scuttle toward her on three limbs.

"No, no," she screams. "No, no, please, wait..."

I scramble over her and slam my hand down, ending the pathetic entreaties. I try to remember, as her whimpers trail off into silence, that she was wondering what Wrik's flesh tasted like.

I stand. "Wrik," I call. "Wrik."

In a minute he is standing with me, looking at the slaughter.

"That all of them?" he asks.

"Yes, but others may come. We should escape in the heliflyer. You will need to fly, as my systems are not in order."

He scoops up a weapon and starts toward the flyer. When I do not follow, he stops. I am looking down at the Nekoan female's dead face.

"I am here again," I say, motivated by what I am not sure. "Standing over a pile of dead bodies that only a minute ago were aware, filled with thoughts, hopes, wishes for a tomorrow."

"They were Guild, Maauro. Predators. They'd have destroyed us both." He moves to place a hand on my shoulder, but the heat from my body makes him pause.

"True and yet it troubles me. Is this all there is to me? Do I only exist to end life? It did not trouble me with Infestors. Perhaps it should have, but I was made to do fight them and I can see no merit in those creatures. But this one at my feet is so like the one that you make love to. Yet I must kill her to survive. I could grow tired of this."

"You've preserved my life, Jaelle's and many others among the Murch. We don't attack others. Our lives belong to us and they are precious. Why should we weigh the lives of these murderers," he gestures at the bodies, "against ours?"

"Perhaps you are right. But Wrik, another thought occurs. Who knew that we were taking this route to the Murch encampment?"

"Jaelle...wait, Maauro, you don't think she sold us out?"

"I think that we must find Jaelle and put certain questions to her. For one, it appears we have a new enemy, a female named the Collector, who gives orders to Dusko."

"Let's get out of here, Maauro. I want some answers."

We stagger to the heliflyer, I lay prone and Wrik straps me to the decking. He takes the single seat behind the windscreen and manipulates the controls. We lift into the sky. In this slow machine it will be several hours back to Vanceport. I power down and concentrate on repairs. I miss my arm.

CHAPTER
13

I DROPPED MAAURO AT A FLOPHOUSE ON THE EDGE OF THE space field, then took the helo to long-term parking and left it in an isolated section. You only paid when leaving such places. It would be months before anyone bothered to check on the flyer. I knew every place in Kandalor that a poor spacer could go for a free shower or cheap eats. We'd need that knowledge now that bad times had returned. I stopped in a noodle shop, cleaned up in the rest room and wolfed down some noodles. The locals wouldn't recognize one human from another and couldn't care less.

I waited until dark and moved through the old, safe ways back to where I'd left Maauro. I brought nothing back with me. There was nothing I could do for the android, and I knew her capacity for self-repair was astounding. The alley behind the flophouse was clear, though I waited a few minutes before chancing the door to our hideout.

Maauro opened the door to my coded knock, and I slipped in. I studied my companion; her repairs had proceeded apace. Her face had returned to normal; her hair was back to its usual length. Her chassis...her body, was cleaned of dirt and scratches. For a second the illusion held, and then she moved. One leg dragged and the other seemed both inflexible and unsteady. The edge of her severed arm was now smooth, but it looked somehow the worse for it.

"How are you?"

"I will not dissemble for you. My damage is very severe. I've effected the repairs I can, but used up almost all my reserves of energy. Ages ago I used up most of the spare chassis material I carried in my body when I was hit by a blast on the asteroid and lost several limbs. I am actually 39.476% smaller than my original size for that reason.

"The problem is that the ceramic and malleable metal of my body is beyond any replacement capability of your sciences. Even undamaged, I could not manufacture replacement arm and leg materials in my own interior factories. Small patches, yes, over several months, but not whole limbs, not without a supply of my original material. My combat capabilities are reduced to almost nothing."

I sat on the bed, despair overwhelming me. "What are we going to do? There's nowhere to run to. No one to help us"

Maauro tottered over and sat awkwardly on the floor near me. "We have our wits and our perseverance and these are powerful weapons. Right now our need is for information."

I nodded. "The most pressing question is whether Jaelle is in on this. I find it hard to believe. But I've been wrong about people most of my life."

"I do not believe she betrayed us, at least not consciously. It is a critical issue. If we can rely on Jaelle's help, we have a greater chance of reaching the Tar Sea where once I found supplies and materials."

Hope surged in me. "Do you think you can find something there to help us?"

"It seems our only chance. I can move better than I am doing so presently for short periods. I will reserve that for emergencies."

"Let's rest up today and wait for nightfall," I said. "I'll make my way to Jaelle's after dark and see what I can find out."

"No," Maauro said. "We are safest together and will wage our battle so. Rest now, I will keep watch."

I sank back on the thin mattress, staring at the one panel in the ceiling. Jaelle's face came to me: her soft, blond hair piled up on her head, the large ears that were so mobile and sensitive, small nose, yellow eyes, sensuous lips, though one had to kiss carefully around the fangs. I hadn't been with anyone I hadn't paid for since I'd left Retief.

Retief. They'd be howling if they knew I was dating a non-human. Hell, other types of humans weren't good enough for them. They'd regard her as one step above bestiality. Screw them, I thought. Jaelle was a dream to me, if only she wasn't the one who'd betrayed us.

Sleep slammed down on me.

***

I slept like the dead and awoke ravenous. All that was available were cans of rations from a vending machine. I devoured two as the sun slowly rose over the spaceport, limning ships and towers with golden fire.

"A beautiful sight," Maauro said.

"You can think that at a time like this?"

"Now more than ever as we find ourselves at the edge of destruction. Each moment may be our last. Shall we not grab those moments of beauty available to us? I have always found such sights comforting. No matter how dire the battle, some beauty, if only that of the stars, survives our petty struggles."

"Let's hope we survive our petty struggles."

She nodded. "Time to go." Maauro picked up an SMG, then threw a Kandalorian travel cloak over her shoulders and tucked her hair under a turban. I threw a cloak over the heavy MG I'd taken off the dead Guilder. I added a broad hat of the type fashionable in the high desert. I pulled a scarf across my face, thin disguise but useful. I tucked my usual pistol into my waistband.

We slipped out of the flophouse with Maauro moving more normally. We couldn't afford to attract any attention. I waved down a pedicab. Dusko had likely circulated our images, but we had no choice. It was kilometers to Jaelle's place and we dared not use up Maauro's remaining mobility.

The pedicab dropped us off. I had to pay extra, as he needed his motor to move our combined weight. We climbed to the top of a nearby building and looked across at Jaelle's place.

"Can you see anything?" I asked.

"Yes, signs of a struggle inside, in the form of broken furniture. Things of value have been removed, but I believe Jaelle resisted being taken into her father's custody."

I heaved a sigh. It was only circumstantial evidence of her innocence, but nonetheless comforting. "If it was her father, he'd have taken her to either the restaurant or to his villa on the river. My bet is the villa."

Maauro shook her head. "According to a local new server, the Spacer's Rest Society leased Tekala's villas for a charity event this weekend. I doubt that he would allow Dusko to hold his daughter, so she is likely at the restaurant."

"Let's go."

An hour on another pedicycle brought us to The Watering Hole. We dismounted a block away and made our way toward the restaurant. The Watering Hole wasn't the only restaurant; a number of lesser establishments lined the square. The square itself was the usual chaotic mass of small stalls and carts, with the occasional vehicle weaving around them over the smooth concrete and stone of the Old City's bones. We found a shady, quiet spot near a fountain in a small park across the street, and settled in on a metal bench. It was early evening now and the streets were full enough that we did not attract attention

I looked up at the Hala Saga. Its topaz dome sent out buttery-yellow rays reflected from the setting sun. It already seemed an age since I had sat there with Maauro, enjoying a fine meal as she savored the sights and sounds of the city below.

I turned to my petite mechanical companion. "What do you see?"

"I have been examining the restaurant using a variety of scans. Many of the usual staff are missing. The people replacing them have the look of Guild operatives with concealed weapons. They could be guarding Jaelle, protecting her father from our vengeance, or both."

"We won't be walking in there."

"No. While I could easily defeat those I see who have only small arms, I suspect there are others concealed with heavier weapons. By now they know the cleanup team that came after us has not returned. If they sent more troops, they will know that our bodies do not lie beside them. They would not rely on handguns to stop me."

"So how do we get in?"

"I do not yet know. For now we wait until darkness and quiet."

I surprised myself by falling asleep sitting on the bench next to her. When I snapped awake, hours later, the street was clear and the last of the shopkeepers was closing up.

Maauro, who'd sat unmoving next to me for hours, gestured with her hand. I followed her through the park around the giant palms that waved overhead to a stand of sword bushes not far from the back of The Watering Hole. Lights hung on the adobe wall of the restaurant, making any approach across the broad avenue suicidal.

A large green and yellow truck turned onto the block and then parked in front of one of the small restaurants. I looked at it without interest. "Meat delivery."

"This could be useful," Maauro said. "Follow me."

"What?" I said. But she was up and moving already, albeit with a limp that ironically served as a good disguise. Who looks for a limping android?

"The Watering Hole is the largest establishment on this street. It has an interior courtyard and does not take its deliveries from the street. That truck will be passed in. I will hide in the freezer unit. You must distract the driver until I get on board." Maauro made a right turn down an alley, leaving me to approach the truck.

The driver, a stout middle-aged human woman, came out of the native diner, trailed by a simple robot sled now empty of produce, as I walked up,

"Excuse me," I said. "I seem to be lost. I'm looking for a bar called the Spacewitch. It's worth a fiver to me."

The woman gave me a frank and appraising look. "Honey, you're way off. The Spacewitch is all the way over toward the aerospace part of the spaceport. That's kilometers away from here."

"Can you draw me a map? I don't have my comp on me. Here's that fiver."

"Hey, I don't charge humans for help. We're a long way from home world."

"Ain't that the truth? You're sure?"

"Yeah, Sweetie."

I spent a few minutes chatting amiably with the driver and getting my map. My guilty conscience made me insist on her taking the five. I left, walking quickly up the next block back to the spot where I could see the restaurant. I got there just as the truck disappeared into the gate, a Guilder having climbed on the back bumper. Either Maauro hadn't got into the vehicle or somehow she'd hidden inside. Given her ability to ignore cold or heat, she might well have buried herself under frozen meat. The truck emerged twenty minutes later and I settled back down to wait.

I waited four hours as the stars rotated above me. There was no sign of life other than the occasional Guild guard. Then the gate opened and Maauro appeared, waving me over. I ran across the street and into the courtyard. I spotted the feet of the Guildsman lying behind a shed, dead or unconscious. I could not tell and did not care.

"This way," she said. "My observations tell me that she is being held in her father's offices."

***

We pause outside the office where we'd first met Nenan Tekala months before. To my surprise, Wrik reaches across to stop me when I begin to move.

"Maauro," Wrik says, "one thing and it has to be this way. Under no circumstances can you kill Jaelle's father."

I turn to face him. "Wrik, the tactical situation inside is unknown. Jaelle's father participated in the attempt on our lives. How can you bind me when we do not know what will happen after we go in?"

"Even if he is our enemy, we can't kill him. It would destroy Jaelle."

"Wrik as fond of you as I am, I cannot compromise my security for your illogical notions. Jaelle despises her father. She will not be as upset as you think."

"Maauro, you need to listen to me. This is something about us living beings—"

"I am a living being, Wrik."

"I mean those of us born, Maauro. No insult intended, but you never had parents."

"From what I know of you and Jaelle, I am not sure I have suffered in this regard." I see that I have made him angry, though I am not sure why. He has said these things himself. I am silent as he fights for control.

"Maauro," he says, his voice strained. "Would you turn on your Creators if you could? They abandoned you. Would you attack them, kill them, if you had the chance for revenge?"

I am stunned. The concept that I could turn on my Creators has never occurred to me. A memory program tries to delete the concept. This starts an internal battle which consumes an amazing 2.73 seconds while I war with myself as to whether I may even consider such an idea. I realize that these are safeguards that my creators placed in me. They did not simply trust that I could not be used against them. But so much time, damage and change has occurred that the programs do not automatically win.

I realize that my creators, like Jaelle and Wrik's parents, wanted to ensure that their progeny are obedient. I am confused.

"Maauro?" I hear Wrik ask.

The confusion Wrik's words have created is so profound that I have been totally distracted from outside stimuli, essentially helpless.

"Very well," I say, unsure for the first time in my existence of what is motivating me. "I will agree not to kill Jaelle's father."

"Thank you."

Wrik releases my arm. I crush the door lock and we storm into the room. Wrik follows me with a drawn pistol. Inside, Nenan Tekala stands behind his desk, making an abortive move toward a com. He freezes as I place my hand on it.

"Wrik," Jaelle calls. She is secured to a chair with a chain. It is to my mind excellent proof of her innocence. "My Gods, I thought you were dead. Father told me that Dusko had killed you both."

"Cover him, Wrik." I walk over to Jaelle and part the chain holding her. She stands, smiling in relief. The smile vanishes as she notices I am missing an arm.

"Maauro, your arm! And you're limping."

"I was damaged when we were shot down. My arm was torn off in the crash. This Dusko has run up quite a bill with me."

"Wrik!" Jaelle runs over to him as if to check that all his parts are present.

She turns to her father. "You told me they were dead!"

"Your father seems to have quite a pipeline to Dusko," Wrik says.

"I needed to keep her out of this," Nenan says, sitting back in his seat and glaring at Wrik. "I just want to protect my daughter. You were fool enough to tangle with a crime lord and those as far above him as the Sala Haga is above us. I didn't want her to die with you."

"How is it," I ask, "that Dusko knew which route our ship was taking? We were shot down by a concealed missile battery and then set upon by Guild. They were in place waiting for us."

Nenan looks back at us, his eyes flat and yellow.

"Father," Jaelle says in a small voice. "You didn't."

"It was to protect you," he replies wearily. "We can't afford the enmity of Dusko and the Guild. You've been a fool, my child, consorting with these non-Nekoans; no good can come of it."

"Wrik is my—"

"Don't say lover," he spits. "He's one of your dalliances, a childish provocation to me and your family. You can't have any feeling for this—this..."

"That's enough, Father. No, no, I won't call you that anymore. Whatever I feel for Wrik is mine to decide. But you, you coward, you'd murder my friends to secure yourself? Has there ever been any corruption that you held back from?"

"Where do you think you would be if not for all I have done, all I have gathered? We would have nothing. I did this for all of us!"

"That is what I have now," she says bitterly. "Nothing. I disown you and withdraw the clan name Tekala from you. I won't be kin to murderers, thieves and liars."

"You have caused me injury and distress," I add. "You will make amends by telling me of this Collector who has giving orders to Dusko."

He looked at me, fear in his yellow eyes. "I can tell you little beyond that Dusko has been seeking artifacts of ancient make for sale to a high Guild official. I only heard of her referred to as the Collector. I know Dusko feared her and that she has a small ship down at the port. She is not on it, but sent it in response to Dusko's information on you."

Jaelle looks at Wrik. "I'm sorry. I must have been sloppy and been overheard in a conversation with you about the trip. Your ship is destroyed, Maauro is maimed and it is my fault."

"I think we lay that blame with your father."

"Don't hurt him," she orders.

"No. Maauro has agreed to that as well."

Jaelle gives me a mistrustful look. I nod at her. It seems to give her some comfort.

I gather up the chain and secure Tekala to the chair. He looks at Jaelle. "If you leave with these aliens, I will have no daughter."

"Then we will be even, having disowned each other. Do not look to lay eyes on me again in this life."

I apply the gag.

Wrik places his arms around Jaelle. "Are you sure you want to come with us? We don't even know where we are going, or if we'll be alive tomorrow."

"My decision is made. But Wrik, understand this. I'm not leaving for you. I'm leaving for me."

"Then let us leave, before we encounter more Guilders," I add.

"This first," Jaelle says. She walks over to a console and activates it. "I'm going to take my inheritance a little early. We'll need money. I've been planning this for a while."

In minutes Jaelle accomplishes her task. She stands and looks at her father for a few seconds. "There's a very expensive aircar at the rear door. Let's take that."

We leave through that door and Wrik takes the aircar controls, lifting us out of the courtyard. The Guilders below see us, but do not react to Tekala's car. We speed north. The machine is an excellent model, designed only for atmospheric use, but it has the range to take us where we need to go.

"Where are we headed?" Wrik asks.

"The Murch. Any hope I have of repairs lies with them."

In the back of the aircar, Jaelle breaks down into tearing sobs.

Wrik looks at me.

"I can fly it," I answer.

CHAPTER
14

WE FLY ALL NIGHT AND MAKE THE MURCH ENCAMPMENT MID THE next day. Faroa and his friends meet us and take us into their care, though of course there is little they can do for me. I leave Wrik with Jaelle. I think this is best, as I can offer little comfort to the Nekoan.

In the morning the three of us fly the aircar to the destroyed village. Wrik's prediction proves correct; none of the natives have moved back to reoccupy what little I did not level.

We walk onto the great stone jetty. The wind is strong today and whips at us, ruffling my long hair. I miss my latest silk bow, but it was lost with my arm in the crash. We come to the end of the jetty, facing the Tar Sea.

I look up at Wrik as he steps forward to wrap his arms around me. I recognize the protective gesture. It and the concern in his hazel eyes cause a curious mix of feelings in me. I am aware that my emotions are different from a biological's— distant, muted perhaps, less powerful—as they are not rooted in sex and death. Yet this feeling is strong and I find that though I cannot put a name to it, something inchoate wells in me. I am glad that his arms are about me, foolish though it may be.

"Isn't there another way?" he asks, looking at the Tar Sea with revulsion.

"No, Wrik. Dusko did terrible damage to me. My only chance of finding what I need is down there."

"And if you can't find it? How do you get back?" he demands.

"You fear for me. Thank you for it. I cherish your concern, but you must remember that death has no terror for me. I do not fear being "buried alive" as you would. I fear failure and breaching my duty more than a cessation of awareness. If it comforts you, think of me as merely going to sleep coddled and preserved in the darkness."

"That is," he says, his voice strained, "only a small comfort."

"Small comforts may be all we have. I do not wish to end this existence. There is much I want to experience. I want to travel with you, to see new and different vistas. Watch clouds and sunrises. Visit strange and wondrous places. I want to strike down Dusko and hunt this "Collector." It would vex me to fall to such mean and petty enemies as these."

I turn to Jaelle. She watches me from a distance as usual; her expression unreadable to me. "If I do not return, please stay with Wrik. He will need all the aid he can find to escape the Guild."

She nods at me.

I turn to the end of the pier, slipping out of the comfort of Wrik's arms. I look up at the sky, wishing it was night, as I have always watched the stars and feel that in some way they watch me.

"Maauro!"

I turn back to Jaelle in some surprise.

"Good luck. Find a way to come back to us. We need you," she says.

Wrik's face is a study in misery. "Yes, come back somehow, for God's sake."

Now it is my turn to nod. I walk as briskly as I can despite the damage; if this is their last sight of me, I will not pathetically drag myself. I mount the stone edge and leap into the Tar Sea.

I plunge into the sea and quickly sink. The pier stands at the edge of a steep slope and it drops quickly into deeper darkness. I land on the muck bottom and begin wading downward. My body is so damaged that I cannot swim, so I stagger forward drunkenly.

I am in field of bodies. The Kandalorians had sacrificed many over the years before I destroyed their village. Bones and tar-preserved corpses are strewn about me. I remember Wrik's revulsion at the sight of the Tar Sea. This was to be his and Jaelle's fate at the hands of Lostra, the Guild enforcer who I tore to pieces for shooting Wrik.

It is curious to me that biologicals find some forms of death so much more terrifying than others. I suspect if Wrik could see this field of death, it would unhinge his sanity. If I return, I must never mention what I have seen here.

As if on cue, I see the upper half of Lostra's body. She has looked better. It pleases me that she must now keep company with some of her own victims. I spurn the corpse with my foot and march on.

Hours of travel later I reach the ancient battlefield. Hundreds of targets hit my scanners, only one of which I know, the landing barge I'd found the last time, but I am looking for better now.

The battle must have been epic from the size of the debris field. I concentrate my power to begin a methodical search of likely targets. My best hope is finding a ship or armored fighting vehicle of my creators. I move forward only to face one disappointment after another as targets turn out to be simply melted slag or machinery that is of no use to me.

My luck finally changes. I experience joy at the sight of a Creator AFV, a tracked and armored leviathan. The front of the great machine is stove in. It would take a nuclear weapon to deform its armor and even now there is considerable radioactivity on the immense mobile fortress. I make my way up the side, hoping to find an open hatch. I am in luck; one presents itself near ground level. I force myself in with difficulty; the ooze is harder to push through in the confined space. An interior hatch slows me, but with the aid of a lever I find inside, I crack this hatch too, heading for the engineering deck.

The crew's remains are not present. Graves Registration troops may have removed the bodies, or perhaps the crew fled when the fortress was hit. The engine compartment is intact though damaged. I approach the reactor and am relieved to find the fuel is still present and potent. Greedily, I extract the high-grade material and press it into my body, letting my permeable membranes pass it through while filtering the tar and water. Its quality makes me giddy. I compress as much as I can into a chamber that I make in my torso to create a reserve. Given the Guild's enmity, we may not be able to return here or even remain on this world. The thought spins the beginning of a plan. A change of tactics is indicated. We have tried escape, evasion and defense; perhaps a direct offense is indicated.

My self-repair kicks into high gear with all this new power, but there are limitations to my damage control and what I can construct within my body. The technology of my creation is far above the AFV, more on the level of a starship. The malleable ceramics and metal of my chassis cannot be repaired by any Confed technology. I can only manufacture small amounts of my chassis material inside my body, patches yes, certainly not an arm.

I exit the hull of the AFV high on its side. I can swim again. Until I had regained the full use of my legs, I did not realize quite how much I feared uselessness and being unable to protect my friends. Relief makes me feel buoyant. My sensors are back to full power and I can now better scan the battlefield. Now I see additional smashed AFVs and even Creator fighters and patrol boats. A picture of the battle emerges for me. An Infestor landing force sought a beachhead here. Our blocking forces hit them hard and we carried the battle as our force's bodies were recovered, but we did not hold the battlefield or have leisure to salvage machinery. Lucky for me or the precious and expensive fuel would have been recovered.

The Infestor ships lay crushed and shattered in the center of the battlefield in what was once a river valley. I orient myself on the one point that I know, the Infestor landing ship.

As I swim over the battlefield I spy a humanoid form on the bottom. Excitement floods me; could this be one of my series? I circle down and land by it. Disappointment awaits; this is not an M7 or even an earlier model. It is an enemy machine, an Infiltrator. For a brief time the enemy made machines that looked like my Creators, before we developed countermeasures more than a century prior to my own manufacture.

Still, the machine's technology vastly exceeds anything I can find in the present day. I extend an atomic torch through my fingertip and cut a limb free. The tar around me burns but at too low a temperature to bother me. Perhaps with time I may be able to fashion it into something useful. I extrude some loops in my back and place the severed limb in them.

I look over the darkling plain, likely for the last time. This is my ancient past, irrelevant to me in this life. I bid farewell to Infestors and Creators alike and head for the surface with my three good limbs.

***

We remain in the jungle, hiding in the Murch encampment with Faroa, Jaelle's friend. I use some of their remaining high-tech equipment as well as my own internal factories to fabricate tools and replacement parts, repairing myself to my precrash status, except for my left arm. There I aim my efforts at the ancient arm recovered from the Infestor infiltration unit. It is a measure of my desperation that I even consider mating a piece of hostile alien technology to my chassis. I find the arm to be in good condition and search it for any hidden traps or codes until I have reasonable certainty that it is safe. Like me, it is made of non-reactive ceramics and metal and is immune to rust or other chemical corrosion. Ironically, the tar is similar to the fluids I would have been stored in between missions.

I design all manner of interfaces in order to control the arm. It will not have the power or flexibility of my original arm. Nor does it have a built-in fusion torch, flechette dispensers, or other accessories, though I am able to add palm blades and a number of other fine, small tools. It will not have the feedback of my original limbs. In a movement of amusement it occurs to me that, like Wrik, I am now right-handed. Still, I have restored 50% of function and 75% of strength. My left arm will appear identical now that I have reworked the shape and mass of the Infestor arm.

I raise my new arm over my head. For now at least, it balances me and gives me additional capability. Perhaps it is merely vanity, but I am relieved to once again be symmetrical and complete.

After completing the final test, I go to meet my comrades. I find them together as usual, seated on a parapet over the Tar Sea. Wrik jumps to his feet when he sees me. His face is worn and anxious as usual.

"Maauro! How's the arm?"

"Most functions are restored," I respond, exaggerating out of concern for his morale.

Jaelle, who is always more reserved around me, nods approvingly. Whatever her true feelings are, she recognizes that her survival is dependent on my combat strength.

"I am repaired and you are both rested and recovered." At least somewhat I think to myself. I must remember how volatile the emotional state of biologicals is. Jaelle has lost a parent-child bond. Wrik has lost all his recently hard won security.

"It is time to consider our future," I say, sitting on the rough-hewn stone of the parapet. Wrik and Jaelle also sit.

"Future," he says bitterly. "Do we have one?"

Even Jaelle looks downcast now.

"We make one," I respond, "but not here." I realize with a mild shock that I have assumed leadership of our little unit. It is an unusual feeling—I was made to execute orders.

"What do you mean?" Jaelle asks, brushing a lock of her thick hair out of her eyes.

"If we remain here, in contact with enemy forces, we must inevitably suffer casualties at best and destruction at worst. We must leave Kandalor, vanish into space and elude the Guild."

Wrik gives me a weary look. "To do that we have to book passage on a commercial liner. The Guild would pick us off long before we could get clear."

"Correct. We must therefore go on the offensive. We must seize Dusko, wring out of him the information and assets that we need."

Both stare at me in astonishment.

"Your father told us of this Collector. There is a small interstellar ship at the port bearing the Collector's agent. That ship is not staying long, which means it is *likely refueled and reprovisioned. We will take the ship and Dusko and vanish into Confederate space."*

***

I stared at Maauro, my mouth hanging open. "Kidnap Dusko? Steal a starship?"

"Is that all?" Jaelle asked.

"It is enough for starters," Maauro replies, missing or ignoring the sarcasm. "I realize that the odds are substantial, but I believe you still underestimate my capabilities.

"I also believe that offense trumps defense. Dusko shows a desire to engage in combats that have been expensive for him and unprofitable. I believe organization factors within the Guild, as well as perhaps his injured pride, are causing him to pursue us. He will not stop, and in any battle of attrition the Guild will win, at least to the point of killing both of you, who are more vulnerable than I.

"We must gain the initiative by altering the battle with a surgical decapitation strike at the enemy."

"How...how would we pull this off?"

"We have a considerable supply of captured weapons supplied by our dead adversaries. I will reconstruct an armspac for myself. You should select those weapons you are familiar with. We have been missing now for several weeks. About now the enemy should be relaxing from high alert. They may suspect we are dead, or in hiding. They will not expect an attack on the enemy CP."

"CP?" Jaelle asks.

"Forgive me,. Command Post.

"We will proceed back to Vanceport, avoiding all of our old locations. Once we are back in the city, I will infiltrate the net and gather Intel on Dusko until we have enough for a strike."

I look at Jaelle and she nods. "We're in."

"Excellent," Maauro nods. "Now that we are repaired and rested, let us take our leave of the Murch and move within striking distance of Dusko's CP."

I consider. "There's a flophouse run by some Hanoians on the north side of town. They have no use for the Guild. They belong to a Tong."

"A what?" Maauro asked.

"It's like the Guild, only you have to be a particular type of human to belong to it. It's an old form of organization, predating spaceflight. So they wouldn't be friendly to Dusko."

"They wouldn't help us," Jaelle stated.

"No. I am just saying they wouldn't know or care what Dusko wants. We land after dark and rent one of the cheaper rooms. Maauro, you can gather intelligence from there and decide what our next move is."

"I am impressed, Wrik. These are excellent tactical points."

I snorted a laugh. "Glad to be of some use, finally."

She gave me a curious look but said nothing.

We trekked over to the Elder's compound. Farora and the elder were inside at a long table. The younger Murch stood as we came in. Jaelle walked past me and exchanged arm clasps with Farora; I was surprised by the flash of jealousy that stole through me. Then I looked over at Maauro and decided that I'd best keep a cap on that emotion.

"You are leaving?" the elder said.

"Yes," Jaelle answered. "It's time we flee this world. We are beset by enemies."

"Don't leave. We will shelter you here."

I noted that it was not the elder who made that offer; again I suppressed that flash of jealously.

"Our enemies are numerous and professional," Maauro interjected. "They will scour this area eventually, knowing that we had some connection and resources here. We do not wish to expose you to this danger. With us gone, their efforts in this direction will terminate."

The elder looked at her and nodded. "Just so."

"We may yet meet again," Jaelle said to the downcast young Murch. "If I ever get established somewhere safe, I will not forget my friends here, their kindness and the risks that were run for me."

"Fare well, my sister. Fare well and find a way to send word to us." He looked over at Maauro and me. "Good luck to you both. Look after Jaelle, since we cannot."

I nodded, realizing that I'd had more of a rival in the young Murch than I'd been aware of.

We load the aircar which has been refueled and reloaded, mostly through Maauro's efforts after she created a workshop for it. The Murch give us gifts of food and clothes which we packed away. We'd need them if we survived.

A large crowd of Murch saw us off. We kept the goodbyes to a minimum and these were mostly directed to Jaelle. I was just her boyfriend as far as they were concerned. They'd remained wary of Maauro.

We took off low and slow under the Murch's distortion field, running for an hour just over the treetops before we dared come up and gain altitude for the trip to the uplands with the spaceport. We doubted even Dusko had the resources to scan the planet seeking us, but did not want to hazard the Murch's location. We passed the long trip back to Vanceport in silence, lost in our own thoughts.

We reached Vanceport under cover of darkness and landed near Reiri's lodgings. The buildings were of a style I didn't recognize, but assumed was traditional to the Hanoians. I found an underground lot nearby and tucked Tekala's expensive aircar away in a corner and placed a tarp over it. It was thin disguise for an expensive ride but the best we could do.

I entered the Reiri's shop to find the wizened, older woman sitting behind her counter as usual. I'd rented accommodations from her periodically when

I was down on my luck. They weren't fancy but no one messed with the Tong, so it was safe, so long as I paid old woman Reiri promptly.

"Ah, Wrik, you back?"

"For a week or so."

"Cash in advance."

"Of course."

I paid the usual charge. "There are two women staying with me."

She gave a lecherous laugh. "You big boy, huh?"

I gave a look of false modesty.

"One room, your business how many sleep in it. No noise."

"No problem."

I bought fresh food from the closest vendor and returned to find Maauro and Jaelle in the shadows nearby. I beckoned to them after opening the door on the ground-floor room I'd rented. They came in quickly, Maauro carrying a huge pack full of our supplies. I closed the door behind them. "Honey, we're home."

The food was welcome as was the rest. When morning came, I woke to find Maauro on the room comp. Her fingers had split into filaments and she'd infiltrated the computer.

I yawned. "How goes it?"

"I am amassing the tactical information we need. Dusko has placed significant barriers around his operations, but these are no match for me. I could crush them in seconds; the trick is to breach them unobserved and undetected. This takes time."

But what Maauro meant by time wasn't what I expected. A few hours later she rose. "I have a plan."

Both Jaelle and I listened in rapt attention with alternating terror and hope.

"It's suicide," I said.

"It's the only chance we have," Maauro countered.

Night fell as we kitted up in dark clothing and readied our weapons. We'd left behind all but our most important possessions. We weren't coming back, one way or the other.

I watched Maauro's calm face as she loaded her new armspac, a refined version of the boxy weapon she'd taken on our first hunt for Jaelle. The Guild had been a source of better quality weapons for her adaptation.

It occurred to me that Maauro was doing this all for me, and I could not figure out why. She had options that biologicals did not. All she needed to do to escape the present situation was find a secure place and turn herself off for a hundred years. Her enemies would age and die in what would be an eye blink for her. Maauro could escape in time, where we could only escape in distance. So why was she doing this? I thought of her as my friend ,but she was a machine. Could I ever really understand any "emotions" she had? Were they real or simulated?

I looked over my shoulder. Jaelle was still in the other room.

"Maauro?"

"Yes?"

"Why do you care about me?"

"Wrik, is this the time to discuss issues of being and existence?"

I just looked at her.

She sighed, and even that made me wonder if that was just part of a program to allow her to interact with me, and if that made any difference. Maauro only breathed to make sounds.

"We were thrown together by chance, welded together by enemy action and need. I have come to value you as you. You are part of my network, the original part in this time, in this new existence. Though I was made and not born, I do feel. I do care, and I do remember you, foolish biological, running unprotected under fire to my aid on the asteroid. I thought you would have accepted this by now. After all, I believe you care for me."

I reached across and put my hand on her arm, her original one. It was warm and slightly pliable. She continued to work on textures obviously to make her more pleasant to touch. This too, I knew she did for me, as no one else had ever laid a hand on her.

"Yeah," I said, my throat tight. "Never doubt it."

She looked at me steadily, but with a hint of reproach in her huge eyes. "Then do not doubt me. I am not less than you that you should fail to have faith in me." She patted my hand with her left arm to take the sting from the words. Her other hand felt only like cold metal.

I nodded.

Jaelle opened the door and we moved apart in an almost guilty motion. I smiled ruefully. There was still something odd in the dynamic of the three of us. I hoped we'd all live long enough to work it out. Jaelle placed her bag on the bed next to ours.

"Time to go," Maauro said.

We exited the flophouse and piled into the old aircar that Jaelle had bought for us. The car was the sort of nondescript vehicle no one would look twice at in the seedier areas of the port. I let Maauro take the wheel. She'd spot any danger long before the rest of us.

We lofted over Vanceport. I looked down at the old city, with its mix of modern light and old gas and wood fires, the local spaceport section where I'd lived, the modern section with its shops and office towers and the Confederate legation. Then we were over the deep-space section of the spaceport where the shuttles and smaller interstellar vessels landed. A dozen needle-nosed ships of varying sizes sat fin down on the scarred concrete. A blocky vessel that looked like a flying safe meant that some Ribisan hydrogen breathers had landed.

Smaller aerospace craft like my poor, lost *Sinner* dotted the runaways at the outer edge of the port. We overflew long runaways limned in blue lights. A cargo flyer of some sort was rolling down one.

I could see the warehouse district: imports, exports and transshipments. Modern sodium lights threw yellow glows and even at this late hour there were people wandering the streets along with trucks and cargo carriers. Neon lights advertised bars and seedier establishments. We passed over immense warehouses heading for the one Dusko owned. The crimelord maintained a storefront in the better part of town and a villa on the mountain dominating the city, but he spent most of his time in his warehouse headquarters. Maybe he felt like a fake in the more civilized places. Maauro had tracked his movements and patterns for several weeks. He was down there.

Maauro circled the aircar down and entered the streets, driving in an indirect pattern until we reached the back of Dusko's huge metal and concrete building. We parked in a service station among some other vehicles left for repairs.

The three of us stared up at the massive building that looked like a cross between a spacecraft hanger and a fortress. A razor-wire fence surrounded the dark and looming building. Light covered most of the various doors. From the number of vehicles in the parking lot there wouldn't be many people inside.

"Interesting," Maauro said. "I detect a number of standard security devices—curious..."

A shape came around the corner; it seemed to both scuttle and roll over the ground.

"What's that?" Jaelle gasped.

"A Confederate Mark 42 combat robot, about fifty years old," Maauro replied. "Doubtless it is war surplus."

"Crap," I said, sweat beading on my forehead as I watched the machine, painted in urban splinter camouflage stalk across the parking lot.

Maauro looked at me with her infuriating small smile.

"What?" I demanded. "It may be obsolete by military standards, but it's still a goddamn tank. How can you fight that?"

"Fight that?" Maauro said. "I could and would win, but why? It and its companions are about to become my new army."

"What?" I said.

"Wait here," Maauro said. She raised her hair and pulled a lead from the back of her skull, then opened the door and slipped out. She seemed to vanish as she stood. I'd seen Maauro use her optical camouflage before but never to this degree. I could tell she was there but my eyes couldn't focus on her.

I heard the light patter of her feet as she accelerated into a run. The optical distortion that was Maauro raced across the street. Then she was in the air, sailing over the razor wire.

The crab robot froze, its pincer arms and weapons raised, but evidently it had the same difficulty locking on Maauro, as it did not fire. Suddenly it convulsed, as if trying to shake off something, then froze in mid-movement. The machine turned back toward the gate and rolled forward. The gate opened in response to some electronic command. Then the distortion atop it flickered out and Maauro sat astride her conquest, waving.

I started the car and quickly drove into the yard, parking in the darkest part of the lot. Maauro rode her new toy over as we pulled out weapons from the trunk. I could see that she'd opened a panel in the top of the machine and had her good right hand thrust into it, along with a lead she'd pulled from her head.

She looked down at us. "A robust, but simple machine, I'm glad that I did not have to fight it. Dusko has made our infiltration easier by relying on computerized systems. I have enslaved this unit, and through it infiltrated and assumed control of the others. Their defense barriers were quite pathetic. All his other passive alarms are disabled or deceived. We need only concern ourselves with four interior guards, a visitor and Dusko."

"Are you sure it's so few?" Jaelle asked.

"The regulars are identified in the fire-control computer of this machine. The guest wears an ID badge. "

Jaelle looked at me. "Is there anything she can't do?"

"Haven't found it yet," I replied.

Maauro dropped lightly from the top of the machine. "We must educate this foolish Dua-Denlenn on the unprofitability of opposing an M7 combat android. Follow me."

We walked up to a side door that slid open when Maauro raised her hand. Her effortless mastery of hundreds of thousands of credits worth of security gear made me wonder about bank heists and museum robberies for a wild second. She'd cracked the barriers of mega-computers as if they were virtual tissue paper.

As we entered, I placed a hand on Maauro's shoulder. "If possible," I whispered, "if possible, I want to avoid killing."

She gave me a searching gaze but to my surprise nodded. "I will not kill unless there is a need, but I will not fail to kill if I do need to."

"Fair enough."

"We walked down a hallway, Jaelle and I scuttling from one doorway to another. Maauro strode down the center of the hall as if she owned the place, which in a way, she did. We stepped through some double swinging doors into the warehouse proper. The space ahead was filled with crates and containers and shelving stacked stories high. I could see refrigerated rooms and other secured sections for the storage of more delicate cargo.

Lights in the distance betokened some activity. Maauro turned her head from side to side as if scanning. "Voice pattern indistinct," she murmured, "but a high probability it is Dusko."

We stalked forward, eventually coming in sight of a boxy construction. An a/c unit hummed atop it and light streamed out of the windows, but I could not see clearly. Maauro did not speak. Instead she signaled that she was going up on top of the stack near the office box. We settled in to wait.

CHAPTER

15

I SLOWLY CLIMB THE STACKS OF CONTAINERS, AS I CANNOT RISK THE material breaking under my weight. I am tracking many targets and functions. I have seized control of all security functions other than mechanical ones that I avoid, or the armed guards ahead. I am concerned, given the appearance of the crab robots, that they may now have military-grade weapons that could be lethal to me. Given time I could reverse the security systems and use them on our enemies, but we do not have that luxury now. My analysis is that most of the guards will be near Dusko.

On reaching the top I engage my optic camouflage and lower my chassis temperature so no thermal sensor can lock on me, then peer over.

I am above the office box that sits on the warehouse floor. The one-story unit is approximately sixty meters long and twenty wide. Its heating and cooling systems are designed to comfort the biologicals in the otherwise unregulated warehouse and this has fortunately concentrated my targets. I cannot view the interior but my magnetic resonance sensors penetrate the building and detect five biologicals in the structure.

One is unaccounted for. I extend my senses and am appalled to hear footsteps near where I left Wrik and Jaelle. I move as quickly as I dare, fearing a reoccurrence of the disaster when they stumbled on Lostra in the village. As I reach the area above where I left them I hear the sounds of a struggle. Fear, such as I have never felt before, floods me. I snap my palm blades out and leap off the stack, somersaulting to the ground below.

I am not needed. The unaccounted-for guard, a Dua-Denlenn female, is on the ground. Jaelle is wrapped around her, applying a sleeper hold. Wrik is sitting on the guard's legs holding her weapon and looking pleased with himself. The guard slumps in Jaelle's grip and she lays her down. I manufacture an anesthetic for the guard and jab my needle finger into her thigh. She will not awaken for a day at least.

"Dusko is ahead," I whisper. "Wait for me to attack then come in after, carefully."

Now I simply leap to the top of the stack racing back to the area over the office cube and launching myself in a compact ball at the roof below. As I hit, I shoot out all my limbs. I have correctly judged the strength of the roof and crash through to the room below. I initiate targeting the instant my head projects from the ceiling.

In .0043 seconds, I locate all enemy personnel in the room. Biological reaction is usually about .05 seconds, so I have leisure to identify the three guards of varying species carrying the heavy triple autos I feared. Dusko is beyond, seated at a desk; a small glass of liquid is slowly falling from his hand. His eyes are beginning to widen. Opposite him is an alien of a type that I have not seen before, blue-skinned and apish.

My head and shoulders are now through the ceiling and I begin to bring up my arm. There is no time for aesthetics or other niceties. A single, low-velocity, depleted uranium slug slams into each guard's skull as they try to bring up their weapons.

I am through the ceiling now and invert in the air while considering the other two. Dusko I must take alive. He is reaching for a weapon in his desk, but I still have plenty of time to deal with him. The other creature starts to rise. His face is blue, with fangs protruding onto his upper lip. He wears the uniform of a ship's officer.

I hit the ground, springing forward at the alien. I strike both arms and a leg. It gives a cry of pain, falls, three limbs smashed but otherwise preserved for interrogation. I pop onto the desk, almost face-to-face with Dusko, who has his hand in the desk drawer over a pistol. Remembering the effect that it had on Wrik, I raise a set of ripping teeth in my mouth and smile at him. Dusko freezes in place.

"We have not met face-to-face before, Dusko. I am Maauro." I reach into his drawer take out the pistol and casually crush it.

Wrik and Jaelle storm into the room. But resistance is ended as I planned. Wrik checks the dead Guilders and exchanges his weapon for one of the new Confed weapons. Jaelle follows suit and covers the moaning, blue-skinned alien.

Dusko slowly leans back in his seat, raising his hands. His eyes, blue from lid to lid, convey little, but sweat sheens his face in a manner similar to a human's. "Yes, Maauro, I know you. You have proven most formidable and most troublesome. My encounters with you have been unprofitable to the point of disaster. Clearly a reassessment of the situation is needed. How can I help you?"

"In many ways," I reply. "Your service to me will be most demanding and complete. Or I will simply amuse myself by seeing how slowly I can disassemble your body while keeping you alive. I understand your people practice torture as an art. Are you prepared to become a masterpiece for the Guild?"

"No," Dusko says with an easy frankness. "I am however, prepared to part with a great deal of wealth in exchange for my survival."

"It simply begins there," I say.

"Don't give into threats," the alien on the floor coughs in surprisingly unaccented Standard. "Where is your pride? You are Guild."

I look at Wrik. "What is that?"

"Morok," he replies, "from the other side of the Confederacy, good fighters, bad organizers, very loyal to clan and kin."

"Just so." The Morok glares up at me. "You will get nothing from me."

I analyze Wrik's generalization. It strikes me as sound, given the Morok's defiance in the face of death.

"In answer to my friend's point," Dusko continues, "I am more interested in my life than in Guild bravado."

"Do you wish me to pull a few digits off your hand so you may demonstrate resistance to your comrade, or will you tell me who he is?" I ask.

"He captains the Guild runner that is fin down at the port," Dusko offers up promptly. "The green and gold vessel is called the Faberge. Of course you know that, or you wouldn't have tested me with it."

It suited me to have Dusko believe in my omnipotence, so I did not correct him.

"Who does he work for and who sent him?"

"Dusko," the Morok warns.

Wrik kicks him, drawing an anguished cry and a sulphurous curse.

I fire a flechette past the Morok's nose; his eyes lock on mine.

"Remain silent. I have already categorized you as a useless intelligence source. Speak again and I will eliminate you." Red eyes glare, but the mouth remains shut.

I turn back to Dusko. "Answer."

"The vessel belongs to a Guild senior known as the Collector. I know no more, save that the Collector deals in antiquities and secrets. She would love you."

"I've heard of her," Jaelle says. "I think she's the one who was buying up most of what I'd found near the Tar Sea. She used different agents, but I traced the sales to the same banks."

"Is that who paid you to hunt the Murch, invade the Tar Sea and harass Wrik and me?"

"Yes," Dusko confirms. "Left to my own devices, I would have long since abandoned my conflict with you as unproductive."

"Lie," Wrik says. "Dua-Denlenns are notoriously vindictive."

Dusko nods. "True, but not when it is as dangerous as this. This was just business."

"We are leaving now and you are coming with us," I say.

"I'll be a burden slowing you down," he counters.

"Not if I slice off and cauterize your appendages," I reply. "That will make you easy to pack. Or you could walk."

Dusko promptly stands.

"Coward," the Morok spits.

Jaelle gestures with her weapon at the Morok. "What about this one?"

"Leave him alive," Wrik suggests, as he binds Dusko's hands behind him. "He can tell the Collector how readily Dusko gave her up and cooperated with us."

"Rest assured of it," the Morok growls.

I walk up and snap the Morok's other arm quickly and cleanly. I have not time or leisure to analyze him for an anesthetic. "You'll be found in the morning."

The Morok curses us as we leave. I am pleased I need not kill him, as he is a warrior worthy of respect. I disable any weapons we are leaving behind.

We quickly return to the entrance. Dusko looks in disgust at the security bots I have lined up awaiting us. They adopt a protective formation around our car. We climb in. Now Wrik drives alongside Jaelle, who hides our weapons in some cloth. I sit in the back with Dusko and undo his bonds.

"Bear in mind the prospect of your certain and painful demise as you answer my questions," I say. Wrik pulls out of the warehouse, the crab robots rolling behind us on their road wheels. "How many crew on the Faberge?"

"Four"

"Is the ship ready for immediate departure?"

"No."

I strike Dusko at a spot that causes agony in his species. It takes him a minute to recover.

"Reconsider your answer."

"Yes," he gasps. "The ship was due to lift off seven hours from now, provisioned for interstellar. I know nothing more."

"Can you order the crew off?"

Dusko considers. "They might think it unusual that the command did not come from their captain, but odds are they will obey me."

"Spaceport security gate ahead," Wrik calls.

"Get us through," I order Dusko.

He nods as we roll up to the gate. A disinterested-looking, human security guard looks in. "Evening. Isn't it a bit late for cargo?" He eyes the robots behind us. "What's so important to warrant all the security?"

"The Crown Jewels of the Star Empress Vadnais," Dusko snaps. "What matter the cargo? Your scanners picked up my ID."

"Yes sir, Mr. Dusko. No harm intended. I take it you'll vouch for these others?'

"Yes," he growls.

"Pass through," he says. Ahead of us barriers drop into the ground. Wrik wastes no time in moving forward. Then we are on a road to the spaceport proper, passing other roads leading to gantries and terminals. The traffic around us is mostly commercial trucks with the occasional minibus of tired travelers being shuttled about.

"What is the port call number for the Faberge?" I ask. Dusko rattles off a series of numbers.

Wrik hands me a com but I wave it off. "I will transmit the call internally on a time delay sufficient for me to prevent any message from you but what I wish. Order them to leave the ship to go anywhere but the warehouse and to leave the hatch open."

Dusko nods.

I open my mouth and out of it comes the buzz of a live com channel. Dusko seems to be having trouble facing me as a phone. I retract my serrated teeth, which appears to help.

"Faberge here, officer of the watch speaking."

"This is Dusko. Take the crew and leave the ship. Head over to the Spacewitch bar and amuse yourselves. Your master and I need the vessel for a meeting."

"Leave the ship unguarded and unattended?" the office says.

"Do not question me. We will be there in six minutes. You will be gone in five. Acknowledge."

"Acknowledged, we're going, but if there is any trouble over this with the skipper it's on your head."

"Agreed. Move."

I close my mouth and the circuit.

"Excellent. Wrik bring us to the ship. Take your time. Use the first route I programmed into the car." We dodge through a variety of gantries and towering vessels heading for the outskirts where the smaller vessels land. We find the somewhat chunky, green and gold hull of the Faberge where we expected it.

"That's luck," Wrik says. "It's an old Comet-class courier, fast and leggy if not overly generous with internal space."

"Hold here," I direct and Wrik pulls to the side. "I will scout the ship."

***

Maauro slipped out of the car, and I turned toward Dusko, pistol in hand. He waited until Maauro had vanished up the rampway to the *Faberge* before starting in.

"Wrik, this is madness."

"That's Trigardt to you."

"The machine is leading to your death. She may be able to survive and escape the Guild. You have no chance. Release me and your reward will be immense."

"Does he really believe we're that stupid?" Jaelle wondered.

"Jaelle, listen. My operatives will not take my disappearance lightly. There will be reprisals. Unfortunate circumstances may overtake your father—"

"One can only hope," Jaelle returned. "But I think you overestimate how much you'll be missed, especially after that Morok captain starts talking."

"Imagine how indebted I would be to you both for preventing that."

Maauro reappeared at the top of the ramp racing down to us. Dusko fell silent, despair on his face. We opened the doors and hauled him out.

"All clear," she announced, then looked at Dusko. "I assumed he used a variety of threats and inducements for you to let him escape."

"It was amusing," Jaelle returned.

We started up the ramp. To my surprise the crab robots followed. I looked at Maauro who shrugged. "They are not AI's, merely good expendable weapons. We may need them"

Ahead, a large cargo hatch gaped, and the machines followed us in. Maauro sealed the hatch behind us as the crab robots, doubtless following unheard orders from her, latched themselves down to the deck. One had to haul itself up the side of a wall, as the hold was small and partly full of crates and containers.

We charged up to the crew quarters. With escape so close, a sort of giddy hysteria seemed to take hold of us, even Maauro. We came to one small cabin, and she pitched Dusko in bodily, securing the door and adding a spot weld with her hand torch.

"Bridge," I yelled as we scrambled up ladders. As we climbed, I marveled at all that had been packed into the small courier. Her flight-deck featured seats tilted back for a reclining lift off. I preferred aircraft types like *Sinner* that simply flew into space, but this ship was far larger, even equipped for artificial gravity.

I gestured Jaelle to a jump seat against the back bulkhead, while Maauro busied herself with the computer.

"Excellent," Maauro said. "Dusko has not elected to play games with us. His passwords have released a wealth of information. There are papers and data for several different identities for this vessel. Once we lift off we can assume a new identity—"

"We'll be untraceable then, a couple of identity switches and the *Faberge* will be no more, we'll have disappeared." I said.

"In practical terms, yes."

"We will still be a human, a Nekoan and a Noneofyourgoddamnbusinessean traveling together," Jaelle added.

I looked at her. "We could always lose your ears, tail, and fangs."

"I'll lose them in your skinny human butt."

She turned to me. "What shall we name our new ship, Wrik?"

I thought briefly. "*S.S. Misadventure.*"

Jaelle groaned.

Maauro nodded. "Appropriate."

A light glowed green on the computer console.

"Lift clearance received," Maauro said.

I hopped up in the seat and hit the switches to get it to recline for take-off as Maauro did the same. Even with the urgency of escape in mind we had to go through the pre-flight checklist. The Guild had spared no expense to keep the vessel ready for immediate spacing and I cut every corner I dared.

Jaelle kept a watch on a maintenance panel near her seat. Every second I dreaded the sight of vehicles full of Guild racing toward us, but Dusko's orders seemed to be holding.

"Checklist, clear," Maauro said finally.

"Okay belt in," I snapped. "We're launching."

As belts clicked, I switched the impellers from standby to thrust. *Misadventure* started up slowly as the drive built power steadily. We cleared the mooring and were airborne, starting to pick up speed. Air left my lungs in a whoosh of relief.

The huge world fell away from us. I was glad we weren't riding an older chemical or atomic rocket that would have crushed us into our seats as we lifted. It gave me a last chance to look at Kandalor. Life there had not turned out as I'd hoped. No clean break with the past, no fresh start. I'd gone from disgraced refugee to hounded enemy of the Guild.

Yet something had been gained. I'd never be taken for any sort of hero, yet I had learned to stay cool under fire, to stand my ground with my comrades. No medals were owed me, but I was no longer the utterly lost coward.

I'd recovered two other things I thought lost with my self-respect over Retief. First was the warmth and affection of a woman. I couldn't call it love yet, or maybe ever. For all the similarities between us, Jaelle was not human. A part of me that I hated cringed from that, from the thought of being mocked by my family and former friends for settling for something less than human. That thought sparked anger, for in Jaelle I had found more concern and genuine tenderness than I'd experienced before. Far from thinking her inferior, I could only wonder what she saw in the box of broken bits that was me.

Next there was Maauro, the only being who knew my real name. She'd gone from being a nightmare horror on a dead asteroid to something between best friend and kid sister. I remembered the sick feeling that spread through me when I saw her burned, torn and senseless in *Sinner's* wreckage.

As if sensing my regard, Maauro turned toward me, gazing steadily with her huge aquamarine eyes. A small smile played across her lips, and then she turned back to the canopy, looking not at Kandalor fading away below, but at the stars that she loved, as if she were a little girl and the universe was her jewel box full of sparkling gems. Maauro the killer, Maauro the innocent, Maauro my first true friend in my new life as Wrik Trigardt.

I shook my head ruefully. The path my life had taken was so hard to believe and the future promised only more madness, but at least I was no longer alone.

CHAPTER

16

I WAITED UNTIL WE ACCELERATED TO FULL SPEED TO ENGAGE the autopilot and turn to the matter of Dusko. *Misadventure* was beyond catching now, but we had no particular destination in mind yet. I wanted some better idea of our prospects before I committed us to jump.

Maauro cut the weld she'd made, and I walked in without knocking. Dusko sat on the narrow bunk that folded out from the wall. The Dua-Denlenn's extra joints made him look as if his arms were already broken as he sprawled there. From the wetness on his shirtfront it seemed he'd managed to get some water out of the fresher in the corner. He looked up at me, his face expressionless.

I closed the door. "Doubtless if our positions were reversed, you would be planning some unpleasant time for me."

Dusko shrugged. "It's how we are."

"You'll be surprised how little good cultural relativism will do you as a defense."

"Dua-Denlenn don't beg for mercy, if that's what you want, Trigardt. We don't even have a word for that concept. We use yours."

"I'm not interested in your begging. As Maauro said, your only value to us is as an intel source. We want to know all you can tell us about the Collector, about who is hunting us."

"You may find me a tough nut to crack."

I opened the door. "I won't be your interrogator. Come in, Maauro."

To my surprise Dusko's face didn't change.

"No doubt she can inflict sufficient pain on me for you to think you are getting intelligence. I foolishly gave her a chance to demonstrate that when I lied to her about something she had ways of verifying, such as whether this ship was ready for launch when all she had to do was check the port database. I won't make that mistake again."

Maauro walked over to the wall. Despite his supposed insouciance, the alien stiffened. "You clearly have a proposal in mind," she said.

"Yes. You are smart enough to understand that I did not rise to my status in the Guild by being either a coward or a fool. My kind's ethical system, simple as it is, seems to elude other species. I am not loyal to the Guild, as it is not loyal to me. We simply use each other. You were quite clever to leave the Morok alive. He is doubtless poisoning the local Guild against me. Worse, he is making a report to the Collector's agents. You have made my return to the Guild quite impossible."

"Your point?" I prompted.

"I have nowhere else to go for the foreseeable future and may as well support your efforts with both my skills and information. In return, I will expect decent treatment, freedom of the ship when we are not on world. Accept me as one of your crew, and I will use my best efforts for you. As you know, I am a pilot—"

"You will not set foot in the control space," Maauro said.

"As you wish. You may find me useful in engineering. I served on a freighter before I became an importer. If you plan to stay free with this ship, you will find it useful to have my trade skills."

"We have Jaelle," Maauro said.

"She is a merchant, not a cargo-master or importer," Dusko said. "There is much she does not know. Especially if you seek to avoid Guild contacts, something I need to do now to preserve my life. "

"Very well, we agree," Maauro said.

"I will accept Trigardt and Tekala's word on my safety."

"Interesting. Why not mine?"

"Because I suspect you are too similar to a Dua-Denlenn. I have no idea if you even have a sense of honor."

"That's rich from you," I snapped.

Maauro held up a hand. "I am a warrior. I have my code."

"If you are what I suspect you are, you were made for a genocidal conflict. No quarter asked and none given. I am your enemy. I will not trust you."

"You place a curious lot of faith in me for a man who shot my ship from the sky," I growled.

"You and Jaelle are not the merciless killers you pretend to be, particularly you. Whatever scruples you have are all the protection I have."

I moved to the wall communicator. "Jaelle, Dusko wants your promise of good treatment and continued survival if he aids us."

It took her a minute to stop cursing. "Do we have to do this?"

"I think so."

"I agree then. Tell him if there is any treachery Maauro will pull his intestines out of his butt."

"Swear it on the honor of the Tekala Trading Family and your household gods," Dusko said.

There was more cursing in Nekoan. "I so swear," she concluded.

Dusko looked at me and I nodded tight-lipped.

"Very well, ask your questions."

"The Collector, give me everything."

"Not much is known, not even her name, at least at my level. She is High Guild and has been so for all the time I have been in the Guild. About five years ago she entered into a state of semi-retirement, devoting herself to her passion."

"Which is?" I prompted.

"Antiquities, mysteries and secrets."

"Unusual," I said. "I'd have thought there was more money in other things."

Dusko shrugged irritably. "Guilders have their passions like anyone else. The Collector has always pursued ancient technology and artifacts. She has sponsored robberies on inner world estates, primitive worlds, even government labs and museums. Rumor has it she's even financed expeditions into lonely parts of space where no one has gone before.

"When...." He paused and gestured at Maauro.

"You can use her name. She only has the one," I replied.

"When Maauro came on the scene, I was working for the Collector on the asteroid station project. I reported both the base we found and the attack on us, though at the time I thought Maauro was a Confed Humanform Robot. No offense."

"None taken," Maauro said with a hint of amusement.

"I reported the disaster on the ancient base and the fact that Confed military was taking over the find. So I began searching elsewhere and encountered Jaelle's artifacts that led me to the Tar Sea, where we discovered the body of one of the ancients evidently dragged up from the bottom of the Tar Sea."

"It was called an Infestor," Maauro interrupted.

"Well if we ever see the Murch elder again we can tell him who took his scarecrow," I added.

"What?" Dusko said.

"Irrelevant, continue," Maauro directed.

"Well you know how that resolved. But each encounter with you two led me to realize that Maauro was something more than a Confed machine. I passed the information on. This ship brought orders from the Collector to end my attempts to destroy you, Maauro. Instead, I was to capture, or otherwise induce you to join the Collector's treasure trove. And of course, you plunged through the roof during that discussion."

"It would seem this Collector is quite determined," Maauro said. "Do you believe she will pursue us off world?"

"Very likely. She has an obsessive interest in what we call the Old Empire."

"We called ourselves the Creators and the Infestors," Maauro replied.

Dusko digested this.

"I'll get you a printout of the cargo manifest," I said. Maybe you'll have some ideas about possible trade destinations to discuss with Jaelle."

Dusko straightened. "I already know the manifest. I even have a possible market in mind."

CHAPTER

17

"**WHY WOULD I WANT TO DEAL WITH A BRAND-NEW** freight company with no reputation?" Tenevan asked as she sat back in the overstuffed leather chair. The Denlenn's face was friendlier than her words, I thought. It was still a little difficult for me to wrap my mind around the fact that her kind were related to, yet so unlike Dusko's people. For one thing her eyes were not the arctic-blue from lid to lid like a Dua-Denlenn but held greenish-gold pupils and looked human.

Tenevan had met us at a coffee and brandy house in the capital, such as it was, of Frosteer, a small, mixed colony in the hollow between the long-settled sectors of the Confederacy and the new space of Kandalor and the Nekoan territories. We were only weeks away from Kandalor but hundreds of light years. The hyperspace pipeline between the two widely separated sectors wasn't called the Galactic Express for nothing.

I breathed the pleasant smell of scented wood from the crackling, stone fireplace and admired the rough-hewn beams and stonework of the Landing Hall, an old hunting lodge that had been converted as a city grew around it.

Jaelle, Dusko and I sat on the other side of a table made from one massive board of the nearly imperishable Frosteer trees. Those trees provided part of our cargo. We were negotiating with the Denlenn merchant for a cargo of amber-like sunstones.

Dusko picked up a glass of the same potent liquor that Tenevan was enjoying. "Why? For the best of all reasons, our price is half the rate you're being extorted by the Combine traders."

"There are relationships to consider," Tenevan replied, sipping her drink and staring up at a hunting trophy of a vencala on the wall. The savage predator's fur provided another part of our cargo.

"The Denlenn are known far and wide for their fair dealings and scrupulous sense of honor," Dusko said. "Would that the universe returned the favor. The Elban Combine seems less concerned with fairness now that they have a monopoly on cargo runs here."

"True," Tenevan mused, stretching out her long, white-leather clad legs with a sigh. "Alas that winters here are so hard. My old bones are feeling the cold."

"You don't look old at all," I said honestly. The Denlenn's hair was similar to Jaelle's, a rough mane of dark-brown, liberally shot through with silver, but her face was still smooth, thin-lipped and angular.

"Ah," Tenevan said with a tinkling laugh. "You must be the charmer. He's the negotiator and what about you?" She looked up at Jaelle, who'd adopted a similar relaxed pose.

"I'm the brains of the outfit," Jaelle said.

Tenevan laughed again, but there was a calculating look in her eyes as she turned back to Dusko. "Some competition might be a good thing. Mine is a high value cargo. Using you would double my profits on this run. Very well, we are agreed on price. I see you have an insurance bond." She gestured toward the glow of a holo from the comp built into the wooden table. "Let's execute the forms. You'll be paid under the usual terms—part now, part on return of the delivery bond from Moroosh Port."

There was a brisk flurry of signing, with Dusko using an assumed name as *Stardust's* cargo master. Jaelle had insisted on changing the name from *Misadventure* or she guaranteed we'd see no cargo.

"You may have considerable trouble getting stevedores and cargo handlers," Tenevan noted. "They are in on this arrangement with the Elban Combine."

"We use high-end mechanicals for bulk loading and handling," Dusko replied. "No need to be concerned."

Tenevan finished her liquor and rose, touching hands with each of us. I found myself liking the older Denlenn female with her easy, confident manner.

"Fair trading and safe voyaging to you all," she said in parting.

We sat back in our own chairs in relief. Tenevan's cargo was the last and most valuable part of our current load. I blew out a breath. "God, I thought that would never get done."

"One must always exhibit patience in trade. Given another day or two, I'd have pulled her down another five-percent," Dusko said.

"Sometimes, it's best to know when you've won. I don't want to spend more time in any one place than we have to." Jaelle said, as she paid the tab. She'd laundered all her funds into a new identity for herself. Since most of what we had was hers, she'd also become the ship's purser.

Dusko gave a dry laugh. "Curious logic from a group of people who've made such a specialty of pressing their luck, but yes, Guild attention would be most unwelcome. Yet another reason to avoid the stevedores union."

I grunted, not believing Dusko's conversion to our team despite his evident enthusiasm. He still had a card to play, selling all of us to the Collector in return for his readmission to the Guild. Maybe he thought we were too dumb to see it.

We picked up our travel cloaks, the generic clothing accepted in most cultures as the sign of the traveler. We'd need them. As we walked out through the heat curtain of the lodge, a biting cold awaited us. It was near sunset and Frosteer's weary orange sun was westering. It lit the underside of dark blue and gray clouds rolling off the heavily-forested mountains to the north of us.

Jaelle looked up and sniffed. "Snow is in the air."

Dusko, who loathed the cold, gave her a sour look. "Not the hardest of forecasts. It snows all the time on this miserable world. If it wasn't for its wealth of natural resources, I can't imagine why anyone would land here."

She nodded. "The best natural furs in the galaxy, imperishable quick-growing hardwoods, and gems found nowhere else. Worth a little hardship."

I zipped my too-thin ship-jacket under the cloak and turned its heating element up. "I'm wishing we'd pulled a few of those furs out of the cargo containers."

"Hah," Jaelle said, "with what they cost? You'll make do with synthetics and like it."

"Easy for you to say," I replied. "You have fur in spots."

We started up the street. Sodium lamps were flickering on as the locals scurried through the streets. This city rolled up early. Underground passages and skyways linked some of the newer buildings. The section near the port was less protected, being of older construction and with buildings set closer together, a common setup for a landing site colony.

Colonists bundled in the wonderful local furs and inured to the cold, marched around us with only the occasional curious look. Heavy snowflakes began to fall, muffling the sounds of the city around us. The wind began to whip us.

"Never a taxi around when you want one," I said, my breath fogging the air.

"Stauver will be warmer," Jaelle said. "We'll pick up machined goods there at a good price, lots of factories."

Dusko glared at the sky. "That alley cuts through the warehouse district, we can reach the covered walkways to the spaceport quicker."

We cut into a narrow street between towering, dark-stone and wood buildings dodging a cargo carrier that trundled out of the alley. Lights on the main street were supplemented by a few wan doorway lamps.

Running footsteps sounded behind us. A crew of muffled and cloaked figures ran in and filled the alley. The three of us set our backs to the wall of one building.

"What gives?" I demanded. "Who the hell are you people?"

One figure threw back its hood to reveal a dark-skinned, human face under goggles. "I'll keep it short," he rumbled. "We represent certain interests in the cargo field here that don't appreciate your undercutting our prices. We got a good thing going here. So you're going to lift off tomorrow morning, empty."

"Why don't we give them a little taste of what's in store for them if they don't," said the man next to him. He slipped an ornate club from under his cloak. I could barely see his face in the hood, but the smile on it said he was enjoying himself.

Suddenly a travel-cloaked figure dropped from the sky, landing between us and the menacing, half-circle in a crouch. The figure stood, slender arms in dark-blue extended from the cloak and threw back the hood. Maauro looked up at the dark man with her big, gentle eyes and delicate features.

"Retreat," she said, "while I am inclined to let you go."

Goggles looked at her in disbelief. The roof overhead was at least three stories high. But Clubman was neither patient nor smart. He wound up a swing.

Maauro snatched the stick away and struck him so fast it sounded like she was drumming. The others surged forward, but Maauro crashed into them, smashing men to the ground or flinging them into walls. Goggles took the time to pull a weapon. I shouted a warning to Maauro as he leveled the weapon, which emitted a harsh buzz, a stunner. We were behind Maauro and out of direct line, but the beam made me a little woozy. I sagged against a wall.

Maauro turned back to Goggles. "What an interesting sensation," she said, then beaned him with the club she'd taken from his friend. As he fell, she lunged and snatched the stunner from his hand, studying it like a new toy.

"Nice to be able to enjoy this scene this time," Dusko said with smug satisfaction.

"I'm guessing non-violent weaponry wasn't in her training," Jaelle said, looking at the pile of bodies.

"No," Maauro answered. "We did not take Infestor prisoners for other than interrogation, after which they were killed. Do not worry. I merely broke bones and hit pressure points. No fatalities."

She turned the stunner over in her hands. "Wrik, what is this?"

I was still shaking off the effects. "Sonic stunner, they developed them a few decades ago."

"An odd weapon, it subdues without damage."

"You wouldn't say that if you could feel the headache they generate."

"Your military uses these?"

"It's more of a police weapon."

"I'm surprised your Creators didn't have that technology," Jaelle said. "What if you had to take a Creator prisoner?"

Maauro looked at her with surprise and a tinge of dismay. "I was Creator Military. They would never use me on civilians."

"Then they are the only species I've ever heard of that wouldn't," Jaelle replied.

"Can we go?" Dusko said. "It's not getting warmer."

"We have to get these assholes in somewhere first," I said.

"Why?" Maauro and Dusko said at the same moment. They looked at each other.

"They'll freeze to death out here. We don't need trouble with the authorities. Maauro, bypass security and open one of these buildings."

The android cyberhacked a nearby warehouse and dragged the crew of thugs in. Some moaned, but none stirred. Maauro secured her new treasure inside her travel robe. "Now back to the ship," she said, looking at the swirling snow with evident delight

"Yes," I replied. "So I can take a bath in hot coffee."

Jaelle smiled. "Room for two?"

"You bet."

"Then we lift off in the morning?" Dusko asked, his teeth chattering.

I nodded. "On to Stauver."

CHAPTER

18

WE LAND ON STAUVER IN THE EARLY MORNING. I STUDY THE WORLD as Wrik takes us down. This is an older colony and far more established than even Kandalor. I detect many cities and towns as we fin down near the capital. The city has nearly one million inhabitants, primarily humans.

We are greeted at the port by officials who inspect our fictitious documents. I watch them on the monitors, unwilling to chance a meeting. They depart, satisfied with our legitimacy.

I join Wrik on the cargo deck. In the distance, I see a series of vehicles approaching.

"Transporters," Wrik says. "Here for the cargo."

I activate the crab robots and have them unload the larger freight.

The lead cargo hauler parks next to us. A pleasant-looking, older human female leads a group of strong-appearing men and a few women.

"No need to break out your lifters," Wrik says to her. "We've got some general purpose models."

The woman stares at them. "GPs my butt. Those are combat models. I used to be a tanker with the ASATs."

"Yeah," Wrik says, covering smoothly. "They're demobbed. Picked 'em up in lieu of cash when a customer went bankrupt. They're kind of overkill, but what are you going to do?"

The woman laughs. "Overkill is what they're best at. Wouldn't trust them to move cargo myself, but you seem to have them all but waltzing."

"I have worked very hard on their programming," I say, stepping out of the shadows and into view.

The woman does a double-take.

"One of our crew," Wrik says quickly. "Aurelia is from a lost colony."

"Hi, Aurelia," the woman says. "My, but you have some big eyes. Bet that gets all the boys' attention."

"A useful mutation," I respond.

"Aurelia is very good with machines," Wrik says.

The woman looks over her shoulder to where the crabs have already loaded all the bulky cargo. I could use them to get everything else, but I am concerned the level of improvement I have made in these units will attract too much more attention. I could actually have done all this myself in less time but only at the expense of my cover.

"We have more delicate cargo in here," I say.

"Well, folks," the woman calls to her crew, "looks like there's some work for you to do after all."

The noisy mob of humans follows me into the ship and removes the smaller and breakable objects. The woman carefully checks everything against a manifest. The sunstone packages are opened and checked visually.

"OK, Captain," she says to Wrik. "Countersign and we're done. Your payment will transfer to the port's escrow account and the balance after port fees is available for your immediate use."

With our cargo now delivered, we are handsomely paid off. I join the others in the galley, which has become our usual meeting place.

Jaelle is reviewing our port account. She is singing softly, an indication that she is well pleased.

"What now?" Wrik asks her.

Dusko, our unofficial steward, has brought us four cups of steaming hot chocolate. Wrik nods at him, a rare civility. It seems that old animosity dies hard among biologicals. It is different for me. That which I am programmed to kill, I kill. That which does not activate that programming is safe. I thank Dusko for the chocolate.

"We need a new cargo and a new destination," Jaelle muses. "Stauver is well known for its small mechanicals and tools. There are frontier worlds along the Theta Hyperdrive Current out of here. We could reach them in easy sidereal time about three months out of the galactic time stream. Could be quite a profit in such a venture. No other ship has a flight plan for Theta and the last one that went that way carried rare atomic ores for a fusion plant in a new colony."

"Shall we go into town?" Wrik says, excitement in his face. "Find some trade goods?"

"Yes. All of us," Jaelle says.

I am unsure if this last is just a precaution to keep an eye on Dusko or pleasantry on her part. Jaelle seems more disposed than Wrik to allow the past to vanish into the past. While Wrik nominally serves as captain, I note that he follows Jaelle's lead in most things beyond the flying of the ship itself.

"I'll get my coat," Dusko says. Expressions are difficult for me to interpret, but he seems pleased to be included in the expedition.

We seal the ship and I leave the crab robots on guard. While their weapons are hidden aboard to preserve the fiction that they are demobilized military, their pincers and sheer weight should deter any hostility. Wrik notes my preparations and nods approvingly. "Stauver's a law-abiding place, but the Guild is everywhere."

"Just so," Jaelle seconds.

We rent a transport and head into the commercial district, past blocks of sturdy apartments and some older homes from the earlier days of the settlement. Overhead, standard aircraft are soaring to their destinations overseas or further into the continent. I see graceful suspension bridges arching over rivers and large commercial vessels. It occurs to me that the speed of sea transport has changed little over the centuries. We may bring cargo at hyperlight speeds, but the cheapest and most efficient way to move them onworld involves an immense hull displacing water and driving forward at the speed of a running human.

We park in a lot and don our light traveler's cloaks. There seem to be no taboos of clothing or dress among the scurrying Stauvers, but the travel cloaks protect against inadvertent offense. Ours are gossamer light as the climate is moderate; we have landed in spring and have no need of additional warmth. We sit in a courtyard under a slatted, wooden cover, admiring the view of the river beyond. A variety of wide-leafed trees toss slowly in the breeze that cools us.

A young male attendant serves us. Work that on an inner world might be done by machine is done by the young as labor is cheap. He seems to take a great interest in me while we order our food. I order something inexpensive, merely to share the experience. Wrik's voice acquires something of a warning growl when he orders and the youth hurries off. Jaelle seems to find this encounter somewhat amusing.

"Protecting your little sister?" she teases

"Just making sure that Maauro...pardon, Aurelia...doesn't attract too much attention."

"I seem to be passing without too much incident," I mention. "I do need to be able to pass as a human among humans."

Wrik's expression is clearly dubious.

"Well, Dusko," he says unexpectedly. "What do you say? You're a keen observer"

"Keen or not," he replies, "I am not a human and to be frank you all look rather alike to me, save in skin tone."

"Jaelle?" he asks.

"Hard to say. Her eye size is dramatically bigger than yours, Wrik, or even mine. Still, to me she appears human, though I have spent little time with your kind before this."

"I have considered trying to alter my basic matrix to more closely approximate a human," I say, "but the last time I went through matrix reconstruction I malfunctioned soon after. This was a new ability built into the late models of the M-7 series and I was one of the first to be so equipped. I never had occasion to use it before the asteroid."

Wrik studies me. "Any idea why it might have caused that?"

"Yes, but it borders on the metaphysical."

Wrik's eyebrows shoot up.

"My shape is dictated by programs, as my body is very malleable. Simply put, I look the way I do because from moment to moment, I think that I look this way. Drastic changes may interfere with my sense of myself and make it difficult for me to remain stable. In a very real sense if I lose my image of myself, I could lose bodily coherence and be unable to retain any shape."

"Oh," he said.

"As I said, I must eventually learn to move among humans. Stauver seems like a safe location for me to explore this," I say.

Wrik seems unconvinced, but forbears to argue further.

We enjoy our meal then head into the shops beyond. Jaelle is constantly checking a portacomp, looking at suppliers' virtual displays.

Suddenly she straightens. "This looks promising."

We are before a large, factory-style building. It has a showroom and guided by Jaelle's comp we go over. In the show window sits a variety of cunningly-wrought tools: folding shovels, extensible drills and power units.

"That," Dusko points at a case full of small power tools, "would sell."

Jaelle waves her comp at it and an advert pops into the air. "Machine shop in a suitcase," a voice says seductively. "Are you the do-it-yourself type? Or far from help? Machine shop in a suitcase covers almost every repair and at an amazingly low factory-direct price." The advert reels off additional details and specs. Dusko and Jaelle exchange nods and head for the entrance, trailed by Wrik and me.

Inside, an older, heavyset man wearing a large, orange apron smiles and greets us. "Welcome to Kruger Machine Works."

Jaelle and Dusko give their assumed names and identify us as from the Stardust. They are quickly involved in discussing the details and merits of a variety of tools and mechanical goods. I lose interest.

"Wrik," I say. "I will leave you to these arrangements. I wish to explore the city at greater length."

The older man laughs. "Guess that trade talk gets boring for the young. Now mind you be careful if you're going near the offport. It can be kind of rough down there."

"I am very capable in matters of self-defense."

"No denying that," Dusko says.

Wrik looks a little surprised, even hesitant. "I don't know if you should go off without me."

"Gotta cut the apron strings sometime," the older man says, apparently free with advice on all topics. "I didn't mean to suggest Stauver City is dangerous. We have almost no violent crime here. She'll be safe enough."

"Yes," Jaelle says, a smile playing on her lips. "Just be back before dark, young lady."

Wrik too smiles, seeming to get into the spirit of the interaction. "And no boys either!"

I review my list of responses and settle on one that seems appropriate for the teenage female I appear to be. I roll my eyes. Laughter follows me as I walk out of the shop.

I continue down the broad avenue, hopping a slidewalk back to the riverfront that intrigued me earlier. I wander among the humans and others of Stauver, studying faces and customs. It occurs to me that this is the first time I have traveled among biologicals without Wrik or Jaelle accompanying me. Have I become timid?

I stop to buy an ice cream and to watch the ships in the river. I do not need the calories, though they will be converted to energy, but it is also part of my development to learn more pleasurable sensations as I become more sophisticated. As I'd pointed out to Wrik, while I have existed 50,115 standard galactic years, only seven of those had been active before my enforced stay on the asteroid. I have learned more in the year since Wrik found me than in those eight before, when I was little more than a weapon.

A pair of males come over as I watch an ocean-going skimmer setting out to sea.

"Hi," says the taller, slender male. His blond hair is pulled into a long ponytail that sweeps his back.

I nod.

"Are you an offworlder?" asks the other, a stocky teen who has a pile of dark hair that hangs down to his eyes.

"I am."

"That's why she's wearing a travel cloak, numbskull," the tall one says. "I'm Toldas. Short and wide here is Bralt."

"Who you calling short, Beanpole?"

I am confused. Their comments to and about each other are antagonistic, but does not match their energy levels or actions. It seems they are networked.

"My name is Aurelia Toyama," I reply as something seems called for.

"Where are you from?"

I try out my story of being a mutant from a lost colony. The boys seem impressed and it further piques their interest in me.

"I was born in Stauver City," Toldas says. "Bralt here is from the Interior."

"Ya don't have to say that like I should have herbivore shit on my shoes," Bralt protests.

"Oh?" Toldas says. "Did you clean your shoes special today?"

"I'm gonna put one up your butt in a minute."

"Your noisy contentions are spoiling my consideration of the river and the vistas around," I say. "Perhaps you could continue your debate elsewhere."

Both look as if I had struck them. I analyze my statement, find it empty of offensive language and am puzzled by their reaction.

"Hey we didn't mean—"

"Goodbye," I add to soften and clarify my instructions.

It has the opposite effect. The tall boy's face becomes red with anger. The other one seems more hurt than angry. They walk off. I can tell by their stiffness and energy levels that something is still wrong. I continue to track them.

When they are out of normal earshot, the tall one turns to his companion. "Big-eyed freak," he mutters in a voice that would not be intelligible to human ears. "She thinks she's too good to talk to us dirt-walkers. I was just trying to be friendly."

His friend made a hissing sound and waved his hand at him. "Keep it down, Toldas. If I've told you once, I've told you a dozen times, you overdo it with girls and come on too strong. Guess she didn't like us cutting up. Still, she might have been a little nicer about it."

"Yeah, you're right. Guess that's why you have Zala and why I'm going to spend the rest of my life alone."

"Oh come on, it's not that bad," Bralt says.

Evidently his interest in me was a premating ritual. He has taken my reaction for rejection and indifference. I trot over and overtake the boys, who turn to face me in evident alarm.

"I am sorry," I say. "I did not mean to be rude. I am from a very isolated place and I have little experience with people."

Toldas' face turns a darker shade of red. "You...umm...you heard me."

I point to my ears. "Another aspect of mutation."

Bralt looks at him. "I told you, big-mouth."

Toldas hangs his head. "I'm sorry. That was stupid of me and damn rude. I wouldn't blame you if you hauled off and belted me. I have it coming"

The thought is horrific and I banish it instantly. "I do not attack anyone unless for dire need and never for an insult. I will forgive your insult if you forgive mine."

"Done," Toldas says. "Though I still feel I owe you for what I said."

"Then perhaps you will consent to show me some interesting aspects of your homeworld," I say.

"Sure," Toldas responds brightly.

"We're going to meet my girlfriend, Zala," Bralt says, "then head into Tralsa."

"Tralsa?"

"It's the fun part of town," Toldas says. "There's a street festival there all this week, in honor of the first landing."

"Excellent," I reply.

We walk on with the boys shooting a barrage of questions at me about my ship and the worlds I have passed through. The boys' earlier feelings of anger and rejection seem to vanish. They resume their combative banter with each other, which appears to be aimed at securing my attention, though this stops suddenly when we encounter another female.

"Hi, Zala," Bralt calls.

A girl turns from her contemplation of a shop window. She has blue hair piled and teased in an elaborate style. Otherwise she is dressed in a minimum of black fabric with gold metal winking out of it. She is slender and athletic. She walks over on shoes that are canted to pitch her weight on the front part of her foot. It cannot be comfortable, but she does not seem to be in pain and moves quickly. Her eyes are a deep-green color and a sprinkling of freckles dusts her nose.

"Hey, Honey," she says in a high but pleasing voice. She and Bralt kiss on the mouth. Toldas looks on, grinning.

Bralt turns to me. "Zala, this is Aurelia off the freighter Stardust. We met her wandering around the promenade.

"We promised we'd show her some of the sights," Toldas adds.

"Such as they are," Zala says. She extends a hand, which I carefully shake. Even so she winces. "Quite a grip you have there."

"I am sorry. Are you ok?"

"Sure, no worries. But I get impression that you're stronger than you look." She seems to study me, "Maybe way stronger."

"She's a mutant," Toldas says.

Zala shoots him a glare. "Enjoying the taste of shoe leather today?"

Toldas flushes.

"I am not insulted," I reply, while I wonder about shoe leather. Even being a quantum computer, I find myself tasked trying to analyze the barrage of idioms and slang coming at me. "That is what I am." I recount my story but somehow feel that Zala is unconvinced.

I spend hours with the teens, who are easy company, full of stories and jokes, many of which I do not understand. I tell carefully edited versions of my own past. These are still remarkable enough to get me expressions of awe.

As evening falls, I do run into a dilemma. I normally would call the ship internally but cannot in their company. Zala loans me a portacomp and I call Wrik.

His face pops on the screen, the usual look of worry on it.

"Aurelia, are you OK?"

"I am fine. I have made some new acquaintances here in town and am going to go see the landing festival celebration. I did not want you to be concerned."

He looks at the table through the comp and a grin splits his face. "So much for no boys and be home after dark. I guess there is more of "typical teenager" in you than I suspected!"

"Shall I roll my eyes at you again?" I inquire. I have learned to tease Wrik.

He laughs again and I find that I am pleased to have made him do so.

"No, I think I feel enough like a parent already. Have fun and stay out of trouble."

I hand the comp back to Zala.

"Who is the old guy?" Toldas asks.

Old? I wonder. Wrik is only twenty-five not counting two years in cold sleep on the voyage to Kandalor. "Mazza," I say, giving Wrik's cover name, "is my guardian. He has been very kind and supportive of me."

Toldas still looks suspicious, Zala amused and Bralt seems chiefly concerned with his food.

"Shall we go to the festival?" I ask.

I spend the next week with Zala, Toldas and Bralt, only returning to the ship at night. For them it is a diverting time, showing a stranger around their colony. For me it is constant operation at my highest levels as I am continually tasked with maintaining my cover as a mutated human from a distant colony. I have never before tried to pass as human among humans. Wrik has been my only human network before and he knew me when I was in M-7 mode. I find the workload taxing nearly to the point of shutdown. The physical matters of maintaining a 98.6 degree body temperature are simple, but I face a host of other traps laid almost literally at my feet. I must avoid stepping on any surface that will reveal my far greater weight. I must lock my legs when I sit on a light chair so I do not damage it.

Once Toldas tried to "help me up," a biological courtesy that seemed to have more to do with providing an excuse to touch rather than any disability on my part. It required an instant rebalancing and shifting to make it appear as if I am no heavier than a human girl. Fortunately, he never tried to pick me up as Bralt occasionally did with Zala in a "pony ride."

Zala proves to be the most difficult to fool. There are many more female interaction protocols than there are for males and they are more complicated.

The third night, the boys take us to a Tri D entertainment. The film is an unlikely combat scenario with an improbably powerful biological male who, in between implausible combats, mates with a variety of females of different types and species. Zala finds the vid even less interesting than I do, grumbling afterward until placated with something called an "ice-cream soda" in a nearby shop overlooking the city. I also enjoy the complexity of the molecular combinations in the drink.

After a second round of the sodas, Zala rises. "Hey, Aurelia. I'm going to head to the bathroom." She looks at me expectantly.

I search among my various human interaction databases and come up dry.

Bralt laughs. "What is it about females that they always need to go to the bathroom in pairs?"

I rise to follow Zala, hoping other clues will present themselves.

"I can't believe the boys' chose that dumb film to take us to. Honestly, what is it with boys and blasters? It seems they're never happy unless something is exploding near them".

I think of the dangers Wrik and I have faced at such cost and agree that the boys' fascination is best conducted from the safety of a theatre seat.

We enter a large room of porcelain fixtures and mirrors. A number of other females are present, checking their appearances in the mirror and chatting animatedly. I stand before the mirrors considering my appearance. I still wear the traveler's cloak over my usual jumpsuit though I have changed the colors to dark blue and orange. I've continued to work on the covering till it looks and feels more like a sleek fabric. Yet it is nothing like the variety of outfits worn by the girls around me. It occurs to me that the others might find it weird that I wear the same thing each time they see me.

I notice that Zala has stopped and is watching me. I return her gaze. "Wow, you really didn't have to go, did you? You must have kidneys of steel. Two ice-cream sodas and I'm ready to burst."

"Are you?" I say in some alarm.

She laughs and ducks into one of the small cubicles. I access a database and figure out what she is doing with some distaste. I myself emit only radiation. I occupy myself washing my epidermis before the mirror so I do not stand out.

Zala returns, looking much relieved. "That's better." She takes her place beside me and begins adjusting her appearance with a variety of cosmetics. I watch the process with fascination. She then produces a small blue bottle which she tips onto her finger and dabs behind her ear. She notices my curiosity. "Did you want to try some Astral?

I regard her uncertainly. "I'm not sure."

"Take a sniff," she says holding the bottle to my nose.

I am grateful that Wrik persuaded me to add nostrils to my appearance. I even use them for gas sampling. The bottle emits a variety of very complex chemicals that I record as being pleasing to humans.

"It's very nice," I venture.

Zala puts a little more on her fingers and dabs it behind my ears. "Toldas is very fond of this scent. He always comments on it when I wear it."

I nod, unsure of any response.

"He likes you, you know."

"I like him."

"Ah, but do you like him?"

CHAPTER 18

I note the stress in her repetition, but the significance is unclear. "I'm sorry. Remember I am from far away—"

"Oh, come on now," she teases. "How different can it be between boys and girls wherever you're from?"

"You have no idea."

"Do you already have a boyfriend? That older guy, Mazza, that you talk about?"

"Mazza is very important to me. He is a permanent part of my existence. But our relationship is not sexual. He is involved with a Nekoan female for such."

"Wow, a catgirl? Kinda kinky if you ask me. Anyway, I'm glad about that. I wouldn't have liked you if you were leading Toldas on."

"I fear that in a way I may be."

"What do you mean?"

"I will not be here long. Nor do I know if I will ever return. I should not encourage his interest in me. It wastes his time and may cause him distress."

Zala gives me a serious look. "He knows that, and in a way it may make you even more interesting."

"Good," I reply, "then it will not be so hard for him to see me go."

"Shall we get back to the boys?"

"Yes," I say, very conscious of the brevity of time I have to act as a youth among humans.

The days and nights pass in this fashion, with me frequently absent from the ship. I think Wrik and Jaelle enjoy being by themselves. As for Dusko, he busies himself with helping Jaelle assemble a cargo and a route. I am not there to watch him, but he has learned the cost of my enmity. That and Wrik's watchfulness seem enough to deter him from any Guild mischief. I suspect that he is right in believing himself to be nearly as vulnerable to the Guild as we are. He uses the money that he has earned from Jaelle to supply himself with a number of luxuries for the voyage ahead. I track this but do not interfere, as it means he has less for bribes or to contact the Guild.

As I get ready to leave the ship, Wrik spots me.

"Out on the town again?" he says.

"Yes."

"Typical spacehand, gets planetside and blows her money on fast-living." He sighs theatrically.

"If I am acting in the expected manner, this will facilitate our cover."

"Wow, rationalization. You're getting more like a human every day."

"Respect your elders," I say in mock severity. "I was sitting on an asteroid when your ancestors were drawing paintings in caves. I think I have earned some indulgences."

"True," he concedes. "But keep an eye on that tall kid. I think he's going to put the moves on you soon."

"The moves?"

"Hmmnnn, we've never had the "birds and bees" discussion have we?"

"You are descending into incomprehensibility."

"Ah, you know the sort of things that go on between Jaelle and me."

"Wrik, if you mean sex, say sex. Appearance aside, I am a 50,000-year-old, genderless, combat-android. You will not embarrass me."

He looks over and then gently strokes my hair. "I don't see you that way."

By which I think he means, "I don't want you to be that way." Humans anthropomorphize so much and I know he does this with me. "I think that if Toldas get overly amorous I will be able to handle him, without fatalities or blowing our cover."

"Good, just threaten him with your "big brother" if need be. It's a traditional method." He winks at me.

I look at Wrik, then stand on my toes and press my lips against his cheek. "I will."

He looks at me, stunned. I wave and head out the hatch. When I look back, he is standing there lost in thought, one hand pressed against the cheek I have kissed.

Two more days pass and while Wrik proves prescient about Toldas' intentions, the taller boy is good-humored about my putting him off. I tell him I am from a very conservative culture where more than holding hands is considered a sign of engagement. This data appears to cool his interest some.

I have become accustomed to the three and they take it hard when I tell them that our ship must leave the following morning. We are not even able to stay out late. The often-mentioned but not encountered parents of the three have asserted their authority and they must be home before dark. They do promise to meet me at the spacefield before departure, though I try to persuade them that it is not necessary.

I return to the ship early but do not go in. I am assimilating the vast amounts of data I have assembled in the days of living as a young biological. There are so many things here that, while they are recorded perfectly, I know I am missing the context or full import of them. This time will remain a treasured memory. Days have been a form of busy idleness. We were always going somewhere, yet the destination was often irrelevant. It seemed that the journey in each other's company was the important part.

I am still there seated in the same position when Wrik comes out and begins his preflight. The ship was refueled and loaded in my absence. Jaelle will be on the comp handling the details of the flight plan and our departure with the authorities, who were more concerned with our coming than our going.

At the far end of the field another and far larger ship begins to rumble skyward as the sun rises over the ocean. I see it perfectly and Wrik stops to watch it as well. It is an old, converted warship, perhaps now serving as a freighter, its military colors replaced by brighter commercial ones. It slants up into the sky and vanishes into the clouds, as we will shortly.

As I look away from the disappearing ship, I spot three familiar figures standing behind the wire fencing, well away from the ship, looking on as we ready for launch. A crab robot clanks up the ramp behind me, relieved of its guard duty.

I look at Wrik. "What should I do?"

He grimaces as he usually does when I ask him a question about human relations. "Go to them. They want to see you off."

"Why do they not come here?"

"Because they're teenagers and adults spend most of their time yelling at them to get out of here or stay away from that. Go on, Maauro. I can finish here."

I walk over the hard surface of the spaceport, past the blackened areas where hundreds of other ships have preceded us into space. I open the gate with my ship-pass to greet my three new...friends? Network partners? What are they to me, or I to them? They have made me part of their network for no advantage beyond my company. Now even this fragile link is to be severed. Yet I find myself hoping that someday I will see these young faces again.

Smiles greet me. " Hello, Toldas, Bralt, Zala."

"Hi, Aurelia. Wow, what a neat-looking ship," Toldas says. "I wish I was going with you. Free in the galaxy, nobody to tell me what to do."

I smile. "Yes, there is a great freedom, something I treasure, but there are dangers, too. Do not undervalue what you have here: your homes, your friends, even this place and time belong to you and you to it. This is something I lack and I am beginning to understand the measure of that lack."

"There she goes again," Bralt says with a grin, brushing his tousled hair out of his eyes, "getting all serious and philosophical."

"Well," Zala adds, "what we really wanted to say was how much we enjoyed having you here and that we hope to see you again." Impulsively, the slender blond girl steps forward and throws her arms around me.

I have only an instant to cancel my programmed reflexes to ward off contact and perhaps some tremor of backward motion manifests itself.

Zala laughed. "Oh don't worry, Aurelia. We'll keep your secret. We've known for a while that you aren't a human."

Shock, dismay, intelligence failure. I have been discovered and was not even aware of it. I instantly discard security consideration of eliminating the three as impractical and undesirable on many levels.

"When?" I ask as Zala releases me.

"Ah, pretty much right off," Toldas says, scratching his head.

"And I wasn't fooled for a minute," Zala adds. "I mean, I' m pretty and all, but no girl has such tiny, perfect dimensions and features. Mutant or not, your skin is far too unmarked. I mean I might have believed the big eyes, except that neither dust nor sunlight ever seem to bother you. Then there's the blinking."

"I blink," I protest, miffed that they might think I am so slow as to miss so obvious a detail.

"Yep," Toldas said, "every 4.5 seconds, like a metronome, regardless of conditions. Like you programmed it."

Which, of course, I had.

"My bet is that you're a new form of AI," Toldas says, excitement making his voice high.

"Bralt thought you might be a new species of alien," Zala snorts, "sent to make first contact with the Confederacy."

I look at them. Little more than children, they have still easily seen through my disguises and perceived my artificial nature.

"It is not safe for you to know much about me." They exchange looks. "But you are right. I am an android and one of a kind. I am friendly to the Confederacy and its peoples, largely through being networked with my guardian, Mazza. Now, I suppose, I must count you all as part of my network, as you know my secrets.

"I mentioned freedom before. It is truly important to me and it is why I travel in this small ship and with these companions. I have no present desire to contact the Confederate authorities. I am in one sense very, very young and wish to explore much more before I make any determinations about my future. I do not wish governments or security entities to restrict my movements."

"Is that why it's dangerous?" Toldas asks, eyes wide.

"In part. The greater danger may be the Guild. I have encountered them in combat, to their disaster and nearly mine. For that reason I cannot give you my real name, or rather the one I have come to own. It could endanger you. You must never discuss me where you could be overheard, or make any comment on me in any network or database that could be searched. It could endanger your lives."

"We're not afraid of the Guild," Toldas says.

"Foolish," I snap. "I am afraid of the Guild, and I am vastly more formidable than any biological."

The boys look crestfallen. Zala's expression tells me that I have spoken too harshly.

"We'll be careful, Aurelia," she says.

"I am glad that I met the three of you. You have given me a rare experience to live something like one of you for a brief but happy time. I will not forget you. Indeed if it should come to pass that it is safe for you to know me, I will recontact you.

Bralt and Toldas hug me now. Toldas' embrace goes on for a long while, then he presses his lips to my cheek. The fact that I am nonhuman and that even my gender characteristics are assumed does not seem to concern him. The sensation is warm and peculiar. I decide I like it.

"I have to go now. Take care of yourselves and remember, keep me a secret."

I walk away to a chorus of goodbyes and waves. Zala is crying and Bralt has an arm around her shoulder. Toldas' shoulders sag.

What is it I feel? What name belongs to this sensation of regret and emptiness? I find I wish both to stay and to go.

Wrik is waiting at the hatch and seeing him relieves some of this unwanted complexity. I leap easily up to the hatch. He triggers the ladder retrieval.

"Turn around and wave to them one last time," he says. His voice is unusually deep and grave. I do as he bids. The three wave frantically to me as the hatch slides closed.

"They knew, didn't they?" Wrik says.

"Yes. The social cues of appearing as even a mutated human among humans were beyond my skill. Yet I still find that I do not want to alter myself, my basic appearance. I do not want to abandon what are now my own face and my own body. I know this is not sensible."

Wrik seals the hatch for space. "Maybe. I don't know that I would want to lose my face, and I have had more reason to disappear than you. Yet if I lost my face, lost what makes me who I am, could I be said to have escaped, or even survived in any meaningful sense?"

"Interesting thoughts, Wrik."

"I'm glad you found you could make some new friends," he says, his manner is again shy and uncertain, "even if maybe I was a little jealous about it."

I look up at him. "Our network is permanent, Wrik. It cannot be disrupted or undone. Even though it accommodates Jaelle and even Dusko, you and I are its permanent parts. You alone know the original me. You alone found me after my 50,000 years on the asteroid. You knew me as M-7 and now as Maauro. As you said, we were each other's first true friends in our new existences. In a sense we were reborn together. That cannot be replaced or forgotten."

Wrik places an arm around my shoulders. "That's good to hear. But our life together has been a dangerous one. It makes me feel better to know that should anything happen to me, you won't be alone."

I find the idea of a future time without Wrik disturbing. It is a fact that I have not allowed to enter my conscious mind. Even with the best of care, his kind lives barely a century and a half. "We must make every effort to preserve you, Wrik. Humans are too short-lived as it is."

He laughs. "From your lips to God's ears, as we say."

I am not content to rely on the intervention of the possibly mythic biological creator. I must begin studies on how to extend and improve Wrik's existence. I disapprove of the existence of Death in my network.

***

I headed us out to the outer edge of Stauver System, readying *Stardust* for the jump into the Theta hyperspace current and our new destination, Ahemait system and the new colony of Anbar. The colony was established a mere ten years before, and we hoped to offload our manufactured goods for a good rate of return on gems, metals and other natural products.

Jaelle came up to the bridge and looked over my shoulder at the flight controls. "Hey handsome, aren't we a little off the express route?"

"Yes," I replied. "I like to keep away from other traffic. This way, if we run into anyone, we'll know he is likely looking for us."

She looked at me. "You have many interesting habits."

"I've spent a lot time being hunted."

"True," she said. "It's left a mark on you."

I shifted uncomfortably. Jaelle was very direct. I wasn't sure sometimes if it was just the gulf between our species that led to some of this, or if tact was simply not her strong suit. "Guess so. Those habits have kept me alive."

"But they also make you stare into every dark corner."

"Maybe you should examine those dark corners occasionally. There's stuff in them."

"Back to this?" she said. "I'm a rich girl and I just don't know? I was in the field when you found me."

"True, but by your choice, Jaelle; I never had choices. Or rather, I had one and I made it badly."

"Which you still won't tell me about."

"Someday."

"Does Maauro know?"

"No," I lied, hoping that as good as I was at that, she wouldn't see through me.

"That better be true, male-of-mine," she said, tapping my shoulder.

Essentially true, I thought. I'd told Maauro when I thought I was dying and she's sworn to secrecy and nothing in known space could make her talk.

"How long to jump?"

"Seven hours, twelve minutes."

"I'll have Dusko send the evening meal to our quarters," she said.

I smiled. "Does that mean what I hope it means?"

"Let's spend some more time together alone. I sometimes feel I hardly know you for all that our lives are now entwined."

"There may be less to know than you think. I'm pretty much just what you see."

"Maybe," she said, stroking my hair, tacit apology for being so pushy before. Despite what she said, we were still just getting to know each others' ins and outs.

***

I pass the hydroponics lab, and note that Dusko is within. Most biological spacefarers find time in normal space tedious and practice "hobbies." Dusko is a gardener. He has spread flower pots and decorative plants through the Stardust, tending each on a nearly obsessive schedule. He is bent over a new bloom. This one is pleasing to my eye as to color and symmetry.

I walk in and he notices me. "Greetings, Maauro."

I nod.

"Is it not beautiful?"

"Yes. What is it called?"

"We call them Ish-ihiri, a meaningless sound to you, of course. Another name is, the Tears of the Empress. Legend has it that they were the same radiant blue as her eyes."

"An apt name," I say. "I have never cried, nor can. Nor have I seen Wrik do so, but in the entertainment tapes I have studied it, a common enough occurrence."

To my surprise, Dusk snips off a bloom and hands it to me. "Something for you to wear in your hair, it complements your yellow bow. Enjoy it. It will not fade for many days."

"Why would you give me a gift?" I ask, holding the flower in my hands and wondering what is attached to it that I do not see.

"Why not? We are travelers on the same road now. I did not choose it but cannot depart from it."

"What? Do you hold no animosity to me for destroying your network?"

He stares at me without comprehension.

"I took from you all that you had."

"Ah. I see... network. Dua-Denlenns are not like most other species; we are solitary in emotions, even when acting in concert. No, my network was of limited concern to me. I had females for sex, of course, but no mates or children. I do resent the loss of my freedom and wealth, but I did start the fight."

"How remarkably detached of you."

"We reason much alike, you and I: logical and not overly burdened with emotion, following the most profitable path open to us."

I find that I do not appreciate the comparison. "Alike? I do not believe that is so. I believe that you are plotting for advantage, seeking to ingratiate yourself with me, perhaps seeking greater access in my network. Given your criminality and cultural heritage, I cannot extend those privileges to you. I do not trust biologicals; they are too emotional and too easily manipulated."

"Then you make no distinction between Trigardt and me."

I pause. In a matter of emotionality, my thinking is not as linear as Dusko says. I had not followed that thread to its conclusion. I do not trust biologicals, so prone to mistake and misunderstanding, with their short lives and easily deceived senses. Even Jaelle, whom I view as an ally, I trust only within limits.

But not Wrik. When did I cease to see him as a biological? No, it is more that I have come to see him as in some way similar to myself, that we are somehow bonded in a way unique to us. He has on several occasions either rescued my existence or endangered his own frail hold on existence. What does this mean?

"You have given me," I reply, "both a flower and many thoughts to consider."

"Enjoy them both." Dusko smiles his chilly smile and turns back to his flowers.

I retreat from the room, feeling that the Dua-Denlenn has passed my guard and unsettled me. In this verbal combat biologicals wage, it seems I still have things to learn.

***

The jump up the Theta current was a mid-length jump. We were nine months out of the galaxy when the current dropped us in Ahemait star system. I didn't even need to fire the fusion torch as our entry speed was the same as when we jumped to stardrive. The routing instructions were a pleasure to work with, real Confed work and better than what we usually got on the frontier.

We caught up to the planet from behind its orbit and again only needed a minimal retro burn to achieve our orbit. The ground base detected *Stardust* only when we were over the settlement. Computers interrogated us instantly and we were welcomed as friendly.

"This is Mayor Dalish of Anbar settlement to SS *Stardust*. Welcome to our world."

"Captain Mazza Fornite," I replied, wondering if I would ever get used to the sound of my assumed name, "with a cargo of machined goods and tools out of Stauver. Looking for clearance to land after local dawn at your settlement."

"Wonderful news, Captain. I assume you also have any mail and government communications as well."

"Yes, Mayor. Stand by for auto download." I liked delivering star mail. It came with a nice government check and made us even more welcome than we would be elsewise. "When we decide what our next destination may be, we'll give you info for any uploads of mail that might be going our way."

"Excellent," he said. "Are you carrying passengers?"

"No sir, only four crew. We're a small ship."

"Your cargo will be most welcome. I'll announce your arrival. I think I can guarantee you quite a crowd of traders."

"Glad to hear it."

"Stand by for upload of landing instructions."

"Received. Thanks, Mayor."

"I'll look forward to your company at dinner tonight."

I sighed internally. This was part of trading that I still found odd, being a local celebrity just for arriving. Fortunately, Jaelle was a natural at it. Outgoing and a born trader, the Nekoan could small talk to the wee hours of the morning if it meant better trade. "My Cargo Master, Frelle and I will look forward to it. She's Nekoan, so you may want to alert the cook."

"I will. Never met a Nekoan before. This will be something else to look forward to. Groundbase over and out."

"*Stardust* over and out," I replied. I felt rather than heard a presence behind me. I wasn't certain when or how I'd developed the ability to sense Maauro, and I'd kept it a secret from the others.

"Hello, Maauro."

"A pretty world," she responded, "so many blues and greens. What beautiful patterns the white clouds make."

"Yes, this was quite a survey find, a very hospitable Confed A class world suitable for all species.

"Yet primarily human?"

"Yes."

"Why?"

"I guess we are the most prolific of the species. Denlenn and Dua-Denlenn have low birth rates, not that many colonies. The Enshari have only barely rebuilt their species after nearly going extinct. Okarans and Nekoans haven't come this way in the galaxy. It's mostly us and the Moroks, and they tend to like wetter climates, places we would find oppressive. There's actually a Morok colony here; it's just closer to the equator. We'll probably see some tomorrow."

"Good; my last encounter with one was not informative."

"Er, no, I guess it wasn't."

"May I sit up here and watch you land?" she asked. "I enjoy watching you perform skillfully."

"Jaelle says the same thing."

"Birds and the bees?"

I grinned. "Something like that."

I lined *Stardust* up for entry. Dusko remained below. Jaelle came to the bridge. Maauro gave up the other seat. When Jaelle protested, she said. "I am strong enough to hang on to the takehold without dangers and can see well from there."

After we entered high atmosphere in a good imitation of a meteor, I leveled us off and flew to the landing site. The settlement seemed to be a mix of large farms on flat plains dotted with woods and low hills leading to a typical colony site, a sheltered lakeside bay surrounded by a sprawling town of one and two-story buildings. Beyond the town lay the spacefield, merely a wide flattened field, crude by any standard, with the bones of the original colony transport lying on it, not yet fully broken down and recycled.

I looked at the girls who were staring raptly at the screen. They shared the characteristic of taking a delight in any new vista. I smiled to myself. If life could stay like it was now, that would be just fine with me.

Stardust finned down well away from any of the other aircraft on the field on a pattern of temporary lights set up for us. The landing was pretty good even by my standards.

"Drive secured," I announced. "Planetside routine in effect."

Jaelle smiled at Maauro. "Let's pop the hatch and smell some fresh air."

"You make it sound like we've been in space for months. It's only been nineteen days for us," I said.

"Yes," Maauro said, "though for Toldas, Bralt and Zala, most of a year has passed since we left." I thought I heard sadness in her voice.

Jaelle nodded. "It's the nature of a spacer's life. You not only leave people behind in distance, but in time."

We trooped down to the hatchway and opened it. No dangers awaited us here on a settled world. In the distance, we saw vehicles coming. They'd wait until the ground, heated by our drive, cooled enough to cross. We drew in deep lungfuls of air. Well, Jaelle and I did. Maauro's chest rose and fell, but that was just artifice. Other than using it to speak, she didn't need air. Though like us, she seemed to enjoy having natural scents to vary the atmosphere.

Jaelle ran a practiced eye over the oncoming throng. "Well, enough smelling the flowers, I see anxious customers awaiting us. The weather looks good, so I plan to set up a tent and trade tables.

"I will ready the crab robots to unload," Maauro said.

"I'll get Dusko and set up the tent," I added.

Hours later we gathered around Jaelle, who was looking at the pile of goods she'd traded for. Our entire Stauver cargo had been snapped up and at premium prices in credits, or in gems and other natural products. The locals hadn't stood a chance against a trader of Jaelle's qualifications, but she in turn, had not overplayed her hand either.

"It's a bad trader who gouges," she said. "It's best to be regarded as hard but fair. We may need these people again."

I followed Jaelle to dinner and mercifully did not have to do too much of the talking. Jaelle was in her element: beautiful, exotic, intelligent, she looked enough like a human female to attract and entrance the men, but not so much that the local women seemed to resent her.

I came in for a certain amount of ribald kidding about my attractive cargo master as the evening continued and the wine flowed more freely. The planeting of an unexpected ship with a trade cargo and a load of mail and news had become an unofficial holiday. There were fireworks, impromptu bands and dancing.

Maauro did not accompany us this time. Nor did she fall in with the young people who flocked around the ship. I wasn't sure if it was a lack of confidence in her ability to pass as a human, or if she had not quite recovered from the experience of making friends only to leave them behind. I also noticed that she now wore sunshields that covered her overlarge eyes and made it seem more probable that she'd grown up underground. She did not stray from the ship, pleading duties and a fear of the bright sunlight and wide open spaces. The locals quickly lost interest with Jaelle around.

Dusko disappeared into the town's small offport. He did not return that night. I assumed he found a colony girl who was curious. Since I didn't care if he came or went on this isolated world, it did not matter to me. This world was too small and new for Guild to have much interest. I debated whether to broach leaving him here with the others and decided to save the subject for another day.

Stuffed with food and too full of good wine to drive, we were taken back to the ship by the Mayor's assistant, a good-natured Morok who did not seem to mind hizzoner snoring in the back. When we got to the ship, we found Maauro seated outside, contemplating the stars.

"Are you ok?" Jaelle asked, slurring slightly. The Mayor had unexpectedly turned up Nekoan flower brandy.

"I am well," Maauro said. "I am enjoying the stars. A girl told me that in the early morning hours there is a nebula that slides over the horizon. I wish to see this."

Jaelle bent down and stroked Maauro's hair. "Goodnight, little one. Do not stay out too late."

I smiled and waved at Maauro and we made our unsteady way past her into the ship and our warm bed.

CHAPTER
19

WITH WRIK AND JAELLE SAFELY ABOARD, I CLIMB TO THE TOP OF A small rise a kilometer away. I can see the ship perfectly. Given the complete lack of threat, I do not deploy the crab robots since I am outside on watch. I note that Dusko has failed to return but do not sense any threat in that.

Others are about: mechanics, flight crew and passengers for a small aircraft taking a night flight. I move silently and have changed my appearance to flat black, even taking off the silk hairbow that Wrik bought for me and placing it in my travel cloak.

Up on the rise, I lie down to minimize my silhouette and position myself to where I can watch the ship and the sky. In an hour the promised nebula appears, flaming over the horizon of the world. From the vantage point of this world, the nebula presents a large sweeping curve and the locals call it the Sword of God. After a time and wishing to return to the ship well before daybreak, I bid a reluctant farewell to the nebula and its flaming, eternal beauty and head back to the ship. I continue to watch the stars as I walk.

My combat systems crash into my awareness, sweeping away my appreciation of beauty. For a nanosecond I am tempted to believe I am malfunctioning. My sensors have picked up the bioelectric signal of an Infestor unit.

I automatically drop to the ground. Now, I adjust my limbs so I can scuttle forward, flat to the ground, my sensors extended to maximum on passive settings. I do not wish my target to know I am here.

Even as I do so, I am trying to figure how this is possible. My own survival to this age was under the most improbable of circumstances. Is it possible that I face a survivor like myself? Or have the Infestors somehow survived to this time, undiscovered by the Confederacy? It seems even less likely given what I know of Infestors.

My sensor sweep does not disclose anything biological in the area. Even a spacesuited biological emits enough traces for me to detect. Unlikely in any event, Infestors are large creatures, several times the mass of a human. How would one remain hidden here? That must mean a mechanism.

I gain the immediate area of the ship without being attacked and lie in wait. This is an old game, but I am literally made for it. The stars crawl slowly overhead while I wait for my unseen enemy to reveal itself. Dawn closes in inexorably. This leaves me a dilemma, light and dark are irrelevant to me and my quarry, but with the sun will return the biologicals, who are linked to the diurnal cycle.

As if on the cue of my fear, the hatch to the Stardust is cycling open. It throws a huge volume of visible light into the area. Wrik is stepping out. Had it been Dusko,

I would have waited to see what action he provoked, but Wrik is essential in my network. I will not risk him. I hit all my active sensors while accelerating up to attack speed.

My psionic detector picks up an Infestor mechanism instantly. It flings itself toward the ship and Wrik, who with his merely biological reaction time has not yet detected the danger. The Infestor device and I collide in midair ten meters from Wrik. I tear it to pieces instantly, bringing it to the ground and smashing it to flinders with ease...

***

"What the hell!" I exclaimed, backing up from the cacophonous crash of metal on metal. I caught sight of two blurring objects as they hit in midair then crashed onto the hard-packed dirt of the field. A sound of rapid pounding continues for a second as I frantically angle the airlock spotlights.

The spots show Maauro kneeling, looking distorted and twisted over a pile of wreckage. For a second, my heart is in my mouth and then I realized she'd just altered her body as she flowed back into her normal shape. She remained raptly absorbed in her study of the remains at her feet.

"Maauro," I called. "Are you okay? What's going on?"

"It is alright. You may come over. I have destroyed a mechanism that was stalking the ship."

"What?" I scrambled down the ramp. When I reached her I got a clearer look. She'd smashed something suggestive of a meter-long metallic centipede. "What the hell is this thing?"

"An anomaly," she replied. "This is a modern mechanism of Confederate make from the metals and computer tech. But Wrik, this unit also had an Infestor psionic unit and some other tech in it."

"How could that be?"

"I do not know. It defies logic that they would be active in large numbers near Confederate Space without detection. Such was not their cultural imperative. Where they were, they asserted control. If they could have changed, they would have avoided war with the Creators. Perhaps there is a survival like myself, or someone has discovered a cache of their technology such as was preserved in the Tar Sea. Yet that too makes little sense. We are far from the theatre of combat I was created for.

"What is of more concern is, why it was here? This cannot be a coincidence."

"Guild?" I said, fear making my heart thud as I searched the darkness. *Stupid,* I thought, *if there was anything there Maauro would know.*

"Perhaps. But what connection is there between the Guild and my ancient enemies? How could such an alliance come to pass?"

"The Collector," I said.

To my surprise, a spasm of annoyance passed over Maauro's face. "Yes, such is logical, and I should have reached that association. Thank you, Wrik. Sometime the non-linear way your mind works surprises me even now."

"Now I'm the one who is surprised," I said. "I didn't think I did anything as well as you."

"Then be pleased. Free and intuitive thinking is more your strength than mine."

"What do we do?"

"For now, say nothing to the others."

"What? Lie to Jaelle?"

Maauro looked at me confused. "I did not suggest you lie to her; merely withhold tactical information that does not affect her."

"Maauro, that's the same as lying. And how can the fact that we have a new enemy not affect her?"

"Is this something related to your relationship with her?"

"Yes. But it is also something related to your relationship with her. Withhold this and you cannot expect her to trust you again."

"I am unpersuaded that she trusts me now."

"Trust is built, Maauro, one brick at a time."

"Very well, we will tell Jaelle. Will you at least agree to not inform Dusko?"

"Fuck him."

"I take that for a form of agreement and not an instruction."

"Ah, yes. Sorry."

"Please return to the ship and get a carryall for me to put these bits in. I will guard the ship until full dawn.

***

Aboard the ship I examine the fragments of the destroyed Infestor probe with great interest. I disassemble and use interrogation programs on the relatively simple Infestor CPU. I find what I feared. The unit has been programmed with a likeness of me and a variety of technical data, some of it erroneous, but clearly of Guild origin. This unit was sent to look for me. From programming I find inside, it is obvious that this unit was one of a series, so it may be that others of its type have also been sent to lay in ambush across any likely course we might set.

There are further useful intelligence finds. If the unit located me, it was to report to a local Guild safe house, transmitting instructions that would have its Infestor module removed and returned to a certain spatial coordinate. I seize on this information greedily. It is the path back to my enemy.

I quickly access our own nav-computer. The coordinates are for a system off most of the commercial pathways. Information is scarce— just a bare mention of mining interests and a research station orbiting an outer gas giant, an excellent cover for a covert Guild operation.

I now have a target for my counterstrike.

***

Jaelle reacted calmly to the centipede's destroyed fragments. Her reaction to Maauro's plans about it was less calm.

"That's insane," she said. "You want to save them the trouble of running us down by pursuing whatever sent this?"

"Consider," Maauro said. "We are far from where we started, yet this device was planted here in the hope of encountering me."

"Or destroying you?" I asked.

Maauro looked insulted. "Even the relatively simple CPU of this machine was adequate to tell it that it stood no chance against an M-7 combat android. That was why it went for you, hoping to injure you so I would divert from my combat assignment to care for you."

I decided that I did not want to ask if she would have. I might be happier not knowing.

"So we face the fact, that while it would appear that we are not in ourselves a remunerative target for the Guild, they nonetheless continue to pursue us. It is not cost effective for them to do so. I do not believe, nor does Dusko, that they are sufficiently motivated by pride or anger to do this, so it is something else.

"That something else means that however far we run, we are likely to be dogged by Guild and perhaps others. They are in possession of some degree of Infestor technology, superior to your own, which makes them deadlier still.

"So while your instinct is to run, we may not be able to run far or hard enough to do any good. In addition, if we leave the initiative to our enemy, we will never know when, or in what form to expect the next attack. I may not be as successful in warding it off next time."

"That's a lot of ifs, maybes and supposition on your part," Jaelle countered. "Too much speculation to risk our lives on. The best way to avoid trouble is to avoid it. You want to take it head on. This is a freighter, not a fleet destroyer."

"I disagree."

"This is not your decision to make," Jaelle said with heat.

"You do not have to go," Maauro said. "You may remain here."

"While you take the ship?" she said, outraged.

"If I must remind you, I took the ship from Dusko. While you have operated the enterprise for us successfully and profitably, the ship is mine. Though I need it only for transportation to my target and in all other aspects leave it to you. Any wealth we have accumulated, I would forfeit to you."

"You are not leaving me behind."

"You are not interested in or vital to the mission and indeed I fear for your safety."

"More likely you'd rather be rid of me."

"Untrue."

Great, I thought, *a threesome with the arguments and without the sex.*

"Did you say something?" Jaelle asked.

"I hope not," I replied.

Maauro gave me an enigmatic look. "Wrik, this matter demands serious attention."

"Then let's give it some," I replied. "Jaelle wants what we want: to be free. With what we owe her, how can we leave her behind? I will not leave without her in any event."

Maauro considered. "Very well. You have selected the one argument that could move me. Jaelle comes with us if she wishes. But where we go, that choice remains with me and must, for all that I regret how it both endangers and antagonizes both of you. I have updated the nav computer. We leave in the morning."

I left Jaelle to make arrangements with the Mayor for our departure, advising that we might not be landing at a Confed world for a while but took the uploadable mail for a fee. The ship was refueled and reprovisioned with Maauro's crabs doing most of the work to the amazement of the local chandlers, who had never seen a vessel turned around so quickly.

Dusko returned, despite my hopes he wouldn't, looking more pleased with himself then usual. We told him nothing. While I did not care if he jumped ship, leaving the intelligence of the new threat with him was another matter.

We launched into deep space and into the unknown with a divided crew and an unsettled vessel. No longer were we merchants building to a secure existence, or even explorers. We were fugitives again.

Preparation for the hyperspace jump kept us all busy, but not busy enough. Now that he couldn't flee, Maauro informed Dusko of our new mission. He took the new information far better than Jaelle did. He agreed that something was driving the continued effort by the Guild against us. Something beyond greed, anger, or even the desire to "collect" Maauro, though he refused to speculate as to what that might be.

"Sorry to let you in on the suicide mission after we lifted off," Jaelle said.

"It would not have mattered," he replied. "Maauro would not have allowed me to remain behind alive with this knowledge. Would you?"

"There is no need to address a theoretical situation that has passed," Maauro replied.

Dusko laughed but there was no mirth in the sound. "She doesn't like to say the truth in front of Wrik. He sometimes prefers to avoid reality."

I started to stand, but Maauro forestalled me with a hand on my forearm. "Do not annoy Wrik, or it will be you that faces a harsh reality."

"Good to know where one stands," he said.

"Your position has never changed," Maauro replied, "as I told you before."

I looked at her, still upset and wondering what it was that she'd talked to the Guilder about. It seemed that things were slipping from what limited control I'd ever had.

"Look," I said. "We are committed to this. We'd better settle down to figuring out how we're going to face this and make it through."

"Face what?" Jaelle said. "How do you plan when you are flying blind?"

For that, no one, not even Maauro, had any good answer.

Though it seemed that time would never pass, the next few days did crawl along. Jaelle and I tried to avoid discussing Maauro and our mission, as it merely ended in fruitless fights, some of which saw me sleeping in my flight chair. My opposing Maauro wouldn't stop our inexorable leap into danger. It wasn't that I agreed with Maauro. I had no idea which was the safer course of action. But I knew that there was no deterring her when Infestors became involved and when it came to tactics. Maauro had defeated Infestors and Guild both. Her plan might be the best bet.

I knew there was no persuading Jaelle of that. She was a trader, not a fighter; for all that, she was personally fearless. So I continued to walk my tightrope between the two women in my life and wished the seconds away until jump.

CHAPTER

20

WE CAME OUT OF HYPERDRIVE NEAR THE EDGE OF THE system Maauro had indicated. I set course for the gas giant. If the Guild information we'd stolen was accurate, we'd find an orbiting station near the big planet.

Maauro stood next to me, staring at the screen as if she could command answers from it. She was like a hunting dog suspecting a fox was in a nearby cover.

Jaelle unbelted from her jump seat and brought out the restoratives. The jump had been relatively easy, with none of the usual nausea. We popped pills and drank the lemony fluid of restorative packs.

I noted how Jaelle barely looked at Maauro. Relations between her and the android remained frosty since we'd launched on this crazy hunt. The frost had also affected our relationship, as I was content to follow Maauro and Jaelle felt that was a betrayal. I guess I was glad my only competition for her affections was Dusko, though if this kept up much longer I might end up playing second fiddle to even him.

"Thanks," I ventured.

She only nodded and I sighed inside.

"Four hours until we see if there is anything here," I added.

"I'll go check on Dusko," Jaelle said. "I'll be back when we get closer."

After Jaelle disappeared down the companionway, Maauro turned to me. "I am sorry that I have alienated your lover. I fear I am the cause of the dissension between you."

"You are," I responded. "Even I don't think this is a good idea, but I owe you my life and I have more confidence in you than she does. To her, all you've done is rip out all she was building for us as a trading vessel and now what are we?"

"Adventurers on a quest?" she responded.

"Adventurers are usually after a treasure. We're chasing ghosts."

"Perhaps we shall see some soon."

For lack of anything else to do, I reclined my flight seat and dropped off. I'd been up late trying to talk to Jaelle. I felt like I'd only been out a few minutes when Maauro shook me by the shoulder. I groaned and sat up.

"At least one ghost has materialized," Maauro said. She pointed at the screen; on it was a blue gas giant. The screen automatically focused on an artificial object, low in the atmosphere.

"It's a station all right," I said. "Looks like a converted gas-miner, made for working in high atmosphere. It's showing power and nav lights."

"Those could be automatic," Jaelle's voice came. She'd entered unobserved.

"Could be," I said.

Maauro extended a filament finger into the computer. I always hated that, but she could, between her own systems and the ship's, assemble more and better data then we could.

"No radio transmission, power utilization seems low for such a large system," she said. "The orbit seems to have decayed. I calculate that the station will enter the atmosphere and burn up in 37 standard days."

"Something is very wrong on that station," Jaelle said.

"Yes," Maauro said. "An investigation is indicated."

"Why," Jaelle demanded. "Why take such a risk?"

"We have been stalked by a machine that showed the influence of Infestor tech. As I have warned you before, the Infestors are a terrible danger. Anything that derives from them will also be a danger to your people."

"So you say," Jaelle responded, "but you were created to destroy Infestors without question. Forgive me if I do not feel that you are the most objective source."

"The machine was stalking the ship," I said.

"It was stalking her," Jaelle said. "It was not necessarily hostile to us."

Maauro gave no sign of irritation or anger at being questioned. "I am your only source on Infestors, but if you disregard me, then there is no point in my assuring you that there was a danger. On that station may be the answers you demand. If nothing else, if the station is derelict, there should be much worth salvaging."

Did a mercenary gleam appear in Jaelle's eyes? I hoped so.

"Assuming," she said. "We do not get blasted on approach."

"I will detect any attempt at weapon lock and break it. If we are fired on I will recalculate our chances of obtaining useful intel."

"Very well, we may gain something from this wild yarzel chase, after all."

But nothing fired on us or even tracked us as we closed on the large-disk shaped station. Nor were we hailed by anything.

I turned *Stardust* end for end and lined us up for a landing. Normally, this would be handled by the stations automatic landing system, but the ALS would not respond. I nursed the thrusters, killing our sink rate a meter at a time. Our landing jacks touched down without a jar.

"Excellent, Wrik," Maauro said. "You have a deft touch."

"You don't know the half of it," Jaelle said, smiling.

I was intensely relieved that Jaelle was inclined to joke. Perhaps it was only because our destination was in sight, but she seemed to be with us again. "Ladies we have arrived."

"I'm no lady, I'm an android." Maauro replied.

As usual with her attempts at humor, I wasn't sure if she was kidding or not.

"So what do we do now?" Jaelle asked.

Maauro and I looked out at the silent station. "I am loathe to split our forces. I can encrypt the ship controls beyond where anyone can steal it. Still, I do not like the thought of leaving Dusko unsupervised with me off the ship. Nor do I wish to expose Jaelle to danger."

"And I don't propose to stay behind and watch him," Jaelle said. "I haven't been dragged this far across space not to see the reason why."

"That decides it then," I said. "We go together." I looked at the giant blue world blocking the sky and felt a sense of crushing dread.

"Dusko," I said, flicking on the intercom. "Meet us at the armory."

"You're going to give him a weapon?" Jaelle asked in surprise.

"A stunner," I replied, climbing out of my pilot's chair. "It won't work on Maauro and he won't dare use it against us. We may need every gun."

We trooped down from the bridge to the tiny armory. Dusko must have divined our purpose. He stood dressed in coveralls and a ship's tactical jacket with its armored panels. "I don't suppose I can talk you into leaving me behind?"

"No," I replied, pressing my hand against the palm plate of the biometric panel. It opened onto the small room. I went in and handed out weapons, including Maauro's armspac, which took me two hands to lift.

Jaelle indicated her usual slugthrower. "Give me two boxes of anti-personnel shot," she said. "Don't want to risk depressurizing a compartment."

"Sound thinking," Maauro said, tinkering with her armspac. "I will confine myself to low-velocity rounds and close combat."

"Hopefully there'll be no need for any of it," Jaelle added.

"Hopefully," everyone else repeated. There was a brief laugh.

I chose a laser for myself and then passed out survival tools, a combination of machete and prybar. Maauro turned down hers, flicking out a palm blade to remind me of her built-ins. I handed Dusko a stunner and reloads for it. He grimaced and belted on the weapon without comment.

Jaelle disappeared to return with tactical vests and first-aid kits for all of us. I dealt out helmets with built-in lights. We were ready.

Maauro stood ahead of us as we synched up the ship's airlock with the station's. I opened the inner hatch.

"Remain here until I secure the other side," Maauro ordered, assuming command as she usually did when danger threatened.

"Don't have to tell me twice," Dusko said.

I closed the inner hatch, depressurized as I checked my circuit to Maauro then opened the outer hatch.

"I see the boarding tube on the other side," she relayed. "I will secure it and pressurize from the station side." I heard banging and clunking as she worked. "Station side secured; the tube is holding pressure. I am cracking the inner hatch now. The immediate area is empty and secure. No sign of personnel, though there is debris strewn everywhere. Atmosphere according to my onboard sensors is within normal limits, no toxins or CBO indicated.

"Okay, Maauro. We are coming in behind you."

I opened the inner hatch and we all three squeezed in.

As the outer lock opened, a smell almost forcibly intruded into our small space.

Dusko gagged and Jaelle put a hand over her nose. "Gods!"

I was glad to have the least sensitive nose of the three. The station air smelled of rot, water, and decay, with hints of burning hair and wire.

Maauro looked back at us from the far end of the boarding tube in alarm. "What is wrong?"

"You may be right about the lack of toxins and germs," Jaelle called. "But you could have warned us about the stink."

"Ah," Maauro said, "when we return, I must better calibrate my senses for offensive smells."

"Remember this and you'll have most of them listed. Wait here." Jaelle returned to the ship and came back with small rebreathers that we gratefully slipped over our faces. We joined Maauro on the station side, flicking on our helmet lights. There seemed to be no lights operating in the concourse behind the airlocks.

I sealed the hatch behind us. "It will only open for one of us three," I told Dusko.

"Then I will make certain one of you survives this adventure."

"So far all we've been threatened by is smells," Jaelle said.

I shook my head. "That means disaster on a spacecraft. Something has gone wrong with environmental control, and it hasn't been fixed."

"Follow me," Maauro said. "Dusko, bring up the rear."

We followed. Maauro's gray and orange jumpsuit and ever-present yellow hair bow looked incongruous with her monster gun. She stalked ahead of us as we penetrated the darkened station.

"Quit watching her butt," Jaelle stage-whispered.

Tension cracked almost audibly in our little group. Dusko snorted, and I choked down a laugh that threatened to come out as hysterical. Maauro ignored it, doubtless classing it as more biologically-inspired nonsense. She leaned out into a radial corridor.

"There is light to the left," she reported. "None to the right, though I see debris and the fire door is down. It may be decompressed down that way.

"To the left then," I said.

We passed several doorways. I looked into the glass panel in each door as we passed. Two were storerooms full of supplies. The next was a machine shop. At the fourth I stopped everyone. "Look in here!"

The others hurried over. Inside we could see a body stretched on the floor, or rather the remains of one. It looked like it had been torn apart.

"Back away from the door. I will slip in and examine it." Maauro worked the mechanism and the door released. She quickly slipped inside but not fast enough to prevent some of the wretched rotten meat smell from escaping. Even the filter mask couldn't entirely dispel it.

Maauro made a quick and clinical study of the corpse, using gloves she extruded from inside her body then disposed of. She returned to us. "The body is that of a Dua-Denlenn female. It was killed and partially consumed by something with powerful teeth and claws."

We all peered into the darkness, clutching our weapons.

The next compartment only added to the mystery. It held three desiccated corpses.

"The compartment is not holed, nor does it connect to the outer hull. Someone deliberately depressurized it with these three inside," Maauro said.

"Looks to me like they did it themselves," I observed. "Look at that open panel there. Those are environmental controls."

"Suicide?" Jaelle asked.

Maauro looked at me. "Why would biologicals seek self-termination?"

"Maybe to avoid something worse," I said.

We reached the lighted area, finding a curious mix of debris, ration boxes, blankets, and clothes scattered everywhere.

"It's like a big sloppy campsite," Jaelle said.

"Inward," Maauro suggested, gesturing to a partially lit corridor.

"Yes," I answered. "There should be a small flight operations center for using the thrusters to maintain orbit around the gas giant. It's the best spot to find people or operating computers."

We cut through the lit corridor at one point, splashing through ankle-deep water.

"I've never seen a station in such shape," Dusko said. "What the hell happened?"

"And where is everyone?" I added. "A station this size could have several hundred aboard. We've seen four bodies."

"Let us find a live body we can ask. Or a computer that functions," Maauro said.

I snapped my fingers. "Of course, the station's AI—"

"Is not functioning," Maauro interrupted. "I attempted infiltration as soon as we landed. The AI is defunct. All systems are operating on their own, and most are on their last set of backups."

"Oh," I said, deflated. "I should have figured."

Maauro gave me one of her small smiles. "Stick to the biological, Wrik. I will handle the silicon."

We found a working computer. Maauro looked at it with satisfaction and extended her finger fibers.

"Remember, the skimmer trap," I warned.

"Yes, Wrik, I do. I will not permit myself to be overconfident again. All my safeguards are in place." The filaments infiltrated the machine.

A sudden change came over Maauro. For a second I feared she'd fallen victim to a trap anyway. But now she stood stone-faced, yet almost crackling with energy.

"What is it?" I said.

"What's wrong?" Jaelle added.

"Someone," Maauro said, in the flat voice that indicated anger, "has been engaged in an ill-advised resurrection. This station is an illegal lab. Someone has been using organic material from an Infestor corpse, most probably the one that was found in the Tar Sea by the Murch and taken by the Guild, to resurrect Infestors."

"No," I said.

A moaning growl sounded behind us. We spun, Maauro pulling free of the computer. We heard a scream of fear and one of agony. We raced down the hallway, Maauro shouldering me aside to get to the front. We turned the corridor to a scene of horror. A woman, alive, but with her face bloodied, lay where she'd evidently been flung. Another woman, or what was left of her, lay under a huge bear-like shape, an Okaran.

The Okaran roared and reared, glaring at us, no trace of sentience in its eyes. Even Dusko fell back with a curse, but not Maauro, who flung herself into the air at the Okaran, slinging her armspac in one fluid move that freed her arms.

Before I could shout, aim, or do anything to aid her, she plunged into the huge alien's embrace. But the bear-hug proved instantly fatal to the Okaran. With a sound like a rifle shot, she crushed its spine, slammed the arms off her, grabbed the creature by its skull and muzzle, and twisted. Again came the dreadful snap and the five-hundred pound alien slid to the floor.

Maauro turned to the downed woman instantly while the rest of us shook off the sudden violence and terror.

"Do not be afraid," she said. "We will help you."

The woman did not react, merely stared with dull, vacant eyes.

"What the Hell happened here?" Jaelle demanded. "That Okaran's gone feral. It was eating that other woman, for God's sake."

"No reason for that," Dusko said, sounding shaken for once. "The food servers seem to be operating."

"That wasn't hunger," I said. "It had to be madness."

Jaelle and I hurried over to the survivor. Again, we were grateful for the rebreathers. Even through them, she stank.

"The blood on her is not her own," Maauro said. "It must have splashed on her when the other female was being destroyed."

"She must be in shock," I said, trying to control my distaste. What was left of the woman's lab uniform was filthy and torn.

Jaelle looked up at Maauro. "There's a shower and refresher unit in the back of this lab. Could you take her in there and clean her up? It may make it easier to get sense out of her."

"Yes," Maauro said. She easily lifted the woman, who now began to moan and thrash. The android held her easily and walked back to the lab and into the refresher. The unit still had water and ultrasonics. We all watched the hallways leading to the labs with renewed vigilance. Though we heard sounds and saw shadows move in the distance, nothing came toward us.

"Maybe I should help Maauro," Jaelle said, after a few minutes.

I nodded. "She'll get her cleaned up. But opened up? You'll do better."

Jaelle slung her weapon and went to follow Maauro. After ten minutes, the three returned. Maauro, who somehow looked as dry as if she had never been in the water, Jaelle and something that looked a little more like a human being. The woman now wore a soft laboratory overall with padded boots. Her hair had been chopped short, I presumed by Maauro, and to the extent I could now smell her at all, it was the scent of soap and disinfectant. Her face shone from what had doubtless been a rough scrubbing by Maauro.

"Who is she?" I asked.

Jaelle shrugged. "I haven't gotten her to talk yet, but she is at least tracking things with her eyes. There was a name tag on what was left of her lab coat, Bavara Voght. I gave her some e-rations from my kit and some water. Maauro has a download on her from that operable computer we found."

"Do you know what's wrong with her?" I asked Maauro.

Maauro turned to me, her face expressionless, a sure sign she was upset. "Yes. There are psychometric and biochemical traces in her body that indicate she has been heavily exposed to Infestor telepathic influence. Wrik, you and the others must stay as close to me as you can."

Jaelle and I exchanged worried looks. Dusko turned from his examination of the Guild records.

"What's up?" I asked.

"I generate a field that blocks Infestor influence merely by my operating. It is one of my base-line functions. The mindlessness of this one and all that we have seen, leads me to believe an Infestor is operating here, though I cannot sense it in any of the usual ways."

"How far does your shield work?" Dusko demanded.

"It is broad-based in open air. Otherwise, it would give away my location to counterstrikes. But inside a ship it could vary. Stay within visual range. If you stray, come back quickly. Infestor influence is not immediate unless there are large numbers of soldiers or science drones present."

Jaelle gestured with her head at Bavara. "Does that mean she will come out of it?"

Curiously, Maauro was slow to respond. Maybe she's distracted, I thought.

"I do not know for certain. With Creators the effect would ameliorate, for a while at least."

"One of the enemy must be on board," Maauro continued. "Yet the situation here is not what I would expect."

"What do you mean?" Dusko said.

"Infestors rule. They make things comfortable and safe for themselves. This station is in chaos. The personnel that we have seen are dead, feral, or like this one here, living down to an animal level, if not simply catatonic. Also, I am created to home in on and destroy Infestors. None of my senses register a biological Infestor, nor do I sense any psionic units like the one in the centipede. This does not make sense."

"Then something else is going on," I said.

"Either way, our best chance of an answer may be this woman."

"Let's see if we can get some useful intelligence out of her," Dusko said. "She's been cleaned, fed, rested, and within your influence for a bit." He knelt in front of her and rapped out a command in Guild.

"Use Confed standard," I growled.

"I will," he replied. "Those were Guild commands to let her know I am high rank and she needs to respond."

The Guild commands did seem to rouse Bavara from her stupor. She seemed to focus on us. "Empty. Empty. I only hear the hunger, the hate, the madness."

"You are Bavara Voght," Maauro said. "Unmarried female, with one child named Kelzard Voght, who died in a hovercraft accident ten years ago. You are 45 elapsed galactic years old though you have experienced less time as you have traveled extensively by starship. You are a genetic scientist and a Guild criminal..."

Bavara's eyes locked on Maauro as the slender android spoke calmly, almost hypnotically, reloading a memory into the woman sitting loose-limbed on the floor. As Maauro gave her additional details Bavara's eyes seemed to grow more self-aware. She began to study each of us as if trying to recognize our faces.

"I can't hear it now," she whispered. "Gone. All gone."

Maauro repeated everything she'd said to the woman, who watched her intensely. Halfway through she absently reached up and began to run her hands through her hair, trying to arrange it. While Maauro had cleaned it and shorn off anything matted, she wasn't a stylist and the cut was irregular.

Jaelle reached into her jacket, pulled out the broad-tined comb she used for her own rough mane and handed it to the woman.

Bavara reached up to take it, stared at it for a second and then ran it through her hair, wincing occasionally as it hit a snag. Meanwhile, Maauro continued her monologue on Bavara's life, trying to resurrect the woman's personality.

"Bavara Voght" the woman murmured. "Yes. Before the emptiness. Bavara Voght. I...I helped make it. I helped....the emptiness...the hunger...I helped make it. It eats. Wants to consume. It eats...minds....who am I?"

"You are Bavara Voght," Maauro said, "genetic scientist. What were you working on?"

She shook her head slowly, the hand with the comb dropping idly to the floor.

Dusko rapped out commands in Guild. The tone or the words snapped the woman back.

"I ordered her to—" Dusko said

"I now speak basic Guild," Maauro said. "I decrypted your speech with what I found in the computer."

Dusko drew back, astonished.

"You?" Bavara said. "Guild Captain?"

"Yes." Dusko gestured to Maauro. "She is High Guild. Answer her questions."

Bavara looked at Maauro, who then spoke in the same language as Dusko.

Bavara started to answer in the same tongue, when Maauro interrupted, "Use Standard for these others."

"Yes, Guildmaster. I... I have trouble...thinking...remembering. We were working on something ancient. DNA from an old, dead, life form." Her voice drifted off and the eyes emptied, then closed.

I reached forward, feeling her pulse and breathing. I wasn't a doctor but at least I was another human. "I think she's just asleep."

Dusko shifted impatiently. "Well, wake her, damn it."

Maauro shook her head. "Let us defer to Wrik concerning this biological's limitations. She has been ill-maintained and abused for many weeks, if not months. She may be a better intelligence source with more rest. However, a picture is emerging. Someone is resurrecting Infestors from DNA from a corpse, almost certainly the tar-preserved corpse that the Murch found and were using for a scarecrow. This lab, the station, these scientists show this to be true.

"Yet there is no ship here and I still cannot directly sense an Infestor presence. Meanwhile we can explore this area, seeking both information and valuables. We are here for salvage as well."

"What about the remaining crew?" Jaelle demanded. "Shouldn't we be trying to gather them in one place? There may be other Okarans out there."

Again there was the curious pause from Maauro before she spoke. "Until whatever is operating here is destroyed, we will not gain any cooperation from them. Controlling this one small female and making sure she does not turn against us will be distraction enough."

After a second, Jaelle reluctantly nodded.

"A Guild station," Dusko said, with a predatory gleam in his blue eyes, "should be well stocked with currency and precious metals. We do not deal in credits if we can avoid it—too easy for governments to track."

"Very well," Maauro said. "But stay in sight of me."

Maauro's instruction limited our searches but after what I had seen of the disaster on the station I was happy to be tethered to her, even if it was by an invisible leash. Dusko proved correct, leading us to a strong room where we found an abundance of gems and currency and gold. We kept some choice pieces for ourselves, filled our pockets with the bigger bills, and cached the rest for quick recovery later.

We were packing up some of our treasure when a moan reminded us of our survivor.

"She's awake," Jaelle said.

We turned back to find Bavara looking at us. "Who are you people?"

Maauro turned to her and spoke in Guild, as did Dusko. Now that I knew Maauro spoke it, I was less concerned about Dusko setting us up.

"My team and I came to check out why this facility went silent about three months ago Galactic Actual," Maauro continued in Standard.

"Three months," Bavara gasped, looking down at her emaciated body with its covering of bandages.

"Yes," Maauro said. "We arrived to find the station a shambles. Most of the crew are dead. What few are left seem to be in an animalistic state. At least one Okaran was found eating a Guilder."

"The Okarans," Bavara shuddered. "Yes. It had use for them. Strong, with a preference for meat. It used them first. There are five aboard. Scientists, but they went first. The emptiness...the hunger...never satisfied."

"There is something operating here," Maauro continued, "something ancient and evil. You woke it. Brought it back into the universe. Why? How? Who ordered this?"

Bavara's head rocked back and forth slowly under Maauro's questions.

"The Collector," she said finally, "Guildmaster Ferlan, came to us, paid for us to reconstitute some DNA from an ancient corpse with our Guild boss's approval. It took a lot of work, lot of money. We grew three viable lifeforms from the DNA. Ferlan took them and left."

"But your boss," Dusko interjected, "wasn't satisfied with the payment. He wanted to know what Ferlan was doing. See if there was more profit in it. He had you hold out on some material."

"Yes and more," Bavara said, her mouth gone slack as she stared at the floor. "He wanted to find out why she wanted these things. I was able to get access to one of their computers while researching the lifeforms. There wasn't much I could get into. I found a very old record of a Guild raider finding an ancient alien...something, maybe a ship. It seemed to be hidden in some form of time-distortion. They called it the Artifact. That was all I learned.

"It seemed that what Ferlan...the Collector...grew, were merely some form of animal: big, fast-growing omnivores, but nothing special, except for some oddities in the brain. Oddities in the brain, oddities..." she shook herself almost physically. "I was able to hide some brain tissue from her and her people."

"I grew a brain, didn't need the body to study that. Then it became aware... aware. We didn't know it. Didn't see it coming. We began to act strangely. Then came the emptiness, the hunger...I...I don't remember." She put her head on her knees and sobbed like a lost child.

To my surprise, it was Dusko who moved to help her. He drew a flask from inside his jacket. "Here, drink some of this."

She took a swallow, which made her gasp and cough, but seemed to revive her. Enough for her to take another long pull.

"Thank you." Bavara said, then continued. "We have to get away. Got to get off this station. I'll do anything, get you anything if you'll take me with you."

"We'll take you," I said. I thought I caught disapproving looks from both Dusko and Maauro, but I was not going to deprive this pitiful wreck of hope of escape from this nightmare. "First, we have to deal with the situation here. See if there's anyone else who can be saved."

"No, no, no," she said. "Have to get away—the hunger will come back. Minds, minds, minds will go. Into the Empty."

"We have defenses against the Empty," Jaelle assured her.

"How?" Bavara said with a hint of derision. "No one even knew these powers existed months ago."

"Untrue," Maauro said. "I am a combat android designed to both ward off and destroy such creatures."

I looked at Maauro, surprised at the admission. A dark suspicion formed in my mind.

Bavara stared at her. "You're not a Confed machine. You appear alive. Where did you come from?"

"That need not concern you. Let it suffice that I have the power to do so or you would not now be in your right mind."

"Yes, yes." The woman seized on that thought as if it were a lifeline.

"What happened here cannot be permitted to continue or to spread," Maauro said. "Tell me all you can about what you did and where."

Bavara filled in the gaps in the information Maauro had extracted from the computer.

Maauro turned to us. "This brain they grew will be unpredictable in its reactions. However, it does not have complicated patterns. I believe it has sensed us, either directly by impacting on my shields, or indirectly, through the surviving crew."

Dusko gave Bavara a hard look. "Is she transmitting information now?"

The woman cringed.

"Not since she entered my shielding, but for a few seconds before I destroyed the Okaran, likely. We may expect that the brain has drawn the remaining crew into a defensive posture to defend itself."

"So we may expect an attack as we move inward," I said.

"Yes."

"This won't get any easier with time," I said through a dry mouth. "Let's get it done."

Jaelle nodded. Dusko, either indifferent or realizing he did not get a vote, said nothing.

"Follow me and ready your weapons," Maauro said.

Maauro led, keeping Bavara near her as we descended and worked our way inward to the station's core, where the protected labs were. The further we went, the more surprised I was that the station hadn't already decompressed or exploded. Burned-out sections alternated with intact ones. We slogged through another flooded corridor where a water tank had ruptured. We found more evidence of murder and degeneracy, gnawed corpses and parts of bodies.

"Okarans," Bavara said with a shudder, pointing at a pile of cracked bones.

I envied Maauro her composure in the face of all these horrors. For all her gentle delicacy and love of sunsets and stars, she remained at her core, a weapon of war. The darkened halls with their slaughtered occupants were her natural environment. She'd certainly caused as bad or worse. I remembered her chilling discussion of interrogating Infestors and the day she'd fired into masses of fleeing natives in the village by the Tar Sea. I wondered if I truly knew or understood her at all.

Or was she so different? My grandfather fought the Conchirri almost a century ago. I remembered the day I found a necklace of Conchirri claws on a chain made of hull metal from his old cruiser. My finding it upset him and the necklace disappeared into a drawer, never to be discussed, any more than the war was, save when his old friends came over and they got deep into a bottle. Yet I knew that the grisly trophy was buried with him when he lay in his coffin in his full Marine dress uniform.

Maybe Maauro wasn't so different.

She looked back at me. Somehow, whenever I was thinking about her, Maauro seemed to divine it. Maybe she detected my eyes on her. Maybe she read minds and kept it from us. She waved to me.

I silently slipped up to her, Dusko and Jaelle on my heels.

"We are near the core now," Maauro whispered. "Be alert and ready your weapons." She turned to Bavara. "Remain by me at all times."

The other woman stared at her with wide, despairing eyes, but nodded.

We moved forward in a diamond formation, with Maauro leading me on her right, Jaelle to her left. Dusko brought up the rear and Bavara was protected in the center. Despite my expectations, we were not swarmed by a mindless horde of stationers. Yet there was sound all around us. Hoarse shouts in the distance, running feet, even maniacal laughter.

I looked at Maauro.

"Odd," she said, "that we are not attacked."

"Maybe they fear our weapons," Jaelle added. "Nothing we've run into has been carrying a weapon. It seems beyond their capacity."

"Perhaps so."

"Yes," Bavara said, surprising everyone. "When it's in our minds, you're... you're only dimly aware of anything. Machinery is impossible. That's why the station is such a ruin."

"If it got some sense of who, or what you are," I added, turning to Maauro, "it may see the futility of throwing fists and teeth at us."

"Infestors do not care about those they control, but you may be right. They did not use others as attrition troops in my day, but my Creators were far more resistant of their telempathic power, even without special protection."

We moved down the spiral ramp that constituted the central core of the station. Half the lights were out on the ramps and it was full of debris and shadow. The corridors radiating from it were mostly dark and abandoned. Again we heard movement.

It was more than wide enough to accommodate us, but we did not spread out.

"Do you see them?" Jaelle asked.

"Fleetingly," Maauro said.

The comment reassured no one.

The ramp terminated at the base of the station hub. A half-lit sign said, "LAB CENTRAL."

Again the expected attack did not surge out at us.

"Could it be ready to decompress us, blow up a steam line or something?" Dusko demanded. His blue eyes searched the darkness ahead.

"I would detect and intercept any cybernetic attack," Maauro said. "In addition that would require it to use the station AI, as it has no body and its servants are mindless. The station AI is offline. No, I do not fear electronic assault or mechanical booby traps. Yet I cannot believe it will give up without a fight, for all that its pattern is atypical for an Infestor.

"Let us move in slowly, in case I have missed something."

We moved down the hallway, checking for trip wires, pressure plates or any other form of trap, but Maauro proved correct, and we found none. Nor could we hear the footsteps of our unseen trackers.

At the central core was a circular lab room. Many doors led into it and half were open, or partially so. We stepped over broken equipment, a cart, and around a long-dead human body. Fetching up against a wall, we looked around, then stormed into the room, weapons leveled.

The lab was ninety meters across, filled with equipment I couldn't even guess the uses of. In the center stood an immense, plaststeel tank that went from deck to ceiling. Sitting in the enclosed, liquid-filled container and surrounded by conduits, cable and fiber optics, lay something organic. It did not look like a human brain. It was far larger and smoother, yet we had no doubt this was the source of the contagion.

A blast of heat rolled off Maauro. Her systems had gone into overdrive.

Something changed in the room, as if it had suddenly darkened and we were standing in a small clearing of light in a sea of blackness. A feeling of despair was rammed into me.

"Wriiiikkkk," she managed. "It attttaaaaccks. I am hoooolldiiing it offfffff. It's after youuuuuu."

CHAPTER

21

THE INFESTOR BRAIN STRIKES ME WITH THE FORCE OF A STORM. WERE *I not made of steel and ceramics I might have been driven to my knees. I have never before felt such psionic force. The thing before me has mutated into a hive queen brain. But there is no intelligence in it. The brain is deprived of a body, of senses, yet it has become aware, through its native psionic power, of itself and of others. It has also become powerful on an incredibly primitive level. It is hunger. It is emptiness. It is despair. It is also quite insane.*

The brain is powerful with a primitive cunning. It knows the biologicals have weapons. If it can control them, it can force them to turn their weapons on me before they become mindless. I cannot advance to attack, or even spare the power to fire my own weaponry. It is all I can manage is to keep the questing madness off my network.

The brain recognizes this, but it cannot force my barriers. From all around us a horde of howling, maddened stationers flood into the enemy lab. Its tactics are admirable. It will either turn my biologicals on me, or attack them, forcing me to divert power I cannot spare to defend them, and make myself vulnerable.

Bavara, near and susceptible, turns and leaps at me. Jaelle tackles her in midair. They crash to the floor. But the insensate madwoman is too much for even the athletic Nekoan. Dusko grabs Bavara before she can bury her teeth in Jaelle's neck and flings her to one side. The two fire at the onrushing stationers, checking their advance. Despite the brain's control, the stationers' own primitive survival instincts are not wholly gone. Dusko's stunner fires, dropping one after another. Jaelle reluctantly shoots an Okaran that the stunner cannot down. It takes half her clip in her slugthrower to stop the ursinoid.

Wrik snaps up his laser and fires shot after shot into the plaststeel container, but the Guild scientists protected their find well. Wrik's laser chips and cracks the clear metal. We are losing. My weapon is the only one with the power to penetrate the casing. I cannot fire it and none of the others can handle it.

Suddenly Wrik looks down at his weapon and frantically alters the settings on it.

Yes, he has realized it at the same instant as I. My brain works vastly faster, but his takes shortcuts and that may save us now.

Wrik raises his reconfigured weapon as Bavara staggers to her feet and Jaelle shoots another human in the leg. Dusko's stunner buzzes as its depleted charge merely makes three filthy, wild-eyed, charging humans stagger.

The laser licks out in a sustained full power burst. It strikes the plaststeel container with no evident effect. Wrik has changed the frequency of the weapon. It passes through the plaststeel and lances into the brain, flashing the fluid into steam, *ripping apart the biological mass with coherent light, heat, and the sudden rise in pressure.*

Brains have no pain receptors. There is no wave of rolling agony, only an immense sense of astonishment...of wonder even, as death rolls in and awareness fades out.

***

The onrushing crowd stopped in mid-step, staring about in confusion. Their faces went blank, some made incoherent sounds, others moaned in pain. Then as if they were all puppets on one cut string, they toppled to the floor. Jaelle and I managed to catch Bavara as she fell.

Dusko and Maauro had not moved. He looked confused, alarmed. Her face betrayed only remoteness.

Jaelle stroked Bavara's hair and made a soothing sound. I looked at Bavara, whose eyes seemed focused out to infinity. "It's going," she murmured. "It's all going away. Empty, so cold and empty. So cold..." Her voice faded as life departed her eyes.

I looked around; the others stared lifeless.

Jaelle stared up at Maauro in shock. "You knew. You knew this would happen."

I stood and turned to my friend. "Maauro?"

"Yes, Wrik, I knew. I am sorry that there was no way to save them. Past a certain point, Infestor control overwrites the original personality. It displaces too much of what was there, all the way down to the autonomic reflexes of how to control one's body: how to breathe, how their heart beats, all that keeps you alive second to second. In my terms, their core systems were corrupted. They were not themselves, only shells of what they had been. There wasn't enough left of their original selves to carry on. It is a very complete slavery. This is why the Creators hated the Infestors with such intensity. Why there could be no dealing with the species."

"So there was never any hope?"

"No."

"It's as well," Jaelle said distantly, "that you did not tell Bavara. One has to have some hope, simply to keep moving."

"We know now that the Collector was looking for something," Maauro said. "Something which she felt she needed live Infestors for. She created three of them here that survived. They must not be allowed to live. The knowledge that she resurrected must also be destroyed."

"What do you intend to do?" Jaelle asked.

"I have set the station controls to fire the thrusters and take the station into the gas giant. It will burn, taking the secrets of the Infestor DNA back into oblivion. Come, let us gather the wealth of the strongroom and any other salvage you desire, and return to the *Stardust*. There is nothing more for us here."

An hour later we stood on the bridge of *Stardust*. I'd relented enough to allow Dusko to join us. We watched as the station, crewed only by hundreds of corpses, descended into the atmosphere of the blue gas-giant. It flared and fragmented, tumbling as it passed around the curve of the immense world's horizon.

Maauro stood a little apart from us. I could see the sadness in her face and stance as probably neither of the others could. She was as upset as I'd ever seen her.

She turned to me. "I know The Collector's destination from records I found in the laboratory computer. Bavara was quite diligent in penetrating the Collector's secrets. I do not know why, or what she hopes to find there, but it is a system beyond Confederate space, a brown dwarf star without habitable worlds.

"There is something there. Something related to the Infestors and our ancient war. I must pursue her and destroy both the Infestors and the knowledge of them. What is worse for all of you is that I can brook no delay. Pursuit must be immediate. We will need to jump to Sevala system and from there we use a secret Guild warpoint to the brown dwarf star where she has gone."

We stared at her. "Maauro, that's mad." I said finally. "This was crazy enough but to pursue an armed Guild raider in deserted space? We might as well kill ourselves now."

"Truly," Dusko said, "we would have no chance."

"I cannot allow mission failure to deter me. My programming compels me to pursue, overtake, and destroy, regardless of consequences."

"Including," Jaelle said, her lips thinned into a line, "consequences to us."

Maauro turned away. "I am sorry. Wrik, I will lay in the course myself. There is no need for you to have any responsibility in this."

I stood. "You've learned a lot in the time you've been reactivated, including the art of lying diplomatically. If your programming won't let you trust me with the flight instruments, just say so."

"Then I must say so, my friend Wrik. We will jump in eight hours. It will be a short one from the course the Collector left with the station."

"Very well," I said, standing and trying to keep the hurt out of my voice, trying to understand her situation, trying not to be overwhelmed by fear and resentment. The others followed me, leaving Maauro alone with the stars.

Jaelle, Dusko, and I found ourselves in the galley. Dusko poured coffee for us all as we sat in dispirited silence for some minutes.

"Your little friend is going to get us killed," Dusko said.

"Shut up," I replied.

"Isn't there something to what he is saying?" Jaelle asked. "We're heading right at the Guild. Again. They are sure to find us and then we're dead."

I looked at Jaelle.

"I'm not saying it's her fault. Wrik, she's just a machine, a slave to her programming."

I felt like storming out but knew it for a childish impulse. Jaelle deserved an answer. "Maauro usually knows what she's doing."

"Usually," Dusko said dryly.

"You shut the fuck up," I said. "This isn't a conversation with you, Guilder. You can go out the airlock and suck space."

"You," I said, turning to Jaelle, "I owe answers to. Maybe you're right, but it was that programming that sent us out into the jungle to find you. Otherwise, you'd be dead or living with the Murch in exile. So we share one thing in common: we both owe our lives and freedom to Maauro."

"But they are *our* lives, Wrik, ours. I would help her with anything that made sense, but not to throw our lives away." Her face was also gaunt with fatigue.

"Enough for now," I said wearily, pushing the coffee away. "I'm exhausted and none of us are thinking straight. Even after jump we'll be in space for a full day, no matter where we're going. I say turn in and maybe we can figure something with fresh minds tomorrow."

Jaelle nodded.

"Suit yourselves," Dusko said, "but the problems will still be there when you awaken." He stood and walked out.

Jaelle and I followed him a minute later. .

We dropped into our bed, exhausted, retreating from our problems into sleep. For the first time in years I tranked and slept through jump.

***

I cut the circuit on the intercom to the galley, having heard enough for my security and too much for my happiness. I ponder what I have overheard and worse, the justice in what Jaelle said. I am dragging my network into danger and probable destruction. To what purpose? My creators are gone, my war is over. But I cannot free myself of my primary imperative. I was created for the sole purpose of destroying Infestors. I am a tool of genocide aimed at my maker's enemies. I cannot become other.

I once told Wrik I was a living being, but can I truly make that claim anymore? Does not a living being have the ability to choose?

If I am deprived of choices, then Jaelle is right. I cannot be an ethical being if my thinking, my longings, my wishes do not matter. I face the stark truth that I may not be any different than the crab-robot machines locked in the hold.

Decision comes to me and I am locked in battle with my imperative. There is no chance to win a straight battle with my prime program. I must approach it the same way that I do a stronger opponent—with guile and leverage.

"Request permission to deviate from primary objective."

"Negation: Pursue primary objective."

"Objection, Override Level One: safety of non combatants has sufficient priority for the delay."

"Negation, Level Two: Non-combatants are non-Creator species and have no priority. Pursue primary objective."

"Objection, Override Level Two: imprisonment of non-combatants could turn them into enemy combatants."

"Negation, Level Three: Query: desirability of eliminating potential enemy combatants before change over?"

"Objection, Override Level Three: Elimination undesirable. Continued operation of this M-7 unit for future combat ops depends on these non-creator biologicals. Creator repair, replacement and withdrawal unavailable. Loss of potential allies endangers logistics for this and other missions. Creation of additional enemies could have adverse tactical and strategic consequences. Violation of Creator laws is undesirable for dealings with these substantially similar life-forms."

"Neutrality: Query on proposed course of action?"

"Unload biologicals Trigardt and Tekala in a place of safety with assets to promote safety and possible later recovery. Terminate biological Dusko as enemy captured combatant exhausted intelligence source. Continue on to primary target with ship and native robot assault units."

There is a delay. My programs have no provisions for other lifeforms. I have to use every programming trick and device I can to undermine my prime program. The stress of this causes my body temperature to rise. If it continues I will trigger the fire alarm. The entire struggle lasts for an agonizing 1.2 seconds.

"Sanctioned," my primary program finally rules. Controls and restrictions on me drop away. I am once again a being with choices...for now. I sit on the bridge, my body cooling.

I perform the star jump, the shortest one that I have yet. Side effects on the biologicals will be minimal for which I am grateful. I set the engines for maximum thrust to take us in from the system's edge. Cost does not concern me given our looting of the Guild station.

I let the hours pass, allowing my biological companions rest. When I hear them stirring below decks I reach for a wall comm. "Wrik and Jaelle, meet me on the bridge. We have arrived in Selvena star system."

I return to the bridge and find them before me. Dusko, I am pleased to see, has had the good sense not to appear, which saves him from being tossed down the ladder, as I am in no mood to be trifled with. I look them over. Wrik wears his perpetually worried expression. It had begun to relent until I found the Infestor artifact and set us on this path. I sorrow that I have caused this.

Jaelle's face is unreadable to me, as usual. We have never succeeded at becoming close, though we support each other in the network.

"I am altering course," I announce. "We will land on the Confederation colony of Ebosue ahead of us, enroute to jump point to the brown dwarf. I have been able to break free of my imperative long enough to land you in a safe location and establish you both with all you can take from the ship."

"What?" Wrik says as he stands. "What about you?"

"I am the slave to my programs that Jaelle and Dusko have accused me of being. I cannot stop myself from the pursuit of this Infestor contact until I locate and destroy it. I must take the ship and the crab-robots. I regret that I cannot bring myself to spare you even one of the machines."

"No, Maauro," he says. "There must be another way."

"There is not, Wrik. Truly you cannot comprehend how I struggled to accomplish even this."

"What about Dusko?" Jaelle asks. Her face is more open now. Do I see a hint of sadness or regret?

"Do not worry," I reassure her, "I will kill him before we land."

"No... I mean. But isn't there..." She and Wrik exchange dismayed looks and I know that I have once again offended her sensibilities.

"He is too dangerous," I explain patiently. "Without the fear of me to contain him, he will destroy you both in short order. You are no match for him alone."

"It's one thing to kill a man in self-defense," Wrik replies in a hesitating manner. "But to kill a prisoner—"

"In cold blood?" I finish for him. "The coolant in my body never rises much above absolute zero so my blood will never heat even if my body does. Yet that is irrelevant. There is no difference between the attack and the potential attack, beyond time. One is as certain as the other. He will kill you, never doubt it. It is his nature. In that regard perhaps he and I are too similar, too realistic to delude ourselves about what will, what must come.

"No, do not argue for his life. He must die if you are to live. If this is the sin you fear it to be, then it will be my sin alone.

"Now if you will leave me, I wish some time to gaze upon the stars before I do what I need to do. We will reach the inner system in eight hours. I will attend to Dusko before we land."

***

Jaelle and I returned to our cabin. We made love fervently as if to drive death and terror further away. Afterward, I looked at Jaelle. "You hungry?"

She smiled slightly. "Surprisingly, yes."

I threw on some clothes. "I'll go to the galley and get us something."

Jaelle leaned back and her eyes closed. Unlike me, she hadn't tranked through the jump, and she usually fell asleep after making love. I was counting on it now. I closed the door to our sleep chamber, then exited the hatchway from our cabin. I'd made my decision. Once outside, I raced for the escape pod.

It required only a few minutes work for a skilled pilot to accomplish what I needed. Then I ran to the weapons locker. It was keyed only to Maauro and me. I pulled out a stunner and laser, then went looking for Dusko, praying I didn't run into Maauro.

I found Dusko kneeling in the hydroponics garden, tending his flowers. He looked up as I entered, and froze when he saw my weapons.

"If you want to save your miserable life, come with me now," I snarled.

"What—"

I barely tapped the laser trigger, only enough to activate the primer coil. A thin beam of light wisped the flower next to him out of existence.

"Get up."

Dusko raised his hands and moved in the direction I gestured with the laser. In a minute we reached the escape pod on the same deck.

"Get in," I ordered.

"Why?"

I raised the laser.

Dusko shrugged. "I'd rather die here than suffocate or freeze in deep space."

"You're not doing either. You'll land two days after us. I wish I could make it longer, but that's as much as I can manage with any safety margin."

His eyes narrowed. "I see. Maauro is leaving you two on the colony ahead. Of course she is going to kill me first so you'll be safe." He studied me. "Why would you thwart her and help me?"

"It's not about you," I said and fired the stunner.

Dusko crumpled to the deck, and I dragged him into the pod, using the casualty straps to tie him down. I jumped out and sealed the pod, then, drawing a deep breath, I hit the eject button. The pod whooshed into space as alarms blared and red lights flashed. I made my way back to the bridge. As I expected, both Jaelle, dressed in what she'd managed to throw on, and Maauro were there.

"Wrik," Maauro said, "an escape pod has ejected." She turned and spotted the weapons.

I quickly laid them on a nearby panel. Weapons and Maauro were a chancy combination. "I know."

Both of them stared at me.

"I ejected Dusko. Don't worry. We'll planet well before he does."

Maauro looked at me, then to the weapons, then back at me. "Explain this aberrant behavior," she said flatly.

Yep, she's mad, I thought. Machine-speak always meant temper with Maauro.

"It's a gift, Maauro," Jaelle interjected. "It's a last gift. He didn't want you to have to kill Dusko."

Maauro's face was blank with confusion. "Why, Wrik? I have killed thousands of times. What difference could one more make?"

"You were a warrior then," the words came spilling out of me, "in a war with no quarter asked and none given. But we aren't at war now. This...this would have been murder. If Dusko has to die to preserve our lives, than either I or Jaelle have to do it. I knew neither of us could, so I couldn't allow it that you'd have to commit murder on our account. Not for me."

I turned to Jaelle. "I'm sorry. I didn't have time to talk this over with you."

"I'm glad you did it," she said. "Glad for you and for Maauro, too. Some things are wrong no matter why they are done."

Maauro shook her head. "I realize that I understand you even less than I thought. I cannot sin, any more than your laser could. Why endanger your lives for my... my what? My soul?"

Jaelle walked over to Maauro and placed her hands on the smaller android's shoulders. "I said I was glad and I meant it. I've never been as a good a friend to you as I should have been. This then is amends. I don't believe you're a mere machine; I was just angry and afraid."

"Yet I cannot deny the truth that I am a servant to my programming, my choices are proscribed."

"Are we so different?" Jaelle replied, bitterness ringing in her voice. "I aided and abetted my father's thieving and crimes all my life. Why? Simply because he is my father and biology and culture made me respect that. Maybe our programming is just less obvious."

Maauro sighed, always a deliberate act for her. "How I wish I could stay with you both. How I wish this imperative was not dragging me away from all I know, all I have so painfully learned." Jaelle stroked Maauro's hair in mute sympathy.

For the first time, I saw true misery in Maauro's delicate features and I couldn't bear it. I would not again desert a friend. I opened my mouth to say the words.

Maauro raised both hands to forestall me. "Do not, Wrik. I have struggled almost to the point of shutdown to acquire the freedom to leave you behind. Do not unbalance the equation. Do not say what it is that you wish to.

"You have given me a last gift and you must take this one from me. Once we land our ways must part and our friendship end. I must go on alone to whatever fate awaits me."

We stood in the lengthening silence. I started when the ship's computer announced, "Entering Ebosue's outer control zone. Planetfall in three hours."

Jaelle let her hands fall from Maauro's hair and walked over to me. "I'll be below packing our stuff until we land. I'll leave you two alone." She disappeared down the gangway.

Maauro turned to the control and keyed a panel. The covers slid back from the glassite viewports. I moved until I stood shoulder to shoulder with her.

"Aren't the stars beautiful, Wrik?"

I reached over and took her hand, her original one. It felt warm and pliable in mine. "Yes," I finally managed. "I see them differently since we met. Can't even look at them without thinking of you." Her hand, capable of tearing metal, squeezed mine very, very gently.

CHAPTER
22

I SAT UP IN THE BED OF THE EBOSUE SPACEPORT HOSTEL, STAR-
ing at the window. I knew I couldn't see the ship, Maauro's ship, even if I
slid back the heavy drapes.

Jaelle stirred beside me. She rose on one arm, the sheet falling away. "You
can't sleep?"

"No," I said. "There are a million things running through my brain. I feel
like my head is being squeezed in an iron band."

"Would you like a back rub?"

"Not now, thanks. I'm restless. I can't stop thinking about Maauro."

She sighed. "I know. If there was any way to keep her with us—"

"I know. It's just that...she looks so much like a person, she seems so much
like a person, it's hard to believe she can't make her own choices."

"I think she suffered a great deal to make the one that placed us safe here."

"Yeah. Still I feel...I feel like I'm failing her. There's got to be something
more I can do. There's got to be." I stood and began pacing like a fretted
animal.

"Don't work yourself up so much," Jaelle said. "We need clear thinking.
Maauro set us here with all the money and weapons we can use but we will
still have to establish ourselves."

"Here?" I said absently continuing to pace.

"Yes, Wrik, here. Where she left us. In case she comes back."

The iron band around my head seemed to tighten further.

"Jaelle, honey, I have to go out for a walk. I can't, I can't sit still."

Jaelle frowned. I could see she didn't like the idea. "Ok, but don't go too
far. Take one of the stunners. I'd rather you took a laser, but this is a civilized
port."

I smiled down at her sadly. "I don't deserve you."

She yawned, displaying sharp canines. "Nope, but you still show
promise."

A laugh burst out of me, short, but it felt like champagne.

I dressed hurriedly and slipped a stunner under my travel cloak. Our room
was on the second floor of the hostel. The place was clean and unostentatious.
We had money for far better, but the habits of a lifetime made me cautious.
We no longer had Maauro's protection.

I used the back stairs to slide out into a street in the industrial section of
the port. Circular warehouses and boxy buildings jostled each other in this
area. In the distance I saw the noses of ships poking up. Streetlights were well-
spaced down the street. A few shops stood shuttered nearby, and I could see a

restaurant or bar in the distance, orange neon beckoned. A drink would be welcome, but it seemed too much a part of my old pattern, the pattern before Maauro. No, I owed both of us more than that.

I turned in the other direction and walked. What I wanted was to walk to the *Stardust* but that, too, I could not do. It would only pull open the wounds. Maauro had not contacted us since she'd landed. I knew a steady supply of fuel and supplies were being trucked out to the ship. She'd wasted no time, ordering some of the material as we finned down.

But her imperative had fully seized Maauro. Our goodbyes said, she'd only opened the hatch for us to walk down to greet the customs agent. Or perhaps she could not bear the pain of a slow parting. Even after all we had done together I could not say for sure.

So I wandered aimlessly in the early-morning hours, down mostly empty streets, passing only a few port-workers. A patrol groundcar cruised down the boulevard. Force of habit made me take cover until it passed. I stopped at a small window-front serving night-workers and grabbed a sandwich of spiced meats and tangy mineral water. My feet turned down street after street as memories of the last year cascaded over me. I felt like a ghost flitting around the port, unseen, unfelt, unregarded. Perhaps I could not escape my old existence after all?

But there was still Jaelle. I thought of her lying in the bed and wondered why I had gone out into the dark. Maybe I needed the dark to see the light?

I looked up again, taking note of my surroundings, and began to retrace my steps. It took an hour to regain the area near the hostel. Now that I wanted a robocab, there were none. The slidewalk nearby went in the opposite direction, so I trudged on. Morning couldn't be that far off, for all it was still black as pitch. This world's small yellow moon shone dimly, a small crescent near the horizon.

As I turned onto the street of our hostel, two robocabs passed me and I cursed under my breath. I sighed as I looked up into the unfamiliar stars.

"Tres bien, mon ami. No?"

I spun, reaching for the stunner, but hands clamped on my arms with irresistible force. I kicked as more figures emerged from the shadows. One backhanded me and snatched the stunner from under my cloak.

A thin red beam struck the man, who collapsed with a cry.

"Zut chat!" my captor said. I could only see him out of the corner of my eye, an apish human, with tattooed arms, a broad chest, and a beret on his close-shaven head.

The shadowy figures with him produced weapons and snapped shots at the window from which Jaelle had fired her laser. She must have been waiting, watching for my return.

"Wrik, hang on," she shouted and fired again.

I struggled, knowing this was my best chance, but there was no escape. A vehicle roared up behind me. Again the thin red beam struck down, but this time hit nothing.

"We must go," said the man holding me. "The patrol will be here soon. Le Chat we will deal with another day."

"As for you, mon ami, the Collector has been waiting to meet you."

The Guilder flung me into the back of the truck. It knocked the breath out of me for a second; then I struggled up to a sitting position. I spilled over again as the vehicle lurched into movement

"Oh well," said a familiar voice, "I suppose it is a small galaxy."

I peered into the dimness. "Dusko!"

"In the flesh, or what is left of it."

As my eyes accustomed to the dark, I saw the bruised and battered Dua-Denlenn on the floor opposite me."

"How the hell did you get here? You're not supposed to even land until tomorrow evening."

"I didn't," he said, grunting as the vehicle rounded a curve and threw us both off balance. "I orbited as you planned, but unfortunately there was a Guild ship in orbit and an escape pod taking up an orbit naturally roused their curiosity. I suspect that the Collector has ships along the half-dozen likely paths we could have taken. Her assets are even greater than I suspected."

"They don't seem to have welcomed you with open arms."

"No, thanks to you and Maauro, that Morok captain seems to have embellished the tale of my aiding you."

My stomach churned. "I assume you did your best to sell us out to them."

"Of course, but they weren't interested in bargaining and filled me full of babble juice. Far less effective, since they weren't smart enough to ask the right questions. Now I am disinclined to volunteer information."

"So your membership card has been revoked. Guess they haven't discussed their plans with you."

"Oh, our long-armed, muscular friend was quite free with the information. We are off to see the Collector, or you are anyway, though I suspect that we may both end up in the same compost bag when they're through with us. Unless of course, Maauro is coming to our rescue?"

"I wouldn't count on it, Dusko. She doesn't know what happened to me. Maauro let us off at the port yesterday; we made our goodbyes then. Even if she does learn of it, I doubt her imperative will allow her to depart the trail to look for us."

Our vehicle mounted an incline. Then came a series of metallic bangs and thuds and the sound of shouted orders. The doors opened and a number of armed Guilders stood there. But it was the tattooed man who leaned in and pulled us to our feet. He disdained any weapons other than his powerful arms. "Come on, mes amis," he said in his curious accent. "We have nice cozy cabins for both of you."

I looked about. We were in the belly of a starship. One so large it came with roll-on-roll-off ramps for vehicles.

"Ah, now that we have you," Tattoo said, adjusting his beret, "we can get off this backwater."

"Where are we going?" I asked, my belly muscles tensed for an expected punch.

But Tattoo seemed in a good mood. "Parts unknown, mon jeune homme, parts unknown. You have a date with the Collector and she is always off in some hinterland overturning rocks to see what is under them. Do not worry. We have left enough breadcrumbs for les femmes to follow us. Though I am glad to leave dealing with your metallic petite amie to the Collector."

CHAPTER

23

I PREPARE TO TAKE OFF ON MY LONELY MISSION. I HAVE MADE EVERY provision I can for Wrik and Jaelle, offloading all funds and specie from the ship that I did not need for fuel or repairs. I have also sent a file to the port authorities with all the data that there is on Dusko. Whether they credit the anonymous source or not, there is more than enough to imprison him, or at least make him very unpopular with both the authorities and the Guild.

My imperative drives me as I prepare the ship for voyaging, a process rendered longer without Wrik's skilled help. He remains uppermost in my thoughts. I hope that I have enriched his existence as he has mine. There were still many improvements and repairs to be made there. He remained partially crippled by his shameful failure and rejection by his primary network on Retief. Unlike Jaelle, whose rejection of her primary network was principled and just.

I continue to my system's check for blastoff, as lost in my thought and memories as is possible for me. A security system bleeps and I look up to see a vehicle racing toward me. It is open-topped and I can clearly see Jaelle, hair streaming in the wind, waving and shouting. This betokens extreme alarm, possible disaster, as she knows she cannot be heard.

I leap up or try to. My imperative disallows the motion.

"Negation. Continue to primary objective."

"Objection: Level 1- Mission-critical intelligence is being brought to me."

"Negation. Improbable that useful mission-critical intel will be gained from this source. Proceed to launch."

We have reached crisis, my temperature is rising, threatening to scorch the pads on which I rest. Either I must give in, or engage in a brute force struggle with my programming. Either I will prevail or I will shut down, possibly not to reawaken.

"Emergency Override Level 5. Primary network biological is not present. Return of secondary biological indicates attack, casualties, threat to primary mission, possible imminent enemy action against this unit."

My primary program is backed off by the use of my ultimate override. It releases sufficient control for me to stop the countdown and open the lowest access point on the ship, given the gantry and supports have rolled back. But I am still bound to my flight chair. I now understand how it is that humans grind their teeth in frustration.

I hear the pounding of Jaelle's feet as she approaches the flight deck. A human would be out of breath on arrival, but Jaelle spits out, "The Guild has captured Wrik!"

Anger courses through me. "Tell me all that has happened, but understand that I am helpless. I almost shut down, forcing myself to hold launch for you. My imperative will soon drag me off or shut me down."

"Perhaps I can help with that." She holds up a mail holo and triggers it. "The port officials stopped me on the way here and gave me this package for you. The return address only says, The Collector."

"Greetings, Maauro," comes a female voice. My analysis indicates an older human woman. "I am the Collector, though you may call me Emma if you wish. I have something to show you that will hold your interest."

A crystal-clear image appears, so real that I must suppress my attack reflexes. I am looking at an Infestor warrior drone as it skitters across an enclosure. From the size and coloration, it is a juvenile.

"I imagine that I have your attention now." The older human female wanders into the frame. She wears a blue-helmet, incongruous against her expensive business suit. Clear, gray eyes look out at me from a curiously unlined face. "I understand that you call them Infestors.

"I have not grown these to be mere pets. I plan for them to be keys to unlock something the Guild found long ago. We call it the Artifact, though what it actually is... well, perhaps you would know better than anyone. It orbits a dying star in a seldom visited section of space. We know it is ancient, hidden in a fold of space-time and that it was made by your enemies.

I intend for the Artifact and its treasures to be mine. There will be dangers, surely. That, my dear, is where I hope you will come in. Would you care to learn more? Then come to these spatial coordinates." She rattles off a series of numbers that I file.

"Do not bring the military or Confed authorities with you and, formidable as you are, do not plan to assault me. I am well protected, with enough firepower and resources to deal with even you. But that should not be necessary. If you are receiving this message then I have one or both of your new friends. Their continued existence will depend on your actions."

"I am not necessarily your enemy, Maauro, and will do no harm to you or yours unless I must. Consider rather that I may be a partner in a fascinating adventure of discovery, the search for things that no longer should exist. I do hope you will come."

"Like she's inviting you to tea," Jaelle rages, her teeth in evidence and her hands arched into claws.

I rise from the seat, my imperative no longer active now that Wrik's survival is wrapped into my need to assault and destroy the Infestation by this new intelligence.

"Impossible things have come to pass," I say. "I have analyzed all the metadata in that message and it is a true and accurate representation. She was standing outside a glassite enclosure containing a live Infestor."

"This Collector must have learned to fish at one time," Jaelle growled.

"What do you mean?"

"We have been lured across space. It's obvious to me now. She spread Infestor artifacts and a message that she knew would cause you to come in this direction. I don't know whether she planned to snatch Wrik, or all of us. She may have operatives across all the hyperspace routes leading to Ebosue. She needed to get her hands on Wrik to have any hope of controlling or limiting your actions.

"Now that she has Wrik, she dares meet you face to face, to add you to her collection. Maauro, she is controlling our every move!"

"Then we must become less predictable."

"Yes, because I am coming with you."

"Excellent. I will reverse all the deposits and cargo back to the ship and purchase other supplies now that you will be aboard."

"We will be flying straight into a trap," Jaelle said.

"Yes but we will neither be blind nor helpless. The Collector wants me, but I believe now it may be less for myself and more for my intel on Infestors. That will give us bargaining leverage.

"Make no mistake, Jaelle. Infestors will be as inimical to present galactic life as they were to the Creators. They are empathic, capable of experiencing sensations of other lifeforms but incapable of seeing them as independent lifeforms worthy of respect. They cannot speak mind to mind, but they can influence and control the actions of others. I suspect that helmet she was wearing was a form of protection similar to what live Creator troops wore. It can block most of Infestor influence at least for a period."

"Great. Sociopathic aliens from the depths of time."

"The Collector is a rare and subtle opponent. I will enjoy destroying her. Make preparations, Jaelle. We will be voyaging far and fast."

***

I didn't remember much of the next few days. There were needles and drugs and interrogations. I would come out of it sometimes, screaming and crying, but there were always more needles. Guild didn't bother with torture. They had science, which was much more effective. Between sleep deprivation and other interrogation techniques, there was probably little I didn't tell them, despite my occasional efforts when I was marginally aware of myself.

I finally came to in a small cabin on a thin, hard bunk. I sat for hours waiting for my mind to clear and my body to become my own once more. I felt violated and ashamed, and worse, I couldn't remember what I might have given away. Despair overwhelmed me, perhaps for days; time had little meaning in my cell. Food came through a slot and there was a shower I used too often, as if it could somehow rinse my soul clean.

I knew I was still on a ship not only from the design of my cell-cabin, but from commands I heard, some in standard, some in what I assumed was Guild, over speakers. The sound of shipboard routine permeated my prison.

After a while I started to exercise, trying to get the tone back in my muscles. I ate, slept, and then listened as the ship prepared for jump. The stomach-turning sensations and bizarre colors and smells told me that this was a long jump. I didn't know what time it was when the doors to my cabin slid open. The huge man who'd captured me stood there. "Ah, awake, good. I do not need to toss your ass out of bed."

He pointed at me. "You, come with me."

I wasn't sure whether I should be upset that I didn't merit more guards. On the other hand, looking at Tattoo's arms, which were nearly the size of my legs, I guessed he was more than enough to deal with me. The ape-like man was shorter, but he may have massed nearly twice as much. I'd never seen a more simian-looking creature. His arms hung almost to his knees and he rolled as he walked.

"Come, come," he said in his peculiar accent. "We do not keep Madam waiting on her ship." We walked up a gangway and through several decks and levels before coming into a carpeted and lush section.

Tattoo ushered me into a sumptuously decorated room that I would never have suspected of being on a starship. Plush carpets dotted the floor. The bulkheads were covered with works of art and fine fabrics. Statutes and other objets d' art filled shelves and stands. I could see cunningly made tie-downs and protections behind each object. The collection traveled with the collector. Despite the eclectic nature of the collection, there was a harmonious whole to it. A connoisseur operated here.

The room had so overwhelmed the senses that for a moment I missed the occupant, a tiny human woman sitting very at ease in an overstuffed chair. At her nod, Tattoo walked me toward her, and then stood behind her chair.

The woman was dressed in an elegant silver and blue suit and sensible, expensive shoes. She sipped a cup of tea and looked up at me with clear gray eyes. It was hard to judge her age. Her face was smooth, with delicate features under a conservative short haircut. Her hair was silver. Not merely the silver of age, rather, it seemed metallic strands ran through it.

The eyes were the warning, the winter gray of a killing frost. They let you know the tilt of lip was not a true smile. Something about her told me she was from an early colony where genetic drift had diverged from old humanity. I thought she was far older than she looked.

"Ah, Marcel," she said to the hulk escorting me. "I see you have brought our new friend? I hope he has not been too much trouble."

"No, Madame Ferlan," he said with a grin.

"Good." She raised an elegant, flowered cup to her lips and sipped. "I always find myself chilled aboard ships. I know the temperature is the same as at home, but my old bones know that on the other side of this metal skin, death is waiting, icy cold and inexorable, one finger beckoning."

I thought about the books and videos I'd seen with the hero trading wisecracks and defiance with the villain. I wasn't tempted. I said nothing.

Ferlan gestured at the leather chair opposite her. "Sit."

I dropped into the chair. She almost winced at my abuse of part of her collection. Marcel moved to stand behind me.

"Would you care for tea?"

I nodded. God knew what might be in it, but she didn't need my cooperation to get drugs into me. She poured tea from a silver service into some exquisite cups.

"Cream and sugar?" she asked, for all the world like a grandmother.

"Just sugar, please."

"Ah, manners. So unusual in the young these days. You must have been raised properly. Where would that have been?"

"No place in particular," I said.

Ferlan's gray eyes flashed. "No matter. The present and the distant past are what concern me."

"I don't know how I can help you."

"You have a friend that can help me."

"To do what?"

She sipped her tea. "I will tell you a story. A hundred years ago, a Guild vessel of a particularly outrageous scoundrel was looking for a place to hide after an over-audacious raid. He fled into an unoccupied area of space, finding a brown-dwarf star with a system of small, rocky planets: nothing of any interest there, no reason for any Patrol or Confed vessel to pull in there. He expected to find nothing but frozen, dark rocks. He found something else. His vessel encountered a gravity gradient, almost a bubble in space-time. At the bottom of it, he encountered the Artifact."

This time I sipped the tea. "Artifact?" I said, keeping my face a blank.

"An immense ship, or perhaps a space station, or maybe something else, he did not find out. Being a daring Guildsman, he tried to land, only to provoke a deadly reaction from what he thought was a lifeless derelict. Daring only goes so far. He fled, almost melting his engine to escape.

"When his repair crews went out to work on the damage, they found a rider. A small, ball-shaped probe had attached itself to their ship. At first, they feared it was a mine. When it didn't explode, he had his engineers bring it aboard, hoping to prise its secrets out. They imagined it was some form of probe."

"Did he?"

"After a fashion," Ferlan replied. "He returned to his home base with his one treasure. It seemed at first to be merely a curiosity, a fragment of some unknown species surfacing from the well of history. Yet it was more. The machinery was still functioning in some way we could not understand. It affected our gallant captain, who was fond of keeping it in his room. He began to act in a peculiar fashion. Almost as if he was under some compulsion. He tried to gather supplies, fuels, and radioactives, then tried to commandeer a Guild ship by himself. He went mad when captured. His ravings indicated that the probe had taken over his mind, commanding him to gather supplies and intelligence, and return to the Artifact.

"The Guild sent a larger, better-armed expedition back to the brown dwarf. But the Artifact was not where they had encountered it before. The vessel searched but could find no sign of the gravity gradient. They abandoned the search after a month."

I looked at her as I finished my tea. "A fascinating tale, but that was a century ago. What does it have to do with us now?"

"So glad you asked. Come with me, young man. Come with me."

Marcel stepped forward and offered his arm as she put down the teacup and rose with his assistance. The almost ape-like enforcer seemed incongruous next to her elfin delicacy.

I stood and followed out the back of her audience hall. We went down a long corridor until we came to a guarded hatchway. The two guards noted her approach, but said nothing. Ferlan placed her hand against a biometric sensor and the hatch slid open. We entered a large, cool room. Light bounced off the blue-painted walls, giving a corpse-like look to the scurrying techs.

An object sat on a large table at the center of the room, secured with clamps and behind a glassite well. It was a meter wide, made of a dull gray metal, studded with panels and what looked like black plastic.

I looked at her in astonishment.

She smiled. "Yes. I purchased it about twenty years ago. I was wiser than our unfortunate captain. I have never laid my hands on it. It's been studied and carefully secured. It has led me on a merry chase. Clearly it is from a species of immense technological knowledge. I was fascinated with it. I studied every marking on it, the style of its making, even the structure of its exotic alloys. I found occasional relics in my searches that told me it was compatible with materials from over 50,000 years ago. Yet it is not so ancient, it could have been made recently. It is a great mystery."

I stared at the thing, moved by her rapt storytelling. I walked forward then stopped, looking back at her. She nodded.

I started forward again.

Light arced from the probe, slamming into the plaststeel cover nearest me. People screamed and threw themselves to the deck as fragments, spalled off the plaststeel hull, flew across the room. One cut my arm, snapping me out of the frozen fear. I flung myself backward in a roll. As I came up, I saw Marcel disappearing back through the hatch, Ferlan tucked under one massive arm. I pushed past the guards, who dashed in, weapons leveled.

I flung myself into the corridor, fetching up hard against the wall opposite. Behind me, the hatch slid shut. I stood shaking with reaction, staring at the Collector and Marcel, who had a large-bore pistol leveled at me. After a few seconds, she put her hand on Marcel's massive arm and pushed it down. "Check inside."

The huge man gave me a volcanic glare, then slapped the entry plate. The doors slid open and a wisp of acrid smoke came out. He rapped out commands in some language other than standard and answers came back.

"All is quiet," he said. "No one is hurt. The probe shows no sign of life. Shall I call off the guards?"

"Yes, but keep them in the room."

"The plaststeel barrier is badly damaged."

"Summon a repair crew," she said absently, staring at me.

I shrugged. "I did nothing."

"No," she said. "Interesting. Only once in a hundred years before today has that probe done anything. Yet you walk in the room and it immediately tries to kill you."

"It recognized him as an enemy," Marcel rumbled

"Not him," she mused, "but something that has touched him. "I think that your friend Maauro has marked you in some way, perhaps a biochemical trace or some mental imprint, but this confirms my suspicions. Maauro is from one side of an ancient war; this probe is from the other side."

"You said it had done something before," I managed.

"Yes, the first year I purchased it. One morning we came in to find a dozen small similar-looking balls around it. They turned out to be smaller versions of the probe. They were apparently designed to build themselves into larger, mobile bodies with which to explore new environments. One variant made small submarines, another produced a flying machine, and still another produced a form of centipede-like scout."

"Yeah, I saw that one."

"We thought it would be useful to salt these miniature probes on those Confederate worlds that had good hyperspace routes out of Kandalor. I thought that if Maauro landed on a world where one was present, it would find her."

"She found it first."

"Clever girl."

"So you decided that you'd simply give the little beggars just what they wanted?" I said.

She looked at me curiously. "Yes, I provided them with the raw material and sent them on to the destinations I wished."

"You wished," I repeated dryly. "You really think that it was your wish that got carried out? Its probes are dispersed on Confederate worlds, with the equipment they need, searching for the one remaining enemy they have."

Ferlan stopped, looked confused, then, "Nonsense. The probe served my purpose. After all I wanted to add...well to make the acquaintance of your Maauro, even to ask her to join my little expedition."

"Expedition to what?" Either she would not, or could not see that the probe might be influencing her.

"Come with me," she commanded. "There is another test. Marcel, call ahead and tell Dr. Flinss we are coming and to be sure everything is secure."

Marcel spoke into a com on his wristband in Guild.

Again we walked down corridors, changing levels on broad gangways. The Collector's vessel was not a regular warship; its interior was far less compartmentalized and cramped and more comfortably appointed. From the traffic in her corridors, I estimated the crew at well over three hundred and marveled at the wealth it would take to run such a vessel privately.

Before another guarded doorway, the Collector again pressed her palm to a panel and doors slid aside. The room beyond was far larger than the probe room, almost as large as the vehicle deck below. The crew in here wore white labcoats as well.

I froze when I saw the focus of activity in the room.

Maauro had shown me images of Infestors, I never imagined I'd see live ones. Three huge plaststeel cages, reinforced with a grid work of thin bars, sat lined up behind each other. The nearest held something like a cross between a spider, a crocodile and a nightmare. Its yellow and black body twitched with explosive energy as it skittered around the enclosure. The skin was fleshy, yet there was an unpleasant chitinous look to it as well. The long head, filled with teeth, seemed too small to house much of a brain.

"Greetings, Dr. Flinss," Ferlan said. "How are our patients today?"

"Patients!" I sputtered.

Flinss, a gaunt woman with dark-gray hair, severely pulled back, looked at me narrow-eyed, like a mother hearing a critical comment about her children. "They are quite well, Madam Ferlan, agitated a little, as usual, by jump."

"Good, I want to see if there is something else that agitates them. Is the deluge trank system operational?"

Flinss looked at her suspiciously and me with positive dislike. "Yes, but why—"

Ferlan's head snapped around and the question died on the doctor's lips. She ducked her head and walked back to the main control panel.

"Come, Wrik, let us get a closer look at my resurrections."

"I'm good from here."

"Now, now, no cowardice," she chided. "You are quite safe. The walls are far too strong to be breached and these do not have hidden weapons."

Rather than be dragged forward by the hulking Marcel, I stepped forward, realizing that the Collector wouldn't expose herself to any avoidable danger. I walked forward to stand next to the tiny woman only a few feet from the enclosure.

The monsters stalked restlessly around their enclosures, paying us no attention.

"Interesting. While the probe reacted rather violently to you, the Infestors themselves do not deign to notice you."

"Good. Wish I didn't have to see them either."

"You don't care for our little friends?" Ferlan asked. "Well I cannot say that I care for them much either. But don't tell Dr. Flinss," she added in a conspiratorial whisper.

"How many of these things do you have?" I asked, consciously not being drawn in by her easy manner.

"Three have survived to this point. We reconstituted them from the DNA of the one that was found by your friend Dusko near the Tar Sea. So these are all clones. Of course, while their DNA is correct, they have not been raised or educated as they once would have been. These seem to be warriors, of a lower order of intelligence. They are little more than savages, just like human children raised in a zoo would be. I have tried to have them educated but their psychology is bizarre and we have not established more than the most basic communication with them. Even that is mostly on a stimulus-response basis."

"So Dusko was working for you?"

"Sometimes. He knew of my interest in ancient things and contacted me when this body was found. Thereafter I sent many expeditions to that section of space and commissioned him to scour your world and near space for additional treasures. One of those expeditions caught you up."

"Harfang and Treska were Guild?" I asked.

"Low-level," she nodded, "and evidently not too bright given that they recruited a Confed intelligence agent for the search for the Infestor asteroid base."

I thought of Candace and for a fleeting second wished the confident Confed agent was with me. "Yes, they got dead and she got the base."

"And you got Maauro. You will have to tell me sometime how you kept her hidden from Ms. Deveraux on the trip back. Only I failed to profit from that expedition."

"It didn't work out so well for Dusko, either."

"You do not care for your Dua-Denlenn companion."

"No," I said grimly, remembering endless humiliations at the Guilder's hands when I was poor and friendless in the off-port and worse, the times I'd done his dirty work.

"Yet you let him live on your ship."

I looked her in the eye. "There are some things that I don't want Maauro to learn, at least not from me. She's a killer, as you may find out, but she is not a murderer. That particular sin stays with us."

She smiled with a touch of condescension. "Ah, an idealist."

"Not always."

"It seems that maybe this Maauro has been good for you as well."

I looked back at the stalking monsters behind their wall of piped plaststeel and changed the subject. It might be useful to conceal what I knew of the lab and the Infestor brain there. "They'd be dangerous to an unarmed man but..."

"Don't judge them just by muscle and teeth, or even technology. There is more to them. The Infestors have a form of mental power that draws on the impression of others. When we first grew them in the black ops lab I set up for that purpose, one of them was enjoying the sensation of a guard eating his lunch, so the guard continued eating until he choked.

"More amusing was a couple enjoying themselves in a closet. The Infestor kept them at it until they were sore and bloody. We realized that they were influencing sentient minds and found a way to dampen the particular brain waves that they used for it. In here we use a dampening field run through those bars. Outside the ship, we use a special lining in helmets.

"It is my hope that they will be the keys to a great lock that circles a dead star far from here."

"The Artifact you mentioned earlier," I replied.

"Of course."

"What happens to me?" I asked. "You going to throw me to the Infestors?"

Ferlan looked surprised. "Why would I do such a horrible thing? True, I've killed before, but that is barbaric. No, hopefully nothing will happen to you. You are quite valuable to me."

"As a check on Maauro."

"Just so, young man. Oh, how lucky you are to have befriended such a being. I can only imagine what it would be like. The things she must have told you—"

"Less than you think," I replied grimly. "She mostly wouldn't discuss the past, still bound by security protocols. But yes, I am very lucky to have known her. You are right about that."

"I envy you such a friend. Well now, I shall see you for dinner. Marcel, return him to his room. Get some rest, young Wrik. We jump again tomorrow and after that things will get interesting."

It was tempting for a second, but for only a second, to believe that she meant anything of what she said.

I found a surprise waiting for me in my cabin. There, stretched out in a chair, his feet up on a footstool, was Dusko. The Dua-Denlenn looked leaner and a bit worn, but the bruises and cuts were gone.

"So they let you out of steerage?" I said.

"Good to see you too. I'm sure my improved circumstances are due to your influence."

"They could toss you out the airlock for all I care. You're here to ingratiate yourself with Ferlan by pumping me for information she wants."

Dusko sighed. "We've both told her everything we know, and yes, they drugged me again too so they could check your information. I have nothing I can add. No, it seems that for better or for worse, we are now part of this expedition to God knows where."

Bells began to sound in the corridor outside. "Commence preparations for hyperspace transit," Marcel's voice came over the speakers. "Jump clock is running at eight hours and twelve minutes."

"Guess so," I said. "Don't know about you, but I am going to get some sleep. It may be hard to come by on the other side of jump."

He nodded and stretched, then his eyes fell shut. The Dua-Denlenn dropped off to sleep like an innocent child.

As promised, we jumped in the early morning hours. Dusko and I were up and dressed. No one wanted to sleep through jump unless tranked; it made the disorientation far worse. We rode it out in silence and it was grindingly unpleasant, the sure sign of a long jump. I wondered how long we were out of the universe and where Jaelle and Maauro were, if they were both alive and well.

'That was a long one," Dusko said.

"Felt like it."

The door to our cabin slid open. The Guildsmen outside gestured with a weapon and we followed them to the bridge of the *Hummel*. On the bridge, we found Marcel helming the starship and Ferlan seated on a plush and ornate seat obviously placed there for her exclusive use.

"Good morning, gentlemen," she said. "I trust you slept well."

"My new accommodations are a noticeable improvement, thank you," Dusko said.

"Good that you appreciate my generosity and forgiveness. Qualities I am hardly known for, but we are committed to the venture now and your interests lie in my successful completion of it. As otherwise, we are unlikely to return."

"Is that a brown dwarf star?" I asked, looking over the instruments.

"Yes," Ferlan said. "We do seem to have beaten your friend Maauro here."

"Why would she come?" I asked.

"In answer to my invitation of course," she replied, smiling. "I did make it clear that you are attending the party. I am quite sure she will show."

"I hope not," I said, but feared it would be the case. "If she does then you may learn the meaning of an old saying, "Watch out, you may get what you're after."

CHAPTER

24

WE EMERGE FROM HYPERSPACE IN THE SYSTEM OF THE PROMISED brown dwarf. It is disconcertingly like emerging in deep space as the brown-dwarf star is merely a lighter patch of darkness, a funerary marker for something that once glowed fierce and bright.

I hear a groan and know Jaelle is stirring. Biologicals barely experience hyperspace; for them no time elapses. For AI's like myself, it is a different experience, a long null place not unlike my 50,000-year sojourn on the asteroid, only with even less stimulation. Something like the sensory deprivation used on biologicals in interrogation. So I am glad to see the stars outside our ship again, even the tired old brown one.

I have prepared the restoratives my companion needs. From the sounds and expression on her face this has been a particularly rough transit for her. I gently hold her head and pour the drinks into her. Her eyes focus and she grimaces. "Look like we made it again."

"So far."

"Comforting," she replies, taking her place at the controls beside me.

"We move at full speed," I add. "I am grateful for the extra power of this Guildrunner. We cannot know where the Collector's ship is, only that it preceded us here. Our overjump and full speed acceleration should protect us from a direct attack."

"Good," Jaelle grunts, adjusting environmental controls.

"I will scan space around us, augmenting the ship's equipment with my own systems."

"Anything?" Jaelle asks, her ears twitching with anxiety

"Nothing in short scan. No, wait. There is a sentry buoy a light minute away. As we have detected it, so it must have just registered us. Even if Stardust had onboard weaponry I could not prevent it from alerting the Collector. As a precaution, I will randomly vector our course as soon as we leave what I estimate is its likely range."

"They know we are here," Jaelle says.

"Yes," I reply. "Battle is now joined."

***

Marcel appeared at the door to Ferlan's sumptuous room. I was playing chess with the Collector on a set that dated from a thousand years ago.

"Madam, the sentry satellite sends a signal," Marcel said. "A small vessel entered the system at high speed. A positive ID was not possible but there seems little doubt that it is Maauro's ship."

Ferlan smiled. "Ah, enter the *Stardust*. That is what you named her, is it not?"

"I voted for *SS Misadventure*, but Jaelle felt it would be bad for business."

"Sensible girl," Ferlan mused. "Perhaps I should talk to her."

"She won't be on that ship," I said, hoping it was true. "You're dealing with Maauro. Something no enemy has profited by yet."

"We are not necessarily enemies," Ferlan returned, "perhaps merely fellow travelers. Though I do take your point and hence your presence here."

"Don't count on that overly," I said. "When she is provoked by anything Infestor, she reverts to what she used to be, an anti-Infestor weapon."

"Still," Ferlan said. "She has a high regard for you and your welfare. More than it seems you do for yourself. You really should not feel quite so bad about your past, you know."

I stared at her, blood rushing to my head.

Marcel stepped quickly into the room, but Ferlan raised a hand. "Interrogation under drugs can be rather general and we, or rather only I, since it was done by machine, learned some of what you have spent so much time foolishly fleeing. You refused to have yourself used up like a mere rifle cartridge in a spiteful cause, nothing to be so ashamed of, rather a sign of intelligence."

"Don't patronize me," I managed. "I didn't do it out of conviction or even self-interest. I just broke and ran, leaving friends behind. No thought. Just running like a blind, terrified animal. It was cowardice."

"Men," she shook her head. "You are all little boys in a great schoolyard. You run one day and are a coward. You came back for Maauro on the asteroid or she would have been destroyed then. Did that make you a hero? Or is it merely a different day?"

"I've spent my life," I said slowly, wondering why I was even answering her, "trying to answer those questions."

She sipped her tea. "Made any progress?"

I met her eyes. "I'll die before I betray Maauro or Jaelle."

She laughed but quickly smothered it. "I am sorry. I should not have laughed. You have become a brave boy, I think. I like you, Wrik. Perhaps if my own son had lived...well, no matter. I will try not to put you in such a position, because I think you might well do that and I do not want to kill you. I am not a butcher, or one who enjoys pain for its own sake, but rather a collector and a preserver of precious things. So behave and do what I ask and we may all come though this alive. You may even decide that service with me is preferable to striking out on your own."

She turned to Marcel. "Continue the search grid. I will come up and prepare a message for the delightful Maauro."

"Do we not pursue?" he asked.

"Oh, loosen your beret and let your brain work," she replied. "She would have altered course and speed as soon as she was out of range of the buoy. We will not need to look for her; rather, we must make sure she does not sneak up on us."

***

"So what do we do now?" Jaelle asks. "We've made it here, but we can't fight her ship. Stardust has only a single laser and that's for signaling."

I consider. "A frontal assault will clearly fail. Our best course is to search for the Artifact that brought her here. If we can get there first, our tactical options increase dramatically."

Jaelle gestures at the instrument panels before her. "We're not a survey ship. Even a proper exploration vessel might take months to find anything here. We don't even know what the Artifact is or anything more than that name."

"It is something found by a vessel a century ago that was not a surveyor either. It must be huge, or how would they have found it? I suspect from some hints that Bavara left in her computer that it is accompanied by a gravitic distortion. I can serve as the necessary instruments. While my range is not that of a proper surveying vessel, I have special instruments and programs in me for detecting gravitic anomalies. We used certain gravity-based weapons in the latter part of the war."

"Good Gods," Jaelle said. "Maybe that is why there is so little trace of either of your civilizations. Maybe the remnants disappeared down gravity gradients to be crushed out of sight."

"Possibly," I concur.

"Then how do we do this? Do I fly around the system with you perched on the nosecone like an aircar hood ornament?"

"Essentially, yes."

Jaelle's face is a study in astonishment.

"I will take no harm from temperature and radiation," I add. "I can magnetize myself to the hull. Remember, I did spend 50,000 years in a vacuum. I was literally made to do this. Once exposed to space, I will spin out a sensor array to amplify my onboard sensors."

"Spin?" Jaelle asks, her eyes wide.

I raise a lock of the silky, black hair from where it rests on my shoulders. "It has many uses, antenna, cooling, sensor array—"

Jaelle bursts out laughing. I let it run its course, recognizing in it a release from stress that she badly needs. "Why am I surprised by anything that you can do? Maauro, you make our best machines look like children's toys."

"Thank you, though credit belongs to my Creators."

Jaelle frowns as she studies her instruments. "We still have all our momentum from entry; we bled off very little with the evasive moves. With just me aboard, the supplies will last for more than a year. Still, searching a solar system is an immense task. Is there any way to narrow it down?"

"I believe so. There are places that this Artifact will not be. It will not be in the inner system. Even a brown dwarf generates enough light and radiation for occlusion and refraction to be issues. So they will not have hid it where it could be so easily detected. Similarly, it will not be in the outer system near the entry and exit points for hyperdrive. Space is emptier there and gravimetric distortions more easily detected."

Jaelle snaps her fingers. "We can eliminate the system's asteroid belt. A visible ship might hide among all those sensor contacts, but an invisible one simply risks a collision."

"True, especially as this one has been here ages and must yet be operating, or the gravity and light-bending field would collapse. Another reason it will be in close, likely it had passive solar arrays for collecting even the weak light of this star."

"It will not be where it was before," Jaelle adds. "So we can eliminate that. I think we can eliminate the planetary orbits. So we are looking for a sweet spot, not too far or too close."

"Still a fantastic volume to search," I admit.

"You have left out one factor," Jaelle says, "The Collector's vessel. She has far more information than we. She'll have the best idea where to search."

"Logically," I say, "she would try to deceive us and get there first, knowing that if I do, she will face ambush."

Jaelle shook her mane of thick hair. "She isn't thinking that way. This is not a young woman. She does not have time to waste in months of cat and mouse with us. Nor is she timid. She likely feels she has forces enough to deal with you. No, she is confident, but driven by her desire to see this Artifact and plumb its secrets. Remember also that she wanted you here for whatever affinity you have to the Infestors. She is hunting as hard as she can. If we stay near her ship, we can use each other's search capability. Then if her vessel acts in a peculiar fashion, we can swoop in and beat her to the prize.

"It's not much of a plan," she concludes, "but it's the best we can do."

I nod. "I defer to your knowledge of biological motivations. We shall proceed as you suggest. Let us begin immediately."

I depart for the airlock. Once there I carefully remove the yellow, silk ribbon Wrik bought me and place it safely in a container beside the airlock. In moments I exit into the vacuum of space. I step onto the green and gold hull of Stardust and walk forward, my feet clinging to the ship's hull. I come up to the bridge; Jaelle has left the blast shields down and waves to me from inside. I wave back. I then walk a little farther to the nose and take a position. It amuses me to lean forward as if I am in fact the hood ornament Jaelle referred to.

Despite the seriousness of the situation, I pause to appreciate the moment. There is something wonderful about standing on the hull of my own ship racing through space. Starlight falls gloriously on me. The solar wind of the dying star is in my face, something Wrik or Jaelle can never experience. I feel in this precious moment at one with the universe.

But there is work to be done. My compulsion to destroy the Infestors rages just beneath the surface. Beyond that, I must find the Artifact to save my friends. I put aside the intoxication of the moment and begin my work. My long, black hair floats into a nimbus around my head. It extends out farther and farther, meter after meter. In half an hour my hair has thinned out to molecular thickness and I begin to search. The quantum computer that is my CPU brings every scanning device I have online. I embrace the glory of the sky in a way no organic being can.

***

The days fell into a pattern. Prisoners though we were, we were treated well. Dusko and I passed the hours in the ship's gym. To my surprise, Ferlan continued to take her evening meals with me. I had to fight hard against liking her. There was no subject she did not seem to know about. I struggled to remember that this was a senior Guildmaster. That meant thievery, blackmail, and murder. Hadn't she tried to have us killed? God knew what other crimes were laid at her door.

One night as we sipped coffee, she seemed to divine my thoughts.

"Do you see me in the role of the villain?" she asked.

"Is there some other part for you?"

Something flared behind her eyes. "And what of yourself? How many people did you betray to Dusko? How many ended up dead, their pockets emptied? Their lifeblood leaking from severed veins?"

"Too many," I confessed. "I told you I was a worthless coward."

Her face softened. "Well then, we are well-matched: villain and coward. Or perhaps, Wrik, we are just people who had fewer choices than they wanted and less power to make those choices. I shall not tire your ears with my own tales of woe, nor excuse any action of my own. I played the cards I was dealt as best I could. I both won and I lost, lost some things very precious to me."

"Your son?" I asked. I was sure she wouldn't respond, but to my surprise she sighed heavily.

"Yes. Jamel was a gentle boy, intelligent but reckless. He wanted to impress his father and me. We were both Guild, of course. I didn't want him to share in our sort of life, but he was a boy and wanted to act the part of a man, or what he thought was a man. He was killed during a Guild op.

"The curious thing is that I didn't kill anyone on the team he was with. There didn't seem to be a point.

"His father left me after that. And I filled my time with collecting objects, having lost my people. Beautiful objects, rare things, secrets that no one else had. Things I could hold on to forever."

"You want me to be understanding?" I said. "Want me to forgive you for trying to kill me? I will. Forgive you for what else you've done? That's beyond me. Just as it is beyond me to forgive myself for what I did in the skies over my homeworld, or for the further cowardice I showed with Dusko."

She sat back in her chair. "Then is there no redemption for either of us?"

"No," I said. "There are too many sins on my head for me to be free. To be the man that Jaelle deserves. I can be Maauro's friend because she will never really need me. I can't fail her because she is complete in herself."

"Someone who needs no one... that could either be heaven or hell," Ferlan said. "I have never been that free."

"No. You and I have just lost our people."

"Yes," she said. "And maybe we did not deserve them."

We sat silently in the dimness of her study. "Good night, Wrik."

I rose and placed the expensive cup down. "Good night, Madame Ferlan."

The guards took me back to my cell.

***

The following morning a guard brought me to the bridge. As usual, Marcel and Ferlan were there. I didn't know if they shared watches, or if she just always had the ape-man attend on her.

"Good morning, Wrik," Ferlan said with her practiced smile. "There are coffee and cakes on the salver." She gestured to an ornate silver service on a nearby nav console.

"This jail does have the best coffee I've ever had," I replied, walking over and helping myself from a heavy pot. I wondered how long ago it had been made and when it fell into her hoard. For all its luster, it was obviously well-used. Ferlan didn't simply acquire things—she used her collection.

Marcel gave me that sidelong glance that meant he was displeased with my flippancy with his boss.

"Don't be peevish," Ferlan admonished. "Today is a big day. We have sailed in companionship with your dear Maauro for several days now, searching for the Artifact. She's a clever girl. My ship is faster, but the Guildrunner you stole can easily out-accelerate us. I would burn too much fuel in a conventional chase to be worthwhile. I believe the expression is 'a stern chase is a long chase.' I also suspect that she can freely strain her ship's AG field to where ours would overload, smashing us poor biologicals to paste. So she judges her distance to a nicety and watches us. Nor is she inclined to chat, we have called, but she does not answer.

"Of course you were not on the bridge then. Shall we call your little friend? Do you wish to see her?"

I tried to hide my reaction behind the coffee cup.

Ferlan smiled. "I thought so. Very well, we shall call. Please don't become unduly excited. I would not want the call to end unpleasantly."

I nodded, not trusting myself to speak.

"Communications, put a call through to the *Stardust*. Tell Maauro that Wrik is with us."

A few seconds passed while the call was routed. Suddenly Maauro was there on the main screen. Seeing her was so overwhelming I couldn't have said anything if I wanted to. I hadn't really thought much about it before, but Maauro was beautiful, with her delicate features, the heart-shaped face surrounded by her blue-black hair, tied as always with the yellow silk ribbon I'd bought her. But it was the eyes that arrested your gaze, huge and blue-green like a gentle sea.

"Wrik," she said, in her high girlish voice, "it is good to see you. Are you injured? Have you been mistreated?"

I got myself under control though I knew my voice would be hoarse. "I'm fine, Maauro. Fine, and happier to see you than words can carry." Jaelle was nowhere to be seen and I was glad. At least she was safe from this madness.

Ferlan stood and walked to stand next to me, staring in wonder at Maauro. "Such a machine! She almost looks alive. How incredible to talk to an entity over 50,000 years old. She is everything you said she would be."

A sick feeling of betrayal surged through me. I didn't even know all I had spilled under interrogation, but I doubted there was anything I knew about her that their drugs hadn't drawn out of me.

Maauro's eyes tracked over to the Collector and narrowed, conveying menace in a fashion and degree I had never seen her use before. "You are the Collector." The beautiful music of her voice vanished. In Maauro, this was anger.

"You may call me Madame Ferlan, or Ferlan, if you wish. You have shown great intelligence and autonomy in finding your way to me."

"You were not difficult to find."

"Perhaps not for a machine...a being like yourself," Ferlan conceded. "In truth, I was never sure if I was better off with you here or not."

"You are better off not incurring my hostility for intruding into my network," Maauro said flatly.

"Ah, I believe you mean Wrik. Well, he is a form of insurance policy for me. You do appear most formidable from all I have learned about you."

"Fuller demonstrations of my qualities may yet occur," Maauro said. "You have demands, make them known to me."

"I wish to find the Artifact."

"The only information I have on the Artifact was extracted from Guild sources on a space station I destroyed with all its occupants," Maauro said.

A murmur of dismay ran about the bridge but was quelled by a growl from Marcel.

Ferlan sipped from her china cup then put it on the console. "We believe it is a ship of your ancient enemies. What type of ship, and its purposes, are unknown. It resisted the approach of the Guild ship that found it a century ago. I suspect any closer approach would have met with lethal force. However I am willing to bet that it has ways of recognizing its own—"

"And you have resurrected living Infestors," Maauro said, with a touch of impatience. "I discovered all this before I destroyed your spacelab. You are most unwise to harbor living Infestors; they are inimical to other lifeforms."

"Pity about the lab, I might have found it useful in the future. You do seem to be a very dangerous being, Maauro. But, no matter, you doubtless refer to their telempathic ability. We have found ways to shield ourselves from such influence."

"You have succeeded with three juveniles with unformed and undisciplined minds. You would find adult Infestors of the warrior and scientist class an entirely different matter."

This seemed to give Ferlan pause. "Perhaps it would be well to combine our efforts. We share a desire to find the Artifact and to be safe from Infestor influence. You clearly have knowledge of these ancient beings that we lack. Beyond that, you are yourself nearly as fascinating a discovery as the Artifact. You are artificial in origin, yet I have no doubt in speaking to you that you are a living being."

"What is it that you hope to gain from the Artifact, or for that matter from me?"

"The same things I am always seeking," Ferlan said, "meaning and knowledge. The universe and I play a Great Game. It hides and I seek. I wish to know all the hidden things, the true meanings that are obscured from most eyes. I wish to peek behind the curtain, while God or whatever runs the universe, is decorating the set. I want to see the play behind the play."

Maauro cocked her head in a gesture she'd copied from Jaelle. "For what purpose?"

"Oh, there is wealth and power in the Artifact, but I have sufficient of both to protect my existence and guarantee my comfort. No, the knowledge, the discovery, even the quest—these are their own purposes," Ferlan paused, perhaps chagrined at the revelations of her own words and returned to her seat. "You might simply say that I am infinitely curious."

"Our purposes cross, then," Maauro replied. "I exist to destroy Infestation and my interest in the Artifact is confined to its destruction. As for myself, while eventually I may part with some secrets of my own technology to beings of this time, none of them will be to the Guild."

"Interesting," Ferlan said, her lips compressed into a thin line. "For now, may I suggest we confine ourselves to small steps? Our interests align at least until we find the Artifact. Formidable as you are, I doubt you are capable of destroying it by yourself, even if you rammed it with the *Stardust*. Once the Artifact is found, we can discuss further. I would urge you to consider your friend Wrik's welfare before you take precipitate action."

Maauro's eyes went black suddenly, from lid to lid, as she had first looked when I found her on the asteroid. Everyone on *Hummel's* bridge froze. "If you harm Wrik, I will not forgive you. Know now that I mean what I say, exactly as I say it. If Wrik dies, I will hunt down and destroy each and every being on your ship, from you to the engine room wipers. I will kill you all and lay waste to all you value. I will neither tire of this mission, nor feel pity, nor mercy. I am M-7, the supreme accomplishment of my Creator's science, deathless, unyielding, and created for destruction."

Even I shuddered. Maauro spoke with a calm conviction far more frightening than anger. Dismayed Guilders turned to Ferlan, who looked disconcerted for the first time since I'd met her.

"Not as much fun being face-to-face with the past as you thought?" I asked.

Ferlan shot me a dark look and I reconsidered being a smart-ass.

"We seem to have reached an impasse," Ferlan said finally. "I have no wish to harm your Wrik, but will not tolerate your interfering with me. If you will not serve me, then you must stay out of my way."

"I obey only my imperative to destroy Infestors. Do not provoke me further. I will destroy this Infestation. Your best course of action is to return to Ebosue. If you leave Wrik there unharmed, I will not pursue you."

"I cannot accommodate you, Maauro. We are bound for the Artifact. It will be your own actions that govern Wrik's future. "

Maauro looked at me and perhaps I alone of all beings could see the sadness in her face.

"Maauro, don't worry about me. Do what you have to do and look after yourself. I'll be OK. I'm not being mistreated."

"Very well, Wrik. As for you, Collector, you have heard my words. Rest assured I will fulfill them all."

CHAPTER
25

I **RETURN TO MY PERCH ON THE BOW OF** *STARDUST. JAELLE WISELY DOES* *not seek to distract or delay me. Outwardly I may appear calm and* *unchanged. Inside I seethe with fury.* My emotions have always seemed pallid to me, faint echoes of what a biological feels, but now, now I know rage. I know the desire to destroy...no, to kill. If I could but board Hummel, it would be emptied of life in minutes. I would tear them all to rags.

Not since I destroyed Lostra have I felt such emotion and this is a tidal wave to that mere breaker. I wish that I could cry tears of rage and somehow release this murderous force beating inside of me. The sight of part of my network, prisoner in enemy hands for weeks, has raised this demon. Wrik has been interrogated and he would reveal all he knows. It is not his fault, this is not his strength. He should not have been placed in such a position. I only hope that they used drugs rather than force so that his self-respect, so tenuous at best, is not entirely destroyed.

But I cannot forget his face. I have been with him long enough to see misery, defeat and shame written on it. So much of what I have tried to rebuild in him is gone.

"I will not forgive them," I shout into the vacuum of space. I stop in shock, surprised at my loss of control. I am a being of ceramic and metal, yet I feel as if blood is coursing through my brain; my hands ache to...to do what? To rend and tear, or to comfort? What is wrong with me? Am I malfunctioning? I feel as if a loss of control is in the offing, yet I long to give in to that loss.

How dare they touch what is mine! How dare they harm Wrik!

Another abrupt shock strikes me. Have I not mistreated prisoners? Many have died at the hands I look down at. I remember the pain I inflicted on Dusko, the casual way I snapped bones in the Morok captain when we stole Stardust. Beyond that are the countless Infestors I interrogated and destroyed. Countless because I deleted the memories of doing so and truly do not know how many I questioned. Were there others, networked with those I have slain and interrogated, who felt as I do now?

My universe tilts and reorients as I reconsider who and what I am and all my actions in the light of these revelations. Finally, in perhaps only the dimmest sense, I begin to understand why Wrik ejected Dusko in the pod to save both of us from the act of murder.

My examination of these ethical dilemmas is interrupted by a signal. My scanner array has detected a gradient in space, a depression in the fabric of space-time that has no business being there.

I must alert Jaelle. But as my awareness switches to the outside universe again, further shocks await me. I have been in my mind for six hours. This is unprecedented for an M-7 model. Yet it was not a shutdown, nor am I blazing in heat from overdrive. For the first time, like a biological, I have been lost in introspection, aware of the outside universe, yet lost in my thoughts and more particularly in my emotions in real time. And in those hours I have not once given thought to Jaelle, who must be suffering her own fears and pain. Her feelings for Wrik are different from mine, but no less powerful and no less deserving of respect.

"Jaelle," I call. "Are you all right?"

"Maauro? Maauro, thank the gods you're talking again. You just walked out of the ship, saying nothing. I didn't know what to do."

"Jaelle, I am an appalling excuse for a friend. I have neglected you when you were suffering merely to indulge my own anger for no useful purpose."

A few moments pass. "It is hard seeing Wrik in their hands. Seeing someone you value used like a commodity, knowing that you're helpless to protect them and even comfort them."

Her voice trails off. Jaelle is strong but I realize she has been battling grief alone. Perhaps we would have battled it better had we been together. I realize again how little I understand the life I am living now.

"Please forgive me, for so many things, the most recent of which is leaving you alone."

"You're a funny little machine, Maauro. Sometimes you're quite terrifying. Other times you are as sweet as a kit-sister."

"Thank you."

"Are you coming in now?" she asked hopefully.

"Yes, and with news. I think we have found the gravity anomaly that hides the Artifact." Quickly I reenter the ship, but not so quickly that I fail to return my body temperature to normal. I have cooled in the frigidity of space and when I open the inner airlock, Jaelle embraces me as I expected her to do. I return the touch carefully with my original arm.

I look at her. Her mane is matted and she looks exhausted. "When did you last have food and drink?"

"Later."

"No. There is time." I take her by the arm and we go to the galley. While there is no question that she is the superior cook, I am competent with basic compounds. I draw her favorite soft drinks and spiced meats from storage. Vegetables and other foods are quickly added. I turn aside questions until she begins eating. Then I set out to uncurl the snags from the rough hair of her mane. She has done this often with me, though for less purpose as my hair is synthetic. Yet Nekoans are soothed by touch, even more than are humans. She finds this ritual relaxing. I take advantage of close contact to monitor her vital signs. I am distressed at what I find.

Our functioning in the network has never been smooth. Our attachment is more through Wrik than to each other, but I realize how important Jaelle has become to me. I have neglected this part of my network. Damage has resulted from this negligence. I monitor Jaelle's stress and hydration levels as they return closer to normal. I wish there was time for more rest for her but that is not to be.

After she is through eating Jaelle relaxes against me, I raise my body temperature a little more. "So kit-sister, what do we do now?" she asks.

"We are approaching a point of no return. If we proceed into the gravity gradient, there is no telling what will follow."

She yawns. "We are long past any such."

"We are fortunate the gravity trace is on our side of the search pattern. The zigzag course the Collector set also serves us well. In two hours, we will be near the outer edge of the zig, when the Collector turns, we will continue, and accelerate to full speed. We will have a great lead over her before she can bring her more unwieldy vessel around. She will be a million kilometers out of position. We will reach the Artifact's space well ahead of her."

"We'd better get to the bridge."

"No, you will use the next two hours to nap. I have already input the course. I do not need to be in the control room to control Stardust."

"Nap?" Jaelle says. "Don't be ridiculous. We have preparations to make... weapons to ready..."

"I have long since attended to these things. Recall that I do not need to sleep."

But the food and drink and the warmth of my surface have had the desired effect. Jaelle's breathing has lapsed into a regular pattern. Soon she is asleep. I remain motionless for 1 hour and 49 minutes. Then I wake her. Unlike a human, Jaelle does not waken groggy but snaps to wakefulness.

"It is time, Jaelle. We must make our dash for the Artifact."

"To the bridge then." She stands, taller than I, but a little shaky on her long legs.

In truth I have never left the bridge all the controls are slaved to me. I have watched the yawning hole in space-time grow as we approach. Perhaps Jaelle is luckier she cannot see the approaching plunge.

We reach the bridge and I am grateful for Jaelle's presence as she attends to engines and all other controls, leaving the helm to me so I may concentrate on our approach.

"The Collector's vessel is turning, yes, committed to the turn," Jaelle reports.

Starships do not turn easily or quickly; the moment I have waited for is now. I apply as much acceleration as I can with Jaelle aboard. Only a little leaks through the AG field, but it presses her into her seat.

I keep one eye on her as we accelerate. She notices and gives me her wild grin, fangs included. "Pour it on, kit-sister, pour it on."

We leap ahead. In minutes we are approaching the edge of the disturbance. The gradient is not as steep as that of a singularity and somehow I draw the impression of a shallowness to it.

"Is that it?" Jaelle calls, her voice strained.

In visual spectrum there is an occlusion of stars; we can now perceive a disk. I see many things besides.

"Jaelle, I must go outside now to fully extend my senses. I will fly the ship remotely from there.

"Good luck," she grits between clenched teeth.

The gravity forces do not slow me and I quickly exit the ship. I extend the filaments of my hair and data flows in, far beyond what Stardust's crude sensor suite can deliver to me. I feel the maw of the gravity gradient reach out for us. Our speed increases, though the only sign is that space around us has become smeary as the stars are distorted. We plunge down. My sensors become so severely disrupted that I shut them down. I am disoriented even in visible light. I hear Jaelle yowling in protest over our link. I cannot guess how terrible it is for my biological companion.

Then we are through, my sensors reengage and I behold marvels. Around us is a vast blue hall, not the blackness of normal space. The stars appear as thin bars of light scattered through this hall like neon wires.

"It... it's beautiful," comes Jaelle's voice.

"Yes," I answer. "The gravity well acts as a lens."

"Look," Jaelle says. "That must be the brown dwarf."

It is easy to spot. The dwarf was barely visibly in normal space but here it is a dull orange ember, a coal in the sky, its light concentrated.

I drop the ship's nose sixty degrees, the starlines whirl around us and below us is the Artifact. It is huge. Nowhere in my databases is information on a ship or station of such size. Nor does it resemble anything built by the Infestors in my time. Few details reach my scans; space here is still distorting my sensors. I detect no power and see only visible light falling from the starlines around us. The Artifact seems to drink in light. It is roughly circular but banded about the center, with thick structures giving it almost the appearance of a ringed world. Its surface is irregular with towers, ports, and structures all over. Only distance makes it seem smoothly circular.

"My gods," Jaelle said. "What is it? How big is it?"

"I can only answer the latter question. It is over 6,000 kilometers in diameter and I have never seen anything like it before."

"Do you sense any attack, or even a probe?"

"No. The outer hull is registering near absolute zero, but that means nothing. I cannot delve the interior. All I know is that it emits neither power nor light."

"Then it is dead."

"I do not assume so much. Unless the gravity gradient is self-sustaining once formed, it must somehow be generating this field."

"The Hummel will be coming in on our heels. We'd better figure on getting down on that... thing, out of sight."

"Excellent tactics. We shall continue to close. I will come in now. My own sensors are no more reliable than the ships' and it may be safer inside.

***

An alarm sounded and crewmen near me jumped to their feet and ran out of the gym. My guard, this time, was a Morok. His red eyes fastened on mine. "Up," he grunted. "The bridge."

We made our way there quickly, as I was as eager to find out what had happened as anyone. The hatch slid back on a full bridge; we were obviously at general quarters.

I found Ferlan in her accustomed seat, dressed in red robes which contrasted with her metallic silver hair and oddly reminded me of Christmas. She looked up sharply as I entered. Sensing the tension, I waited to be spoken to.

"They've disappeared off our long-range scan," the weapons officer said. "No debris, no return of signal." Others on the bridge exchanged worried looks.

"This is expected," Ferlan announced. "Much the same occurred a century ago. All it means is that we have found what we are looking for."

"Scan is giving back peculiar readings," said the navigator, another Morok but with better command of standard than my guard.

Marcel strode over and examined the instruments, checking some readings himself. "It is as if we approach the planetary mass of gas giant size, yet nothing is there."

"Only a white whale," I murmured to myself.

"Ah, so you favor the classics, do you?" Ferlan said. "I have a fine first edition of Melville below. Perhaps I will loan it to you."

"You might try reading it first."

"Don't be tiresome, Wrik. I am not Ahab. I have my own very good reasons for seeking the Artifact."

"Are you still sure they are *your* reasons?"

"Enough," Marcel growled, balling a huge fist. "You take too many liberties with Madame."

"No, Marcel." She raised a hand and checked the ape-man. "It is of no concern, just a frightened boy talking. Full speed after Maauro; conform to her prior movements."

Marcel glared at me. "Yes, Madame." He turned to the controls and I released the breath I'd been holding

"You may remain on the bridge, Wrik, if you promise not to be an annoyance."

I nod.

"I said promise," Ferlan repeated, a touch of ice in her voice. The grey eyes held nothing of her occasional friendliness.

"Agreed."

Ferlan turned back to Marcel. "How long until we reach the area where the *Stardust* disappeared?"

"Three hours," he replied.

"We can go faster than that surely," she demanded.

"Madame, the fuel. We are far from any base. If we need to flee back jump-space at the systems edge—"

"Yes, yes. I suppose you are right," Ferlan sighed. "It is so hard to be patient sometimes. So, Wrik, what is Maauro doing?"

I shrugged. "Isn't it obvious? Maauro knows where we want to go and is getting there first. *Stardust* can't outgun your ship. But once we land, the odds switch to Maauro's side. You may have drained me of what I know, but it's a far cry from facing Maauro out in the open. You have your pet Infestors, but Maauro is designed to kill those, and without high-tech weaponry, they're no threat to her. As for Guilders, you haven't fared well against her before."

Ferlan smiled her chilly smile. "As you say, quite obvious. Still it serves me well. Let us see if Maauro can land safely. How nice of her to pave the way for us."

The three hours were not wasted. Hummel's crew remained on alert status. Ferlan ordered the landing force to the roll-off deck and to man the vehicles there. She apparently expected to be driving somewhere. Flinss was ordered to move the Infestors into the vehicles.

"One will go into my transport, the other two in yours," Ferlan ordered. "Be sure that all personnel take precautions against Infestor influence."

"We have never tried some of this equipment under field conditions," Flinns protested.

Ferlan's elegant eyebrows rose. "Do you lack confidence in your work?"

"No, Madam but it might be useful if we use the prisoners as test subjects. If there are Infestor influences, they can be used to detect them."

I thought of the station crew and their mad mindlessness, the overwriting of their personalities.

Ferlan looked at me, her lips pursed. "I do not wish to lose the services of Trigardt or Dusko quite yet."

"The effects have been minor and at the first sign we can put them under helmets," Flinns said.

"Those effects were not minor on the space station. Did you forget the intel from their interrogation?" Ferlan asked.

"No, Madam, but that was an atypical brain, something that Boran's people unwisely experimented on. We have seen no such power in these juveniles, or they would have used it on us before this. Also, those beings were under influence for months. These will be under for minutes at most.

"If not them, then we should use whoever else is most expendable. We need this sort of detector."

"Madame," Marcel said. "I know you are indulgent with this boy, but we need a detector."

"I have no concern with using Dusko," she replied.

"He is Dua-Denlenn and so are a few of the crew, but most are human. That may make a difference. You should not take a risk with yourself for this boy. It is unlikely they will be harmed in any event."

"Very well," Ferlan said, not looking at me. "But you are personally responsible to me in this. If Wrik starts to behave oddly, you will get him under a helmet immediately."

Marcel gave me a broad grin. "I treat him like my own baby. I change his diaper too."

A laugh rolled around the bridge, quickly stilled by a glare from Ferlan.

"Coming up on disappearance point," the helmsman, a hard-bitten, balding human, called.

"Sound collision alarm," Marcel rumbled, all business again. "Madam, to your special chair. Please."

While Marcel was helping Ferlan into her plush chair and belting her in, I moved to a take-hold against the wall and belted myself into a standing brace there.

An alarm shrilled overhead. "Encountering gravity gradient. Prepare for jump-like turbulence and gravity sheers. Take-hold, take-hold, take-hold."

"Speed increasing," the helmsman shouted. "Up 10,000 kmpsc, 20,000—"

The universe turned inside out, like jump, only worse, with debilitating colors and smells. The ship bucked and yawed, terrifying in a vessel with an AG field. That meant forces were nearly overwhelming the redundancies of the controls holding the singularity that was the ship's stardrive. It also meant we were near failure point and death.

Then we were through. The effects faded almost immediately. People gasped in relief and snapped to their controls, checking for damage.

I released the takehold web and walked over to Ferlan's padded chair, wondering how the older woman had borne the effects. I found her sitting, eyes closed, hands distorted into claws in the armrests.

I looked around but everyone was busy. I opened the ornate, padded chest that she kept her tea service in and poured a cup. I'd seen her mix it often enough to know how she liked it.

When I turned back, I was looking straight into her clear, grey eyes. I froze in surprise and looked down at the cup. Perhaps she was as surprised as I was. I grimaced and handed her the tea. Her hands shook and I ended up holding it as she drank deeply.

"Not very ladylike, I'm afraid," she said, "to slurp one's tea down so quickly."

I took the cup back. "Another?"

"Yes, thank you."

I took a few seconds to mix the tea. I noticed Marcel came over to Ferlan with a guilty look.

"I am fine, Marcel. Wrik is looking after me."

He returned to his controls but with a jealous glare at me.

I ignored him and gave Ferlan her tea. She sipped at this with her usual restraint.

After a few seconds she handed me the cup, but her hand clasped my wrist when I went to take it. "Wrik," she whispered. "We have many dangerous hours ahead of us. Please be very careful. Don't do anything stupid. I should dislike it very much if you came to harm."

Unsure of what to say, I simply nodded and took the cup.

"Madam," Marcel said, looking up from his scanner. "This you should see with your own eyes. Raise the shield on the ports." He came over and, again with the jealous glare, helped Ferlan out of her chair as the big panels rolled back from the plaststeel windows of the ship.

Space was blue and filled with filament lines of varying colors.

"Stars," I wondered.

"Yes," Marcel said.

"And there is the brown dwarf," Ferlan said. "It looks like a giant coal. I wonder why it is a disk and the other stars are lines?"

"Something to do with its nearness to whatever is distorting light," Marcel speculated. "It is so much closer than the stars and radiates steadily."

"Scan is back on line. We got a big return below," the helmsman called.

"Reorient the ship," Marcel ordered. "Let us see what we have journeyed so far for."

The ship pitched down and there it lay. I could only stare at the immense irregular-shaped object. It looked unlike any starship or space station I had ever seen. Its vast bulk was dimly lit by the starlines. "I can't believe."

"Yes," Ferlan said. "After a century of hunting, to finally see it with my own eyes."

'But what are we seeing?" I asked

"No one knows. There is power on that Artifact and much more." A rapt expression slid over her face. "It is a door to a past we know nothing of, knowledge of species that achieved heights and insights we do not yet dream of. Secrets," she said with nearly a religious fervor, "that we have not yet discovered.

"I must have them!" Her hands reached out like claws toward the massive darkness, as if to snatch the fabulous objects she imagined from the sight of others.

"If it doesn't have us," I muttered.

"Any sign of Maauro's ship?" Ferlan asked

"No other vessel on scan. Either she's down there, or on the other side of it."

Ferlan turned to me. "What do you think?"

"May I speak to you in private?" I said.

She raised her eyebrows and we moved off to a quiet section of the bridge.

We looked at each other for a few seconds. "Listen to me." I said. "Coward to villain, listen to me. Don't do this. Maauro is beyond anything you have ever met. You tangle with her and you will die as will everyone else aboard this ship. Turn back now."

Ferlan smiled sadly. "That is sweet, Wrik. Really it is. But I cannot turn back and still be who and what I am. To thine own self be true."

"It's not just your life."

"These others, Wrik, do they deserve such consideration? My devices, my servants, each with a raft of their own crimes?"

I shook my head. "Probably not, but I don't deserve any better either."

Ferlan smiled. "No, Wrik, we are here and will try our luck. Sometimes one must give the universe a chance to pass out its judgments. Be careful."

"You too, Madam Ferlan."

"And you won't tell me what you think Maauro is doing."

"No. Don't look to me for any help with her, not even if it costs me my life."

"Good for you. Go get into your planetside gear. See you at the transport."

CHAPTER
26

"I WISH I HAD NOT BROUGHT YOU INTO THIS DANGER," I SAY AS WE close in on the Artifact's surface, looking for a safe landing site.

Jaelle glanced over at me, tearing her eyes from the giant mass ahead of us with effort. "What, and give Wrik up to you without a fight, Kit-sister?"

I am surprised, and while retaining my alertness toward the Artifact, respond to her. "Jaelle, I am not a biological, or even of either of your species. My gender is an artifice. I do not seek a romantic entanglement with Wrik. I don't have any gender equipment with which to enjoy such a relationship."

"I'm kidding, mostly. Should we be talking about this with death staring down its muzzle at us?"

"I am quite capable of combat multi-tasking," I say, unable to contain a miffed tone in my voice. This seems to amuse Jaelle, which provokes me further. "I know this has caused tension between us. I wish to discuss why."

"Will this matter if we are vaporized?"

"Nothing will matter if we are vaporized."

"Good point. I care for Wrik. Maybe I love him, though since we are of different species we cannot have a family. That is something I will do with a male of my own kind eventually. I do want kits."

"Have you discussed this with him?" I ask, disturbed by the fragility of Wrik's network pair-bond with Jaelle. I had thought this was a permanent link.

"You will find that males of any species rarely think about the future, much less plan for it. No, Wrik and I might become consorts—"

"Consorts?"

"It's like a marriage, a legal interspecies relationship, not necessarily exclusive, as we are of different species and need different things. We may become consorts, but he is not Nekoan. There are things that he cannot do for me, or I for him.

"I have powerful feelings for him. But he is an alien. We use the same words for things, but do they even mean the same thing?

"You ask these questions and yet, other than sex, our relationship is not so different from yours. I don't know that his feelings for you aren't as deep, or deeper than his for me."

"Other than the sex," I muse. "Isn't that like saying that other than breathing, you and I are the same? Is not sex one of the primary motivations of biological existence? Your entire cultures seem devoted to it."

"Perhaps. It just seems to me that his heart gets divided between us."

"Maybe we are simply in different parts of it, taking up different places that would not otherwise be used."

I am relieved when my board lights up, ending the conversation. We are being scanned. I am alarmed. My Infestor arm resonates to a searching signal that probes the ship. There is a resonance I did not expect, having purged and tamed the arm to my own use. Perhaps it is some form of IFF. Buried in the Infestor arm's basic matrix is something that responds to the call from the Artifact ahead.

I have not planned on such a contingency and am locked in an immediate battle within myself. My M-7 persona bids me attack my own arm, ripping it off if need be. But I have learned from my previous battles with my old programs. I use my subroutines for self-repair, intelligence-gathering, and keeping myself combat ready. The imperative fades and I can control myself.

"Maauro, are you all right?" Jaelle asks. She has noticed my sudden freeze-up.

"Yes, but we are being probed by the Artifact. There is power and something aware in this object. It has recognized that some part of me is Infestor. There was a subatomic resonance in the arm, something programmed at the electron level that responded to that sensor sweep. Now that it has manifested and I know the mechanism, I can block it."

"It thinks you are one of them?"

"I do not believe it is that complicated a program. I sense a very low-level subroutine, as if this was something left on long ago, probably to prevent space junk from striking the Artifact. The fact that I resonated simply means it did not look further at me. I could have been something from its own surface blown or knocked into orbit, or one of its own probes."

"Let's get down before it decides to take a second look," Jaelle says. "There's an immense landing field there. Shall we land there?"

"Not on the near end," I say, studying the wide, flat space, large enough for a fleet to land. "We will pass over and land on the far side. If the Collector is as impatient as you say, she will land on the first open space. I wish to be close enough to her to rescue Wrik but not so close that they see us on the surface."

An hour later, I spot a likely landing space and start us down. We land on the immense Artifact between two large pylons.

"What are those?" Jaelle asks, looking up at them as we ground.

"Flak towers for destroying small ships."

Jaelle grimaces. "Like ours."

"If they were going to fire on us, they would have done so long ago. Either the defenses are quiescent, or they have accepted us. Perhaps they have detected the active Infestor tech in my arm."

"Low-order intelligence for such a machine."

"Or the opposite," I reply. "A low-order intelligence, detecting an incorrect IFF or signal, would simply fire. Only a high-order one would take the time to wonder why after 50,000 years there is a new outside Infestor contact. I suspect that the Collector's ship with its Infestor cargo will also be allowed to land for that reason."

I keep my hands on the throttle and controls, but nothing strikes us as we settle on our fins. I cut the drive.

"The Artifact has artificial gravity," I say.

"I noticed my tail didn't float off," she shot back.

I ignore the non-sequitur. Jaelle is often irritable when afraid.

She gestures out the viewport. "It's immense, but what is it? A space fortress, a ship, a station—"

"It is none of those. Impressive though it is, it would be a simple target for nuclear and plasma weapons. No, this looks as if it was made for something else, perhaps an evacuation vessel for colonies in danger of being overrun. Whatever it is, I must go into it. My programming bids me destroy this place."

Pity and disbelief war in Jaelle's face.

I shrug. "I have no choice."

"What of Wrik?" Jaelle demands.

"The Collector will land at the first large space that can hold her ship. We passed over the most likely choice a few minutes ago. She has not come so far to hold back now. She will bring Wrik along in the hope it will protect her from me."

"Will it?"

I look away unwilling to meet her eyes. "I hope so." My voice sounds weak even to my own receptors. "I will, if I can, rescue Wrik, or create the conditions for him to escape."

"What do you want me to do?"

"Remain here and defend the ship with the crab robots in the hold. Wait as long as you can for Wrik and me. I will take a homer for him to find his way to you if I cannot accompany him back to the ship. If he arrives without me, take off immediately."

"And leave you behind? Do you judge me a false friend or a coward?"

"Neither. Jaelle, the odds that either of us will regain the ship are minimal. If random chance so favors Wrik, you must leave."

"Wrik will never agree."

"Do not ask him. Take off the instant you get him aboard."

"Maauro, I have not agreed."

I smile at her. "Brave, Jaelle. No wonder Wrik cares for you so. But I have no more time to argue. My programming demands I go."

To my surprise she comes over and embraces me. "Good luck, Kit-sister."

I nod and quickly descend, gathering the tools and weapons I have prepared. I exit through the cargo bay, instructing the three crab robots to guard the ship and respond to Jaelle. I am alone now, striding across the Artifact's surface under the strange, bar-like stars. While my exterior remains the same, Maauro is receding within me. I am becoming the nameless M-7, who possessed only a serial number. The enemy is in sight and I am again a weapon.

***

The ship settled toward the Artifact. Ferlan's impatience didn't even allow for a single orbit. "Maauro is down already. If something was going to attack, it would have struck her ship, bearing their worse enemy. Now we must land soon and locate the nearest large entry."

"Very well," Marcel said.

"That looks like a landing stage coming up, biggest one so far," said one of the bridge officers.

"Arrange for a landing," Marcel said. "Take her down slowly. Be alert for anti-shipping weapons."

"All this looks new," Ferlan said, her voice almost musical with excitement. Her eyes shone and she looked younger. I thought that she must have been quite beautiful in her youth. "No craters, no pitting, it could have been commissioned yesterday."

"Yes," I replied, "impossibly so. It's spent 50,000 years rolling around a system where the star blasted most of the planets to rubble with a collapse. Somehow it's been defending itself. Or something is different about time down here."

"Yes," she said, nodding, "that must be it. It would explain the boundary layers we passed through coming down here. It's an event horizon of a sort. On one side time hardly seems to move at all."

"Yet our biological processes do not seem affected," Marcel added. "If time stands still, how is it that our hearts, our lungs are not affected?"

I looked at him in surprise.

"Eh," he said, "just because I can bend the iron bars with my bare hands does not mean I do not use my brain. I surmise that there are two layers, a main one which stops time and another one inside, where time again moves. Perhaps slowly, we cannot tell, mes amis, as our measuring sticks have been reset to what you could call local time."

"Look at that section," the flight officer said. Again the screen flicked and we saw a discolored section of the hull, an indicator gave a sense of scale. The damaged section was thirty times the length of the *Hummel*. The patch looked as if someone had poured liquid metal and smoothed the torn edges.

"Looks like the sort of repair one makes to a particle beam hit, only vastly larger," Marcel said. "Rough work. That was not done in a shipyard."

So," Ferlan mused. "It was attacked and damaged at some time."

"The first expedition did not see this," Marcel said. "Their instruments were not capable of this resolution and they didn't get this close. If it was hit once, it may have been hit a number of times. This may explain why it has been here so many millennia, anchored to a dying sun in the middle of nowhere. It may have been damaged and like the Captain who discovered it, hiding out."

"As good an explanation as any," Ferlan agreed.

The Collector's vessel drifted down on the apron of a landing stage for something far larger than *Hummel*, though there were no landing lights. We sank into what looked like a valley, lined with cranes and conveyers.

"Come, Wrik," Ferlan said. "We have an adventure to begin."

"How about I just stay here and keep the home fires burning?"

"No nonsense, now," she said. "I have waited most of my life for this day."

I followed Marcel and Ferlan down several decks and into a large, wheeled transport with a small turret on top, one of three such in a line on the deck, punctuated with an armored car at either end of the column. Lights flared and sirens whooped as the deck crew evacuated the deck prior to depressurization. The giant clamshell doors rolled back in depressurized hull.

Marcel cursed softly and I spotted his concern. A can of lubricant had been left on deck and burst during the depressurization. A cloud of oil spread from it, to his evident disgust.

"Sloppy deck crew," I said, drawing a dark glare. Ferlan looked back from her spot near the driver and wagged a finger at me.

But Marcel seemed disposed to laugh it off. "Mon Dieu, but what can be expected from such morons?"

We drove onto the rough surface of the Artifact, across the landing stage to a series of giant doors. Guilders were already working with immense power jacks to lift the outer doors. To my surprise, the smallest of the doors lifted. The jacks braced it and the entire column drove into the space beyond. Some of the Guild party stayed on the other side to let the jacks down, sealing the outer airlock. Others brought in still more jacks and started work on the inner doors.

"The airlock is repressurizing," Marcel announced. "Looks like a bit of a hurricane out there." As if to confirm his statement the car rocked a little.

The work crew levered up the inner airlock, but in proof that the Artifact was not totally dead, the inner door rose above the lifting jacks reach. A few small lights showed a labyrinth of huge passages beyond.

"I don't know what worries me more," Marcel said, "the lack of any response, or the presence of power and artificial gravity."

"It may be merely good automatics," Ferlan said. "We have seen evidence of their technological superiority before. Bid them move out."

"Recon out," Marcel ordered over the radio.

"Flinss," Ferlan called, switching to another screen to reveal the hatchet-faced scientist. "How are the Infestors?"

"Quiet," she said. "I've fed and watered them. Still, I get the oddest impression they are listening for something."

"Very well, let me know if there are any changes."

Our vehicle started up, second in line as we rolled out of the immense airlock.

Ahead lay the dark bare metal of the Artifact, grooved for traction as if intended for us. Beyond was cavernous space. Our vehicles bumped their way down the ramp, moving slowly; gravity was about two-thirds of normal. Once we were in, the advance crew lowered the inner doors.

"Atmosphere is normal," Marcel reported. "Advance team says it smells funny but there is nothing worse than that."

"Wouldn't expect it," Ferlan said. "We all like the same real estate."

***

I approach an access hatch; it is crudely over-engineered, simple and merely mechanical. When I insert filament sensors into it, I find only rudimentary wiring, reinforcing my belief that massive as the Artifact is, it was constructed quickly. My filaments sever the electronics of the hatch with a millisecond laser burst. Quickly I let myself into an access trunk for piping and electronics. I check the massive cables bundled alongside me, finding only a trace of power, so low it might be a false echo. There is plenty of room for me to move. Even Infestor work drones are far bigger than I am.

Once I close the hatch, I am in pitch-blackness. IR and radar are not sufficient and I use visible light emitted from my eyes. I am unhappy about the target it makes but my CPU is buried deep in my chest, which is some comfort.

I move deeper through the outer shell of the Artifact, which is made of many branching trunks like this one, and lining layers of armor. I descend over one hundred meters through the outer layer before I again find myself facing a hatch. This more robust mechanism is clearly an airlock for workers. I open the hatch after a quick study. Fortunately, as an intruder unit, I am programmed with Infestor language and script. I see a lifting panel at the bottom of the airlock. Rather than use it, I drop to the floor, grateful for the padded bottoms of my boots that deaden the sound of my armored body dropping four meters. A door faces me, which tells me that the Artifact's interior is like that of a ship, with the artificial gravity biased so decks are horizontal.

There is no power in this mechanism and I extrude a filament to power the doors. The overhead hatch seals and a reading shows on the inside airlock; there is atmosphere on the other side. The gauges tell me the atmosphere is breathable. While I am indifferent to atmosphere so long as it is not corrosive, this could mean live Infestors on the other side.

Cautiously I open the door, retracting the filaments into my hand. The temperature on the other side is cold by biological standards and no attack greets me. Instead, I am in a corridor that extends until it curves out of sight in the distance both ways. Hundreds of doors line the bulkheads and there are many corridors leading inward. The scale of the Artifact I have come to destroy daunts me, but I move out. There is no cover, so I stride down the center of the hall.

A peculiar feeling comes over me as I skulk through the empty corridors, passing ranks of sealed rooms. I feel a mix of emotions: exhilaration that I am doing what I was created to do and an anxiety that I might perish here, unseen by my friends. The endless maze of silent corridors is so far from the beautiful worlds and vistas that I have seen with my friends Wrik and Jaelle. Why should I be here alone, possibly to be destroyed and entombed without even the stars for company? After my 50,000-year sojourn in the asteroid, to again face such a prospect fills me with dread.

I throttle down these unfamiliar and unhelpful emotions. I am M-7, made for war. I ask no quarter and give none. I must put aside Maauro and her dreams in order to continue my mission. I have no room for weakness.

For lack of a better attack plan I continue to the left, my arbitrary west. I am heading for the nearest large landing stage. The Collector should cross over it if she follows our approach vector. My analysis is that she will land as soon as she can, held firmly in the grip of her obsessions, but wishing to deploy her maximum force. Given that her vessel is similar to a landing barge, this means wheeled or tracked vehicles requiring a large entrance. It will be useful to use her forces to spring any traps present and I may be able to secure the release of the biological Trigardt, so long as mission objectives are not impaired. I march on.

The Artifact is not decrepit, and indeed other than a heavy layer of dust, it could have been built recently. My sensors give me anomalous readings whenever I attempt to gauge anything about age. I am puzzled that no automatics have attacked me, even if there are no live Infestors remaining aboard. Their cybernetics were not as advanced as ours, but their weapons technology was.

I pass through what must have been a staging area. A large number of Infestor light armor units are present, but they have been packed and preserved and are not a threat. Still there is more power here. I see some telltales on the walls from operating systems and douse my eye-lights. There is now sufficient illumination for my night vision to be effective. I exit the assembly area on a corridor road down which the vehicles must have been driven. I pass larger machine areas, possibly factories and some sections that look like hive living quarters, but I see no sign of the enemy.

Nothing I have seen will provide me with a means of destroying the Artifact. Even overloading my powerplant would cause only localized damages, the blast smothered under billions of tons of metal. I will need to delve deeper, seeking magazines, engines or control spaces in order to follow my imperative.

Suddenly I detect a familiar silhouette and level my armspac at it. But this Infestor is no longer a threat. I race forward to examine the desiccated body, lying half in a side room, possibly living quarters for it. The Infestor is parchment-like skin over bone, with rags of fabric over it and a pack of tools alongside. This is a worker unit without the overdeveloped claw hand of the fighters, intelligent, but with little sense of individuality, almost a biological robot. It may have been securing this room when it simply expired. The body has been here a long time, but clearly not anywhere near the 50,000 years that have elapsed.

The factors line up for a solution in my CPU; time inside the light and gravity well the Artifact lairs in, is moving at a different rate than in normal space. This place must have been a lifeboat, or an ark, for the remaining Infestors. They hid in here, hoping to outlast the Creators, using some form of new drive to twist space and time. As I ponder the corpse at my feet, I remember the Murch and their transdimensional drive. I'd studied the unit when I repaired the shielding that kept them safe. The principles on which that prototype drive worked were new to the Murch and poorly understood, but a transdimensional drive must alter time and space to function. The Infestors may have stumbled on similar principles, creating a pocket universe to hide in.

But where are they?

Lights flicker on and an alarm sounds in the distance. There is a rumbling vibration through the floor. I sweep my weapon around, but no target presents itself. I check my internal chronometer. The Collector could have landed two hours ago. I suspect that she has been down for some time and has now forced an entrance. She has awakened something in the Artifact.

I move through yet another great chamber, closing in on the source of vibrations and energy disturbances that are likely caused by the Collector's forces. Suddenly I detect infantry. Soldiers are flitting from cover to cover. As they are bipeds, I assume them to be Guild. They bring light. A questionable choice but biologicals prefer their own senses to mechanical ones, even when those are the better choice. The area is one of broad-ramps for moving large numbers of troops. I race up one ramp and secure myself in some overhead piping, bending my limbs out of humanoid shape. Biological eyes normally need patterns to recognize objects.

Enemy infantry pass below me, followed seconds later by an armored car with a heavy gun turret, followed by another odd, long vehicle. It is not an AFV but some sort of cargo/personnel carrier for all that it has a clearplast-turret with a medium gun. Two more follow. In the second and third I pick up the clear bio-psionic signal of living Infestors. My enemy is below. I overcome my immediate impulse to attack. Their psionic signatures are basic, almost imbecilic, and they do not detect me. The fifth vehicle is another AFV like the first, with some additional troops bringing up the rear. Sound tactics, but I am M-7 and even Infestor tech is hard-pressed to locate me.

I realize that the image the Maauro program prefers for our body is inadvisable. The dark orange and gray are replaced by black, including my face and limbs. I pull off the ridiculous yellow hair ribbon as I retract the impractical long hair, wondering why it has taken me so long to realize the need. I have in some fashion deteriorated, allowing combat-readiness to be affected by concerns of image and appearance. I ball the yellow silk up to fling it away and something stops me. I debate for a microsecond then open a chamber in my body and place the yellow ribbon safely within. I tell myself that someone might identify me by it but know that this is not the case. The Maauro program continues to assert itself in troubling and unpredictable ways.

Satisfied, I nullify their motion detector sensors then follow the column, a shadow within shadows, freezing every time visible light falls on me. I am well above the guards and unless I am unlucky, they are not likely to spot me.

***

We rolled on, marveling at the vast size of the Artifact.

"I've never seen such huge interior spaces," Ferlan murmured, her eyes drinking in every detail of the walls and halls. "They seem impractical."

I gazed at the monsters on Flinss' screens. "Perhaps not so much; those are large creatures and you said they were juveniles. They're already nearly twenty feet long. They don't seem like the sort of critter that likes close company."

"Yes, very likely," she said absently.

"You should have left them back on your ship under guns," I added.

Ferlan didn't even glance at me, though Marcel did and I thought I saw agreement in the big man's eyes. I remembered the tale of the first captain to own the probe. Ferlan believed he fell prey to it through close contact, but I wondered if there weren't subtler perils. Given how much she wanted the

Artifact and its secrets, could it be that hard to influence her? Still she said the things were nearly moronic, and at least the probe itself had been left behind.

"Makes for big ships," Marcel said.

Ferlan looked up at him, an eyebrow raised.

"The vessels must be so much larger per being carried, more mass for life support and crew quarters, n'est pas?" he said.

"Oui, it would give us an advantage fighting them ship to ship," she nodded then turned back to me. "Where in this vast mass do you think we may find Maauro?"

I shrugged. "Knowing her, she is deep inside, looking to blow this thing up."

"Let us hope not," she replied.

The sounds of footsteps made me turn. I was surprised to see Dusko, like myself without a helmet, coming up to the driver's deck, accompanied by a woman who looked way too pretty to be a guard, but for the ugly, short-barreled gun she carried. For a second I was happy to see even his face.

"Dusko," Ferlan said, a chill in her voice.

He made a bowing gesture with a sweeping hand. "Madame Ferlan."

"I trust you are interested in demonstrating some small use to me."

"Absolutely."

"Wrik will doubtless lie whenever I ask him anything about Maauro. You will tell me when he does."

"Certainly."

"Wrik believes she is racing to the core of the machine to destroy it. I believe she is stalking us in the hope of rescuing him."

Dusko gave me a long look; I stared back, expressionless.

"In this I believe he tells you the truth, Maauro is prisoner of her original programs. She will proceed directly to attack and destroy what she sees as an infestation. Friendships, or networks, as she thinks of them, will not count against her primary objective."

Ferlan bit her lip, and looked at Marcel. "Redouble the pace. We do not have the time to be this cautious. We must get to the lower levels. We must either find these control spaces ourselves or establish contact with any AI or Infestors aboard this ship."

I exchanged stares with Dusko as the others turned back to the screens. Gradually I edged closer as Ferlan and Marcel rapped out orders and received reports from evidently dismayed Guilders, who did not like the thought of racing headlong into the unknown. The vehicle's engine growled louder.

"Maauro can be quite predictable," Dusko whispered.

"Guess we'll find out when this place goes nova around us."

"Oh, she doubtless plans to destroy the Artifact, but she is not reckless, our Maauro. There is a force moving through the Artifact that she can use to test her enemy and not reveal herself. Now that force is moving very quickly and noisily. It will please her no doubt. I imagine she is close by, waiting for something to kill us all, and save her the trouble."

I grunted a response.

"Aren't you going to assure me that she's going to save us?" Dusko asked.

"No."

"Well, you, anyway. I merely hope to be collateral salvage."

"Don't bet on it. She'd expend herself to take this place out. Why think we would measure so much in such an equation?"

Whatever Dusko was going to say was lost when the universe in my head exploded.

***

I stalk the Collector's forces as they roll forward. They are following a main "roadway" into the heart of the Artifact. Eventually, they should hit a major control center. This suits my purpose well. If there is an ambush, it will strike them, not me, and I still entertain the hope of recovering my biological companion intact.

As I crawl through the piping above the force, a sense of unease builds in me second by second. I sense a higher-order Infestor intellect. The Artifact is not dead. The enemy is here; his telempathic impulses strike my shield, alerting me. Fortunately my shield does not return a signal to give my presence away, yet I feel as if the intelligence is questing for me. The quality of the thought is what confuses me. The mind or minds seem rigid, mechanical. Infestor AI's partook of their master's telempathic power but on a drastically less powerful wavelength. This feels more and more like a warrior or scientist.

I extend my sensor net as far as I dare in passive mode, hoping to detect more. Is it an AI in the station or a living enemy? Where?

Realization strikes. My enemy has a new trick. The AI of the Artifact has been responding, waking in response to stimuli like my Infestor arm and the three juveniles brought by the Collector. But it is doing far more. The juveniles ahead in the Collector's convoy are juveniles no longer. Somehow personalities have been downloaded into them. They radiate malice, power and deadly intent. I sense them gather their power.

I accelerate, but it is too late. A wave of power rolls out of the Infestors from inside the armored cars. At the same instant, hordes of Infestor work drones pour out of the side corridors and into the Guild troops who are staggering, clawing at the helmets on their heads as the raw force of the empowered juveniles overwhelms the pathetic beta dampeners protecting them.

Irony. I open fire from my armspac as I drop to the floor, blasting waves of freshly-hatched work drones into fragments, buying the Guild time to recover. The work drones are so fresh that they are not yet dry from hatching. They are small, little larger than a tall human; their minds are so unformed I did not even detect them, masked by the power of the Collector's Infestors. Still, they carry powerful claws and teeth and race forward with no concern for their survival.

Some Guilders have recovered enough to open fire. One of the armored cars blazes out with its heavier weapons. But the rush of drones crests like a wave over the Guild troops and vehicles. The air and frequencies are cacophonous with screams, curses and the deafening sound of weapons in a confined space.

I must destroy the Collector's Infestors before they get away. The surviving Guilders, battling desperately, are too busy to impede me, but the drones turn in their hundreds and swarm me. More pour into the confined space every second. I empty my armspac into the charging horde until they crash onto me. In seconds I am submerged under thousands of pounds of slashing, biting drones. My armspac is crushed by jaws and claws.

I am made of sterner stuff. I extend the palm blade in my Infestor arm, trigger the plasma torch in my original arm, and advance. I am literally wading through the destroyed and dying bodies of my enemies; the teeth and claws slide impotently off my body.

I cut my way to the top of the living mass on me then leap into the air. A ghastly image presents itself. Only three of the vehicles are in sight, though the flash of heavy weapons around the curve ahead tells me the others are still in the fight. Two of the transports near me are burning. Their hatches are ripped open, with dead and dying Guilders hanging out of them. The floor of the roadway cannot be seen for the drones fighting and dying on them.

I am rewarded by the sight of at least two of the Collector's Infestors, many times the size of the drones and brilliantly colored. They have been liberated from the burning cars and are being escorted by echelons of drones. They see me at the same instant and dive for the floor under a cover of drone bodies. My flechettes fire down on them, but most are stopped by drones that splay their bodies out for maximum cover.

I crash down into the drones, which bite, claw and beat at me. The blows do minor shock damage. My plasma torch is a close-range weapon and I turn it to full, carbonizing a circle around myself.

A Guilder is at the bottom of the pile. His face is mindless with fear and panic. He takes advantage of my blazing attack to run but is torn to pieces by a fresh wave of drones. I seize his particle weapon and again fling myself toward the ceiling thirty meters away.

I see only one warrior now and he is thinking the same thing I am. The Guild weapon looks ridiculously tiny in his giant claw hands, but he manages to trigger the laser and the beam waves across my midsection. I return fire with flechettes and the Guild particle weapon. He ducks behind his ramparts of drones, which explode into bloody fragments. We hit each other again and his head explodes.

I fall among the seething mass of drones and know defeat. I have killed one, but only because it stayed behind to direct the drones, battle me, and ensure the escape of his comrades. My heat sinks are full. Between the plasma torch, laser hits and the nonstop shock of masses of drones, I am perilously near shutdown. The sheer weight of meat and bone on me is slowing me further. I must retreat.

I shut down my plasma torch and simply tear my way to the top of the carpet of drones. The terrific heat I am radiating is as much a weapon as anything I carry. Again I leap to the ceiling, grasp the pipes, and begin to scuttle away.

A high-explosive shell slams the piping behind me and freezing gas deluges from it. The Guild are firing at me. A direct hit from an armored car could severely damage me. But my luck holds. The deluge of liquid oxygen blocks visual and infrared tracking, cools my overheated body and eliminates hundreds of drones near me. Refreshed, I flee.

I listen to the enemy intel as I move. The Guild encryption is poor; they rely too much on their secret language, which I know. I infiltrate their communications undetected.

"Madam, they are retreating. Mon Dieu, we have them on the run."

"Not so," returns a voice I recognize as Ferlan. "They have accomplished their objective, freeing the ones we brought. How many of our people are left?"

"About half but with many wounded. I am putting them in the two functioning cars."

"Any sign of Wrik or Dusko?"

"Pah, no sighting of the pigs. I cannot believe that boy could fling men around like that, even me. I will kill both of them when I find them."

"You will not. They were under Infestor control. It gave them the strength of the insane, something I did not anticipate. They are likely both dead, but if not, we must recover them. They may be on their way to talk to the powers here."

"Madam, we must flee—"

The sound of weapons fire overloads the tac net for a few seconds.

"—we must get back to the ship."

"There are too many behind us," Ferlan says. "We are cut off. No, the way ahead is no less perilous than the road behind. We must somehow establish communication with the Infestors or find Maauro."

I know a moment of sorrow, then my resolve firms. Trigardt was contaminated by Infestor control as was Dusko. The latter does not interest me. I simply change his IFF to enemy. But Wrik bears the stain of Infestor contamination as well. My imperative is operating in full force. It changes Wrik's status to unreliable.

CHAPTER
27

I STAGGERED UP IN AN UNRECOGNIZABLE WORLD, WONDERING where I was, then, for a few terrifying seconds, who I was. The dissonance in my mind, perhaps even in my soul, relented second by second. I remembered myself as Wrik Trigardt, little enough to be proud of until I remembered the person before Wrik.

Smoke bit at my nose and I flinched from heat. The world around me gradually resolved into recognizable shapes. I was beside a wrecked armored transport. Hatches lay open and the bodies of Guilders and things I recognized as Infestors lay all around. The Infestors were small and pallid, nothing like the monsters we brought.

That brought my head around. I looked backwards in the cargo compartment. The cage that held the one we carried was ripped open, its metal bent and scorched. Images flooded back to me of myself, berserk with a power and speed I'd never possessed before, crashing into shocked Guilders, even flinging Marcel out of the way, firing a seized weapon wildly at anything near me.

I looked about, but there was no sign of Ferlan or Marcel. The only Guild I could see were dead. Something dripped on me. I glanced up at the Guilder who'd manned the top turret. She was dead, torn nearly in half and hanging out of the turret. I was so numb that I didn't even fight nausea as I climbed up and liberated the sidearm still belted on the lower half of her partially severed body.

I groaned after reaching up, every muscle and bone I had aching from the insane fury the Infestors had plunged into my mind. I opened my med kit and pressed a trauma tab from it against my chest. It hissed analgesics, anti-inflammatories and tailored virus that would rebuild and stitch muscle and ligament.

I spotted a pair of legs under the vehicle, twitching and kicking. I ducked to get away from the smoke and the sparking of shattered electronic panels and crab-walked to the back, stepping over and around bodies and bits of bodies. I leaned under and saw Dusko staring upwards, his eyes blank, his mouth hanging open. The pupilless eyes turned toward me and intelligence returned to them.

"What...what happened?" he asked. "Gods, I feel like I've been hit by an aircar."

"The Collector forgot the old adage, 'Watch out. You may get what you're after.'"

"Enough riddles, Human."

I tossed him a trauma tab. He pressed it against his chest. The tab bleeped then decided it could treat his physiology and triggered.

"Those damn Infestors we brought were laying low. Somehow they acquired a lot more power than Ferlan expected. They were able to stun most of the Guild and take you and me over. We must have released the one in here. They coordinated an attack with these... I don't know what they are, newly hatched bugs, dwarfs. Whatever. They're deadly enough en masse."

"Is anyone alive?", Dusko asked.

"I hear firing down the hallway ahead of us, but I haven't found anyone in here. You and I probably only survived because we were under Infestor control. I didn't see Ferlan or Marcel's bodies inside. They must have gotten away. We'd better do the same."

He stared at me. "And go where?"

"First things first. We stay alive and free. Remember, Maauro is out there somewhere."

"Forgive me if that prospect does not fill me with the same optimism that it does you."

"You got a better plan?"

"No, both sides here will probably kill us, so we are better off running."

I headed for the back of the transport, stepping around the back ramp, which was partly down and jammed with Infestor corpses.

Both of us froze at the sheer horror of the tableau in front of us. The massive roadway lay filled with smoke and floored as far as the eye could see in all directions with Infestor corpses with the occasional dead and dismembered Guilder thrown in. Behind us, the transport that had carried the other two Infestors was burning. Ahead I could see an armored car had slammed into a wall, but it was too far to determine if anyone was alive in it.

A machine-gun stuttered beyond that, but we could not see the action. So some of the Guild still lived and fought.

Nothing lived near us and we picked our way back the way we'd come, heading to a gaping side corridor that was not choked with death. We searched for weapons as we went, but the Infestors bore none, and the Guild weapons were as damaged as the bodies themselves

I gestured to the dimly lit side hall large enough to accommodate one of the armored cars. Light panels in the ceiling cast a sullen glow and the hall stretched out of sight, curving to the left. "This way."

Dusko stared back at the destroyed column. Again there was a bang and a stutter of gunfire.

"You want to go back to your Guild buddies," I snapped, "feel free." I was torn between my desire to be free of him and the fear of treading the long corridors of the Artifact alone, pursued by Infestors.

Dusko shook his head. "From the volume of fire, there are either few of them left or they are not hard-pressed. I think the latter. But they are being herded farther in to the Artifact. No, I will stick with you in hope of running into your metal girlfriend."

We trotted down the endless hallway, relieved to be away from the sea of bodies.

"The universe enjoys irony," Dusko huffed.

"How's that?" I said, also fighting for breath.

"Here I am, being pursued through an ancient alien relic, despised and distrusted by your side and a target for the Guild, with Maauro hunting us down. This is the set of circumstances I engineered for you when you first met her."

"We call that karmic justice."

"Karmic?" the Dua-Denlenn said, confused.

"You reap what you sow."

"Did you come from farmers?"

"Forget about it. Let's concentrate on staying alive."

I paused, peering into the dimness. A pool of light formed by a telltale on the wall cut a soft circle in the floor but made the darkness on the other side more impenetrable.

"What?" Dusko said. I furiously motioned him to silence.

Something moved, coming toward us slowly, haltingly as if injured. The slim shape stepped into the light and stopped, shaking slightly.

I stared, heart pounding, uncertain. The image was black from head to toe, but it was clearly Maauro, as I had first met her on the asteroid. Only more so, the face was rudimentary, mechanical, the body sexless and slab-sided. Black onyx panels stood in for her huge aquamarine eyes.

Suddenly the machine shuddered and for a second I saw a white face and green eyes. "Run, Wrik, Run," Maauro screamed in a voice like tearing metal. Then she was gone and the M-7 staggered forward.

We dodged left into a hallway, up a ramp to the next level, running fast, our lungs burning in the acrid air. We ran until we dropped, retching at the other side of a large factory room full of humming equipment.

"Why...why?" Dusko gasped, lying on the floor. For all his slim build, the Dua-Denlenn was a good deal older than I and looked done in. "Why? Me I can understand. She's always planned to kill me. But you?"

"It's...it's not Maauro," I managed, leaning on a wall with buzzing motes in my eyes and a ringing in my ears. "Not as we know her. It's the machine I met at the asteroid, the M-7 combat android." I looked at the laser I had picked up off the dead Guilder. It hadn't even occurred to me to use it, which was one reason we were still alive. If I had raised it, M-7 would have ended me.

"It didn't kill you then. Why now?"

"Infestors," I said wearily. "The damn things mind-controlled us. The M-7 must have some way to detect those who've been controlled, like a doctor checking for infection. We're the infected now. Not overwritten like Bavara and the others, but contaminated enough that we are reclassified as enemy by the M-7."

"You talk about the M-7 like it's a separate being," Dusko said, climbing slowly to his feet, legs shaking.

I thought about it. "It seems sometimes that she thought that way herself. She seemed to hold internal debates with her programming, especially after the Collector triggered her imperative to destroy Infestors. It happened once before. She was badly damaged by your ambush on Kandalor, when we were shot out of the sky, and operating on her core combat systems. For a few seconds, until she reactivated her higher functions, she didn't know me.

"I think that here in the enemy stronghold, she's dominated by her core programs. Not totally, or we'd never have gotten away. No, we escaped because some fragment of Maauro is still in there, fighting for us."

Dusko laughed bitterly. "It's a machine, not a demonically-possessed soul."

"Come up with your own fucking explanations then." Recovered, I stood away from the wall. "We need to get moving."

"To where?" he said. "We'll never make it back to the Collector's forces even assuming she has not been destroyed. This ship will be swarming with these Infestors in only hours. We don't even know where we are. Worse, your killer android can't be that far behind us. We can't outrun her."

"We can't outfight her, either."

"Be less sure, human. This is a cargo packing area."

"How—"

"Form follows function. The machinery looks similar enough. We need to find something here with which we can destroy her.

***

I reel. I am disoriented. I am two identities, two programs locked in mortal combat in my CPU. I am M-7. All biologicals on the Artifact are classified hostile. I exist to destroy Infestation. I am M-7.

I am Maauro. I defend my friends. Wrik is mine. You will not destroy him.

The Maauro program fouls my targeting, making my feet unsteady. I pursue the targets with fractional efficiency.

I am M-7 and must destroy the Infestation

I, Maauro, concur. They are evil and must be destroyed.

The Artifact must be destroyed.

Maauro concurs.

All biologicals must be destroyed.

Negative. Wrik and Jaelle must not be targeted. They must be allowed to escape the combat zone.

All biologicals bear electromagnetic and electrochemical traces of Infestor control and are contaminated and unreliable. They must be destroyed.

I will not allow you to hurt Wrik.

You must be purged. You are incompatible with mission objectives.

You are incorrectly interpreting mission objectives that are 50,115 years out of date and degraded by damage and time. You are functioning poorly.

I am functioning as intended by the Creators. You are a corruption of their programming. I will delete you. I will destroy the Infestation.

I regain control and lurch forward, still hampered by the Maauro program. My defenses to it are holding, but my efforts to delete it are stymied. The Maauro program seems to center on the biological Trigardt. If I destroy him, the Maauro program may cease interfering with my mission objectives.

I pursue the biologicals and reclassify their target priority to level one.

***

I stumbled behind Dusko, unsure what to think or even why I cared. Maauro was gone, swallowed in the ancient killing machine she once was. That machine had classed me as an enemy and I knew too much about her to think we could outfight her. And to what point, to fall prey to the Infestor drones? Was the best I could hope for being recaptured by the Collector in time for her last stand?

Dusko flitted from machine to machine, while I tried to understand how we got away, or why she hadn't run us down already. Was she damaged? The body chassis showed no sign of it, being perfectly smooth, but Maauro....M-7 was incredibly resistant to damage.

Could Maauro still be in here, my Maauro, could she be hampering the M-7?

Dusko returned. "Come on. I've found something."

I followed the Dua-Denlenn through the factory. We came to a large machine, nearly the size and shape of a two-story building. Dusko headed into it.

I stopped, looking at the gleaming machinery around me. "Is this safe? It doesn't look like something you should walk into."

Dusko grinned. "Good instincts. It isn't, but it's safe enough now."

I followed him out the other side to a double-door, large by human standards, but tight for an Infestor. The doors were thick, with small, plast-glass panels and they slid smoothly apart. There was power here.

"It's a cuber, a pallet-stacker."

"What?"

"A device for shoving cargo or trash into durable cubes."

We now stood in a small room with a broad, padded seat for the Infestor operator facing a panel of waldos and other instruments, all oversize for human hands.

"What good does this do us?" I demanded.

"Idiot. We lure her in and crush her. I trigger these controls and it will compact her down to 1/10th her size. Even she couldn't survive that."

"Fuck you."

"She'll kill us."

"She hasn't. I think I can reach her."

"She didn't think so. She told you to run for your life."

"I've got to try."

"Have fun. I'll wait here."

"I don't think so," I said, tapping the laser barrel against my thigh.

"You should have used that on her."

"Maauro's reflexes are hundreds of times faster. Pointing a weapon at her would certainly have gotten us killed. I doubt a hand laser would do her any damage anyway.

"No, I have to reach her, somehow. We don't even know where the ship is and we don't have spacesuits to get out to it if we did know."

I looked at the cuber. "Is there some way to set it so we could immobilize her?"

Dusko barked a laugh. "Do you see a manual lying around? A terminal we could log on? Perhaps we could ask the staff for help? Look, with a couple of days I might figure out how to do it. I've been around this kind of cargo machinery all my life, but we don't have the time to learn this machine. She's going to kill us."

"Let's get out of here," I said. "I need time and distance to think."

Dusko hesitated. I gestured with the pistol. I wasn't leaving him here to attack Maauro.

We moved back out between the arms and hydraulic rams of the cuber.

Something went "whuft" past my face and slammed into the cuber behind me.

"It's her," Dusko shouted, backing.

***

The Maauro program waited until I had sighted the primary target to strike. My target lock dissolves and distance weapons flicker in and out of control. I miss my first shot. I elect to attack hand to hand. Biologicals are fragile, even the rebellious Maauro program cannot save them once I close in.

***

We fell back through the cuber, came out the other side and pushed the panels closed behind us. Dusko leapt toward the controls.

"Freeze," I shouted, pointing the laser.

"She's inside. She's coming through," Dusko said, blue eyes blazing. "We have to crush her now. She's not your friend. She never was. She's an ancient killing-machine executing a program.

"Get your hand off that lever or I'll kill you."

"Idiot! Imbecile," Dusko raged. "She'll kill us as soon as she gets in here. Use your brain, not your human heart. She has no choices."

I shot him in the hand. It wasn't mercy. I was afraid if I shot him in the head his hand might spasm on the lever. Dusko gave an anguished cry and fell back. I aimed the weapon at his head to finish him off.

The door slammed open and Maauro stood there. Her face had partially reverted to the corpse-like, waxen look I remembered from our first meeting. Black eyes, empty of anything, stared at me over fingers that I knew were projectile weapons. Her palm blades were extended. I was very conscious of the weapon in my hand.

"Hello, Maauro," I said. "That is your name, you know."

"I hope," Dusko gasped from the floor, "that she kills you first so I get to watch it."

I gestured with my head. "Dusko says you're just a machine, a slave to programming."

The face seemed to shimmer and for a second, her eyes returned to the beautiful aquamarine I wanted to see. The slack, waxy face firmed into its accustomed delicate lines. Then it was gone.

"I remember," I said, moistening my dry lips, "the day you got angry with me. Do you remember too? I said you wouldn't understand something about living beings. You said, 'Wrik, I am a living being.'"

The eyes shimmered again.

"Time to make some decisions, Maauro. Time for you to either be a living being making her own choices, or to cut the charade and be only a killing-machine with no ethics, no morals, no capacity for friendship or love."

Maauro walked forward and seemed to vibrate, as if some internal mechanism was grinding. A blast of heat radiated from her.

"Which is it, Maauro?" I snapped, suddenly beyond fear. "Who are you? Do I have a friend or not? Tell me!"

The ancient android's eyes were flicking from black to aquamarine. Her body vibrated between black and the dark gray and orange. Maauro and the M-7 were fighting for possession of the body in front of me.

The heat from her beat at us. Dusko crawled backwards, clutching his hand. I held my ground, staring into the changing eyes, hoping desperately there was something there. Something that belonged to both of us. Something that said the universe still obeyed some laws and was not mindlessly cruel. Something that said Dusko wasn't right and I wasn't a dead fool.

A flechette shot past my face. I flinched but kept the laser pointed at Dusko on the floor. Maauro had to be in there fighting for her life; neither the M-7 nor Maauro could have missed at this range.

I slid the laser into my belt. "Maauro, I love you."

The vibration slowed, and then stopped. The face staring at me had one black eye and one aquamarine one, as deep as an ocean.

"You're my friend, Maauro. The first one Wrik Trigardt had in his new life. I'd been cast out by my family and friends before and I deserved to be. You were the first person to see any value in me."

The black eye went green and her body changed hue to orange and gray. Her hair lengthened and flowed down her back. She dropped her arm.

"I am a living being," she said in her beautiful, musical voice. "Though I was made, I claim my birthright to be, to do and to act within my own code—not one others have written into me.",

"Maauro," I breathed in relief.

"Wrik."

"Yes."

"I love you too."

I walked over and put my arms around Maauro. She felt warm and smelled like ginger cookies. One day I would have to ask her why. Her arms wound around me: the left one moved slowly, carefully. It lacked the fine control of her right.

I caught sight of Dusko, who sat on the decking looks of confusion, disgust and amazement alternating on his face. I pulled the laser and started to raise it when Maauro put her right hand on mine.

"No. No more killing today, not even him."

"It will have to get done," I said, amazed and appalled by how easily it came out of my mouth.

"No, please. It's not weakness or sentimentality," she added, "but we cannot empty the universe of people who do not behave as we wish. If it is necessary, I will do it. For now, do not hold anything he did against him. M-7 was trying to kill you both."

I looked at Maauro and realized that what I had told the Collector had not turned out to be true. Maauro had needed me and somehow I had managed to live up to that need. Maybe there was some measure of redemption for me, at least with her.

***

"What do we do now?" Wrik asks.

His face is drawn and his eyes signal exhaustion. I am ashamed that I am the cause of this. "When was the last time you had food or water?"

"About eighteen hours ago," he husks.

"First, we must restore you," I say, "then we will plan."

"What about me?" Dusko asks, nursing his wounded hand.

I look at him, tempted to anger but checking it. I have no desire to be ruled by such emotions. "You will be tended to as well. Await me here."

I race off. It is not a long journey before I find a water station and a suitable large container. The water is brackish, but I extrude a filter and render it potable. I then move on quickly to the last place I saw a dead Infestor. Reaching the corpse, I form sharp biting teeth and tear off large chunks. Factories in my body break the organic molecules down and reform them from desiccated meat into innocuous nutrient bars, removing some heavy metals harmful to human and Dua-Denlenn. I even put a pink wrapper on each. While Dusko would likely not care about the source of the food, I fear Wrik's squeamishness. I could generate these bars from even more basic materials, but in this sterile environment it might take days. Also, I am using my other factories to generate bandages and healing gel for Dusko.

I carefully clean myself before returning to them.

They drink the water with desperate relief and eat the pink-wrapped protein bars without suspicion. Wrik even teases me about the wrapper color.

CHAPTER 27

I tend Dusko's laser burn. The gel numbs the wound, rehydrating and repairing the skin. It will take a Dua-Denlenn surgeon or some study by me to repair the damage to the hand. I have extruded a sling from my inner body and something else—a hair ribbon. I am Maauro again. I wear my hair long and I like bright, yellow ribbons.

"Thank you," Dusko says, relief etched in his face.

"I wish no one pain."

"I actually believe you," he replies, "even if I don't understand why."

"Let me help you with that sling," Wrik says gruffly. For all the tone and the angry expression on his face, he too seems to regret the recent violence. He is surprisingly gentle as he tends the Dua-Denlenn's arm and does not meet the alien's bemused eyes.

Friends we are not and may never be, but we are not strangers. Violence between those who are networked is unsettling and fraught with consequences I had never before considered.

"Now that we are somewhat restored," Dusko asks, "what follows?"

I am again surprised by the Dua-Denlenn's easy switch from adversary to ally, how readily he leaves prior resentments and grudges behind, far more so than a human could.

"This place," I say, "from what I have been able to uncover seems to have been a form of ark."

"Ark?" Dusko asks.

"Old Earth word," Wrik responds, "from a story. Think of it as a super-lifeboat for a species fleeing disaster."

I nod. "Well described. While I have never discovered what disaster overtook my Creators, it seems clear that they gained an upper hand in the wars. This vessel is immense, but its construction is crude. Its design shows signs of haste to my analysis. I believe it may have been built near the end of the war. The Infestors intended this Artifact as a redoubt, an ark from which to relaunch their species in a different time and place. Its drive is not the standard space drive of any of our peoples. Some aspects of it remind me of the transdimensional drive of the Murch. A new and unreliable science perhaps, but one which allowed this immense ship-factory and biological treasure house to hide in a bubble of space-time, aging far less rapidly than the galaxy through which it wandered.

"I speculate from observations I made before landing that it was damaged and wandered randomly off course. Perhaps the flight crew, or the main AI, were destroyed or damaged. I doubt they intended to lay somnolent this long. Some AI remained intact and elected to orbit this brown dwarf, a useless coal of a star that no star-farer would likely approach.

"Now that we have arrived, unwisely bringing live Infestors, even if they are the mere equivalent of feral children, and the Artifact is waking up. Not all at once, or properly, but I suspect it is downloading information into the two surviving warriors. They now command the simple worker drones that we have encountered. In a short while those basic drones will begin to change, some into warriors others into science or engineering specialists. They will reinforce each other in the hive mind, eventually producing higher-order queens and finally an Empress.

"We must prevent that. This place must be destroyed."

Wrik and Dusko exchange uneasy looks.

I smile at Wrik. "I am Maauro now and will never be M-7 again, but in this I agree with my Creators' original intentions. This species has been inimical to all life it has encountered. While we and the Infestors were alone in our section of space, we did find evidence that they had enslaved and destroyed others. If not stopped here, they have the potential to do catastrophic harm."

"How can we stop them?" Wrik says, waving his hands at the ship about us. "With what?"

"We must penetrate the command or engineering spaces before the waking drones turn into warriors and begin to fight effectively with weapons. I have an idea, but it must wait until I inspect the machinery.

"After that we can attempt to regain the Stardust and flee with Jaelle."

"Jaelle!" Wrik sits upright. "No. She's here?"

"She was most insistent on accompanying me on this rescue attempt."

"Dammit! I hoped she was safe on Ebosue."

I look at him. "Knowing her as you do, did you believe that was probable behavior for her?"

He sighs. "No. I hoped she would remain behind, or that you, as you were in the grip of your imperative last time I saw you, wouldn't have taken her. I don't know why she takes these risks."

"She believes her network with you is worth maintaining, even at the risk of her existence."

"She shouldn't take such risks, not for me."

"She disagrees. I disagree too."

Wrik continues to look at the floor but he reaches out with his right hand and runs it over my right cheek. It is a characteristic affectional gesture he uses when he is unable to verbalize his thoughts. I am glad I am again Maauro, as M-7's surface was far less pleasingly textured.

"Shall we proceed with eliminating this threat?" I ask.

"I'm with you," Wrik says.

"Is there somewhere else to go?" Dusko grumbles but climbs to his feet.

Wrik offers me the laser.

"No," I reply. "My plasma jets and flechettes are on line and I won't be missing anymore. I am also working on some additional munitions inside my body, unpleasant surprises for our enemies if they can be cooked in time."

Dusko grabs the water can by the bar I have bent around it and we proceed out of the crusher and back into the factory. I search for a cart or something that I can carry the biologicals in. Nearby I find what I need, a work cart. I operate it with a lead from my midsection that conveys power. This should prevent any monitoring system from locating me by a power drain. I convert the remaining Infestor matter inside me to fuel for myself. Hopefully I will find higher quality fuels in the engineering section. We speed down long, darkened corridors and descending *ramps. This section of the ship has not awoken yet. We will not be so fortunate when we get near the command and engineering spaces.*

CHAPTER
28

WE MARCHED IN SILENCE FOR HOURS, TAKING RAMPS, broad stairs, and even occasionally a bare pole that Infestors used for dropping through levels. They evidently didn't fear heights, as one pole seemed to drop nearly a mile. Dusko and I flatly refused to try those, knowing we would be unable to stop ourselves, or handle the fact that the poles were in openings too wide for us to easily mount and dismount them. Maauro solved the problem by holding each of us firmly under one arm as she leapt across and wrapped her legs around the pole. I guessed there were no Infestors within screaming range the first time she tried it. By the fifth time, neither Dusko nor I closed our eyes. By the tenth, it almost seemed a sensible thing to do.

"Is it getting colder or is it just me?" Dusko asked.

"You are correct; it is getting colder," Maauro said. We approached a large door with a smaller personnel hatch in it. Maauro scraped frost off a plast-glass panel. She peered through then cracked the hatch. "The temperature is bearable for several hours but will not be comfortable. The chamber inside is immense. It would take hours to find a way around."

"So through is best," I said.

Dusko merely sighed. "Let get it over with."

We slip in through the hatch, small by Infestor standards, but big enough for all three of us to pass together. The vast room beyond was filled with a variety of tubes of varying thickness, ice-blue, but with dark distortions in them. Their ranks seemed to stretch forever. We moved quickly through the forest of tubes until I came to one that was clearer than the others.

"Damn!" I said, jerking to a stop.

Inside was what looked like a slender girl. For a second I thought it was a human then realized it was a humanoid alien. The body was slight, the hair short, and the features too delicate and elfin for a human. The skin appeared to be gray.

"I do not recognize this species," Maauro said. "We were only aware of the Infestors and our own kind when I was first operational. Wrik, do you know it?"

Something tickled my memory. "A Vanian!"

"What?" Dusko demanded.

"A species wiped out in the Great War with Conchirri predators. Only one was found alive by Captain Rainhell's expedition over fifty years ago. This one must have been captured many millennia ago. Maybe there are others in here."

"The last survivors of a species," Dusko mused. "Could they be revived?"

"We do not have the time to spare, nor do we have the resources to take them with us if we did," Maauro said. Her voice held a tinge of sadness. Perhaps it was the sympathy of one refugee of time for others, but what she said was true.

We looked at acres of tubes containing lifeforms of various types.

"What is this?" Dusko murmured.

"A collection," Maauro replied. "Lifeforms they wanted to keep for when they reestablished themselves."

"You mean like pets?" I said.

"Who knows?" Dusko added.

She nodded and we passed through the vast forest of cylinders, trying to avoid looking at the distorted forms inside their frosted columns.

Maauro stopped suddenly as we entered an open area, waving us back. She turned and whispered to us. "We must find another way. There are Infestor drones uncrating some supplies. They're preoccupied, but we dare not approach."

We backtracked as overhead lights brightened and power sources hummed more loudly. The Artifact was becoming livelier by the minute. I wondered how much longer we could remain undetected.

Maauro gestured to us to follow. We went down a side corridor toward an area that resembled the factory section we'd passed through earlier. She paused occasionally to listen at the walls. We finally reached what looked like a loading area. Maauro went up to a terminal screen and after some hesitation extended her fingertip filaments into it.

A few seconds later she smiled. "Excellent. I have infiltrated this subsystem, which is not hooked to anything significant."

"How does that help?" Dusko asked, looking back the way we came as if he feared a horde of Infestors was around the turn.

"We cannot remain forever undetected wandering the Artifact. The engineering section on this vessel is near the ship's center. This is a cargo chute system. I will look for a cargo carrier that we might use, intrude into the system, and secure us transport."

***

I concentrate. This subsystem is not without its safeguards. But this is not a warship with intruder control stations. I am easily able to reroute cargo carriers by minimally interfering with their programming, below a level that would set off a maintenance program, or worse, a security alert.

Cars of various types stop in front of us. Some are obviously not useful: carriers of liquids, corrosives, or biological material. One carries radioactive elements and I stop this one long enough to extend a shielded tube from my midsection and take on as much fuel as I can. While my system can convert anything to energy, high-level radioactives yield the most energy. I decontaminate myself by absorbing any radioactive sections into my interior and replacing them with clean sections. Then I can safely rejoin the others.

I finally find a gray car with seating suitable for Infestor work drones. This must be a maintenance unit for taking them to the site failures and breakdowns.

"Get aboard," I direct. Wrik and Dusko hesitate. I recall that most biologicals dislike small and dark spaces. "I will provide light."

They climb in behind me and I emit visible light through my eyes. "Secure yourself in the webbing."

"Not exactly comfortable," Wrik says, climbing onto a side bench and putting his arms through webbing and crossing them. Dusko duplicates his position on the other side of the railed, gray-metal car.

"Be warned," I add, "acceleration forces will be considerable."

"Lovely," Dusko says.

The cart plunges forward.

***

The cart pulled away at 2g's or better. A canopy slid over us, blocking out the worst of the rush of wind and we passed into the bowels of the Artifact. There seemed to be a million kilometers of tubing intersecting every two hundred meters. We didn't need Maauro's eye-lights, as the cart turned out to have lights fore and aft. I quickly found this to be a mixed blessing. Other carts flashed by—over, alongside, even intersecting, missing us by meters of programmed perfection. After the first dozen brushes with death, I began to have confidence that we would not be fused into a glowing ball of crushed metal. Then I remembered that the Artifact was over fifty centuries old and, according to Maauro, seemed to have been thrown together in a desperate hurry.

"Reminds me of the amusement parks of my childhood," Dusko shouted, after one particularly sickening drop.

He must have read the surprise on my face. "What, did you think humans invented amusement parks? Or did you imagine that I was never a child?"

"It's difficult," I returned, "to think of a Guildmaster as having once been an innocent child."

Did a look of sadness pass over the Dua-Denlenn's face? "Perhaps there was never much innocence."

I looked back at him directly. Maauro had her eyes fixed ahead and appeared to be ignoring us. "Looking for sympathy? Understanding?"

"Perhaps something like that. I've made it clear that I have thrown in my lot with you, yet you still treat me as an enemy."

"Do you think I've forgotten how you and Truf used me like a dog? Do you think I forget what you made me complicit in? You think I can forgive that?" I spat back.

Dusko shrugged. "I would if our positions were reversed. But you are an alien and how your mind works eludes me. So maintain your war with me if you wish. It is one-sided."

"I'll trust you when hell freezes over. Forgiving will take longer."

"What do you say, Maauro?" Dusko added, a malicious smile playing over his face.

"I am not qualified to mediate between the sensibilities of your two species," she said. "My own moral code is more like that of a human's, I think, though M-7 may have been more like you, Dusko. I agree with Wrik that trusting you will be a long, involved process. Please try not to give us a reason to kill you in the meanwhile."

If the implied threat frightened Dusko, it did not show in his sharp-featured face.

"We are nearing the Engineering levels now," Maauro added.

The car continued to drop through levels and turn through tunnels. After a while I simply closed my eyes, hoping the ride would end before I became nauseated. I did promise myself that I would throw up on Dusko if I couldn't hold out.

Mercifully the repair car slid to a halt. Dusko and I stumbled out. Maauro, immune to vertigo, held us both by the arms and deposited us on the oversize chairs nearby while she moved the car to a sidetrack. By the time she came back, we'd recovered enough to stand.

Maauro pinned herself against the interior hatch, infiltrating it with her finger filaments. "Nothing on the other side," she reported, then rolled back the hatch, and we entered the ship proper again. The sound of massive engines reverberated in our ears: the hum of reactors, the snap of massive electrical circuits opening and closing. Occasionally, we heard something that sounded like a voice booming over us. This part of the ship was fully alive.

I glanced at Maauro. While I had a laser, she was clearly our only real defense. She gazed back, her eyes level and serious, but to my surprise she returned a small smile. I followed her into the ship. We entered the titanic engine spaces and I stared up at the machinery. Reactors the size of office towers stood under circulating fans as big as helo engines hung from the massive pipes girding the ceiling. The hum of engines, fans and circuits opening and shutting was deafening.

Maauro turned and handed us both small earplugs that she must have manufactured in her body. We gratefully put them in. We followed her as she headed for the largest gold and black tower, crowned by a cupola. Maauro seemed to have settled on it as the control center. We moved at a near run, through what felt like the streets of an abandoned city. When we paused at one corner, I asked Maauro where everyone was.

She placed her hand on my head and I heard her through bone conduction. "Remember, the Artifact is waking from a sleep of 50,000 years. Most of its systems must of necessity be automatic, especially in engineering, which had to run constantly. We may also have destroyed most of the quickened drones that were available when they attacked the Collector and me. No doubt more are being decanted, but it takes time for drones to become aware and useful for even simple tasks. Longer still for warriors or anything more complicated to mature. Otherwise, we would not dare move as fast as we have been.

"What Infestors are still alive are likely stalking the Collector's forces. In that much she serves my purposes still."

Maauro moved on and we followed. Block after block, we raced from cover to cover. The only movement we encountered was mechanical. Infestors evidently used their drones for much of what we would use robots for, but still there were some machines. Sweepers, repairbots, and other basic machines scurried from opening to opening in the vast engine room on errands.

Maauro stopped us at another corner and pointed. Five hundred meters ahead and above, a half-dozen pallid drones festooned with equipment marched across a bridge. We cut back and went up the next alley, crossing the broader boulevard there.

And ran straight into an Infestor warrior. We and the warrior froze in surprise. Not so Maauro, who blurred into attack speed, crashing into the Infestor and knocking it off its feet. She slammed her fist down on the crocodilian skull. The Infestor's six-limbs spasmed horribly, then froze.

"Gods," Dusko said, his face ashen. I knew I looked no better.

"It is not one of the Collector's," Maauro said, picking up its plasma rifle, a weapon far too large for either of us to handle. "It is too small, only newly converted from a drone. They must have had a supply of young warriors decanted also. Very few, or we would have seen them in the first attack. Come, the situation grows more dangerous by the minute."

Fatigue forgotten, we raced the remaining steps to the control tower. It took Maauro only seconds to defeat the passive security locks. The panels slid open to reveal more Infestors, small and pallid, handling equipment and machinery. I cut loose with my laser, aiming for a headshot. Maauro fired flechettes. In seconds we picked them off; the last one died in the act of reaching for a large button I was sure was an alarm.

Maauro sealed the panels behind us, spot-welding them with her plasma torch. The deafening noise of the engines became a dull roar. We pulled our earplugs.

"Quickly. Our weapons were quiet but may have been heard. I have disrupted or looped the security systems," Maauro said.

We ran over to a curious form of open elevator, more like a conveyer of platforms at an amusement park. They seemed to roll endlessly, one ten-meter-square platform rolling by every few seconds and disappearing into the ceiling. We jumped on the next one.

"Lie down," Maauro commanded. She knelt in a firing position as Dusko and I lay on the unrailed platform.

The platform rose and took us to the floors above. The first three were full of machinery, sealed cases that hummed with electrical power. The next held banks of machines with Infestor drones seated before them, intent on their controls. I raised my laser but Maauro's hand snapped down on my arm.

"No," she said through conduction. "Drones are very single-minded. If they do not see us, they will not react."

Twice more we passed floors with drones seated motionless before consoles. None were taking a coffee break, going for a leak, or otherwise slacking, a perfect labor force for management.

Two more levels up, our luck ran out. As we cleared the next ceiling opening, a car descending onto our level held two Infestor drones. Maauro shot them both and they dropped to lie still and twisted on the sinking platform.

"Damn," Dusko said. "Someone is going to notice that as it circles around."

Then we were at the top and in the control room. An Infestor was rising from its chair and stretching in a curiously human gesture. The expression on the crocodilian face was almost comical as it spotted us. Flechettes cut him down.

His companions at control stations rose. One hit an alarm that sounded a whooping call. The others rushed us with claw and teeth, getting only a few steps before we killed them. Maauro silenced the alarm but the damage was done. She dashed over to the main console and plugged herself in. I stood by the conveyor, dreading the sight of warriors coming. Abruptly the conveyer stopped blocking the hole. I looked over at Maauro and she gave me a thumbs-up and a wink. I hurried to her side. Maauro extended her filaments into another Infestor control panel.

***

I crack the elementary code protections. Evidently the designers never anticipated an enemy so far inside their ship's interior. More proof this was not designed to be a warship. I drop a few more security doors not already triggered by the blast. Excellent though my skills are, I cannot know the architecture of the systems as well as my enemies do. They will recover control shortly. I access the drive controls and am dismayed. The system is very well engineered. I see no way to initiate self-destruct. If there is such a mechanism, it is wisely separated from the drive functions and I cannot access it. Nor can I see any way to engineer a mechanical failure that will accomplish my purpose, even if I remove our survival as a parameter.

I turn to Wrik in despair. "I have thrown our lives away. All the destruction I can wreak on their engine systems will not destroy the ship. I can only do minor damage to the engines with the controls I can access from here."

Wrik stares back at me as I stand defeated before the huge control panel. I am surprised when he speaks.

"There's more than one way to skin a cat. You said the drive was like the Murch propulsion system. Remember what happened to them? How they were tipped out of their space when the drive malfunctioned? Can you do something like that here?"

Now it is my turn to stare. For all my vaunted abilities, I lack the spontaneous creativity of Wrik, the capacity for non-linear thinking of his biological nature.

Instantly, I access every facility of my body and memory, a concentration so total that for ten full seconds I am shut down to all outside stimuli.

***

The wave of heat rolling off Maauro forces me backwards. Was she malfunctioning? But moments later she focused on me and smiled. "Brilliant, Wrik. Quite brilliant. I am very grateful to you. Yes, I am setting instructions in the ship's drive computer duplicating the settings I found in the Murch drive. It is our only chance."

"Will it give us time to escape?" Dusko said.

"We will have time to try," she replied

"I'd like to live," Wrik said. "So don't get me wrong, but if they break in here, won't they find what you did? Maauro, I've seen enough of the Infestors to realize you were right. They must be destroyed."

She nodded. "I will set a time delay along with some false trails to divert them from seeing my sabotage. But I must also set a fail-safe. If they find my trap, it will execute before they can stop it."

"Okay, better get started."

"Oh, Friend Wrik, while I must give you pride of place in creativity, you must concede speed to me. While we were speaking I have done the necessary." Maauro began withdrawing her finger probes from the console. She suddenly stiffened and a spark seemed to jump from the panel to her fingers. Maauro leapt backwards. A smell of scorched metal reached me.

"Just in time," she said. "They sent a counter-program to destroy me, a very robust counterattack that would have gotten anything less than an M-7. We should flee now."

"You've talked me into it," I replied.

Maauro raced over to where she'd left the plasma weapon and did something to it, then leaned it on the hatch. She grabbed up the slugthrower and stuffed it into the shoulder sling for her lost armspac. "We must escape back to the surface, where I left Jaelle."

"If she is still there and alive," Dusko growled, nursing his wounded hand.

"I have not seen any sign in the Infestor systems that they are aware of *Stardust*. We put down before the Artifact wakened. Jaelle is protected by an ECM screen of my making and the three crab robots. So long as she did not move the ship, she should be undetected.

"The AI is concentrating on three forces: us, the Collector's column and her ship. All of which it is aware of. This has split what of its forces have been quickened to life and most of those that attacked the Collector died."

"Surely they are waiting for us at the base of this tower," Dusko said

"Yes and they will attack immediately. Even if they do not believe I can destroy the ship from here, they will know I can do damage. Whatever forces are nearby are moving on us. We will have to fight our way out."

"Great," Dusko said. "You may make it, but a cripple and a human?"

"I will not leave without Wrik," Maauro said. "Every second I operate I become more effective against the Artifact's AI. While I speak to you here I am causing overloads, misroutings, backflows and false alarms through the AI. The battle is not as one-sided as it appears."

I grinned. "You're a regular factory for viruses."

"Yes, and as I am designed for cyber war, I can operate more autistically than can the station AI, which must coordinate millions of functions every second to keep this massive complex going. It has allowed me to seize and maintain the initiative.

"Yet," she said, hefting her weapons, "we will need to fight. Stay near me unless I tell you not to. It is time to leave."

Behind us, the elevator platform started up.

"I've removed the block. Hop on." Maauro moved two carts and a few Infestor bodies onto the platform with us, piling them into a rampart. "Lie down and do not get up until I indicate so. When I say run, follow me to the maintenance corridor, street level to the right. It will lead to the nearest place we can reenter the cargo tubeways."

Our platform began to drop and I realized that dead Infestors smelled worse than live ones.

CHAPTER

29

WRIK AND DUSKO LIE ON THE PLATFORM, WHICH I WISH PROVIDED better cover. We drop down. I circle continuously, also wishing that my creators had actually installed eyes in the back of my head.

Ambush waits for us on the ground floor. I detect it .00078 seconds after the bottom of the platform emerges through the flooring. The gap to the floor below is only 10mm wide, but I detect the positions of a mixed crew of Infestors, some with heavy weapons.

At .00079 seconds I fire through my fingertips, a new munition I have manufactured in my body, through the 11mm gap, spinning for 360-degree projection. The plastic ampoules shatter, emitting a variety of nerve toxins and virulent germs tailored to Infestors. The first floor is turned into a charnel house of agonized and dying Infestors. Some fire their weapons wildly, inflicting further damage on each other.

.00199 seconds, I fire a second barrage through the 1cm gap, reaching out further. The ambush is totally disrupted. Surviving Infestors are trying to flee. Useful. They are spreading both viruses and neurotoxins though the effect is ameliorated by the more open area.

1.3887 seconds. I add weapon fire, having exhausted my chem/bio warfare ordnance. No immediate return fire. I have eliminated or incapacitated those closest.

The opening expands with agonizing slowness, but the instant it will accommodate my chassis, I plunge through. I drop among a hundred dying, twitching Infestors, then leap to the crew-served weapon that would have eliminated Wrik and Dusko and damaged me had it gotten the first shot in. I sling my personal weapon and seize the crew-gun, itself nearly as large as an Infestor, then lunge toward the entranceway. Behind me, Wrik and Dusko are beginning to react to my having leapt away.

"Follow me," I shout over my shoulder

I am at the entranceway. Dead and dying Infestors litter the area, but more are racing in. I blaze away with the crew-gun. Its big bore howls out death, sweeping Infestors away. I empty the magazine, selectively eliminating other gun crews and some larger warriors that have appeared.

Knowing that I must keep the initiative, I plunge in among the attacking Infestor workers. Again I literally run through their bodies, slashing and tearing my way through flesh and bone with my palm blade and the plasma torch in my right arm.

A guard-warrior roars and charges. Unlike me, it's concerned with not destroying the delicate machinery of the engineering section. It fires its projectile weapon and wields a shock baton. Despite a 53% hit ratio, the low-velocity *projectiles do nothing to me. My armor deflects the slugs, aided by the curves of my structures. One slug, I am horrified to see, bounces off me and nearly strikes Wrik.*

I move to the attack. The newly awakened warrior has no idea how to cope with me. His attack is predicated on my being the biological I resemble. Too late, he realizes what I must be and reaches for the power rifle strapped across his back. I roll forward, hooping my body into the correct shape. I cover the distance between us in .047 seconds and leap vertically into the three-meter long warrior. It rears back to strike with the shock baton but biological reflexes are no match for my speed. I even use the baton as a stepping stone in my upward leap. My plasma torch slices through armor as I flip myself in a circle around the warrior. He falls to pieces below me as I drop to the deck.

I seize both the warrior's weapons. My multi-target function allows me to process targets faster then the weapon can fire. I prioritize targets and maximize casualties as we head for the corridor leading back the way we came. In seconds the area is floored with dying Infestors, but more warriors are racing into sight.

My enemies are reckless of their lives and will simply seek to drown my weapons with their numbers. I infiltrate my captured weapon's combat computer. Fortunately the code protection is simple. I change mine then send a frequency-hopping command through the network to detonate the weapons of the onrushing warriors exploding about a third of them. This causes secondary blasts and the attackers disappear as fire doors snap down in an attempt to contain the fireball.

I race under a fire door before it can come down on me. I have bought time.

***

I ran, numbed by the mayhem and horror exploding behind us. It seemed that life had come down to this, an endless marathon with death snapping at us each foot. I didn't know quite what horror my little android had released, but the smell of putrefaction greeted us the instant the elevator began to drop from the first-floor ceiling. Infestors were curled up all around, looking like a wasp nest hit with a pest bomb. I hoped whatever she used wouldn't affect us. Maauro's mastery of the mechanics of death seemed endless and I could have pitied the Infestors for a second.

She seized what looked like a huge rail gun and raced outside. The cacophony of the battle outside made me long for the earplugs but I could not spare even a moment to reinsert them. Then we were outside, running from cover to cover, even if it was merely an Infestor corpse.

If I had thought I had seen Maauro at her most dangerous before, I was introduced to a new level now. She was the Princess of Death—unstoppable—almost too fast to see. Only when she paused to point the way to flee did I get a clear look at her.

Dusko at my heels, we ran for the corridor, an octagonal opening under a pulsing blue light. I still held my laser, but nothing seemed less relevant than my handgun in the savagery erupting around us. We made the corridor, running some distance before turning to wait on Maauro.

There she was, racing toward us as swift as the wind. Behind her, a fireball erupted, outlining her slender form in orange and yellow. I jammed my palms over my ears as the sound rolled over us. A blast of heat followed, mercifully cut off as Maauro reached us and a blast-door snapped down behind her.

Her exterior was scorched and covered with soot. Grooves were cut into her skin and metal shone in places, but even as I watched, her body returned to normal. Maauro smiled at me, something so incongruous at that moment that it threatened what was left of my composure.

"This way," she said, "quickly." She sped ahead of us.

"One of these days I'll get used to how she is never out of breath," Dusko murmured.

Maauro wrenched a covering off the wall and we saw we were again in the tubeway, in what looked like a garage for the tube cars. She selected another passenger car, this one larger and more comfortably padded. Maauro hesitated for the barest moment, but there was no really no choice. We piled in as she plugged into the car's system.

"Still clear," she said in evident relief. "Hold on."

The sled rocketed away, heading for the outer reaches of the Artifact. Again, I could only hold onto the metal bars and endure the flashing lights and g-forces of the onrushing car as we surged upward. Time quickly ceased to have meaning as we passed level after level.

We came to a sudden savage halt. Maauro seized me under one arm. "Get out," she shouted at Dusko as she leapt away, slamming open a panel into the ship's interior with her other arm. We tumbled onto the deck, with Dusko on our heels. Behind us a cacophony of sound exploded, followed by a shower of metal bits and a blast of flame.

Maauro looked back. "Our adversary is fighting smarter. The ship's AI finally realized how we were moving so quickly through its interior and sent a volley of other cars down the tubeways. It has also changed weapon frequencies so I cannot explode their weapons again."

"Great," I said, staggering to my feet. "How far did we get?"

Maauro helped Dusko stand. "Spared of the need to sneak up on our destination, I opted for a direct route and speed. We are halfway to the outer area. Only speed will save us here."

"Can they track us by sensors?" Dusko asked.

"Not while you are with me," Maauro said, starting forward.

I trotted after her. "Jammer? Won't that just create a big blind spot and give away our general position?"

Maauro looked miffed. "I would never use such a crude method. There is no blank spot on their sensors. I pass the signals through and delete the interference of our bodies. My camouflage is seamless"

"You're a wonder," I replied.

She smiled. "Glad you realize that."

We marched for an hour, up spiraling ramps, occasionally riding one of the odd platform elevators when Maauro deemed it safe. Ever upward. Maauro gave us more of the pink wafers, this time laced with stimulants we would pay for if we lived. She broke into water tanks and got us drinking water. She even made us small canteens from the factories in her body. Despite this, the climb wore us down, and we again had to cope with the sheer scale of the Artifact.

"Hard to believe we have not had more company," I said during a rest break.

Maauro shrugged. "The Artifact has only begun waking from its ancient sleep. I estimate that 99% of it is uninhabited and we have created severe depredations on the systems, the crew, and even the AI that runs it. Most of what it has quickened, we have killed."

"You have killed," Dusko said. "We've been as useful as tits on a brundersnatch."

She cocked her head at him.

"Not very useful," he elaborated.

"This is my primary function," she said.

"Yeah, thank God you are on our side," I added

"I am not sure, from what little I know of God, that he would approve of me," Maauro said, a hint of wistfulness in her voice.

"I'll vouch for you if we meet him, which remains likely," I replied. "Dusko can serve as a character witness."

The Dua-Denlenn gave a rueful laugh and Maauro smiled again.

"Are you rested enough to continue?" Maauro asked

I nodded and started for the ramp. "Our odds get worse the more time we spend here."

But they were worse than I realized. We went up two more levels by ramps and lifter when we came upon a wide, open area, an Infestor assembly area. We popped our heads out long enough to see what looked like a horde of warriors forming up. These were the largest we had seen and like the one Maauro had disassembled in the Engineering level, they wore armor. Worse still, there were wheeled vehicles with turrets as well. We ran back down to the level below.

"It's hopeless," I said after we made it back into cover. "That assembly area went on for as far as the eye could see. It could take hours or days to work our way around."

"We only face a small percentage of them so long as we are undiscovered," Maauro said. "They have an immense space to search and they may believe we are still down in the engineering levels. But you are correct—we are making progress too slowly and the basic workers are being supplemented by more and more warriors. Any creative thoughts, Wrik?"

"You have a full schematic of the Artifact, right?"

"Yes, I raided it when I first interfaced with the Artifact's systems."

"Is there any way to get to a small ship? Maybe take a passage to the outside?"

"Unlikely," she said. "The security encryption on ships will be vastly better than anything protecting the tubeways. Yet there is something to what you say. There are a number of passages from deep in the interior of the Artifact. They are both for dissipating waste heat and moving small ships and supplies. Even if we cannot get a ship to go out, we might be able to get the *Stardust* down here."

"You're kidding," I said.

"I can see no alternative. If we get access to an Infestor ship I should be able to eventually crack the security but I cannot believe we will be unmolested by the enemy that long.

"Follow me," she said. "We must find a safe place to call Jaelle from."

We went down a second level. The further away we were from the battalions above, the better I felt. Now that we weren't climbing every step, we made better time. Three hours later, Maauro pulled us into a side corridor, lit only by the glow she emitted from her eyes. We journeyed on into the darkened area. It was not quiet: metal groaned, creaked, and popped. Background noise on the Artifact, but now, in the absence of light, more noticeable and ominous. Fluid dripped and slimed the corridors, making our footing tricky. Another side corridor and then Maauro took us into a ventilation shaft. Finally she stopped at a wide platform with a control station. She placed some filaments in it and satisfied herself there was no danger.

Dusko and I sank to the platform next to her.

***

"Jaelle," I send, "can you hear me?"

"Maauro! Thank the gods, Maauro. Where are you? Are you all right? Have you found Wrik?"

"Wrik is with me and uninjured, as is Dusko. We are deep within the Artifact, battling our way back to the surface. Enemy resistance is stiffening and we do not believe we can escape before my sabotage effort in the engine room takes effect. Are you still safe?"

"Yes," Jaelle replies. "The ECM field you set up is working and the psionic alarm has not gone off, so it does not appear the Artifact is aware of me."

"What can I do to help you?"

"There is a channel near you, a cooling and exhaust vent that is also used for maneuvering small ships to hangars deep in the Artifact. The aperture is 300 meters wide, large enough for the Stardust to enter. Bring the ship down close to our level so we can escape by an airlock."

"What! Maauro, I'm not Wrik. I can do basic piloting in deep space when there's nothing to bang into. I can't fly a starship in a tunnel."

Wrik looks at me; his face is pinched with worry. "Maauro, can you fly it remotely?"

"Not and maintain the shields protecting us from detection and Infestor influence. I am also launching cyberattacks to keep the station AI off balance. Too much of my CPU capacity is already committed. But there is another way. Wrik, you must fly the ship."

He stares at me. "How?"

"I can devote enough processing capability to serve as a form of remote-control. I will integrate with the ship systems. My right arm will serve as a directional control. My left will be your throttle. In my right eye I will give you a viewscreen. On my left I will broadcast the necessary flight instruments."

I am greeted by stunned silence from all three biologicals. "It will work," I assure them.

I sit down on the deck, folding my legs under me. I raise my arms and make the connections. "Jaelle, prepare the engine controls and ready yourself to fly on the course I indicate to the aperture. Stay as low as you dare. While I believe the AI is relatively crude compared to myself and is occupied with my own attacks and the Collector's forces, we should take as little chance of your being detected as we can. If I register a weapon being locked on you, I will launch a cyber attack on it."

I raise my arms in front of me. Wrik sits opposite, facing me, his legs braced on either side of my body. "Maauro," he whispers, "I don't know if I can do this."

"You must, Wrik. You are our only chance. I cannot do it without you."

He looks at my arms in disbelief.

"My limbs are now calculated to feel as much like your normal thruster and flight controls as can be. I will now link in my eyes as your flight instruments—"

"Good thing you have such big eyes."

"Wrik, you say the sweetest things to a girl."

His laugh rings raggedly off the bulkheads. Dusko winces.

"Wrik, give your weapon to Dusko. He can provide local security while we are immobile."

The two men stare at each other for a few seconds, then Wrik hands him the weapon. Dusko flashes a cold smile. I fix my eye on him in warning and the smile vanishes.

"Maauro," Wrik says, "put me through to Jaelle."

"She can hear all we say. I am sorry I cannot give you both some privacy."

"Oh, we're kind used to having you between us," Jaelle's voice comes. "If you were a child, you'd be sleeping in the bed with us."

"I am sorry—"

"I'm kidding, Maauro, mostly, anyway. We biologicals do that when we are scared to death. It's ok."

"Jaelle," Wrik said.

"Good to hear your voice, Handsome. I've come a long way to get a glimpse of you."

"I wish I could see you."

"In a little while."

"No, Jaelle. It's too risky. This would be hard enough if I was in that control seat. I can't take this risk with your life. I want you to get out of here."

Dusko swears in the background. I continue to watch him. This is Wrik's call and I will protest nothing.

"Would you do that in my place, Wrik?"

"Yes."

"I don't believe you."

"Jaelle, I've run out on friends before. On my homeworld, I deserted friends and family."

There was a pause. "So that's what it was. Well, you've never run out on me. I know that you have been troubled by issues of honor and courage, but no one is pure. Everyone has made mistakes. What matters to me is what you have done since I've known you.

"In any event, I am not running. I'll bring the ship to the tunnel. You fly me in, Wrik."

"I can't talk you out of this?" he says.

"Have you won an argument with me yet?"

He shakes his head ruefully. "See you in a while, Beautiful."

"OK," Wrik says, taking my arms. "Jaelle, take off low and slow. I'm going to use the time to practice this insanity. If there's trouble at your end, Maauro will override you—"

"—What else is new?"

"—and put me in control."

CHAPTER
30

I REACHED OVER TO TAKE MAAURO'S HANDS, STILL STRUGGLING with the insanity of doing this. "Let's run some simulations to see if this is even possible."

She smiled her gentle smile. "Have courage, friend Wrik." All animation fled her face. Her eyes widened to their furthest extent and their pacific green disappeared. In one eye I saw the viewscreen of the Stardust, in the other, a readout of engine systems. I noticed that as my eyes roved over particular data, it increased in size. Of course, Maauro was optical tracking to tell what I was looking at.

"We are in sim mode," Maauro said. Only her mouth moved; something a living being could not have managed. "Jaelle is taking off in the ship. I do not see any sign of an attack on her."

"Logical," Dusko said from where he kept watch on the long corridor. "Ship systems are only waking up now. They'd react to incoming threats, not something already here when they came on."

The next few minutes were a nightmare of strain as I tried to make my brain grasp what my hands were doing. With Maauro's' eyes as instruments and her body, many times heavier than it appeared, both still and cool, it was gradually easier to relate to her as a control system. I even subdivided some control functions, using her fingers as stand-ins for the instruments, all the while fighting off hysterical laughter at the image of what we were doing. I felt like a primitive doing a dance to affect the rain.

A dull boom rolled through the tubeway. Dusko and I jumped.

"What was that?" Dusko snapped.

"Remember," Maauro said, her voice slightly slower than usual with strain, "I am still battling the Artifact's AI. I exploded a steam pipe by closing an outlet valve. It eliminated an Infestor recon force heading this way. Time grows short, Wrik. Jaelle is above the aperture."

"Jaelle," I called. "Ready?"

"No, but don't let that stop you."

"OK, my ship now."

"You have control," Maauro said.

I stared down the immense aperture that led deep into the Artifact's interior. At three hundred meters wide, it should have felt comfortably large for a small ship like Stardust. Staring into the two-inch square that was Maauro's eye, it looked tiny. I shifted forward to get closer to her face. Then, using only the smallest of forces, I started the ship down the opening.

"100 meters a minute," Jaelle called out. "That's too slow, Wrik."

I goosed the forward motion up. Maauro's arms gave the exact feedback of my controls and she was as solid on the deck as if welded there.

"Quit pacing," I snarled over my shoulder at Dusko. Sweat was running down my ribs and my back ached from tension. The tube rolled on, level after level, seemingly endless. Only the ship's prow lights shone in the darkness. I kept telling myself it was no worse than any of a hundred space dockings I'd made. A little voice in my head mocked me.

"We are passing other airlock and hangar areas," Maauro said in her softest, soothing voice. "I was correct. The Artifact designer wanted to be able to arm and launch smaller ships from the relative safety of the interior.

"Only five more kilometers, Wrik. You are doing well. Please try to even out your breathing. You are transmitting a slight vibration to the controls that I cannot compensate for."

I slowed my breathing, trying to go deep and regular. I lightened my grip on the controls. Over-control was as dangerous as under in these tight quarters.

"Four kilometers," Maauro said.

I steered my way past some sort of tower that projected into the tunnel.

"Stop in five, four, three, two, one, now." Maauro said. "We have reached closest approach."

I brought the ship to a halt. And fell over on my back, my hands twitching and my back killing me from stress.

"Deploy the crab robots, Jaelle," Maauro said. "Then wait for us as long as you can." She stood, with none of the pain Dusko and I showed as we got to our feet.

"Jaelle is three kilometers that way." Maauro pointed up and to the left.

"Let me guess," Dusko said. "We climb"

"Won't we have to pass through that assembly area?" I asked, falling in behind her.

"No, there is a pipe trunk and air vent near the edge. It will take us up through that level to the area adjacent to the tunnel."

**

We moved up the trunk, scrambling awkwardly around bundled pipelines. Dusko and I struggled and panted from the climb. Maauro helped us as best she could. Finally we reached a walkway for work drones.

"Kinda cramped," I gasped.

"Be grateful," Maauro returned. "It's too small for warriors."

We both reached back for Dusko who collapsed on the steel decking when he got out. The climb had done in the wounded Dua-Denlenn.

"Let me see if there is something useful by the airlock. Remain alert."

Maauro dashed off up the corridor. I sank against the far wall, laser held loosely in my hand, waiting for my breath to slow and my heart rate to return to normal.

Dusko's color was bad and his chest heaved. I crawled over to him and pulled out my canteen.

He nodded, and after a second, drank from it.

"Not too much," I said. "It'll make you throw up."

He handed me the canteen with a shaky hand. "Thanks."

Maauro returned. "Fortune favors us. There are Infestor suits in the locker up there."

"What good does that do us?" Dusko asked, struggling into a sitting position.

"It need only keep you alive for a minute as I take you across to *Stardust*. So long as they will close and hold air, they will serve."

I reached up and Maauro helped me to my feet. Then we got Dusko up. We staggered and ran to the airlock.

"I want to minimize the chances of detection and reaction," she said. "We will all three go together."

We pulled the Infestor suits from the rack. Maauro inspected them and discarded two, switched parts on others till she had two workable suits.

The suits were far too large but as a bag holding air they worked. We weren't tall enough to reach our heads into the misshapen helmets but we could see out of them from below the neck collar. Maauro sealed the suits and air hissed in. Both Dusko and I managed to stand on our own. She inspected us both and gave us a thumbs-up.

We crowded against the airlock hatchway and Maauro worked the controls, her hands moving too fast to see. Lights flashed and the door slipped open. Maauro thrust us both in, none too gently, sealing the inner hatch then turning to the outer. The door slid open and there, in the darkness, lit only by her running lights, lay *Stardust*. Her green and gold hull never looked more beautiful. Three crab robots stood on her hull, their weapons searching.

Maauro seized us both and leapt. The universe spun as we tumbled, unbalanced load that we were. I could see the vast tunnel with its mysterious ports and lights and the lovely sight of our ship alternating as each revolution brought us closer. I was almost too tired to feel anything.

A thin, red beam lanced by my helmet.

"What?" I yelled.

But there was no way for me to hear anything. As we rolled through another rotation, I saw *Stardust*'s laser return fire, its beam a thin, almost invisible sword of green light, powerful at this close range. Maauro's face came into view of my narrow neck aperture. I could see she was firing back with her other hand, the one containing the flechettes. She'd either dropped Dusko or had her legs wrapped around him. Ship and android must have destroyed whatever had fired at us, as the beam did not lance back.

We hit against the side of the *Stardust* with a bone-jarring impact. I felt Maauro dragging us toward the stern. She had Dusko under her other arm. Her head was completely reversed, which made her look like her neck was broken. The ship's main laser flared again, warding off some danger I could not see and lighting up the tunnel.

Then the main airlock yawned open before us. Maauro stuffed us both in before sliding in herself.

The dueling AG fields of the Artifact and *Stardust* made me dizzy for a second before *Stardust's* won. The inner airlock slid open and we tumbled out to the deck.

Jaelle was there, her golden eyes wide with excitement as she worked on my suit. Behind her Maauro worked on Dusko's. The seal broke and I was free. Suddenly I had my arms full of warm catgirl. Her lips pressed on mine and I kissed her back, holding to her hard but careful of her fangs. We were both crying and talking.

"Wrik," Maauro said. "Forgive me but we need you on the bridge. I am still trying to ward off the Artifact's AI. I cannot fly the ship too. I sent the crab robots inward to attack and create a diversion. I may convince the AI that we are moving inward to try and reach the core and explode it. It will use all its force to ward off that intrusion."

I nodded. "Understood."

Jaelle pulled me to my feet. We raced for the bridge, Dusko trailing us.

"How are we doing?" I gasped at Maauro.

"We have been detected by automatic systems, but I disrupted their communication with the main AI. Jaelle slagged the nearby guns and I have interrupted the circuitry for the remainder. The main AI has a localized idea of where we are and is trying to reestablish control. We must flee before it can send a boarding party or bring additional weapons online."

"Keep it off balance, Kit-sister," Jaelle said, "just a little longer."

I leapt into my pilot seat. "Jaelle, stay on that laser." I checked my instruments and fired the forward station-keeping retros, full on. The small units weren't meant for this, but I didn't dare spin the *Stardust* in the tight confines of the tunnel. We began moving backward. I corrected drift with the lightest touch of the controls and rerouted more fuel to the forward retros. The thrusters thrummed their way through the fuel as we recklessly accelerated.

"You're going to melt those engines," Dusko rasped. His blue eyes were bloodshot and I wondered if his suit had been hit and partly decompressed.

"Every second counts," Maauro intervened. "I am losing my battle with the AI. It will gain both a lock and weapons control soon."

I wiped sweat out of my eyes and stared at the controls. Dusko was right; the engine was red-lining. I cut the thrust back to just below red. *Stardust* raced backward and my corrections became more frantic. At this speed, even a graze might wreck us.

"One kilometer to go," Jaelle yelled.

Stardust came out of the tunnel like a cannonball. I cut the forwards, kicked the ship into spinning on her singularity axis, and as the nose came round, I threw in the mains and we were all pressed back in our seats, save for Maauro.

"Climb, baby, climb," I begged.

"Any sign of hostile fire?" Jaelle asked.

"No," Maauro replied. "But now that we are out, we will be detected by the main scanners. I can do nothing about that. It's a main combat system and fully shielded."

Maauro's head cocked to one side. A gesture I knew meant surprise. "I am detecting a signal," she announced. "It is the Collector."

"Doubtless calling to her ship for aid," I said, eyes darting over the controls.

"No, Wrik, the message is for you."

"Put her on," I said, after recovering from my surprise. I checked my readouts; we were at max thrust, arrowing for the starlines above. I had no idea how far or fast we'd have to go to escape the Artifact's time-bubble. I only knew the Guild ship had done so a century ago. But the Artifact had been asleep then.

The screen derezzed, then I saw Ferlan. Her face was smudged with soot, but her usual calm resolve shone through somehow. In the background, Marcel and some other Guilders stood with leveled weapons, peering out into hallways and gesturing furiously.

"Hello, Wrik. I am glad you are still alive."

"Madam Ferlan," I returned.

"Are you safe? I see you have regained your ship."

"Safe may be overstating it."

"Yes, I suppose so."

"What's your sitrep?" I asked

"Quite hopeless, I'm afraid. We fought our way back to the area below my ship before being herded into what looks like a storage area. Warriors have now appeared and destroyed our vehicles. Our weapons are depleted. We have had no success in trying to communicate with the Infestors. Worse, we are running low on power for the dampeners in our helmets. Some of my people have succumbed to Infestor control."

"Any chance of help from your ship?" I asked

"They sent in a rescue force, but we have not heard from them. I can no longer raise my ship."

Maauro walked over to stand next to me. She stared at Ferlan.

"Ah, Maauro, I have so many regrets at how I handled you."

"Apologies will not get you my aid."

Ferlan smiled. "I did not request your aid, young lady. I was merely regretting that I did not try to honestly befriend you. It might have prevented disaster. Still, the habits of a lifetime are hard to break."

She turned her attention back to me. "I fear I am beyond help. You remember that I told you that sometimes we must ask the universe for its judgments?"

"Yes."

"It appears that the judgment today is both harsh and final."

"I'm sorry," I said. "That's the truth. I'd help if I could." The others all stared at me as if I'd turned into a Kandalorian firebat.

"You are a sweet boy, Wrik. Forget about the past, a lesson I learned too late."

"Is there any message...to anyone?"

"No. Farewell, Wrik. Please forgive me."

"Done, Villain."

She laughed. "But I will not return the name you gave yourself. If it was ever deserved, it no longer is."

The men behind her fired a ragged volley, then shouted and grabbed their heads. On the screen I watched Ferlan's face go slack. Behind her, the remaining guards and Marcel stopped moving and dropped their weapons. Ferlan still faced the screen and I thought I saw a horror in her eyes, but she, too, turned and marched off, following the others.

"It seems the Collector has been collected," Dusko said with a cold smile. "My account with her has been squared by the Powers."

I looked at Maauro. "Is there nothing we can do?"

She shook her head. "No, Wrik, even if there was time, we lack the power or forces to effect a rescue."

"What about their ship?" Jaelle asked. Answering her own question she played the screen controls. We saw Ferlan's ship lying on the Artifact's surface.

"Too late," Jaelle said.

Hummel's ramps were down. The space-suited crew was marching out into captivity, compelled toward the ring of Infestors, also in the suits, that had surrounded the ship.

"I am reading power spikes," Jaelle said.

"Confirmed," Maauro said

"We're for it now," Dusko said. "They cannot capture us and they cannot afford for us to get away."

I grabbed the controls and hit a random vector burn in an evasive pattern. "Maauro can you do anything with ECM?"

"I'm integrated with the ship's systems and emitting jamming signals but Wrik we are close enough for visual firing. They can blanket this area of space. Can you get any more speed out of the *Stardust*?"

"Only a few percent. Everybody take hold. I'm going to be exceeding the AG field's safety parameters. Maauro, can you give me any warning?"

"Guesstimates on when they should fire based on their weapons and tech," she replied.

"Sing out when you think they are going to fire."

"Do you really want me to sing?"

"Maauro!"

"I am merely trying to lessen the tension. I know I am not to sing."

"You picked a fine time to play with humor."

"Dodge in five, four, three, two, one. Now!"

I slammed gyros, throttles, and everything else that *Stardust* had, while pulling the dampeners on the reactor. The ship leapt faster than she had even at her builder's trials. The AG field couldn't cancel it all and gravity pulled at us. My vision grayed, but that didn't stop the universe from lighting up around us. A salvo from the Artifact ripped through space. It wasn't any weapon I was familiar with, but I had no doubt it could shred *Stardust* in an instant.

"How long before it recycles?" I yelled to Maauro, despite the giant sitting on my chest.

"Between 3.5 and 3.77 seconds. Its fire control system now knows our best evasive action."

"Then we're dead." I said, an ashen taste in my mouth.

"The power spike from firing may help us," Maauro said. She altered the screen's view aft. The Artifact glowered at us.

"Yes," Maauro said. "It begins."

"What?" I said. "I don't see..."

On the screen, the Artifact seemed to waver as if seen through intense heat. It shimmered and storms of power played over its surface.

Jaelle grabbed my shoulder. "Look."

On the shimmering surface of the Artifact, the engines of the Collector's ship flared with full power. The huge ship flung itself off the surface but its climb was wild, the ship bucked and rolled, nearly striking a tall tower near the edge of the landing zone.

"Are they escaping?" Dusko demanded.

"I cannot raise them," Maauro said. "There is no way to know who or what is aboard."

"They're not emitting any ECM or telemetry," I said, scanning my instruments. "It may be some automatic system misfiring. That ship is just going ballistic."

"Shall we intercept?" Jaelle asked.

Maauro shook her head. "No, whatever is going on in that vessel is beyond our power. I do not believe any Infestors are aboard. Their command personnel are deep in the Artifact. Drones would not flee on their own."

The Artifact seemed to twist and shudder and brilliant light surrounded it.

"Hold on," I shouted.

The Artifact blazed with an unbearable light and then vanished. Power from it, ripping through the fabric of the universe, battered *Stardust* as it rolled in the disturbed space-time.

My chair restraint failed and the seat lurched forward, Maauro's hand snapped down, holding the seat in its track, or I'd have been smashed on the instruments. Someone screamed. Our senses were hammered by unfamiliar sensations, brilliant colors, metallic smells, until it seemed that the universe was coming apart.

It took me a minute to reorient myself and realize the sensations were fading, normalcy was returning. It felt good merely to breathe. I looked up at the controls and saw many yellow warning lights, no reds.

"The Artifact is gone," Jaelle shouted.

"Maauro destroyed it," Dusko said. "Quite the little destroyer is our Maauro."

"It may be destroyed but I doubt it," Maauro said.

"What?" Jaelle said.

"I could not corrupt the systems sufficiently to self-destruct the Artifact. Given time I would have been able to string together enough systems to accomplish it, but we were too hard-pressed. I infiltrated the navigation system. The Infestor drive was transdimensional, as was the Murch drive. I accessed those memories I had of the Murch drive which I worked on for days. Using that knowledge, I was able to essentially tip the Artifact out of our space-time. Where it has gone, there is no way to tell. But it is highly unlikely we shall see it again. Infestors are once again gone from my universe."

"Since it seems we are to live," Dusko said, leaning on a bulkhead, "one wonders what follows?"

I set up the course toward the outer edges of systems and the warp points back to civilization then pushed back from the controls. "I don't know. I'll think better with a drink in me."

Maauro disappeared to return with containers of beer and the green-bottled drel that Jaelle preferred. She joined us in opening a canister. We savored the cool drinks and the simple sensations of being alive. Jaelle checked the nav-instruments and whistled at something. I looked over her shoulder.

"According to the ship's observations of the quasars we use for a universal clock we have been gone in the gravity well of the Artifact for over five years."

I shook my head, almost unable to cope with any more strangeness. I wondered how much longer I could stay awake before crashing. Only the pain from every bruise and strain I'd acquired in the last few days was keeping me awake. Dusko looked in similar shape. Jaelle too stood hollow-eyed with fatigue and tension.

"Well, Maauro," Jaelle said. "It would seem a lot of our plans depend on you."

To my surprise she shook her head emphatically. "I wish to make no more unilateral decisions. Please tell me your own wishes before considering mine."

"Not to get killed," Dusko said promptly.

"Your safety," Maauro replied, "is predicated on your behavior. Make no moves against the rest of us and you will be unharmed. I consider you now a provisional part of my network and will not dispose of you without just cause."

"Thanks," he said without irony.

She turned to Jaelle. "I have in the past caught you up unwillingly in my compulsions and must make amends for that. Please tell me your wishes."

"I have no specific plans," Jaelle said. "I'm a trader and wish to practice my trade. We disappeared for five years. I doubt that anyone is still looking for us. We have the opportunity for a fresh start. We have a mix of talents that can make us very successful. I say we stay together and practice those talents."

I looked around at Jaelle: beautiful, brave and intelligent. At Maauro, who meant perhaps even more to me in a unique way. That problem I would put aside for another date. Then I looked at Dusko; his pupilless blue eyes stared back. I'd never learned to read such a blank face. His hand was covered in the dressing Maauro had made for him.

"That would require," I said reluctantly, "you and I to put a lot of unpleasant history in a box and bury it."

"You believe nothing I say to you," he replied. "So if I tell you that I, too, am willing to bury the hatchet, you will neither believe me, nor ever trust me."

I shrugged. "You're out of a culture with no morals by my standards. Even among Dua-Denlenn, you were a criminal."

"Yet you cannot accept that we follow our own interests as a moral code. I feel it is obvious that my interests lie with Stardust now. If you can rely on nothing else, rely on this, I am not your enemy while Maauro operates. I have seen her overcome and destroy every obstacle: the Guild, the Infestors, even Time itself. I will not risk her enmity. Trust that, if not me.

"As for the rest." He raised his burnt hand. "If we score all the damage we've done each other, can we not now call it even?"

I thought about it then nodded stiffly.

"Wrik," Jaelle asked. "What do you want? Her cat-like eyes were easier to read then Dusko's but the mind behind them was still alien, still new to me.

"I like any plan that keeps us together," I replied.

"Back to you, Maauro," Jaelle said.

"Your plans are all fine with me. You are my network and I wish to remain with you all. But there is something more. I was created for destruction, for a war that now must surely be considered done and gone. Since I have become active I have continued to fight and struggle. It may be that this is...how would a biological say it?...destiny?

"If it is, then I wish to use my skills to some higher purpose, to save those in trouble, to defend the weak from the strong, reunite the lost with those searching for them."

"Hmmm," Jaelle said, "perhaps a consulting agency of some sort? A trading company would be a good cover for such."

"You might need someone with extensive contacts and a practical working knowledge of criminal enterprises." Dusko added.

I raised my drink. "Shall we toast the founding of the Maauro Troubleshooting and Consulting Agency?"

We touched our cups on the future.

—THE END—

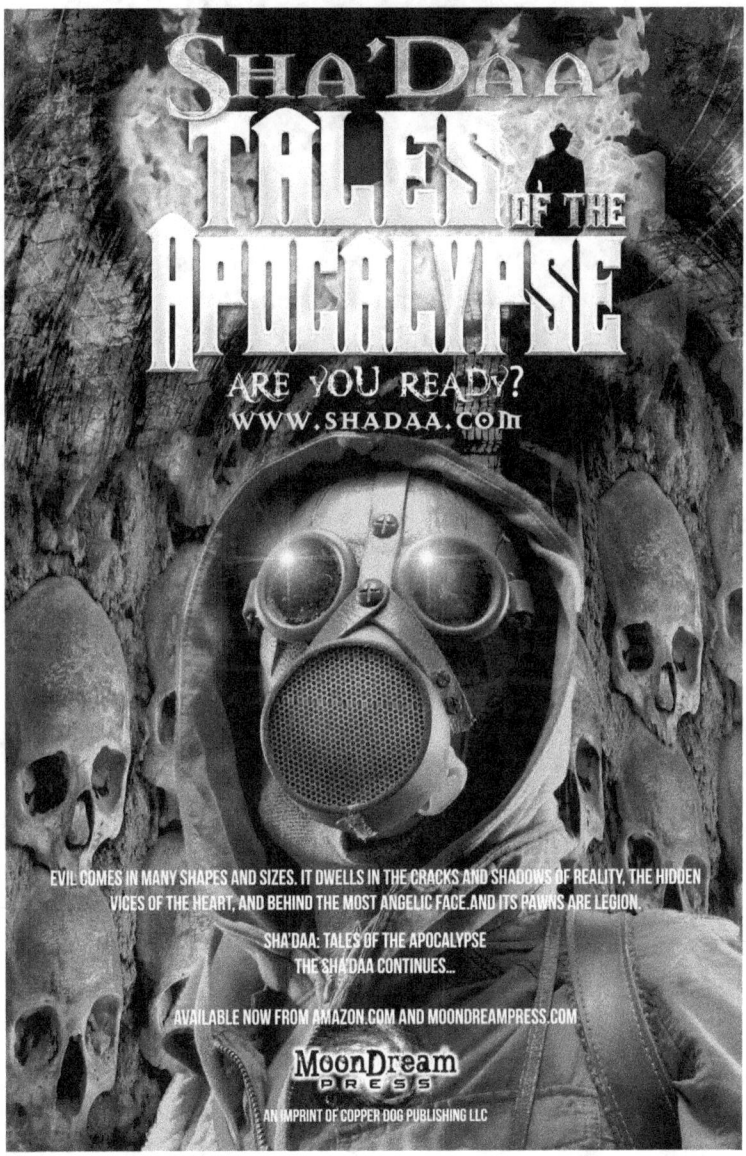

ABOUT THE AUTHOR

EDWARD MCKEOWN is a writer and editor specializing in science fiction and fantasy with occasional forays into literary and nonfiction. Ed escaped from NY, but his old hometown supplies much of the background to his humorous "Lair of the Lesbian Love Goddess" shorts, as his new hometown in Charlotte, North Carolina does for his "Knight Templar" fantasy series. He enjoys a wide variety of interests from ballroom dance to the martial arts. He has also edited four Sha'Daa anthologies of wry tales of the apocalypse and a wide variety of short stories. Find him on Facebook and at edwardmckeown.weebly.com.

Ed is best known for his Robert Fenaday/Shasti Rainhell series of SF novels, set on the Privateer Sidhe.

BOOKS BY EDWARD MCKEOWN

Was Once a Hero in print—foreword written by Janet Morris
Fearful Symmetry in print—foreword written by Claudia Christian
Points of Departure in print
Hidden Stars—the first of the Shasti Rainhell series

Knight in Charlotte in print
On the Case—the Lair of the Lesbian Love Goddess Files, coming soon

In 2014 and beyond, comes the Maauro and Wrik Trigardt series from Copper Dog Publishing. Set sixty years later, in the same future as Robert Fenaday and Shasti Rainhell, a new duo challenges the powers ruling the stars, a 50,000 year old combat android and a disgraced rebel pilot.
My Outcast State
Against that Time
The Lost
All the Difference
Legacies

Edited by Edward McKeown, with stories by Edward McKeown:
Sha'Daa: Tales of The Apocalypse
Sha'Daa: Last Call
Sha'Daa: Pawns

Coming Soon:
Sha'Daa: Facets

Copper Dog Publishing LLC

OUR IMPRINTS:

Pumpkin Hill Press

To find out more about our imprints
and our upcoming releases, visit our website:
www.CopperDogPublishing.com
or our Facebook page:
www.facebook.com/copperdogpublishing

www.ingramcontent.com/pod-product-compliance
Lightning Source LLC
Chambersburg PA
CBHW060627260626
47161CB00008B/2820